INTO

AUSURNIA

ALISHA TRENT

First edition July 2023

Cover design by Rena Violet

Edited by Earley Editing, LLC

This is for anyone who was ever told their dreams weren't practical.

Newcomer in Pontagu

There was nowhere to go but forward. Behind her lay only pain and sadness. At least she stood a chance by running away. It wasn't cowardice; it was survival.

Thick, white steam rose from the ground, blocking her way. She navigated around the tunnel grate and then between a strewn pile of empty crates. No light from the moon or stars helped Annika this morning. Every painstakingly slow step threatened to expose her presence. The sharp tang of rotting garbage crept through her upheld sleeve. She dry-heaved once, twice, forcing her steps forward. The smellier the alley, the more deserted—and safer they were. Generally. Something behind her tumbled to the ground. Annika slapped her other hand over her mouth to stifle the bubbling scream. A small, dark shape ran past her, and she breathed again. Just a cat, or a gigantic rat. She shuddered, peeking around the corner, and wondered at her next move.

Brown exhaust and low-lying gray fog swirled together in the street. Phantom-like cars pushed through, their yellow headlights bouncing off dense air. Walking commuters disappeared and reappeared in front of store windows bathed in orange light. The train station's entrance doors whirled as bodies entered and exited. It was now or never. Annika turned up her collar to hide her face, picked up her suitcase, and ran across the street.

She entered the low-lit diner to the left of the train station. "Coffee," she muttered at a passing server and sat down in the booth furthest from the door. The same tired-eyed server set a steaming mug on the table, avoiding eye contact and saying nothing. Annika didn't blame them; conversation was dangerous in public these days. She cradled the warm mug in both hands, took a quick gulp, and grimaced. This level of bitterness should be illegal. She sighed. Another person entered the diner and her eyes darted up. *Would they know where to look for me?* She looked at the clock on the diner's wall. Twenty more minutes. She dug an icy hand into the depths of her wool jacket pocket. The sharp edge of her one-way ticket poked out of the inner lining. *No more second guessing. I'm doing this.* She threw coins onto the counter next to the black sludge they called coffee and left.

"Ausurnia is a dangerous, old country. Rovalkia never does business with them. We don't associate with those monsters. Never venture there, Annika," a voice echoed from memory. She looked at her suitcase. *It couldn't be any worse than here.* This one roller suitcase and the ratty bookbag slung over her shoulder reflected the image of a poor traveler. Staying inconspicuous was the name of the game today. She tightened her grip on the handle as she strode past the train station's ticket booth. *Mom and Dad shouldn't realize I've gone until James and Sarah wake up.*

2

She glanced over to a huge bulletin board being ignored by everyone. Resumes of people looking for employment crowded half the board. People requesting housing placement eclipsed the other side. *It shouldn't be like this. So many of us need help, and nobody has anything to give.*

A large clock above the platform boomed six times as orange streaks of sunlight tinted the horizon above the perpetual smog that enveloped the city. Waiting travelers queued up where each train car door would open. Annika took her place in the third-class waiting area that always smelled of urine. *For being touted as a modern capital city, Karaxin is a miserable place,* she mused, glancing around. Most others in line were bleary-eyed men in wrinkled suits. There were also small families huddled together, their suitcases in worse condition than hers.

Two soldiers in green wool uniforms strolled by with large rifle muzzles poking up over their shoulders. Their eyes were flinty, darting between travelers. Annika lowered her eyes as they made a beeline in her direction. She sighed in relief as they passed her, but then sucked in a breath as they pulled apart two men embracing one row over. Commuters standing around them shuffled away. Annika ran a hand over her collar, moving further over in line as well. *I shouldn't have worn Grandma's necklace.* With her other hand, she pulled her thick, silvery-blonde hair forward around her face, should the soldiers decide to scrutinize passengers in her line.

An argument erupted between the couple and one soldier. The taller male pushed the soldier and then the soldier punched the man in his gut. His partner let loose a string of curses. Annika scrunched her eyes together. *One day you'll help the innocent, one day.* When she reopened them, she saw the soldier had pulled the taller man's arms back. The couple kicked at both soldiers, shouting about abuse of government power. One soldier struck the shorter man in the head with his rifle, and he dropped to the ground. His partner began sobbing, holding his stomach, begging for mercy, but the soldiers handcuffed both and forced them away from the platform. Annika tracked the soldiers until they were out of sight, exhaling her held breath slowly. The soldiers were acting like police. That was new. Come to think of it, she hadn't seen any police officers walking the streets in the last month. Was the government replacing them with soldiers? She shuddered at the thought.

The transcontinental passenger train pulled up, its brakes screeching, covered in graffiti. Passengers reformed the line. "These vandals and rioters think they're working toward a better future, but *they're* the bad guys. Our country and its public service members deserve more respect. But don't worry, my smart girl, bad guys never win. Remember that." She shook her head, trying to quiet the voice.

But the trains have more paint each time I ride, she mused, tilting her head left and right. Different colored words of love and hate in diverse handwriting competed for attention. *Either the vandals are outpacing the police or they're arresting all the wrong people.*

The travelers shuffled forward, stepping toe to heel as the doors creaked open. People pressed Annika forward from behind, jostling into and down the train's corridor. Each cabin door slammed shut before Annika could reach it. She squeezed past people arguing over a seat and slipped into the last train car. A cabin door stood ajar; she peeked inside. *Small, but empty.* She wrinkled her nose, looking at the muddy boot prints covering the floor, the dust-layered surfaces, and the greasy fingerprints smearing the window. Sighing, she hoisted her suitcase upon one of the bowed wooden shelves and sneezed as a puff of dust rose when her bookbag landed on the faded floral seat cushion sporting multiple rips. *Ten hours in this dirty coffin, but it's also ten hours in a direction away from Karaxin and Rovalkia.* Annika sighed again. "This *has* to be worth it," she muttered, sitting down next to her bag and looking out the window.

"Excuse me?"

Annika startled, turning toward the voice. A tanned, round-faced woman poked her head into Annika's cabin. The stranger motioned to the empty seat across from Annika. "Is this seat taken? All the other cabins are full." Annika gave a stiff shake of her head. If she said all the other cabins were full, she was probably right. The woman's shoulders loosened and a grateful smile followed.

Her short, round body squeezed in sideways. Her gray woolen coat matched her cropped gray hair. As the older woman moved to stow her bags, her body bent backwards. Annika pressed herself into her seat and turned her face away, frowning. She remembered when the government had boasted about all the money they were putting into more spacious cabins on their rail cars. Liars. The woman fell into her seat, causing dust to powder the air. Annika coughed and waved her hand, clearing in the air.

The woman smiled at her, the corners of her eyes crinkling. "You must have the weight of the world on your shoulders this morning. Are you traveling alone?"

"I'm just tired," Annika answered, avoiding the question. Her travel status wasn't any of this lady's business.

"Well, it's brave of you if you're alone. I shouldn't say it, but Rovalkia isn't what it used to be. So many businesses boarded up in Karaxin—that surprised me." The woman tutted. "And so many missing persons signs plastered everywhere. I'd never let *my* kids travel alone through here." Her eyes went wide. "Oh my gosh. You're from here, aren't you? Forgive me for my rudeness. Karaxin used to feel so vibrant thirty years ago." She looked out the window. "Where'd all the businesses go?"

"Moved on, I suppose." Annika tapped on her knees while glancing out the window. *They were like me. Cast out because they were different.*

5

"Ah, but you're young, huh? I can tell. Your eyes are so fresh. Those emerald eyes and silver hair are a beautiful combination. Very Rovalkian. Life hasn't placed a single crease on your face yet. Just wait until life catches up. Then bam," she slammed her hand into her fist, "you're old."

Annika frowned at her, and the woman let out a nervous laugh. "But what do I know? Anyway, tell me about this new leader. What's his name, again?" She tapped her chin. "Anyway, he promises considerable progress. People must believe him, with those polling numbers. I've been reading all about his speeches in Calageeh. It astounds me that Rovalkian's want more of an extremist in charge." She slapped her hands on her legs, causing Annika to raise an eyebrow. "But what do we coast folk know about the workings of inlanders? My name is Frida." The lady smiled and reached her hand out toward Annika's face.

She regarded the woman, looking at her calf-length floral skirt, which was as faded as the seat fabric, down to meet her wrinkled beige stockings tucked into black clogs. Not the type of clothes someone working as a witch hunter looked like. Her father had pointed them out in the streets to her on several occasions. They all wore perfectly tailored business suits. But one could never be too careful. An old rose scent traveled with her hand, and Annika held her breath, returning the handshake with a tight-lipped smile. "Nice to meet you. My name is Sarah." She tried to read Frida while the woman smiled back, none the wiser. *Let's see if you are a potential threat to my freedom.*

Annika pushed her psyche forward, connecting with the unsuspecting woman's mind, and found no malice lurking beneath her agitation and lingering sorrow. *Frayed nerves from a funeral or meeting gone wrong, I suppose.* She released her psychic hold and settled back to stare out the window while Frida rummaged through her purse, now talking about her garden. Or was it her kids' garden? The train picked up speed, lulling Annika's anxious mind with its swaying motion.

Karaxin's cityscape transitioned abruptly. Annika scooted closer to the window to see the parts her father never let her travel to. Buildings on the outskirts of Karaxin were in disrepair, and huge chunks of wall crumbled near the train tracks. She spied a tattered Rovalkian flag hanging limp on a bent flagpole; the sun-bleached green serpent eating a sword looked more sad than intimidating as they whizzed by. *The flag's supposed to symbolize us devouring conquering enemies, but it should show the truth: the government devouring its own citizens.*

Countryside farms eventually replaced the dilapidated buildings. Annika turned her attention to the cabin and fished through her book bag for lunch. "Frida, how long does it take to reach Ausurnia's border?"

"About an hour more if my memory serves me correct. I see you brought lunch. I may walk down to the lunch car to—"

BANG! The cabin door slammed open. Frida yelped, and Annika's hands flew up to shield her face. Seconds ticked by in silence; Annika peeked through her fingers. A Rovalkian police officer stood in the doorway, staring down at her. He wore a black helmet and a Rovalkian flag patch upon his bullet-proof vest. One hand gripped a small notebook; the other rested on the butt of a pistol strapped in its holster.

"Sorry to disturb you, ladies. We're looking for someone—a young male with black hair, black eyes, and dark features. We suspect he's an Ausurnian spy. Nothing to stress about, but we need to know if you've seen anyone matching this description?" he asked as his narrow gray eyes searched the cabin, eventually falling back on Annika.

She picked her wax paper wrapped sandwich up off the floor, her heart thumping loud in her ears. "No officer. You're the first person to pass by here, sir."

The officer looked at Frida and she gaped, "I don't know of any such creature. I'm going home to Calageeh. I'd *never* cover for someone from that accursed country."

He pursed his lips and turned his attention back to Annika, looking her up and down. "Well, I guess you two look respectable enough. A couple of my men and I are two train cars up if you spot the boy. We have until Ausurnia's border to make an arrest. And you are, Miss?" His eyes pierced into hers while he waited for a response.

She swallowed the bile rising in her throat. "My name is Sarah. I'm visiting my boyfriend who's working in—in Calageeh." The police officer frowned, so she tilted her head toward Frida and smiled, trying for a quick recovery. "Don't worry, we'll keep an eye out for any *unsavory* looking characters."

The officer drew his eyebrows together. "This train makes one stop in Ausurnia. If you see anyone getting off, try to get a physical description and come find us." Then he scribbled in his notebook.

"Yes, yes, we will," Frida rushed out, pointing toward the door. "But right now, I'd like to get lunch while it's still available."

"Uh, yeah, okay." He touched his helmet, looking at Frida. "Ma'am."

Frida waved him away. When the door clicked shut, Annika exhaled, slouching back in the seat. The older woman smiled at her. "You handled that situation very well, Sarah. Police officers or not, Rovalkian men frighten me with how they stomp about. I'm sure he would've acted more forcefully had it not been for your lovely face and demeanor. Thank goodness he was a police officer and not a military man, huh? Don't worry, I won't leave you alone. I just wanted him gone."

"Thank you, Frida." So even non-Rovalkians knew about the Rovalkian military's martial law antics. She turned her attention back to her bag and threw the sandwich inside. The folded paper containing cryptic notes for her potential new life lay next to the discarded sandwich. She stared at the folded page, letting her thoughts travel back to the plan: First, get to Ausurnia without being arrested. Try to find a job. If that doesn't pan out, move on to the next town, heading west. Once settled, find someone who knows where the rebels hide out. According to rumors she'd heard, most everyone on this continent could speak Truscan, so it wouldn't be necessary to learn the Ausurnian language right away..

Annika took a deep breath and pushed the bag off her lap. She moved her hands up the front of her jacket, her fingers playing over each of the six black buttons, checking they weren't loose. First impressions are of the utmost importance was lesson number three. Every week had been a new lesson. Every week she's had to repeat them all, starting with number one: never have your back to a stranger.

Looking back outside, Annika watched the rolling hills and far away shadows of the Abaxan Grasslands grow closer. Spring flaunted itself in different shades of green, adding depth to the landscape in a watercolor effect. Would there be sympathetic Ausurnians in these wild lands? Would they know where to find the underground base of rebels?

She glanced over at Frida. The woman had a Calageeh newspaper propped in front of her face. The date in the corner read 2200 AC. *At Calageeh. Our Rovalkian year is only 99 AR. What would our year be had they not restarted the clock after the revolution?*

The front headline facing Annika read:

TWO MORE FEMALES MISSING IN NORTH ROVALKIA.
WHO TO BLAME?

The articles beneath highlighted recent riots and protests, and a graph in the corner showed the percentage of people who didn't believe the landslide victory of the recent election. Forty percent. *He'll be the most fanatical leader the Rovalkian government has ever sworn in. Can anyone even afford his tax and housing proposal? What's his name again? Terry? Jerry? His face is on posters everywhere, but not his name. So strange. I'd put money on him being the perpetrator behind the increasing number of disappearances, too. The rebels have their work cut out. Just another reason to get out now. Who knows what he has in store for our hundred-year anniversary celebration…*

Annika leaned her head back and stared at the ceiling speckled with different colored stains. *The citizens' eyes are opening. Mine certainly are. I'll figure out the truth. My generation will be the one to reclaim Rovalkia. And I'm going to help them do it.*

A tugging sensation in her psyche made her glance down. Frida peered at her over the newspaper. Annika faked stifling an enormous yawn and kept watching the landscape go by. Her stomach nausea increased. She swallowed hard and closed her eyes. Every sensationalist newspaper and gossip television host painted Ausurnia as a country full of heartless monsters who prey on people venturing too close to the Land of Shadows. They couldn't be any worse than the uniformed monsters that preyed on the citizens in Rovalkia, could they? She built up a psychic wall around herself to nudge away the woman's stares.

Their cabin door opened. Frida and Annika's heads turned, and a young train clerk asked to punch tickets. Frida handed hers over first. He took longer looking over Annika's ticket. "Pontagu stop is coming up soon, miss. Collect your bags and head to an exit."

Annika nodded and got her luggage down. She turned around and froze, seeing Frida's dilated eyes and her mouth forming an O.

"What? What is it?" Annika swiveled her head around, looking for clues.

"Pontagu? That's in Ausurnia. Why are you getting off there? Didn't you say you're going to Calageeh? Did they make a mistake on your ticket? It's not safe there." Frida stood, shaking her hands. "Why do they still have that place as a legitimate stop? I'll flag the boy down. He must allow you to ride on to Mortainy Station."

Annika fell back into her seat, and her bags spilled out into the hallway. She gritted her teeth as she climbed over the side of her chair to get around Frida. "Frida, no. It *is* my stop. Let me out."

Frida gasped and clutched at her heaving chest while her other hand stretched out. "No, you mustn't. Those people, that land—cursed! No one enters the country and comes back—alive or dead. Please, stay and ride on to Calageeh with me. You can stay with me until you get your itinerary sorted out."

The train car lurched, and Annika tripped over her luggage. She balked and stumbled to one side. "No. I don't know you. This is my stop. It's as far as I can afford to travel. It's all a bunch of conspiracy theories, anyway." She slung her bag over one shoulder and dragged her suitcase down to the train car's main exit door.

"Come back, Sarah."

"Mind your own business," Annika hollered, flipping her loose hair over one shoulder as she stood facing the exit door. Then she froze and scouted the hall. *How long would it take those policemen to get back here?* Frida still leaned out of the cabin's doorframe, staring at her. The train chugged to a full stop, and Annika hastened out onto a wooden platform. The door jerked shut, and the locomotive sped off into the afternoon sun. *If Frida ever discovers what I am capable of, she'll be glad I got off.* Taking a few steps forward, the sun-bleached floorboards creaked underfoot. The openly constructed shelter had no building or ticket office. A wooden sign's white, chipped letters were the only indication she had got off at the right stop.

She turned in a slow circle, seeing the sloping landscape go on and on. Cool air breezed through the cloudless sky, causing the tall grass to ripple. Annika gazed back eastward. *Someday I'll be back, James and*

Sarah. The sinking sun illuminated the land, unhindered with no other person or car to be seen.

Annika looked around once more, tugging at her necklace and chewing on her lower lip. As silver wisps of hair tickled her cheek, she took the road headed north that snaked its way through the surrounding hills before her.

* * *

The overgrown dirt road continued with no sign of civilization. Small birds chased each other across the endless pale blue sky. Annika smiled at them. *There's nothing scary about this place so far.* She glanced down at her clothes and wiped the kicked-up dust from her pants and shoes. *So much for shining my boots last night.* The breeze picked up speed, dragging loose hairs across her face. She stopped to spit out wavy mid-back length strands and pull the now unruly mass over to the other shoulder.

A house materialized in the distance, small and forlorn in the countryside. *Well, it's a start.* Annika picked up her pace. The quantity of homes increased around every hill, and each house appeared to be built closer to the next. Finally, buildings resembling a midtown area rose beyond the homes. The dark greens of a forest beyond that hugged the northern outskirts, and she spotted ephemeral cars and bodies moving in the twilight.

She froze. "What the—?" Something moved in her peripheral vision. *A small animal?* Annika resumed walking, now looking to her left and right. Her scalp tingled. *I sense you watching me. Where are you, little creature?* She stopped behind a tree and peeked around. *What the— ?* Figures darted between homes, keeping in the shadows. *Are those kids?* She scrambled to the middle of the road and detected movement in a nearby shadowed recess out of the corner of her eye. She looked over, but it ran off before she got a good look. Annika walked faster. *Ausurnia is called the Land of Shadows. So, what lives in the shadows?*

The Land of Shadows

Colonial style buildings lined both sides of a busy street. She looked up at a street sign. Main Street. Annika tightened her grip on the bag and suitcase and strode forward. The cobblestones carried traffic sounds much better than the asphalt covered streets of Rovalkia. People passed by and paused their conversations or stopped walking to gawk. Annika stared back, observing their bland clothes. No wonder they were staring. Her red jacket was the brightest piece of clothing around. She watched other Ausurnians cross the street. Those who didn't have big black hoods shrouding their faces had long black hair that they wore either wrapped up on their heads or billowing down their back, swirling in the breeze.

Her sweaty palms slipped on the suitcase handle. *Come on, Annika, keep going. I'm sure they're more afraid of you than you are of them. Now ask someone for directions.*

Across the street up ahead, warm light beamed from a blue storefront. The breeze picked up speed, blowing aromas of baked goods and fresh brewed coffee into her face. Her stomach growled. *What I would give for a Sunday roast.*

She paused just outside the glow of a lamppost to observe the people entering and exiting the building's front door. Those leaving appeared to be carrying bags, similar to what restaurants offered back home. The neon sign in Ausurnian didn't help, though.

Annika crossed the street and peeked through the front bay window. It had the setup of an eatery, and one lone stool sat unoccupied at the counter. She backed away from the window, twisted her hair into a knot, and dusted off her pants for the umpteenth time. Standing tall with her suitcase in hand, she made her way inside, focusing her eyes on the white-tiled floor as weighty stares and silence descended.

Annika felt a penetrating stare coming from behind the counter, and when she looked up, a pair of warm chocolate eyes gazed at her. She took in the thick, black braids wrapped around the woman's head; her smile striking with a warmth she hadn't experienced in a long time. The woman leaned toward her.

"Hello stranger," she said in accented Truscan. "Where're you headed, sweetie? The nightly fog is rolling in quick and thick. I'll help you if I can." She winked and slipped Annika a tall glass of water and a cookie.

"Thanks." Annika took a sip of water. "I've a room at the local hotel. Can you give me directions?"

"Of course," she said, pointing left. "If you follow this street—"

Suddenly, a strong presence buffeted her from behind. The woman put her hands on her hips, and a small frown formed on her lips, looking at whoever it was. Annika's seat squeaked as she turned to glance that way. A tall figure blocked the entrance. Control and suspicion emanated from him in waves, making Annika clutch the counter for support. *Damn!* Her chest tightened and an invisible weight pressed her head down. *I should've put up my shield.* The mysterious person strode forward, bringing into view a strong jawline veiled in day old stubble. A stern frown was visible from beneath his hooded uniform, and his shoulders were further broadened by his black leather vest studded with three medals and striped patches on one side.

The place fell silent. Annika glanced around to see the patrons looking back and forth between him and her, their expressions ranging from curious to worried. His psyche continued to press against her own. She fought against the mental invasion, staring back; never breaking contact with where his eyes should be. The uniform he wore had an attachment on the hood, masking his eyes. The ensemble resembled the others she'd noticed outside. Instead of the cape draped down, though, the bottom right corner was tied to his belt. There was a large badge above the medals that she hadn't seen on anyone else so far. He closed the remaining distance with silent, quick steps. One hand rested on the black hilt of a knife sheathed at his hip, the frown deepening on his lips. Her gaze zeroed in on the weapon, examining its size and shape. Rule Twenty: Know what weapons your enemy carries and position yourself on their non-dominant side to evade attack.

"You're causing quite a stir with your presence here, miss. What's your name?"

Annika narrowed her eyes. "None of your business." She rotated back around to the counter, even though her heart was pounding. *Can he hear it?* The friendly server looked from Annika to the man.

"Nephew, it'd help if you introduced yourself first. The poor girl thinks you're trying to arrest her."

Annika spun back to face him, intrigued by the familial connection.

"I'm Captain Donauska, of the Ausurnian military. I got a call to inquire about a suspicious girl walking into town alone. My job is to keep my people safe. So, I'm only going to ask you one more time. What is your name and business here?" His gaze continued to penetrate her psyche while his aura, still solid, still powerful, retreated. A thick, whispered accent punctuated his Truscan, sending tingles through her. Annika shivered and looked back to his aunt.

The lady gave her an encouraging nod and a look that said do as he asks before saying, "I'm sure he'd be happy to give you a lift to the hotel. I'll call Tiana to reassure her of your safe arrival since you mentioned your phone's battery died. Now run along and don't forget your cookie."

Annika stood, nodding in understanding, and wrapped the cookie in a napkin, pocketing it. "Thank you," she whispered and picked up her bookbag. Then, turning to the captain, she asked, "Would you be able to give me that ride?" Captain Donauska's hooded face remained stony. Then he gave a curt nod, turned, and left. She rolled her eyes, raised her chin, and followed, muttering, "What a gentleman."

The captain opened the front passenger door of a large, black four-door vehicle and paused. "Put your roller suitcase in the back. I had my car's interior cleaned today."

She went around and pulled at the trunk's handle. It didn't budge. She shouted around the side, "Is there a trick to opening this?" Instead of answering, the car door opened, and she saw the car bounce as the captain got in. Annika released her grip on her suitcase and used both hands to tug at the handle. It eased open inch by inch, as if it weighed a hundred pounds. She looked at the doorframe, perplexed by the unaccustomed weight; the frame of the car was twice as thick as any she had been in. Shrugging, Annika smacked at the dust covering her suitcase, then heaved it up into the car.

After shoving the trunk closed, Annika marched to the front passenger door, glancing at the tires on her way. *They're as tall as my waist! This car must be bomb-proof.* She bounced on the balls of her feet and hauled herself up into the passenger seat. Captain Donauska waited until she had buckled to start the car.

17

Annika stole glances at him out of the corner of her eye as he turned the car westward. Power emanated from him, but it washed around her instead of attacking. Ambient light within the car allowed Annika to admire his black uniform, from the dyed leather of his gloves to whatever blend of cotton his fitted pants were. Completely shrouded, he excited her imagination, reminding her of the mysterious character in her favorite novel. Was the body underneath this man's clothes as muscled and tight as the contoured fit suggested? Taking a deep breath, she forced herself to look away, pushing the fantasy aside.

"This car is a beast. It reminds me of the military cars back home." She snuck another peek while drumming her fingers on her knees. "So, do you have a first name?"

The captain didn't answer.

"Your aunt is nice. How far to the hotel?"

He remained silent.

Is this guy for real? It's like talking to a mannequin. She smirked to herself. "Have you reached your word limit for the day?" His gloved hand clenched around the steering wheel, and she flinched at her overconfidence. "I was only kidding, Mr. Donauska. Just trying to make conversation."

The captain parked in front of a five-story, white-washed building. A single desk lamp was on in the lobby; she could just make out a head poking up behind the desk. He turned off the engine and pointed up to a neon sign Annika couldn't translate. "We're here."

She unbuckled her seatbelt. "That didn't take long. I could've walked here. How far was that? Three blocks?"

"Yes. But unlike you, I worked all day. I'm exhausted. And call me Captain Donauska, not mister." He turned toward her. "Before I let you out, you need to tell me your name and how you know my cousin." His finger pressed down on the power-lock button.

18

Annika's heart thumped, and she gulped against her constricted throat. She did her best to form an innocent smile, but his frown didn't waver. She swallowed once more and sat up taller. "My name is Annika Mullway, and we are international pen pals." She tapped the bookbag at her feet. "I've got her phone number in my phone if you want to see it— tomorrow when its recharged. Who are you anyway? Chief of police?"

A loud exhale flared his nostrils. "You know nothing about the Kingdom of Ausurnia, do you? Soldiers double as law enforcement. And I *will* find out if you're hiding something—don't try anything. I'll have my eye on you." Then his finger released the locks.

"Be my guest. Waste your time looking for something on me," Annika snapped as she hopped out, grabbed her bags, and hurried inside.

Sheilds Up

S he stood in front of the bathroom mirror, roping her hair into a knot atop her head. "Stupid, stupid girl. You shouldn't have snapped at him. Now he really is going to look into you," she chided herself. The room's phone rang, and she jumped, releasing her carefully wound hair. No one should know she was here. She hastened to the phone.

"Miss Mullway, this is the front desk. Tiana Donauska is here. Can I send her up?"

Tiana who? Oh, no.

"Hello? Miss Mullway? Are you still there?"

"Ah, yes. Just, ah, tell her I'll meet her in the lobby in a minute." Annika laid the phone down. Should she try to slip out the back? But that may be even more suspicious. The woman from last night must've known this Tiana person may be a good alibi. She had lied so smoothly for a complete stranger. Perhaps Tiana would make an ally. Annika pinned up her hair, stabbing her scalp several times, grabbed her bookbag and trudged downstairs.

Chatting with the receptionist was a lanky girl with straight, black hair down to her waist. Her hands waved as she spoke Ausurnian, saying something that made the receptionist double over with laughter. As Annika edged forward, the tall Ausurnian spun around. Annika stopped short.

"There you are," the girl, presumably named Tiana, said in Truscan. "Mom said you got in late last night. Want to get some breakfast?" Even from the six feet between them, Annika could feel the girl's calm aura and see the kindness in her sparkling brown eyes. Her mother's eyes. Annika nodded and followed her outside.

Once they had made it to the sidewalk, the tall girl stopped and turned. "Mom said you looked like you needed a friend when my cousin came around. He hasn't called me yet, but we should get our stories straight before he does."

"Oh, yes. Thanks," Annika said, taken aback. Tiana smiled, signature Ausurnian sharp fangs pointing down. But nothing about this girl felt threatening. "My name is Annika. Annika Mullway. From Rovalkia. I said we were pen pals."

Tiana tipped her head to one side and held out her hand. "Nice to meet you, Annika. I like your name. And that red coat is fantastic. I was serious about breakfast, if you don't mind. Mom wants to treat us."

"Sure." Annika nodded just as her stomach growled, eliciting a laugh from Tiana.

"Mind if we stop by my grandmother's shop on the way? Mom wants to know if I can bring her any food, too."

"Sure. Is your grandmother or mother hiring at all? I'm looking for work in-between traveling."

Tiana clapped her hands together. "How serendipitous! Gran mentioned needing help at the shop just last week. Then she had a dream

21

that help would arrive. That must be you! Let's go, quick!" She grabbed hold of Annika's hand, and they ran across the street and into a pale green shop. "Grandma! I found you an assistant."

Annika allowed herself to be pulled to the checkout counter at the rear of the shop as heady smells of herbs and spices enveloped her. Shock from Tiana's words had fried her brain. She'd never had a psychic dream. *These people may be more powerful than theorized.* A woman about Tiana's height walked out of the small, adjacent room. She wore a black, floor-length skirt with a black blouse, and her swept up black hair pinned in a bun like Annika's. A single thick streak of gray originated at her left temple. Deep brown eyes observed Annika from head to toe. Slow and thoughtful. A calm aura radiated from the woman, just like Tiana, and it put Annika at ease. She stood as tall as she could and glanced around. A small shop that sold spices? She could do that.

The woman's eyes paused on Annika's forehead. Annika felt a slight tingle in between her eyebrows. "You have quite the psyche, young lady. What's your name?"

"Annika Mullway, ma'am," she gulped. Her hands twitched at her sides. The woman had just called out the one thing Annika kept secret to keep herself alive. Tiana's grandmother offered a hand to shake, and Annika accepted. A powerful energy flowed from the older woman and embraced Annika like a plush robe. Yes, she could work here. She sent that desire as a thought to the woman, hoping it would help.

"I can start today if you need me to, ma'am."

"Call me Tracy or Mrs. Donauska, whichever you're more comfortable with," Tracy said with a smile. "Why don't you start tomorrow? And if you'd like, I have a small apartment available for rent upstairs that I only charge utilities for?"

She couldn't believe her luck. A job and an apartment on the first day? There had to be a catch. Annika looked around and stretched her psyche upward to the second floor, searching for any sign of a trap.

"Does that amount to very much? I'd be only able to pay you what I make from this job."

"Oh no, no, dear. I pay a livable wage and utilities amount to around three percent of that. The last girl to live there got married last month, hence the vacancy. I understand your hesitations, but I am very transparent. How about you give both a one-week trial? No contracts to sign." There was a sense of safety in Tracy's words, like she somehow understood Annika's predicament without being told. There wasn't an ounce of suspicion in this woman's aura; Annika would've felt it. She retracted her psyche and nodded.

"I appreciate that, Mrs. Donauska."

Tracy picked up a purse from behind the counter. "Wonderful! Let's show you to your apartment, then. Oh, and if you haven't already noted, military personnel—which there are many here being that it's a military base town—are never called by their first name, so don't take it personally if they don't offer it up. I don't suppose you have a car?" Annika shook her head. "No worries. Main street has all the shops to buy essentials. Ask Tiana or myself where to go for anything else."

"I'll make sure she has me on speed dial, Gran. Oh, and Mom wants to treat you to breakfast with us."

They went up wooden, sun-bleached stairs behind the shop. Tracy unlocked the door and flipped on a light, revealing a one-room apartment. The kitchenette, with white countertops, sat to the right, and an open door revealed a bathroom beyond. The single bed, complete with a mattress and slate gray sheets, sat along the east wall. Opposite the bed stood a wood stove.

"I picked out the blue paint after the last girl moved out," Tiana said, sweeping her hand around. "Isn't it a happy little room? And all yours."

Annika craned her head around Tiana. On the north wall, a four-paned window overlooked Main Street. A dark blue lounge chair and

23

wooden bookcase sat next to it. She stepped further inside. It smelled of fresh linen and lemon oil. Annika arched her eyebrows up as she turned in a circle. "Mrs. Donauska, this is more—"

"Oh, let's go. I'm starving," Tiana interrupted. Annika spun around. "My stomach is going to eat itself if we don't get food soon. It's an apartment. We get it." Tiana grabbed Annika's arm, tugging her back outside.

Annika blinked. "Let go."

Tracy handed over the apartment's keys to Annika. "Tiana, let the girl go. You need to learn self-restraint. But yes, let's get some breakfast."

Tiana let go of Annika and muttered, "Sorry," as she skipped ahead.

Crouched figures darted around the nearest corner. Annika stopped short, pointing toward the dark recesses of the alley. "Please tell me those are kids or pets running in the shadows. I saw them last night, too."

The two women tittered; Annika felt her cheeks flush. Tiana waved her hand in the direction Annika had pointed. "Yeah, how else would they work their energy out? My little brothers run somewhere around here and in the woods—"

"You let kids run in the woods?"

"They're fine," Tracy assured.

Annika stared down the dark alley. "But they're kids." The faces of James and Sarah popped into her head and her heart ached. "What if something or someone grabs them?"

"Ha! If they're stupid enough to try, the kids would teach them a lesson. Just pretend they're not there." Tiana grabbed Annika's arm and tugged her back. "It's hard enough to get them to sit for a meal. Try babysitting them. It's a nightmare. They're safe in their little packs and will go home when tired. My siblings always do."

"So why is Ausurnia called the Land of Shadows?"

A passerby bowed to Tracy. "Good morning," Tracy said and then turned to Annika. "Hmm? Oh. Shadows is an Ausurnian translation. It means soldier. Ausurnian soldier, to be exact. The Land of Ausurnian Soldiers. And they're the best in this world. Here we are."

Best in the world? Annika turned back around to see they'd arrived at the same eatery from last night.

"Welcome to my parents' diner," Tiana declared as she opened the door. The same woman from last night strode up to them. "Hi, mom. This is Annika, grandma's new employee. Annika, this is my mom, Jenny Donauska."

Jenny offered her hand to Annika. "It's a pleasure to meet you, Annika. Welcome to Pontagu and Ausurnia. Hello, Tracy. I'm glad to hear you have brought on an assistant. Come sit down, you three. I'll bring out the food."

Moments later, Jenny presented Annika with a steaming plate piled high with food. "A local favorite," Jenny explained. Red powder heavily coated the fried eggs and vegetables. "On the house as a welcome to Ausurnia." She set identical plates of food before Tracy and Tiana.

"Thank you," Annika said, and picked at the foreign meal. She nibbled a chunk of potato. Her entire mouth lit up from whatever pepper hid in that red powder. She resorted to chewing and swallowing in quick succession, trying to control her watering eyes.

"Our capital, Fringur, is good for boutique shopping." Tiana counted out each fact on her fingers next to Annika. "The next country over, Calageeh, is the best for buying wares in bulk, and our south coast is best for vacationing. The forest isn't scary if you go in with someone." She took a deep breath as Annika snorted into her cup.

"What's so funny?" Tiana scowled, her eyes flashing. "I'm trying to help you."

Annika held a napkin to her mouth. "I'm sorry. It's just, you claimed to be hungry, but you keep talking instead of eating. It's endearing."

Tiana's scowl turned into a blushing grin, and Annika relaxed back in her seat.

"Unlike my stupid cousin, I enjoy helping."

"We don't talk ill of our family members, Tiana," Tracy warned.

"Well, he is," Tiana mumbled.

Annika nodded and winked at her. "I appreciate all the help I can get. Thank you."

The Ausurnian girl bounced in her seat. Between bites, she asked, "So what brings you here? I thought Rovalkians distrust and hate us?"

Annika glowered at her. So much for a cover story. Tiana's widened eyes told her she had realized her mistake. "I mean, you had said you'd wanted to visit sometime, but I thought you were just being nice," she lied.

"I've been told the same," Annika said, annoyed, glancing around. Tiana's mouth formed an O and looked down at her own plate. *Great, Annika. You're alienating yourself already.* She tried again. "Never mind. I'm not a huge fan of my country right now, to be honest. I'm hoping to make something of myself abroad. Then I'll go back and help reshape Rovalkia. And reunite with my family."

Tracy held one finger to her lips. "Take care of who's around when you say such things, dear. You're in good company at this table, but I can't speak for everyone." Annika slumped down in the chair; her eyes darted back to the front door, half expecting a line of soldiers to come rushing in to arrest her. She'd seen it happen back home frequently. Tracy fluttered her hand at Annika. "Don't assume that of all Ausurnians. Just be aware of your surroundings. So, what do your parents think about your, er, extended visit here?"

"They don't know," Annika whispered.

Tracy raised her eyebrows. "Oh." Then a softness settled in her eyes. "Okay, ah, then what of yourself do you desire to refine?"

Annika pushed her plate away, drained her water, and looked Tracy in the eye. "I wish to become smarter and stronger—a fighter." She smirked, imagining herself in a military uniform with war paint on her face.

Tiana clapped her hands together. "Oh, Grandma, don't you just love her spirit? We're going to have so much fun, Annika. I'll teach you *everything.*"

"Tiana, remember our rules," Tracy said and gave her granddaughter a stern look. "One day at a time. Annika said she wants to learn, not *become* an Ausurnian. It's time I got back to the shop. I just need to speak with Jenny."

Annika tracked her employer's walk to the counter while she asked Tiana, "What rules?"

"There are laws that govern how we interact with outsiders. Don't worry, I'll find a loophole. Come on, we'll walk back with her." Tiana hopped out of the booth and headed to the front door.

As they trudged back to Annika's apartment, Tiana turned to her. "Do you like shopping?"

Annika kicked at a large pebble. Then she jumped away from the sidewalk's edge as a military truck rolled by. *I'm an outsider who looks like one. Who knows when they'll try to snatch me up?* "Um, Mom hires out the shopping and we only have one car dad takes to work. The streets of Karaxin are dangerous." She looked back at the receding armored truck.

"Oh. Well, it's quite safe here as long as you follow the rules. Did she give you your pretty necklace?"

Annika's hand shot to it. "No, uh, it's a gift from my maternal grandmother."

"When did she give it to you?" Tracy asked.

"Well." *Do I tell them the truth?* "My mother inherited it after she passed away, but she threw it in the trash since it's a symbol of the old, forbidden gods. I dug it out and hid it away. Today's the first day I've ever worn it. It's all I have to remember her by."

She saw the two women exchange a look, then Tiana slowed to Annika's pace. "We have old horseshoes nailed to the walls of the barn for good luck. The horses are an old breed that we keep around for sentimental reasons. We should go to the beach with them. It's exhilarating when they splash through the waves."

Annika perked up. "I've never ridden horseback, but I do love the beach. We went to the southern Rovalkian coast every so often." She stifled a yawn as they reached her apartment. Constantly being on guard was exhausting. Tiana wrapped an arm around her shoulders.

"I'm so glad you're here, Annika. I know we'll be the best of friends."

Tracy pulled her granddaughter away. "I'm sure you will. You're welcome to move in today if you'd like, Annika. I hope you find what you're looking for, whatever it is. But don't forget to find inner peace. Sometimes terrible things happen. But those things can drop us on a path to the best things that could ever happen in our lives."

Annika tilted her head to one side. "I don't understand."

"Grandma's always speaking in riddles. You'll get used to it. We'll catch up later, okay?"

Annika nodded and turned to climb the stairs. The Donauska women gave one last wave and slipped back into the shop.

Uneven Ground

Captain Donauska

He was a master of his craft: accurately reading the inner depths, the truth, of anyone within seconds. Friend or enemy—it was one or the other, no exceptions. That his cousin had *invited* a Rovalkian, their sworn enemy, into the country made him worry, though. He shook his head. His conclusion had landed in the middle. The dreaded gray area. Annika's posture had exposed her as someone in unfamiliar surroundings, and yet, she was confident in a way that said she was telling the truth.

As he laid down to sleep, his thoughts argued. *What if she's a spy? I bet the new Rovalkian leader is itching to get hold of our state secrets. I won't let those apple-green eyes enchant me. No, they're darker than that, like the deep greens of our forest during the first weeks of summer. Damn.*

Annika

She stepped outside and took a deep breath of the crisp morning air. "I will make this a good day," she said as she opened the back door to the shop. Tracy stood at the counter, opening a box. "Am I late, Mrs. Donauska?"

"Good morning, Annika. No, you're not late. I wanted to get an early start since it's your first day. Let's make tea and chat."

Annika turned to where her boss motioned. An electric kettle and boxes of tea and coffee sat in the corner. Her mouth watered at the sight of a glass jar full of biscuits. "I'll make the tea." She hurried over to the kettle. "My mother always had me make the tea and offer two biscuits to guests. Let me know if you like it any different."

"Your mother taught you well," Tracy said, and sat down in her office chair while Annika took a seat on the adjacent little couch. Tracy brought the steaming blue ceramic mug to her lips. Annika noticed how elegant her boss looked in the natural light from the small window. That single patch of gray stood out in her black hair was once again swept up in a bun. Lines around Tracy's eyes were those of life and laughs, her makeup light and flawless. *She's as classy as Grandma Mullway had been.*

Tracy set down her mug. "Now, let's see where you are in your herbal knowledge. Can I assume you know basic remedies found in a kitchen?"

Annika's fingers traced the edge of the sage-green couch's square armrest. "I might identify common herbs and spices, but I couldn't tell you what the medical uses are. My parents say traditional medicine is as false as the old gods." Annika raised her eyes to meet Tracy's and felt her pulse quicken as the woman's gaze hardened. "Not that *I* am opposed to learning—I don't recall from yesterday you needing me to know any medical knowledge. But I'm a diligent worker. I'll clean." She searched the room and her eyes fell on a calculator. "And can add in my head and will do anything else you need—"

"Annika, stop." Tracy raised her hand. "I want you, nay, will *require* you to learn everything I know to run this shop. It's my goal to leave you in charge on days when my garden or family require my attention. You have more skills than you would admit to, young lady, regardless of any book knowledge, and I can prove it. Come, stand with me on the sales floor." Tracy strode out of her office. Annika downed the last bit of tea, shoved another biscuit in her mouth, and hurried after the lively older woman.

"We're going to try an exercise. Close your eyes and hold out your hand."

Annika obeyed. Through lowered eyelids, she stared at the floor. Never have your back turned or eyes closed around a stranger; an extension of rule one. The dry scrapping sound of a lid being unscrewed perked away her thoughts. Annika steeled herself as she closed her fingers around the object placed into her hand, feeling the edges and texture. An earthy smell reached her nose above all the spice dust lingering in the air.

"Now, tell me what you feel," her boss commanded.

"I think it's a dry mushroom."

"No, not what it is. Listen to it. It *is* a dried mushroom. But what does the mushroom *tell* you?"

Annika took a deep breath and emptied her mind. Words popped into her head one at a time. "Grounding. Minerals. Strength."

"Ah, very good," Tracy cheered. "That mushroom is good for stamina."

Annika looked from the mushroom in her hand to Tracy. "My parents told me any random words or thoughts were a dark entity trying to speak to me. It never feels evil, but I don't know where it comes from." She looked out the front window. Her forehead was tingling again. *A warning? Or is Tracy reading my mind like yesterday?* "The words pop into my head. Words and images are always popping into my head..." *I've said too much.* She glanced at Tracy's face to gauge her reaction.

"It's because you're psychic."

Annika sucked in a breath. She was going to get arrested for sure. "You shouldn't say such things out loud."

"Calm down," Tracy said, and placed a hand on her arm. "You're safe here. Why do you think I hired you? We're kindred spirits. Ausurnians are born with the same innate abilities as you've shown."

Dammit, I've got to learn to stop being so transparent. It's best to pretend not to know what she's talking about. "But I'm Rovalkian." She looked down at her own hands. They clenched and unclenched as a constant feeling of energy flowed through and around them.

"I don't define souls by where they land in the world. It's what goodness lies within and how you choose to use the gifts given to you. Just because your people look like Kraxxan, God of Winter, and we look like Bandau, God of Summer, doesn't mean we're completely different. We're all still kin of the Void. Let's try more."

Annika followed her around. *Can I use these gifts to save Rovalkia?* Tracy replicated the exercise with various products. Annika closed her eyes and let the answers come to her.

"Well, I'll be. You have a strong connection to the Void, *and* you trust enough to listen. But it's a bad idea to have others know of your abilities until you become more established here." Tracy paused. "We'll go to the library at lunchtime. Since I'll be employing you, I'll act as your sponsor here, in case your government asks questions. There should be traditional medical literature written in Truscan, so you can learn the names and science-based uses. It's best to keep your psychic shield up all the time, too."

"H—How do you know about that?" Annika took a step back. Psychic shield. The term that had prompted her to bring home that accursed book. She should've put it back. She shouldn't have opened it. But she wanted to understand. Who could blame her?

"From that astonished look, you know what you're doing. I wondered." Tracy regarded her. "I'm guessing you found a book on the old Rovalkian faith and tried to understand the concept of a psychic shield?"

Annika gaped. "How'd you know? I wasn't even thinking about anything."

Tracy smiled. "Your people's old polytheistic faith morphed to reflect much of ours after years of cultural exchange. Long before the Religious Revolution in Rovalkia, all three countries got along splendidly. That's when we built the transcontinental railroad, back before the World Intelligence Committee even existed. See, in the Ausurnian faith, we believe in the Void—does your faith still talk about it?" Annika shook her head. "I didn't think so. It's where everyone and everything originated from and will return to when we die, including the gods. It's the source of our power. We believe the Void imparts the gift of energy manipulation. Some, like you, are born with the gift without the awareness." She lowered her voice. "But between you and me, anyone can be psychic if they understand the science behind it. Thoughts and intentions are more like wavelengths. That's how they can move *through* people and objects. It takes practice, but I believe anyone can thought-project. It's just energy and we're all made of it. Having a well-built psychic shield around oneself will protect you from others with the same gift. Shields are of the same energy wavelengths as the projections. Elders here teach it from an early age, and meditating will build your psychic potential."

Annika shuddered at the memory of Captain's energy in the diner. "That's good to know. In the Rovalkian faith, only the devout get to join the one mighty god, Kraxxan, in paradise. Your faith sounds more interesting and inclusive. Who's the strongest god in your faith?"

"There's a god we thank for each season. They all have a role to play, like the seasons. None are *more* powerful than another," Tracy explained. "And we Ausurnians are just evolution at work."

"Oh. Ausurnia is an old country, huh?"

"We tell outsiders that Ausurnia is 3642 years old. But between us, I think we as a people are much, much older."

"Whoa. How old is Rovalkia in relation? I mean, in total?" Annika asked.

"Good question. I don't know. Let's put it aside, though. I need to show you the layout of this shop and go over how to clean."

* * *

As Tracy showed how to file invoices, Annika's stomach growled. Tracy chuckled and stood up. "That stomach of yours is correct. We'll get lunch at the grocers before going to the library."

They locked up and strolled westward on Main Street. Ausurnians on the street stared at Annika, just like they had the previous night. The few children around pointed at her until adults slapped their hand down. Annika shook her head at Tracy. "Have they never heard of social politeness?"

"Give them time, Annika," Tracy stated. She grasped Annika's shoulder, causing Annika to stop walking, and looked into her eyes. "As your confidence grows in both your personal and work life, they'll come around. Foreigners staying here are a rarity. Ever since the Rovalkian sponsored assassination of our leader fifteen years ago, distrust of any outsider is still strong in their hearts. And I've never seen a more pure-blooded Rovalkian looking woman than you."

"There's no such thing," Annika argued back. "We come from all over the continent like everyone else. Except for you Ausurnians."

Tracy let go of Annika and started walking again. She said over her shoulder, "No offense dear, but you are a poster child. Silvery-blonde hair, colored eyes, *and* cool colored skin? A mortal descendant of Kraxxan himself, your leaders would say, and the opposite of us Ausurnians—the way they like it."

Annika grimaced as they entered the grocery store. *A mortal descendant of Kraxxan? Ha. I'd love to spit in his unholy face.* Annika stopped short and gazed around. *These vegetables are enormous. And their bread is so much darker than the traditional Rovalkian loaf. They must have better soil than Rovalkia to grow such an abundance of food.* Tracy ushered her forward, pointing out good things to eat while they meandered the aisles. They decided on pre-made cheese sandwiches wrapped in brown paper for lunch. Annika pulled money from her pocket to pay.

"Put your money away and spend on groceries later," Tracy said, pushing Annika's money back into her hand. "Lunch is on me. The registers are back up front." She led Annika down another aisle. "But it reminds me, we need to get you set up with a bank account here. I can have your paychecks deposited using the computer. You'll then be able to use Ausurnian cash or a charge card. We use these electronic cards to make most purchases." She showed Annika a plastic disc with raised symbols on one side and a silver stripe on the back. The cashier scanned her card with a wand connected to the electric register.

Cards representing money? And my parents told me Ausurnians live in the dark ages. I wonder why my parents pay cash for everything when this technology exists?

Annika wanted to ask the cashier how the wand knew how much money to take and where the technology came from, but the next person in line crowded her away. She made a mental note to ask on her next trip; then she could tell her dad about it.

Tracy led the way down a side street; Annika glanced over at a newspaper stand. She froze. *Was my name on the front page?*

"Come along, Annika. We need to get back soon."

"Yes, Mrs. Donauska. I thought I saw something." She hurried to catch up. *It must've been someone with a similar name,* she thought and looked beyond Tracy, where unoccupied benches stood in the shade of oak trees, in front of a two-story stone building.

"Here's the library, Annika. Once you learn Ausurnian, you'll know what each store and business is."

Stone is an excellent building material to house such precious things. "Those benches look nice to sit and eat."

Tracy nodded in agreement and asked, "I just realized I didn't ask what other jobs you've had in our initial meeting. Did you have any?"

Annika gazed across the street. "My mother had me watch my siblings and teach them some lessons for an allowance. Mom and Dad said I'd be of more help that way, and I didn't mind being home most days. I felt safest there. It felt good teaching the twins what I know."

Tracy stood and stretched. Then she threw away their trash and led the way up the library's steps. Once inside, Tracy walked up to a lady standing behind the front checkout counter. "This is Lettie, the head librarian. Lettie, this is Annika Mullway." The woman, dressed in a gray business suit that reflected her stony expression, nodded once. "Here is the list of books we require. Annika will check them out today." Tracy handed her the piece of paper.

Lettie gave Annika a withering look. "I'll need to see *authentic* identification to make a profile before lending out any of my books to you, Miss Mullway."

Annika produced her Rovalkian identification card with a haughty smile. Lettie sniffed and made up her profile, then left to collect the books.

"Don't take it personally. She's like that with everyone," Tracy proclaimed, shaking her head.

After Lettie finished scanning each book, she laid a hand on top of the stack and glared at Annika. "They're all due back within the month. We charge by the day if not returned and for the entire book if there's any damage. I suggest you wash your hands before handling—"

"Oh really! That's enough, Lettie. You'll have your books back in the same condition. Come, Annika." Tracy gestured to Annika to grab the books as Lettie bowed her head.

Tracy motioned to the shop's counter when they got back. "Put the books over there. I think it'll be best for you to start your learning by my side."

Safety In Silence

Annika followed her boss around learning the job and pretending to tidy nearby while Tracy helped customers. "Try to use the same exercise of reading the herbs to read the customers. Some people may not be aware of their real ailment and that's where your gift comes in. Try your best. I don't expect you to be right on your first try," she told Annika.

"Don't worry, I know how," she admitted, raising her chin.

"You do?"

"I found the concept of aura reading in a history book. I skimmed each chapter to find things to try. After days of practice, it became easy to do, with people being none-the-wiser. Like you said, practice makes perfect."

Tracy pursed her lips and nodded. After that, each time a customer left the shop, Tracy asked, "What did you sense?"

If the customer's psychic shield was down, Annika got an accurate reading. "That lady hurt her shoulder," and, "That couple is struggling with headaches as the energy from their heads felt heavy." Tracy then went over remedies and how to quote scientific texts from each reading.

On their afternoon tea break, Tracy interrupted Annika's deep concentration on one of the library books. "You remind me so much of my grandson." Annika's narrowed eyes flicked toward her, taking offense, but Tracy prattled on, unaware. "You're both a quick study. I'd like to bring you to a dinner with his parents tonight. It'll bode well for you to know them."

Annika drew her eyebrows together. Meeting more people was the last thing she wanted to do, but the way she said it would "bode well" made her curiosity override her fear of a trap. She stared at the far wall, weighing the pros and cons, then turned her head to face Tracy and nodded once.

* * *

After closing the shop together, Tracy drove them to her son's house, which was ten minutes northeast of town. She turned down the private gravel road as purple clouds turned dark blue, causing her to flick on her headlights. Annika gazed out of the side window, her head whirling with anxiety. Her parents had warned about going to unfamiliar places in the dark, and here she had done just that.

"Their house is just down this road. They own acres of land and like their privacy. It'll be a pleasant evening, you'll see."

Annika remained staring out the window and gripped the edge of her seat, stretching her psyche out and in, over and over, just in case a danger presented itself. *I should've just said I was too tired. If they're anything like Captain, it won't be very pleasant for me.* They approached a three-story white house with an even whiter pillared porch and electric torches illuminating the area with an orange glow on either side of the double wide red front door. The house shone in the dark like a beacon, with light spilling from every window.

Tracy sighed as she got out of the car. "I love this house. Such wonderful memories. Such wonderful, old bones." She then placed an encouraging arm around Annika. Annika tried to stand straight with her chin up, but felt herself tremble beneath Tracy's tight grip.

The front door swung open; the immense form of a cloaked man filling the doorway. Annika tried to step back, but Tracy held her firm. "Hello, son. Can you please pull back a bit? I forgot how solid you are to an outsider. Annika, this is my eldest, Commander Donauska."

Her son stood looking at them, not retracting his powerful aura. He spoke in a deep baritone. The sound emanated from the depths of his hooded military uniform, weighed down with medals. "Hello, mother. So, this is Annika. Welcome to our home, Miss Mullway. My wife is eager to meet you. She's in the dining room. Come in." Warmth and a bright interior emanated from behind him.

After shedding their coats in the entryway, the commander led them down a hallway. Annika peered at a portrait on the wall. Two civilian-clothed figures smiled while the two military-uniformed figures' lips remained neutral. Tracy stopped alongside and explained, "That's their latest family portrait. Theodor isn't a soldier by trade, so he's not obligated to wear the uniform." She then pointed to each face in the photo. "Captain, their eldest who you met, takes after his father with his facial structure and broad shoulders. Once someone becomes a full-time soldier, they wear the uniform every day for the entirety of their service. Theodor takes more after their mother—softer facial features, you see. Theodor is less, let's say, larger than life, than his brother is. You'll like him. He's closer to your age, too. Come along to meet Ista."

She led Annika to a dining room connected to the family room. A woman set down the linen napkins she held and came around the table. The black diamonds dripping from her ears and neck complimented her pressed dark-blue cocktail dress. Everything sparkled in candlelight, flickering from the carved, black taper candles; their lacey spiraled print caught the light, enhancing each rise and dip.

Tracy smiled at the woman as Annika closed her gaping mouth. "Ista, this looks magnificent. You always outdo yourself. This is Annika Mullway, my new employee from Rovalkia. Annika, this is Ista Donauska, my daughter-in-law."

Ista approached them, wearing a soft smile, with her hands held out in front. Annika sputtered when Ista went in for a hug, her voice coming out smaller than usual. "Oh. Nice to meet you, Mrs. Donauska. You have a lovely home."

Ista pulled back and grasped Annika's hands, looking at her with sparkling, caramel eyes. "Thank you, the pleasure's all mine. Please call me Ista. I leave all the formalities to my husband. And look how pretty you are! Please have a seat. Dinner is ready."

Annika jerked her shoulders back as Commander Donauska's heavy presence entered the room. His energy crowded the space, and he shook his head at his wife as he sat down at the head of the long table.

As Ista frowned at her husband, Tracy restarted the conversation. "I told Annika she reminds me of your boys."

Ista gestured for Annika to sit next to her and said, "That couldn't be possible." Annika raised an eyebrow at her. "What I mean to say, Annika, is my boys were little monsters growing up. How did you draw this conclusion, Tracy?"

"She follows me around like a shadow to learn the job. It's endearing."

Annika's cheeks warmed, and she stared down at her plate. *Why were they being so nice to her?*

41

"But it's what I told her to do. It was her first day, and she's already doing so well." Annika sat up straighter with a sharp intake of breath. "It was a compliment, Annika," Tracy added.

Annika offered a small smile and took a dainty bite. Ista grinned, watching.

Tracy set down her fork. "Like I was saying, Annika is my little shadow. Do you remember when Captain tried to be a literal shadow for a week? You told me he never showed up for meals, but food would disappear. Goodness knows where he slept," she chuckled.

Captain's parents exchanged grimaces. "We had to put an end to his game within the week," Commander Donauska said. "It had put his mother on edge. I found him behind the curtains one morning. He had a bit of shoe sticking out. Scared him half to death when I snuck up and grabbed him." A hearty guffaw erupted from him. Sharp incisors stretched down from the man's gums. Annika's mouth dropped open, her eyes widening. They were the longest and sharpest she had seen. What would make people evolve in such a way? What in their environment was so different? She glanced out into the darkness beyond the glass doors and felt herself attempting to stand up before she knew why.

Ista turned in her seat, put her hands out. "What's wrong?"

Annika's foot caught the chair leg, impeding her escape, and she fell back into her chair. She looked at Commander Donauska, her eyes re-widening as he stared back. Annika felt her face flushing, and she gulped air, attempting to slow her heart.

"Did you hear something, dear?" Tracy held out her hand toward Annika after glancing out the patio doors. "Or was it my son's teeth? I forgot to mention we have sharp canine teeth—a genetic trait. Knowing Rovalkia's education system, I'm sure they left out that little detail. We're not monsters. We don't bite like the outsider news sensationalizes. I promise."

"Unless provoked," Commander Donauska deadpanned.

Annika gulped again. Ista giggled and smacked her husband's arm where he sat to her right. "Don't listen to him, Annika. His sense of humor is the driest. No one's going to bite you." Then her eyes darted around. "Dessert anyone?" she asked, springing up and collecting everyone's plates.

Tracy turned on her son. "You're not helping. Annika won't stay if we don't make her feel welcome." Annika shrunk down in her seat.

"Mother, leave it alone." He cracked the knuckles of one hand. "One dream and one girl won't change anything. The outside world is evolving to our level of technical knowledge, but it doesn't mean we're going to disappear tomorrow. Nor does it mean we need to make friends."

Annika wished she could excuse herself as Tracy clenched her napkin until her knuckles turned white. "It doesn't matter what you think," said Tracy. "Where's the support you showed when I broke the news of my hire? Have you forgotten all I taught you about compassion? Annika is a *gift*. You need to figure out how she can help you, too."

Ista reentered with dessert as Annika sat up. *A gift? Is she talking about my psychic gifts?* Her eyes traveled from face to face, looking for clues. They stopped on Commander Donauska. When he turned to her, his thin-mouthed expression was down turned.

"I think we'll skip dessert, Ista. Come Annika. We have a lot of work to do tomorrow." Tracy stood from her seat, staring down at her son.

"No, wait," Commander Donauska said, motioning her back. "Please sit. You're right, mother. Something my son said is clouding my perception of her. May I ask you a question, Annika?"

Annika lowered her eyes. "I'm sorry about my reaction earlier. I knew Ausurnians have … different genetics, but never realized how different. During homeschool, my mom focused more on Rovalkian subjects. I'm still adjusting, I guess."

43

"No offense taken. Let's start over." He leaned toward her, pulling a plate of chocolate pudding closer. "Mother tells me you come from Karaxin. I'm curious. What's it like?"

Annika shifted in her seat, her eyes darting from one person to another. She felt a sinister undertone in his words.

Ista leaned closer to her. "You aren't in trouble, dear. We've never been, is all. Is it grand?"

Annika glowered down at the pudding in front of her, remembering why she left. "No. Tall buildings block the sun, and the traffic is loud. I hate the pollution. But it's home," she sighed.

"And the people?" Commander Donauska's voice lowered to match hers.

Annika eyed him for a long moment; the Donauska women leaned forward.

"The truth? Worse. Their feet pound the cement like robots. They let anything natural die. No one smiles. There's no money. There are no jobs. No one wants to feel. Because if you feel anything," she sneered, "you'll disappear." Her fork stabbed into her pudding.

Commander Donauska kept leaning forward, unphased by her abrupt display of aggression. "And you, Miss Annika? What do you feel?"

She raised her eyes to him. "I feel everything." She intended it as a warning: *I'll know if you try anything.* But from the way both Donauska women brought a hand to their hearts and exchanged sympathetic looks, she guessed they heard it as a plea for help. *It is, in a way...*

"And how do you feel about the guy voted in?" the commander pressed; the exposed lower half of his face was impassive.

"Voted in is one word for it," she said through gritted teeth.

Commander Donauska leaned back, a satisfied smile playing on his lips. He brought his napkin up to dab at the corners of his mouth. "So, you don't believe the landslide victory either? Being so close to the action, I wonder if you have any insights? I'm sure we can help each other out—an arrangement perhaps, to help you stay longer."

She smiled, feeling villainous, and gazed at the commander's hooded face. "If you help me find the rebel headquarters, so I can join them, I'll tell you everything I know about Rovalkia. But first, I need to figure out *how* to help—so they'll accept me."

"Goodness. Do your parents think the same way?" Ista wondered.

"All brainwashed," Annika sighed. "My parents kicked me out when I brought home a book I found on the old faith. They claimed I was going to get them all killed by bringing it into the house. Dad burned it to ash. Then he told me not to return home until I understand the real world and repent." Annika looked around the table, pausing at Commander Donauska. "That's why I applied for this job with your mother when the opportunity arose. I want to learn the truth of the world—the truth behind the lies—and to gain a new perspective. Dad wants me to follow blindly. But if I ever return, it'll be to reform the government and expose their twisted laws."

"Interesting," Commander Donauska said, jotting in a notebook pulled from his pocket. "And what does your dad do?"

Annika glanced at Tracy. "Um, he's an office clerk." Then she put her first finger up to the commander in sudden panic. "But it's not their fault. They're brainwashed. I don't understand how, but everything taught to me feels like half-truth. Like they don't think I can handle it. But when I push them on anything, I'm punished."

Ista reached over and laid her left hand on Annika's right. "Don't worry. We're in the business of taking out bad guys, not the misunderstanding innocents. You should give your parents a call, though. There's a missing person's announcement about you in today's paper. It said you disappeared in the night last weekend, and it's assumed someone abducted you. Your parents must have misunderstood your travel arrangements. We'll help in any way we can."

45

Tracy locked eyes with Annika. Her eyes begged a question to which Annika shook her head. Tracy nodded.

Commander Donauska finished writing and tucked his notebook away. One side of his mouth ticked up before saying, "Yes, we will, Miss Mullway. You have my word."

* * *

With one of the herbal medicine books in hand, she curled up in the blue chair and looked out the window into the dim, fog-engulfed street outside, wondering what her family was doing; wondering if they were thinking about her tonight, as she was them. What had her father expected her to do? There were no jobs or housing anywhere in Rovalkia. Perhaps in a week she would call them once she had settled in.

Halfway through the first chapter, Annika glanced up to rest her eyes and rubbed her stomach, full of Ista's dinner. Her still-packed, open roller suitcase lay on the floor near the bed. *Might as well unpack.* She deposited the book on the seat of the chair, sunk down to the floor, and removed one item at a time. All of her folded clothes filled two out of the five dresser drawers. Next came her baby photo album and an extra pair of shoes. These were black like the high-top leather boots she wore but made of canvas and had low tops suited for warmer weather.

She then turned to her worn-out bookbag, that lay slumped over with the corner of her favorite novel sticking out. The story of an angel falling in love with a demon and restoring its soul; another secret found from deep within the dusty depths of the old bookshop. Reaching up, she placed it on top of the dresser.

Then Annika turned back to the suitcase. She pulled out a framed photo of her and her siblings together on vacation. It was from two years ago when they were all smiles on a beach in southern Rovalkia. James and Sarah took after their father with their sandy blonde hair and blue eyes. The one person with silver hair like hers had been her maternal grandmother. *But was she born with it like me? At least I have mom's green eyes.* Annika remembered that trip: the heat of the sand, the salty air, and the fresh-caught fish grilled over an open fire. It had been easy to forget the loud, crumbling capital when one had their feet in the ocean. *One day, I'll come back to you, James and Sarah. I'll make everything right again.* Her finger trailed over their faces in the picture. *But sissy must help herself first.*

She placed the picture on the dresser and leaned back on her heels, musing over what had transpired that got her on the train. *One week. One week to go from being part of a family to being cast out and living alone in a foreign country. One week to be running away for fear of what my compatriots would do to me.*

Was it the memory of her father's heartless words, or her mother not taking her side that made her heart ache more? It would be something she vowed never to forget:

"Look what I found in my favorite bookshop today. I've been reading it all afternoon. It answers everything. The things you claim are unnatural about me were actually normal in great-grandma's younger days. Look."

Her father ripped the book from her hands. "Where'd you find this? Are you trying to get us all killed?" he roared.

Her mother gasped, pointing at the book. Annika reached for the book again. "But it's okay. Stop freaking out. It's just a history book."

"You shut your mouth, young lady. It's *not just* a history book, and you know it! This is the last straw. I've had more than enough." Her father marched to the fireplace and threw the leather-bound book onto the burning logs.

"NO!" Annika launched herself forward to save the book as the flames licked the edges. Her dad caught her by the waist and hoisted her away while her mother ran over.

47

"Quiet, Annika. Please hush before the neighbors call the police. What've you done?" her mother whispered wide eyed. "Foolish, foolish girl. Orrin let her go. Please."

Her father's grip loosened as Annika squirmed her way out of his arms. "This is *it*. You've put us all in danger. We can't keep covering up for you. If the authorities show up, so help me—you need to go."

"Go?" Annika stopped trying to yank her arm out of her father's firm grip. "Go where?"

"Mommy? What's happening?" Little James and Sarah padded into the room, rubbing their eyes.

Annika tried to go to her siblings, but her father still held her by the wrist.

"Nothing, my sweets. Mommy will come tuck you back into bed." Annika's mother threw a warning look mixed with concern to her eldest daughter. She then took the kids' hands and led them away.

"I'll give you a week to find a job and move out. You will stop talking about feeling energy or using your mind tricks or anything deemed ungodly, as our faith dictates. You know people are disappearing every day. *I* keep you safe. Yet, here you are bringing the most forbidden of books into our home."

Annika glanced at the fireplace while her heart ached. The leather cover curled into itself, charred beyond recognition. Tears had built up in the corners of her eyes, but she dared not cry. Rule Fifteen: Tears are the absence of strength.

"Keep your mouth shut until you move out, or we'll kick you out sooner. Then spout all that nonsense and see how long it takes to land in jail." Her father poked the fire and strode out of the room.

Annika held her hands up, palms facing forward. "But I can't help what I am."

"Yes, you can," came her father's voice from the stairs. "Nothing in that book would've helped you in the real world. Your ancestors didn't work hard doing the will of Kraxxan the past one hundred years for you to throw it away. I won't let you. It's time for you to get a dose of reality. When you understand, we'll welcome you back home. Now, go to bed."

"But Dad—"

"BED. NOW."

* * *

You wanted me gone. Out of the country far enough away? She wiped a single hot tear off her cheek and flicked it away, hoping the action would toss the memory away, too. *I've found the others like me, but I'm still the outcast.* She rubbed at the fantom pain in her wrist, which had ached for days from being twisted in her father's grip. Now unpacked, she pushed the suitcase and bookbag under the bed. *Rovalkia will regret the day it deemed people like me the enemy.*

* * *

Tuesday at the shop started like Monday. Annika listened as Tracy told of the various local farms from which they ordered products and how she also grew specific herbs and prepared them at home. "The more local a product is, the higher the nutritional value. Feel an old package of food and you'll notice how it doesn't speak. All the life force is gone. I wish more people were sensitive to what they put in their bodies," said Tracy, ending the most recent lesson and gazing out the window.

At lunchtime, Tracy took Annika to the town's three storied cement bank with thick panes of opaque glass in every window. A man hurried toward them as soon as the front door closed behind Annika. His black suit of impeccable fit resembled the military uniform material: a strange blend of cotton, wool, and silk. It was thick but shiny, and light

49

reflected off and then got absorbed, confusing her eyes. This man's jacket also had the Ausurnian flag embossed on the breast pocket, which comprised a constellation of stars in a white diamond with inverted swords situated on either side. Its background was the same shade of red as the Rovalkian flag. The middle-aged man bowed to Tracy, showing the gray that peppered his full head of black hair. *This bowing nonsense again?* Annika scoffed as a whiff of heady cologne stung her nose.

Her boss dismissed the man's gesture with a flap of one hand. "That's enough, Mr. Talbot. I've brought Miss Mullway here to create an account."

Mr. Talbot looked Annika up and down, rubbing the back of his neck. "I'm not sure about that, Mrs. Donauska. We don't make money accounts for foreigners."

"I beg your pardon, Mr. Talbot?" Tracy Donauska set her hands upon her hips as her eyes narrowed. "I'm Miss Mullway's sponsor and her employer. How do you expect me to pay her? How is she supposed to manage her affairs? I suggest you reconsider. I'd hate to call your father out of retirement for such an issue."

Whoa, thought Annika. *This woman has pull in this society. Is that why it's beneficial to know her family?*

The manager tripped over himself. "Mrs. Donauska, please forgive me. I forget myself. It's been so long since—"

"Just do it, Mr. Talbot, before you say something you'll regret."

Now sweating, he led Annika and Tracy to a private office. Tracy sat, staring daggers at the man as he typed in haste. Annika remained still. This was a new side of her boss she never wanted directed her way. Mr. Talbot handed over her new account information and a charge card.

"Your account balance will be zero until Mrs. Donauska deposits your first paycheck," Mr. Talbot explained. Then he bid the two women a good day while mopping his forehead with a handkerchief.

Outside of the slate gray building, Annika leaned close to Tracy. "People respect you, I've noticed, Mrs. Donauska. Very much the opposite from my home, where they cast grandparents into a retirement home in the countryside to forget them."

"That's sad to hear," Tracy sympathized. "You may notice Ausurnians treat me differently than other adults my age because of my position on the Elders Council." Suddenly, her pace quickened.

Annika scrambled to keep up. "So, you work in government too?"

"Yes … and no. See the ornate building bigger than the others down this side street?" Tracy paused and pointed as they got to a four-way stop. There stood a two-story whitewashed building with a spire roof. Its eaves were unpainted wood with curled up corners. "That's our town hall. It's the oldest building in town and also doubles as our house of worship on the first day of each season. We Council Elders meet there and discuss issues at the town level."

Annika squinted at a gigantic Ausurnian flag rippling in the wind atop its flagpole on the building's front lawn. "Do you get to pass laws?"

Tracy ushered her across the street. "No. We more discuss than act … We aren't the *actual* governing body. I'll explain another time."

"I don't mean to pry, Mrs. Donauska. But I learned nothing about your country growing up. Well, nothing useful."

"That's because we don't share any socio-economic statistics with the world," her boss said with airs.

"Why is that?"

They'd made it back to the shop, and Tracy went to sit down at her desk. "You're full of questions, aren't you?" Annika stared back, confused. "Get yourself settled first, is my advice. Your questions will answer themselves in time. We still have to get work done." Mrs. Donauska turned to her paperwork. The conversation had ended.

The Red Dahlia

A tall, smartly dressed woman sashayed into Mrs. Donauska's Herbs and Remedies. Annika tiptoed up to her, plastering on an enormous smile. The customer clutched her purse when she noticed Annika's approach and gaped.

"May I help you today?" Annika ventured in broken Ausurnian she'd learned that morning.

The lady looked at Annika with wide eyes and glanced over her shoulder. "You? No. Where is Mrs. Donauska? She always helps me."

Annika took a breath and rolled her shoulders back. She switched over to speaking Truscan. "My boss is busy. I'm her new assistant. I can help you."

The lady backed up towards the front door. "No, no. I'll come back later." She opened the door and left.

Annika stared after her. *What did I do wrong? Am I that off-putting?* She shuffled back to the office and slumped onto the office couch while Tracy filed paperwork. "I'm trying so hard, Mrs. Donauska. I am. But customers still look at me like I'm going to rob them. Shouldn't it count you trust me, being an Ausurnian Council Elder?" She picked at the arm of the couch.

"I'd hoped it would, my dear, but these are still early days. Give it time. Once they understand you can help, they'll regret their behavior."

Under her breath, Annika grumbled, "I don't *have* time."

"Hello?" a female voice called out from the shop floor.

Annika ambled out of the office. Tiana was standing at the counter with a brown paper sack in hand. The Ausurnian girl wore a dark blue button-down shirt and black slacks. She had plaited hair and didn't wear makeup or jewelry. Annika attempted to speak Ausurnian once again. "Hi Tiana. Nice to see you. Can I help?"

Tiana bounced her way behind the counter. "Hi Annika. Your Ausurnian is coming along. Grandma is a brilliant teacher, isn't she?" She pushed the office door open, and said over her shoulder, "Try to let it flow out of you, so the words won't sound so forced. Come on, I've brought an afternoon snack." She went and hugged Tracy.

Tiana pulled out the food she brought. "I made us all my favorite sandwich: veggie and dried fish."

"Dried fish?" Annika made a face, lifting one side of the bread.

Tiana giggled. "Try it, Annika. It's good, I promise. The fish comes from our lake and they smoke it to perfection," she said, giving a chef's kiss.

Annika nibbled at a corner. "Oh wow, it *is* smokey and not at all spicy. You Ausurnians sure like your spice. And I do like fish—it was the dried part that concerned me. I thought there was going to be a dried-up fish with its head on."

Tiana threw her head back, laughing, and Annika felt her cheeks warm up. Tracy clucked her tongue. Tiana stopped and gave an apologetic smile to Annika. "I'm glad you like it," Tiana said, bouncing in place on the couch, energized anew. "We should get together, Annika, and we can bake something. I'm the baker at mom's diner, so can teach you."

Annika nodded, smiling gratefully back at Tiana.

Tracy stood. "You know, we need fresh flowers for the vase in the front window. Tiana, why don't you take Annika to the flower shop for a fresh bouquet and show her how it's ordered? I'll call your mom to let her know you'll be back later."

"I'd love to, grandma." Tiana skipped to the door and gestured for Annika to follow.

They trudged down Main Street and turned up a different road, following the forest on the north side of town. Smells of cedarwood and warm grass enveloped Annika's senses; she hummed in solace. Tiana turned and grilled her with questions. "What's your favorite pastime? And your favorite color? Not just for the back story. I genuinely want to know. I want to be your friend for real. I like your energy."

Annika inhaled, filling her lungs with fresh air while taking in the cloudless sky above. Then she looked at her new friend. "That's the nicest thing anyone has ever said to me. I like yours too. Yours and your grandmas. To answer your questions, I love to swim. Rovalkia's rivers dry up before summer's half over, and we're too far away from the coast or mountains to get any substantial rain in Karaxin, so I have to wait until we take a vacation to the southern coast to swim in the ocean. And red is my favorite color."

"I like to swim, too. We have the best lake to swim in. It's deep, cool, and fed by fresh snow melt year-round from the tall mountain to the north. I'll add it to the bucket list I'm making for you," she said, and pointed at the forested, snowcapped mountain skirted in low-lying puffy white clouds. "My favorite color is blue—all shades. I wear muted colors, as is customary for everyday attire. Except for our festivals. Our special occasion outfits are extra loud with color and design. I like your bright, everyday style, though."

Annika nodded. It was the *only* jacket she owed. Tiana opened the door to the florist for Annika to enter first.

A stooped man dressed in a dark gray suit and full-length black apron approached from the counter. He ran a hand through his white hair after doing a double take of Annika. "Hello, ladies. How may I be of service?"

"Hello," Tiana offered back. "Grandma Donauska needs a fresh bouquet for her shop window. Can you make one up to her usual specifications while we peruse the shop?"

The shopkeeper bowed at a forty-five-degree angle and ambled back to the counter. Tiana pointed out her favorite plants on the other side of the shop. Annika turned to a flowering plant that caught her eye. She sidled over to it and whispered, "What's this?" The plant had a playful feeling, causing the energy in her hands to tickle when she touched the multitude of petals and leaves. Most plants in Rovalkia felt half dead or angry. Landscapers torched their thorns and poisonous flowers every summer in the city.

"That's a red dahlia," Tiana said as she walked over to where Annika stood. "Aren't they pretty? It's more than an ornamental plant, too. Grandma taught me the roots are edible, and there are medicinal properties in the stem. But they like warmer weather, so we keep them indoors." She picked up the potted dahlia and marched to the checkout counter. "We'll take this, too," she told the florist.

"Tiana, I didn't bring any money other than the amount your grandmother gave you for the bouquet."

Tiana pushed Annika's reaching hands away. "No, I'm buying this. It's a welcome present. You should've seen your eyes light up when you saw it. Its energy must be what you need. Your kitchen window will have the perfect amount of sun for it."

"Thank you, Tiana. I'll take good care if it. You're sweet ... but you already know that." Annika smiled at her new friend, feeling the girl's warm, glowing aura next to her.

"Yes, yes, I do." Tiana swung her plaited black hair behind her. Her smile expanded to show gleaming white teeth; her sharp incisors poking out. Before Annika could comment on the girl's dental work, Tiana engrossed herself with paying the florist. She pointed further down the street when they exited the shop. "Over there is the clubhouse. It's that big whitewashed one-story building with large windows. They have classes for all ages, a game room, and a gym. Come on, I'll show you."

"Every business here is open. I don't remember walking one block back home without at least one shop already boarded up."

Tiana flashed her a smile. "We take care of our people. People before money. It's what is right."

Annika picked up her pace to keep up with the long-legged girl. "Rovalkia could learn a lot from you guys. But Tiana, I have to ask, why do Ausurnians bow to you and your grandma?"

She shrugged. "Oh, that. It's because we're royals."

Annika stopped walking. "What? Your grandmother said she was on the Elders' Counsil. Now you're telling me she's the *Queen* of Ausurnia? Was it her *husband* that was killed on the World Intelligence Committee's island years ago? Oh man, what am I saying? That was so rude. I'm sorry."

"Relax. She *is* on the Elders Council." Tiana stopped and grabbed hold of Annika's arm, pulling her back into a walk. "*And* she's the king's mother. After assassins murdered Grandpa Donauska at the W.I.C. headquarters, she retired from her royal duties and opened the herbal shop. My uncle, Commander Donauska, is now the leader of Ausurnia. We only use royal titles at international events, and sometimes the veterans address my family formally, since it was more common back in the day." Tiana paused. "It almost broke our faith in the goodness of

56

people. My cousin, the captain, lost his mind to grief for a while. He put all his energy into his military training and became the youngest captain in our history. I wouldn't be surprised if some of the monster stories originated with him." Annika saw her shiver. Then Tianna took a deep breath and continued. "Even though heartbroken, our grandma stayed strong. Then she started having dreams. But she only ever told me about the one—about someone coming to work for her."

"Oh, wow." Annika looked around the street. "Now it makes sense why your cousin called it the Kingdom of Ausurnia instead of country. So, your cousin, Captain Donauska, is a prince too?"

"Prince and heir to the throne."

Annika gaped. "Oh, my god. And here I've been lying to him from the beginning! He'll fillet me alive if he ever finds out! How did I not know this?" She threw one hand in the air, her other cradling the dahlia plant. "I don't get that vibe from any of you. And where's your castle? Does the Town Hall have a throne room? My parents taught me you have a governing system akin to Rovalkia. Why did your mom help me? Why are you?"

"Because my mom could tell you were innocent. Like I said, we take care of our people. You don't exactly cover up your psychic abilities very well. My cousin has the problem with outsiders, not us. We know you belong here." Tiana suddenly tittered. "Did you say a throne room? You're so old-fashioned, Ro."

"Why'd you call me a fish egg?" Annika asked, distracted.

Tiana smiled a toothsome grin. "I called you Ro, not roe. Short for Rovalkian, not the fish egg. *That* would've been an insult. It's a little nickname for you. Anyway, we stay low key in our ruling style. It's about ruling fairly, not flashing our wealth. Flaunting our assets would bring the wrong attention from home and abroad. Other countries teach what they *think* they know. I bet they taught you we're a poor country, huh?"

They stopped in front of the clubhouse doors. Annika stared at Tiana for a long moment. "I've never had a nickname." She tilted her head in thought. "And yes, they taught us that your country was poor. Wow, so I know royalty—"

"Ugh, stop. Don't make it weird." Tiana rolled her eyes. "Treat us like anyone else. You don't need to bow or anything, either. I hate all the extra attention, and so do my cousins. Well, except for some in Fringur …"

Annika gave her a sly smile. "Are you sure, princess?"

"I'm going to slap you if you call me princess again." Tiana raised a fist, then paused as Annika raised a hand in self-defense, winked, and lowered her fist with an apologetic smile. "Sorry, I'm used to dealing with my brothers. Yes, I'm one-hundred percent sure. Grandma will tell you if an occasion calls for formality." She then ushered Annika inside the clubhouse.

A group of women were lounging in the main reception area. The open space boasted overstuffed white chairs surrounding opaque glass coffee tables. Sunlight streamed down from the skylights and bounced off their clunky gold bangles and shiny black hair. Each wore a tailored dress suit in various muted brown and beige colors.

Their conversations ceased as they turned and glowered at the newcomers. Two held teacups up to their lips as if too shocked to move. Annika and Tiana looked back at them. "You'd think we'd stumbled into their private homes," Annika muttered. One woman stood as Tiana nudged Annika toward the reception desk. Tiana rolled her eyes at the receptionist, who giggled behind her hand.

"Well, well, well. If it isn't Annika Mullway, the missing girl from Rovalkia. Haven't they told you we don't have room for any more of your kind here?"

"*Your* kind?" Annika choked out. She and Tiana spun around to glare at the tall woman who stood with her arms crossed and a predatory

58

glint in her eyes. Her hair and makeup reflected an unnatural sheen up close, and Annika built up her psychic shield as Tiana stepped in front.

"Bugger off, Ciara. She's none of your concern."

"Ha. You think you're so powerful because you're a Donauska." Ciara's hands went to her hips. "Does it make you feel big and important?" Ciara taunted, tossing her head back as her long gold earrings danced around her neck. Then her voice rose. "Everyone knows my father's money could buy more loyalty than your name. We just choose not to. Yet." The women still sitting in the chairs nodded. A complex, flowery perfume penetrated the air around Annika. "Little Rovalkian, why are you here?"

Tiana let out a high-pitched, mocking laugh and held her sides. She stopped short and glared at Ciara. "*Loyalty?*" Tiana spat out as her eyes narrowed more. "You forget your place, Ciara."

Annika stepped around Tiana's protective stance while the other woman blinked. She attempted to insert the same edge into her voice. "I'm here to learn how to crush anyone who puts money above friends and selfish desires over their countrymen's needs. Include yourself in there, too."

"Ha! I see right through you, outsider." Ciara squinted, pushing her aura down on Annika. "Your people are lazy; always running into other countries, looking for handouts. How long do you think you have before Commander and Captain Donauska figure out your little game of fortune grabbing? It would be so sad if something were to …" she flicked her hand in Annika's direction, "… happen."

A wave of energy bounced off Annika's psychic shield, forcing her to take a step back. She planted her feet further apart, steadying herself.

"You have psychic shields?" Ciara's face fell. She looked at Tiana. "You can't teach outsiders our secrets." She pointed a sharp nailed finger at Tiana and screeched, "I'm going to turn you in. They're below us. This is unacceptable."

"And it's illegal to use energy blasts against civilians," Tiana shrieked back.

Ciara's friends stood in unison. They all took a step towards the three girls, exchanging worried looks. Annika looked from them to Tiana. Her new friend now sneered open mouthed, her sharp incisors exposed as she took a step toward Ciara, her free hand reaching for Ciara's pointed finger. Annika stepped forward, forcing the potted dahlia plant into Tiana's open hand. "Tiana, hold my plant. This cow wants to tango, and I'm in the mood to dance."

Ciara sucked in air through her teeth. She raised her pointing hand above her head. Annika bent her knees, readying herself for the blow. Rule Thirty-two: Never throw the first punch.

"Oh, no you don't," a dark, masculine voice growled at the same time as a gloved hand suddenly grabbed Ciara's raised wrist. "No one is going to fight *anyone*."

Ciara gasped.

Annika shuffled back two steps.

Ciara looked behind her and simpered, "Oh, it's you, Captain. You came just in time. This Rovalkian animal was about to assault me. Tiana's been training this runaway witch our ways. I was trying to defend myself."

"Shut it, Ciara." Captain threw her arm from his grip. "No one cares. I heard everything. Go back to your friends." He pointed at Annika and Tiana. "And you two. Why aren't you at work?"

Tiana frowned. "Grandma sent us to get flowers for the shop and Annika hasn't been here—"

"You'll rue the day you came into my country, witch!" Ciara yelled from behind.

"I said shut it, Ciara. Stop wasting everyone's time. Now I'm taking you two back. March." Captain reached out to Annika and Tiana.

Annika stepped away from the hooded soldier. "Don't touch me. I'm more than capable of walking myself." She tossed her hair back over her shoulder, took the potted dahlia from Tiana, and marched off in front of them, allowing the front door to close in the captain's face after Tiana had passed through. His startled grunt brought a satisfied smile to Annika's face.

"*Oh Captain, my captain. Save me from these mean little girls,*" Tiana mimicked Ciara's simpering voice when they were outside.

"*Oh Captain, save me. How am I to defeat such a wicked Rovalkian? She could've poisoned me with her inferior touch.*" Annika joined in, wiggling her fingers in Tiana's face. They flung an arm around each other's shoulders while cackling, doubling over.

Captain Donauska turned around from unlocking his car, wearing a smirk on his face, but when Annika smiled back at him, he pulled his mouth down into a frown. "Enough, girls. Get in."

"Awe, cousin. Have fun at Ciara's expense with us. I won't tell anyone."

"I have plenty of fun on my own, Tiana." He secured their doors and went around to the driver's side. "You wouldn't attract so much attention, Miss Mullway, if you didn't dress so loud."

"My clothes are the only identity I have of myself. I won't become a plain-clothed drone for your benefit," Annika grumbled.

Tiana cautioned, "Don't pick a fight with my cousin, Ro. You'll never win. And he doesn't have fun. All he does is work. Oh, and did I mention work?" She turned back to her cousin. "And no one cares about her clothing choices. I like it, and I'm going to teach her about being an Ausurnian. She'll be fine here."

Captain mumbled under his breath as he pulled up to the diner.

"Yes, she will be," Tiana shot back. "Let them stew back in Rovalkia. You'll see. She'll do great." Tiana turned to Annika. "Come sit up here."

Annika took her place in the front passenger seat. "So, I hear you soldiers are the best in the world. Would it be possible for an outsider to take lessons or observe? With your position and knowledge, and my desire to join the rebels, I could learn how to help Rovalkia become a better country."

"My *position*? Wait. Are we talking about *you* taking military lessons?" He chortled. "You wouldn't survive a week in basic training. Only two top soldiers outside of Ausurnia have survived long enough in training to join us. Besides that, our economy runs on us being hired out as mercenaries, and even with that, we research the contracts to ensure the people we seek are bad. We don't go raiding other countries for fun. You couldn't afford us if we did. There's nothing you can do about Rovalkia. It takes a monster to kill a monster." He pulled up to the herbal shop. "And whoever is running Rovalkia *is* an evil beast."

She turned toward him while unbuckling her seatbelt. "Well, something needs to be done. Tiana informed me you are the rulers of this country, so who better from which to request guidance? Your dad even said we may help each other. I've decided I want to become a warrior to fight back home. And if it means becoming a monster, according to others, so be it."

His mouth stretched into a thin line. "*You*? You don't have what it takes. No, you don't have the right build and you wouldn't be able to stay who you are on the *inside*. Being labeled a witch isn't enough to instill fear. There aren't witches anymore, anyway. Just stay here, help my grandmother, and leave the politics to us."

Annika blinked once, twice. "I—but it's my plan. The witch label was Ciara's, not mine. My parents labeled me as a bad person because I don't follow the Rovalkian doctrine, but I crave to learn the truth.

Fighting skills would be useful because that seems to be the first step to making changes. Your grandmother is teaching me Ausurnian, and I'm learning more about myself. What do you mean, I don't have what it takes?" She crossed her arms.

"There's *more* to you? I suspected as much." Captain scratched his chin. The sound of his leather gloves raking against the stubble caused a sudden lust in her to stroke his face; to feel the sharp hairs prick her fingertips. She blinked out of the sudden daydream, and she and the captain turned their heads toward the shop window. His grandmother strode out of her office and stood looking out at the car. Annika glanced back at Captain Donauska. Out of the corner of his mouth, he said, "You sure are acting comfortable for having not seeing us Ausurnians' true nature yet. I wouldn't let your guard down if I were you." He turned to fully face her. "Monsters are real, and they look like people. Like your people. Like mine. Stay out of it if you know what's good for you. Besides, there's a catch to being trained by us. You'll need to *become* an Ausurnian if you want to become as strong as us."

"Like a legalized citizen?" Annika stared at him, but he didn't respond.

Tap, tap. Annika turned to see her boss standing outside the car. Captain hit a button, rolling down the window.

"What's going on? Where's Tiana? Why have you driven Annika back? Are you okay, Annika?" Tracy craned her head to peer inside the car.

"Everything's okay, Gran," Captain answered. "I ran into them fighting with Ciara. I thought it'd be better to drive them back to work."

"Oh. Annika, don't waste your time with Ciara. She's a jealous, self-absorbed girl. Who's the dahlia plant for? I know I gave you exact change for the bouquet."

Annika got out. "The dahlia is mine. Tiana bought it for me as a welcome present. And I couldn't help but react to how awful Ciara was.

Captain stepped in after she threw energy at me. My shield protected me."

"Yeah, about that," Captain called over from his seat. "You want to explain to me how you have a psychic shield?"

Tracy grabbed the flowers. "I'll contend with that. Thank you for dropping her off." She ushered Annika back inside the shop with her chin. "That's enough of that. All right, back to work, Annika."

* * *

As they finished the day, Tracy held Annika's red dahlia plant to the light, turning it this way and that. She handed it over when Annika approached. "This is a healthy plant. I'm curious. Did you or Tiana pick this out?"

"I did." Energy radiated from the plant as she stroked an outer leaf. "I love the color, and Tiana said my eyes lit up when I looked at it. Right now, I want to smile while holding it. It feels like such a happy plant."

Tracy smiled at her and opened the back door for Annika. "It *is* a happy plant, my dear. A plant of love. Of true love. If you ever feel the same way around a person, they say you've found your soul mate. Have a good evening," Tracy said, closing the door behind her.

Annika set the potted plant on the windowsill above her kitchen sink. She settled herself into a chair to visualize her psychic shield through meditation. The amount of information she learned during the week had left her feeling vulnerable. She envisioned a gray fortress of stone surrounding her. *I thought learning there were others like me in the world would make me feel safer, but I may be in more danger than back home ...*

The thought triggered a memory that surfaced as she drifted off to sleep. Her parents had been discussing what to have for dinner. Young

Annika desired to eat something different. She stared at her parents, fixating on what she wanted to eat. Without missing a beat, her mom turned and barked, "Stop trying to influence our decision!"

Annika awoke to her alarm. She lay there in bed, staring at the ceiling, reliving the past twenty-four hours. She then remembered the dinner she'd gone to and called Tiana. "Hey, Tiana. It's Annika. Do you have time to talk tonight? I want to talk about the dinner at your uncle's house."

"Good morning, Ro. Of course. Call when you get off work. I should be home by three o'clock."

* * *

"Hi Ro. So, how'd dinner with my family go? Tell me everything."

Annika pulled off her shoes, pinching the phone between her ear and shoulder. "First off, your uncle is intimidating. The man *exudes* power. I can see how he doesn't need royal attire or a castle. Same with your cousin. But your Aunt Ista and grandma were a perfect counterbalance. You could've sliced the tension between your uncle and grandma with a knife at one point, though."

"Ooh, I wish I had been there. But yes, there always seems to be an argument going on, and you sure add extra spice to the pot," Tiana giggled.

"I'm glad you find my situation so amusing. Oh, and I got to see your uncle's fangs on full display while he laughed. I can't believe you grow them naturally." She shuddered, recalling the memory. "No wonder outsiders speculate you guys are vampires or werewolves."

"But you don't?"

"Uh, no. Sorry if it upsets you, weirdo. After they proved your grandfather's murderer came from my country, Rovalkia showed programs trying to prove you are all monsters. It desensitized me to a degree. I'm guessing the so-called documentaries were to rationalize Rovalkia's actions. Then after three weeks, they banned the same shows." Annika snickered. "I guess they were mad when the monster shows gained more viewers than their religious programming."

"Geez, Rovalkia sounds like a lot of fun." Tiana's voice dripped with sarcasm. "They taught us to never to quell the monster rumors. It's part of what keeps enemies from challenging us."

"Huh. Anyway, I made a breakthrough in my plans while appeasing your uncle. He's interested in what I know about Karaxin. In exchange for that information, Tracy says I can stay here longer. I'd like to know what's going on in the government, too. It's a win-win."

"Whoa. You *are* serious about doing something. I just assumed you had a poor home life and wanted out. No one would blame you. But I'm glad to hear you might stay longer. And my uncle will keep his word, trust me. It probably won't take long to figure your government secrets out, though. We've always kept a close eye on our neighbors. Did you have a poor home life? Do your parents support your intentions?"

Annika harrumphed. "The short answer, no. The long answer is they kicked me out of the house and forbade me to contact them till I repent my sinful ways. But I'm going to do the opposite. No more, 'Be fearful of our vengeful god, Kraxxan. Bow to the men who represent his interests.' Blah, blah, blah. Heck, every word Rovalkian leaders say is mean and twisted. I'm going to become stronger and more enlightened." She took a breath. "Speaking of which, would it be possible to join you on a worship day once I learn more Ausurnian? You know, to become more cultured?"

Silence followed. "Tiana? You still there?"

"Um, oh, I don't know, Annika. You'll have to get special permission from my uncle. No outsider has ever entered our city hall, at least to my knowledge."

"Huh. I'd think you'd want to be hurling pamphlets from airplanes to spread your faith. That's what my government does. The litter is terrible, but effective," Annika sighed. "Let's change the subject for now. Can you explain Ciara's attitude toward me? I've met mean girls before, but she was something else."

"That would never happen here. The pamphlets, I mean. We *hate* litter. And Kraxxan isn't vengeful. He's the inert God of Winter. He represents introspection and death—it's not that I don't want you to learn, but our laws about outsiders are so strict." She let out a sigh as a door slammed shut in the background. Tiana whispered, "I locked my bedroom door, so my nosy little brothers won't listen in. Now I'll explain Ciara's deal. She grew up with wealthy merchant parents, who thought flaunting a rich daughter was enough to gain a marriage proposal from the heir to the throne. In Ciara's fantasy, Captain would help her gain worldwide socialite status."

That grumpy hunk? "But the guy doesn't act rich or popular. He acts surly."

"It's not about money or how many friends you have here. It all comes down to who is married to whom. Literal bloodlines. We could be the poorest family, but still rule the country because our families' genetics produce the strongest Ausurnians. Money is just a bonus."

"That's the opposite of my culture. Money rules everything in Rovalkia. And since only the highest-ranking officials and government butt-kissers have any, everyone is miserable. Most families, including mine, live in the same type of houses, too." *Why can't everyone get along and fall in love for love's sake?* She let her fingertips graze the contours of her horseshoe charm necklace. *Grandma Mullway would be so disappointed.*

"That isn't the craziest part," Tiana baited. "Our wedding bands and soldier identification rings have our DNA injected into them—literal blood. We've been doing it for hundreds of years, but I like it. It's dark and fantastical, right?"

Annika made a gagging noise.

"Okay, okay. Back to Ciara. With my uncle's position comes serious people connections. Plus, all the parties and traveling. So, if married to my cousin, who will one day be king, one would get all the spotlight and attention a heart could handle."

"That'd be a volatile coupling. Ciara and your cousin, I mean." Annika pictured them holding hands with evil grins on their faces.

"You're telling me. Lucky for us, there's no need to worry. None of them, meaning my cousin or anyone in his friend's circle, are interested in her. She can't get anyone to propose to her."

"I'm sure she has a backup plan. There'll be another poor soul for her to attach to soon enough." Annika laid back in bed.

Tiana guffawed. "Poor soul, indeed. Her seeing you already in with us Donauska's will drive her mad. I'd put money on the possibility she's having her friends work to find anything on you they can. Be extra careful around her, Annika. I don't want you to get poisoned by her."

Annika raised her eyebrows. "Whoa, that bad? You don't have to tell me twice. It sounds like she's trying to create a reality from fake delusions and insecurities. It's sad. Everyone deserves to be happy. And everyone will be happier once she is. If she ever is …"

Making Waves

Daylight stretched its hours. The sun beat down hotter. Annika took a break in the shade of an alley after walking two blocks, pulling at her blouse to allow air to flow over the beads of sweat condensing on her chest. She stared up at the sky. *I wish my psychic shield could block me from this heat.* A female passerby stopped short and turned to her.

"So do I. This heat is the worst, huh?"

Annika gaped. "Excuse me?"

"You're the new girl working for Mrs. Donauska, right?" She looked Annika up and down. "There's a new clothing shop one block down with the newest summer fashions." She pointed westward. "There are lots of short dresses and short sleeve blouses."

Annika tugged her long sleeves back up her arms. "Thanks." The stranger smiled and continued on her way. Annika leaned back against the cool cement building. Could all Ausurnians read her mind?

She straightened back up and forced herself to walk toward the shop, suffering in the unbridled heat. After flipping through the various racks, she pursed her lips and slipped out with slumped shoulders. The skirts were too short and the prices too high. She cursed her instilled modesty as the stifling air engulfed her on the walk back home, wavering in the air like an electric current. *If I could see my aura, would it look like that?*

* * *

Annika squinted up at the sun on Monday morning before entering work. The giant, rising ball of yellow beamed down.

She reached for the sweating water pitcher after only a half hour's work. *TINLKE, TINKLE.* A tiny bell alerted her of incoming customers. Annika spun around; the cup still pressed to her lips as a gaggle of older women entered the herbal shop.

Mrs. Donauska rushed over, hugging each woman. "What're you all doing here?"

The other women talked over one another with increasing rapidity, their voices full of excitement and laughter. Then one woman pointed at Annika and whispered to Tracy. Her employer shook her head and ushered them back to the front door, replying in hushed tones. Annika scrunched her nose and ducked into the office to avoid more stares from the other customers.

"Annika?" Tracy came walking around the corner. "Oh, there you are. Don't mind them. Word has spread that your name is in the newspapers again. A woman quoted in the article, Frida, said you seemed delusional or under the influence of a drug when you got off the train. My friends claimed the article also said you gave the wrong name. Did you interact with this Frida person? What happened?"

"Oh, no." Her stomach twisted. "I don't want to be in the news. I don't want anyone from home knowing I'm here. That's why I gave Frida the wrong name—my sister's name, Sarah. Frida was this nosy, old lady who shared my cabin, and there were Rovalkian police officers on board, searching for an Ausurnian." Annika scrunched her eyelids shut. "I didn't want them to search my documents and arrest me. The disappearances happening in my country scare me and I don't fancy becoming a statistic." She dabbed at her moist forehead with her sleeve.

"Hmm, I wouldn't be too concerned. It sounds like uninteresting gossip—same as the disappearances. People disappear for many reasons. It's not always about abduction or murder. Arrests and runaways like you are probable."

"It doesn't matter. If they want you to be their bad guy, there's nothing you can do to convince them of your innocence. They'll destroy you, regardless of whether it's true."

"Well, whoever 'they' are, Annika, they will not get you here. It doesn't do any good to worry about a problem that doesn't exist." Tracy waved her hand to fan herself. "We need to help you cool down. I know Rovalkia doesn't reach these temperatures. Though we are further north than your capital, we get strange heatwaves unlike anywhere else. Why do you keep wearing pants? Do you need a pay advance for new clothes?"

"No." This conversation wasn't helping her nerves or her sweating pores. And she wasn't about to take a handout. That was Rule Seventy.

"Okay, okay. I won't ask you twice." With raised eyebrows, her boss turned to the counter and poured two fresh glasses of iced water, handing one to Annika. "Speaking of which, would you like to join me at the lake this coming weekend? Ista is organizing it, and Tiana will be there, too."

Annika lowered her glass, debating, but finally relented. "Okay. I have a bathing suit, too."

"Great! And it'll be a valuable experience for you to stretch your legs past these few streets and meet more people." Tracy paused when Annika grimaced. "Don't fret, there's plenty of room for everyone to spread out. You don't *have* to meet more people if you don't want to."

* * *

Annika put on her bathing suit underneath pants and a shirt and threw a towel into her bookbag as she waited for Tiana and her mother, Jenny, to pick her up. Once buckled in, Annika tried speaking into Tiana's mind. *"Should I have brought food?"*

"No, Ro." Tiana turned around in the front seat. "When you spend time with us Donauska's, you never go hungry. Aunt Ista and Grandma Tracy make a ton of food, and next to you is a batch of my dark chocolate dessert bars. Good thought-projection, by the way."

"I *can* do it!" Annika immediately clamped her hand over her mouth as Tiana and her mom exchanged a look.

"Is grandma teaching you the projection technique? You're doing it perfectly. It's as easy as speaking aloud. We're born with the innate ability. And now you can, too."

Annika shook her head. "I didn't mean to shout."

"Awe, isn't she the cutest mom? It's like when the kiddies learn for the first time. It's okay, Ro. Make sure you have your psychic shield up when you don't want to be heard; especially when you are thinking loud thoughts." Tiana turned back around in her seat. "We still prefer to talk aloud, though. And there's also *throwing* energy, but that's a different lesson for the most advanced learners of self-defense. I studied the concept but haven't done it myself. Mom, did I tell you Annika's shield deflected Ciara's energy attack the other day?"

Jenny chuckled. "I'm cutting down your coffee intake, girl."

Annika looked at the empty seats beside her. "Didn't you say you had brothers? Where are they?"

"My other grandma took them to the lake earlier this morning. I'm sure they'll find and annoy us when we arrive. Make sure not to encourage them, or they won't leave us alone. And mom, I think I would die without coffee. Take it away and you'll have an *actual* monster on your hands. I mean it. I'll start burning the bread."

They continued to argue about coffee consumption as Annika gazed out the side window, wishing James and Sarah were here. *She* wouldn't mind them hanging around.

Tiana and Annika waited in the kitchen as Ista pulled Tracy and Jenny out of the room to grab more supplies. Annika opened the lid to Tiana's dessert bars and inhaled their aroma. Her mouth watered. Black chocolate icing laced the tops. Tiana reached in and broke one in half, handing a piece to Annika. She popped it in her mouth and the chocolate melted as it hit her tongue.

"Mmm, this is the most delicious chocolate I've ever tasted. And the spices are so complex—so warm. You could charge a fortune for these." Annika felt the sugar hit her brain in a sudden rush.

"We do," Tiana and her mother crowed in unison.

"But I'd never charge you for one," Tiana said with a wink.

Tracy, Ista, and Jenny came back into the kitchen, and whispered amongst themselves in Ausurnian, ignoring the young women. Their whisperings stopped, and Tiana and Annika looked at each other, turning to the women. Annika jerked her head up at the sight of all three women staring at them.

"What? Why are you staring at us?" Tiana squawked.

"Oh, calm down, Tiana. No need to be so sensitive. I swear, young women these days." Tiana's mom waved a dish towel in their direction.

"We were catching up on who's going to be at the lake today. And Tiana,"—Ista leaned forward—"rumor is, men from Pontagu Base will be there. Maybe Second Lieutenant Baar." She winked.

Tiana's cheeks pinked.

"Who's that?" Annika wondered aloud.

Jenny wiggled her index finger at her daughter. "Her crush or boyfriend. Or is it fiancé?"

"Mom, stop." Tiana rolled her eyes. "And I'm not his until he makes more time for me. He says he's going to marry me, but I'll only believe it when I see the ring on my finger."

"Geez," Annika winced. "I'm glad I've never had a boyfriend. It sounds complicated."

Tracy leaned away from the sink. "I'm sure you will have a boyfriend soon, Annika. Both of you girls grab a lot of attention wherever you go."

Tiana and Annika whipped their heads toward her and asked in unison, "From who?"

The three older women howled with laughter. Tiana's face turned bright red as Annika's own cheeks became hot.

"Mother's talk." Jenny smirked and wiggled her shoulders, making her layered gold earrings jingle as she made eye contact with Annika. "Tell us who you like, Annika, and I'll have their mother tell them to ask you out."

Captain Donauska's hooded face flashed in Annika's mind. She shook her head, and her silver braid whipped around, smacking her on the cheek.

"Ooh, you like someone already." Tiana pointed at her. "I saw it in your face. Didn't you see it, everyone?"

Annika shook her head again, slower this time, and rubbed at the stinging side of her face. Tiana elbowed her in the arm. "I'm sure he'd like you back, whoever it is. I wish we could synchronize our work schedules, so we could spend time together more. Hint, hint mom." She turned her head toward her mother.

"Whoever heard of a baker not working until eight in the morning? No one would get their breakfast. Or lunch," Jenny chided back. "Come over here a moment, Annika." Jenny wrapped and pinned Annika's platinum braid around her head. "There. Now you look like one of us. I love your hair color. It looks like a proper crown of silver."

Annika felt the bumpy mass pulling on her scalp, a wash of emotion welling in her throat. Ista loaded the last of the corked drinks into a separate cooler. Both coolers that rested on the kitchen floor had wheels and extendable handles like a suitcase.

"I agree. Both of you girls are natural beauties," said Ista. "Oh, and keep your backpack here, Annika. We packed towels and anything else you may need. Come on, we're burning daylight and giving away prime shade spots. It's a solid mile hike to the lake from here. Everyone, pick up a bag or a cooler. Let's go."

The air's temperature cooled once they reached the dense forest lining the trail. Annika imagined each tree fighting for a bit of skyline, their leaves like thousands of hands grabbing at the sun's rays. Hot white sunlight beamed through the gaps in the foliage to create sporadic spotlights while they hiked along in silence. Once again, Annika wondered why everyone back home believed Ausurnia to be such a dark, scary place. Besides the off-putting fangs and the military uniforms, the land didn't feel at all intimidating.

Tracy slowed to a stop at the front of the line. She pointed over to a small clearing of weathered tree stumps. A squirrel stood on the nearest one.

"Look at its wee paws," Tiana crooned.

75

Annika watched as the squirrel crossed its paws in front of its chest while his tiny black eyes stared at them. The white stripe down the squirrel's belly looked velvety soft. Its bushy brown tail curled up into the air. *If I'm to bolster my abilities, I need to practice. I wonder if I can thought-project with animals, too?* Annika extended her psyche to the small creature and whispered, "*Hello.*" Its tail twitched once before the creature scampered off.

"Now, which one of you girls scared him off?" Ista turned on Annika and Tiana.

"Not me," Tiana squeaked out in defiance. "I didn't have a thought in my head."

"I'm sorry." Annika looked down at her feet. She looked up again to see everyone had turned to peer at her. "I wanted to see if thought-projection is possible with animals."

Tiana threw her arms up, cackling. "Where do you think you are? Fairyland?"

Tracy turned to her granddaughter. "Be nice, Tiana. I'm sure you tried something similar when you were learning. At least she's practicing." Her expression softened when she turned to Annika. "Annika, thought-projection only works with people who can speak your language."

"But imagine the possibilities …" Ista mused as she looked to where the squirrel had run into the woods.

Annika rubbed at her burning cheeks and pushed past everyone to continue down the trail. Following close behind, Tiana whined, "I practice. But I prefer to talk out loud."

"We know," her mother quipped.

The air near Tiana became weighted as Tiana's energies darkened. Annika thought-projected to her friend, *"I like you more outgoing, Tiana. Don't mind them."* Tiana's aura quickly reverted to its usual lightweight nature. Looking behind her, Annika caught the flash of an appreciative smile. Everyone fell back into step on the trail, with Annika in the lead.

"Annika, I forgot to ask. What do you think of Pontagu so far?" Ista wondered.

"What?" Annika started. *Wasn't Tiana behind me?* "I like it. It's much quieter here. All I used to hear in the city were planes and cars, and explosions rattled the windows when riots took place."

"We in this family like it quiet, and since we are in charge, it stays quiet. We have planes, but ensure they fly high up so you wouldn't notice them." Ista strolled next to Annika, changing the bag she carried to her other shoulder. "I can't imagine the horrors your people have seen. Humanitarian aid can only do so much when you live in a concrete world. I think that's why we prefer to live close to nature, with its abundance all around. Our capital, Fringur, sounds much more like the big cities around the world. But us Donauska's are proper nature lovers." She spread her arms wide.

"What about big predators?" Annika wondered. "Should I ever be worried if I walk out at night since the forest is so close to town?"

Tiana hopped around her aunt and made a clawing motion at Annika's face. "No animal would dare. Ausurnians are the top predators of the world."

"Tiana!" shouted Jenny and Tracy, startling the girls.

"What? We are, aren't we?" Tiana argued.

Her grandmother shook her head with a glint in her eye. Tiana cowered and turned back around. "The short answer is no. Between the packs of kids running around at all hours and the soldiers running drills, the larger animals have moved deeper into the northern woods and mountain range. Anywhere within walking distance of Pontagu is safe."

They hiked through a break in the tree line. Up ahead, Annika spied a glint of sunlight bouncing off a body of water. Noonday heat swallowed them up as the coolness of the forest canopy fell behind.

Smoky air and food cooking replaced the aromas of pine needles and fresh earth.

The trail ended in a clearing that led down to the lake. Groups of Ausurnians sat around as little barbeques were hard at work, their long blue wisps of smoke rising in the air. Annika spied lake goers plastering their bodies and the bodies of their squirming children with white paste, their sun-kissed skin now a shade lighter. She looked down at her own pale arm.

"Don't worry, we packed sun-cream, Annika." Ista's voice rose over the wild chatter of a group of kids racing by.

"Thanks," Annika barked while still focused on the scene in front of her. People had traveled far out on the water in canoes. Kids were leaping off a ramp made of boulders, ascending high over the water. Picnickers hailed the Donauska women as they picked a shaded spot off to the right. Tiana directed Annika to keep walking.

"Let's stop here," Tiana instructed. "It's close enough to grab food, yet far enough to have privacy."

They stripped down to their swimsuits and helped apply sun-cream to each other's backs.

"What is this witch still doing here? And how old is that swimsuit?" Ciara's high-pitched, forced cackle followed.

Both girls froze. "Ciara," they groaned in unison. Annika looked down at her one-piece red swimsuit with the attached modesty skirt, then turned toward Tiana. Ciara stood just feet away with her hands on her hips and a scowl twisting her face. More women stood behind her, wearing mocking sneers of their own. They all wore matching black bikinis, each with gold metal gromet details along the straps and waistline.

"We could ask the same of you," Tiana sneered back. "Wearing matching outfits all the time is lame and unoriginal. Does your daddy get a bulk discount?"

Ciara gaped as Annika plopped her arm around Tiana's shoulders. "Oh Tiana, leave her alone. She's just jealous because we have actual curves filling out our bathing suits. No padding required." She stared Ciara down. The woman's mouth opened wider, and her eyes bugged out.

"Good one, Ro." Tiana let out a haughty laugh. "Go away, Ciara. Nobody likes you."

"As if," Ciara shot back, tossing her black curled mass of hair over one shoulder. She locked eyes with Annika again. "You're digging your own grave by staying here, Rovalkian. I've already told *certain* important people about you; people with political power. Whatever scheme you're working on, you'll never win. The authorities will collect you long before."

"Tell them anything you want. I'm here legally. They'll laugh you out of the room."

Annika felt her friend's energies transform while her own picked up speed. She shifted her gaze to witness Tiana's eyes blaze open and her teeth emerge. "When will you understand running to your daddy won't make the world kneel to you?" Tiana growled.

"I have more influence than you think, princess," Ciara hissed, taking a step forward. "And stay away from my officers."

The girl standing closest to Ciara took a step forward. "Except for Captain Donauska, right Ciara? The Rovalkian can have him, huh? It's not like he can do any better," she scoffed.

"Shut up, Marna," Ciara snapped.

Tiana crossed her arms. "What're you talking about?"

"I saw you with Second Lieutenant Baar," Ciara interrupted, pointing a sharp nail at Tiana. "He's mine."

Tiana clenched her fists. "In your dreams."

"Come on, Tiana. They're goading us. It's a pure waste of time. Let's go cool off." Annika tugged at her friend's unyielding body. She didn't fancy picturing Ciara in the captain's arms. *"We need to get away,"* she thought-projected to Tiana. *"There are too many people here for a proper fight."*

Ciara ran a hand across her exposed stomach. "I know he'd much prefer—"

"Dare you to jump off the jetty with me, Tiana," Annika shouted above Ciara. She ran full tilt in the ramp's direction, hoping Tiana would follow.

"Wait!" Tiana called after her. "No. Come back!"

"Not if it's what gets us away from Ciara," Annika thought-projected back. Ausurnians turned toward them as Tiana pleaded for her to stop once more. Annika ran faster as the burning heat of the ground seared her feet. People scrambled out of her way. She raced past kids cheering, beckoning her to jump.

She flung herself in a wild kicking leap past the edge and dropped feet first. Blue sky and water blurred together, and a fleeting sense of weightlessness followed. Icy water enveloped her, and Annika popped her eyes open. She looked around as her body adjusted to the sudden cold. A smooth, sandy floor sloped down toward darker depths. Brownish-gray boulders, broken tree trunks, and large tree limbs lay here and there. She saw no creatures other than the legs of swimmers. Annika swam forward, waiting until her lungs ached before resurfacing.

Tiana admonished her while doggy paddling over. "Never do that to me again. I wasn't ready to come in yet. And how'd you stay underwater for so long? You freaked me out. I thought you'd drowned. I must've looked like a lunatic trying to swim out here so fast."

Annika rolled her eyes. They moved toward the shore as whooping kids cannon-balled off the ramp. "I told you I love to swim. This place is gorgeous, and the water is so clear. It's like being in a whole other world down there. I never want to get out." She splashed Tiana playfully, but her friend frowned. "Awe, you can't be mad. I got you away from Ciara. Are you jealous I jumped? Have you ever jumped off? It's like you're flying. When the cold slaps your body, you feel so alive."

"Alright, alright, stop splashing." Tiana held up a hand. "I'm cold enough as it is. And yes, I needed to be pulled away from her. See what I mean about her poison? Anyway, us older girls don't jump off the jetty anymore because we're self-conscious around the boys our age. I don't want them to laugh and make fun of me." She turned, looking around.

"Looking for someone?" Annika teased. Tiana didn't respond. Annika swam up to her, feeling the sadness radiating from her. "Look, I grew up leaping off piers and cliffs with lots more people around and no one has ever laughed at me. Let's go up there and jump together. You'll remember how fun it is. Ciara doesn't hold a candle to you." Annika looked around. "We should also borrow one of those floating balls to play a game called volleyball. We're here to cool off and have fun, remember?"

They made their way back up the shore just as a large group of soldiers walked through the clearing. More stood at the water's edge, talking with Ciara and her friends. They turned and pointed at Annika and Tiana. Annika looked at her friend, who stared ahead, her lips pressed into a thin line.

"Was Ciara really in a relationship with your cousin?" Annika asked, fighting back the bile that swelled up.

"Yeah, but I don't remember when or for how long. Who cares, anyway?"

I do, Annika moped in thought. Then she noticed none of the soldiers were stripping down to swimming trunks. "What's up with all the soldiers in their full uniforms?"

"They can swim if they want to, but they must keep their uniforms on. My cousin Theodor told me the material feels like a second skin. Staying in uniform is part of the Ausurnian military creed. Don't ask me why. Something about keeping their identity a secret."

Two dripping-wet young boys ran up to Tiana and hugged her. Tiana tried to nudge them away, shouting over to Annika. "See what I mean about my brothers? They're little leeches."

Once her brothers let her go, she asked who wanted to join in a game with her and Annika. "Me!" they all shouted.

"Okay, little leeches. Go grab your friends and meet us in the shallows. Annika, let's jump quick before I change my mind." Tiana's little brothers made whooping sounds, and they leaped off the edge into the lake one after another.

Captain Donauska

Excited murmurings rippled through the group of soldiers when Annika and Tiana waded back up the shore.

"That Rovalkian is pretty."

"Look at all the women."

"What a body."

"Thank Bandau for lake days."

Captain Donauska eyed the girls, watching Annika spread her arms, her fingertips grazing along the surface of the water while Tiana marched ahead. He stretched his psyche out to see if Annika had her guard down. *I want a taste of what's in your mind, Rovalkian,* but averted his gaze when Annika looked in his direction a second time. *She's sensitive, I'll give her that much.* But she would slip up eventually, and he would be present to take advantage and learn her truth.

His father's words from that morning replayed in his mind. "Your grandmother seems to think that Rovalkian is a gift to us, but we will be the judge of that. I'll nudge our family to include her in outings and Ausurnian affairs to make her comfortable, and then we will slowly draw information out of her. I could tell she was withholding information at our dinner party. It will be *your* job, son, to get that information. I can

82

feel our victory over the Rovalkian government soon. We just need one last push. That girl will be it."

He turned to find his family's picnic set up as he stood in the shadow of the trees. Those in the water looked to be forming teams to play a game in the shallows. "Did she come with you?" he asked his mother as she handed him a drink.

"Yes. She's a sweet, innocent girl underneath her self-imposed walls."

"So now you like her, too? I noticed she's still wearing the horseshoe necklace, though it's a symbol not allowed in Rovalkia. Makes one wonder if she's wearing it just to blend in here—not like she could with that hair and those clothes."

Annika and Tiana directed a gathering crowd. Both girls wore braided long locks wound atop their heads, proof of Aunt Jenny's handiwork. Annika's silver braid stood out amongst all the black-haired Ausurnians.

"Enough with your knit-picking," his grandmother shouted over to him. "For your information, it was Annika's grandmother's necklace that she hid away until she arrived here. Stop being such a quick judge of character and give her a chance. You're as bad as Ciara sometimes. Annika ran and leaped off the jetty to distract Tiana. At least *she* has common sense." She pointed at her grandson. "You two could learn from each other. Observe her. You'll see what I mean."

"Trust me, I am," he proclaimed under his breath.

The two girls were standing on a rock rising above the lake's surface. He observed Annika's blood red bathing suit against her moon-colored skin, admiring the diamond cutouts around her midriff. *At least the red color she's chosen suits her.* Ciara and her posse were standing aways off with drooling soldiers stuck to them. *Poor lads. Those girls will eat them alive.* The game began. All the players cheered and shouted for the ball.

"Now look at that, son," his mother pointed out. "The children like her, and there are adults your age out there having fun, too. They're accepting her. It wouldn't be such a bad idea to give her a glimpse into our culture. Give her lessons. Your father mulled it over the other night, too."

"Ha!" Captain barked. His mother, sweet and innocent to the core. Not a suspicious bone in her body.

"What's so funny?" all three women sitting on the blanket wondered aloud.

"Give it a rest, you three. My priorities rank like this." He used his hand to emphasize the various levels. "Ausurnia is up here. Then family, then friends, and way down here is everyone else, especially an outsider." *They shouldn't let their guards down around this girl. There must be a catch. Dad and I both agree she's a spy for an agency, on the run from her government, or both. But if that's the case, why is she popping up on the news so much?* The possibilities played a tune of suspicion in his heart. "She's bad news for Ausurnia," he mumbled.

His mother threw both hands into the air. "Like father like son. Ugh, we get it, but someday, you'll need to let go of the control you think you have. Heir or not, the gods like to scramble the rules to teach lessons. I just hope you don't learn your lesson too late." Captain shook his head in reply.

"Speaking of which," his grandmother said and faced him. "Have you seen the articles about her? Who's writing them? They're calling her a witch now in the Calageeh Times. But why do they care? It started as a concerned message about her disappearance in the Rovalkian Times. It's like two different people are submitting vastly different stories. Annika said she didn't tell anyone from Rovalkia where she was going. So, who in Calageeh would know her? Something is going on, and I don't like it."

Captain drummed his fingers against his belt. "Yeah, the contrasting articles are peculiar. We're aware of them. Dad doesn't like it, either. He wants her as a secret informant, but it wouldn't work if the world knows her name and where she is. Is Ciara still causing trouble? I wonder—"

A sudden rise in the volume of yells from the water diverted everyone's attention. A group of soldiers had stolen the ball, and the soldier in possession shouted, "Keep away from the girls!" The genders charged each other. Taller males kept the ball soaring high in the air, and the girls resorted to climbing onto the men to disarm them. One girl grabbed the arm of the soldier with the ball. He threw the ball, and it flew low above the players' heads.

Annika jumped up, and her fingertips caught the ball just as it passed overhead. Gravity hauled her back down with a *splash*. Captain kept his eyes locked on her, impressed with the interception.

Each gender, both on land and in water, cheered or cursed in unison. Captain unfolded his arms and stepped forward, keeping Annika in his eyesight. She swam further away from shore, still holding the ball. "That blasted girl shouldn't be trying to show off her swimming skills while there are so many soldiers around who can out-swim her."

Three soldiers broke from the crowd and gave chase. His grandmother stood up and grabbed his arm. "Do something. She's going to get hurt. Didn't anyone warn her about how competitive we are? Please, do something."

What does she expect me to do? "I'm not her protector, Gran." He watched as Annika swam in an arc towards the jetty where girls had congregated.

"No, you're a protector of the innocent," his grandmother argued, pointing toward Annika with her other hand.

The three men in pursuit were gaining on Annika. Captain pulled his arm out of his grandmother's grip and jogged up to the pinnacle of the jetty. Kids hanging over the side stepped back out of his way.

Annika looked behind her mid stroke and yelped, the sound severed at its peak by the wind as the three soldiers closed in. She hurled the ball to the nearest girl. He scanned the area to see the others in the water, who all had their attention on the ball, oblivious to Annika's potential predicament.

Annika had spun around to face her pursuers by the time he looked back her way. He could just make out the mouth of the nearest soldier, his teeth sharp and sneering. *That's not good.* In the next second, the soldier ducked beneath the surface, and Annika's body jerked and disappeared without a splash. Captain arched over the edge. He extended his psyche, feeling Annika's anger shift to fear. The clear water allowed him to track their descent straight down.

He counted the seconds ticking by while the other two pursuing soldiers were still bobbing on the surface. Suddenly, they dove. Seconds passed. Bubbles rose to the surface. More people gathered at the shoreline with both hands up, one shielding their eyes from the intense sun and the other pointing. Tiana splashed through the shallows, looking around. A ripple from the depths caught his eye. He dove in.

Annika

"Hey, I threw the ball. Get off me."

"Not until you learn your lesson, witch."

Annika kicked harder. "I'm not a witch, you turd." The soldier dove, and she felt her body being dragged down; her inhalation of air replaced by water. Bubbles escaped from her nose and mouth as she struggled in his grip. Her heartbeat sped up. The lake floor came closer. Annika clawed and kicked at him, but the water's resistance slowed her efforts.

More air escaped. She paused, remembering her swimming lessons. One should never panic. Panic would make you drown. The heightened sensation of rippling energy went through and around her hands. *"There is also throwing energy."* Tiana's words snaked through her head.

Annika closed her eyes and raised her hands with palms facing the soldier still holding her ankle. She thought-projected a scream while imagining the energy from her hands shooting toward her captor. His grip released, and she opened her eyes. The soldier writhed backward through the water, one hand holding his chest and the other covering an ear. She kicked toward the surface with the last of her waning energy.

A disturbance up above caught her attention. Another soldier had dove in from the jetty. *The surface looks so far away. Am I sinking?* She still made determined strokes. The soldier veered toward her in their descent, so she aimed her body away from this person, worried they were going to drag her down again. Her lungs screamed, the ache radiating through her torso. *Don't swallow water,* she commanded herself. *Don't breathe.* The newcomer caught up and wrapped an arm around her waist. *"No,"* she thought-projected. Annika attempted to pry herself from their grip.

"Stop struggling, you blasted girl," a masculine voice spoke in her head.

They broke through the surface. Heat penetrated Annika's senses in a new form of suffocation. She gasped, her mouth opening wide to force air in. She coughed water out, trying to refill her hungry lungs. Her heart pounded. Pain radiated from her lungs and the sound of her blood pumping clogged her ears.

Captain Donauska

Holding Annika tight to his side, he observed the three boys still below the surface, twisting in circles. *Wait. Are they the ones in trouble?* Two cadets righted themselves and pulled the third to the surface.

He called over the first cadet to surface, but the young man froze, pointed at Annika, and yelled in Ausurnian, "She did it! She did it, your Highness. Tell her to stop. I can still hear the screaming in my head. Tell her to stop screaming—"

"Shut it, cadet. She's not doing anything. I saw the whole thing. She kicked you in the head," Captain said surreptitiously, using his most commanding tone.

The other boys chimed in, their voices sounding panicked. "No, Captain Donauska. We heard it too. It hurt. We weren't near her. She's a witch like the reports—"

"No, she's not. Listen to me. You three are in the same troop, correct?" He waited until all three nodded. "That's what I thought. You all share a mental connection, deeper than you know, through the brotherhood of service. If one of you is in pain, it's common the rest of your troop will sense it. It's what makes us strong. We are Ausurnians. We're better than pointing fingers at a weak outsider. Now, get out of my sight. Report to my office tomorrow at zero-six hundred hours for your punishment."

"Yes, Captain Donauska, sir." They said as they turned and swam away further down the shore.

Now I have to punish those boys to cover this girl's transgression. Annika coughed again, her grip tightening on his arm. Captain's thoughts ripped back to the present. He pulled his arm away, spinning her around to face him. Then he grabbed her arm so she couldn't get away. "What were you thinking? Are you trying to incite an international event? They claim you screamed underwater. I had to cover for you." He jabbed his thumb towards the shore. "They may not have figured it out, but I'm on to you, girl. It's called Psychic Thought

Projection. How'd you get through their psychic shields? Are you aware you can do that? No, don't answer. I'm sure you'll just lie." She gaped at him but said nothing. "Did you goad them on purpose? Is this Gran's doing? Did she teach you? I'll give you one last chance to tell me why you're here." He tightened his grip on her arm. "So, what is it? Are you a spy or a psychic running from your government?"

Annika shook her head while her eyebrows furrowed, coughing once more. "Don't speak to me like I'm a child. It was his fault for holding me down for so long."

"They were *playing*," he forced through gritted teeth. "Nothing was going to happen to you. Answer my question."

"Well, I'm not sorry, and I don't have to answer you. You wouldn't believe me if I told you, anyway. Your grandmother knows my story if you care to listen." She turned to the sound of Tiana's voice calling her.

"Stop right there, Tiana," Captain shouted. "I'm not finished." His cousin froze in place.

Annika turned to him. "Yes, we are. I'm seeing who you truly are and that you're resistant to helping me. Foolish me for hoping you would. I don't know what I expected from a busy prince up on his high horse."

"Stop being so dramatic. I just don't buy the story you sold to Tiana and Gran. It's too convenient—too easy. And I'll talk to you however necessary, to get my point across. You can't waltz into a different country, knowing nothing about their way of life, and expect to be treated as an equal. Reality is going to wallop you, and I have way too much on my plate to deal with the fallout of your actions."

She stared back, her green eyes flashing. Wet strands of hair clung to her cheeks, and her pouting upper lip curled. "Why can't you—"

"Don't waste your breath groveling. If you want to stay, here's your first lesson. We're trained to be deadly. Every single one of us. And cadets coming out of basic training are extra volatile." He lowered his voice to a whisper. "If you ever want to leave this country alive, don't get bit." At that, he turned and waded away through the shallows.

Once he'd gotten a hundred yards away, he looked over his shoulder and watched as Annika waded toward Tiana and the rest of his family who encircled. "No one's that innocent," he mumbled to himself.

He stood in the shadows a while later. Annika and Tiana, wrapped in their towels, drifted along the shore in front of him. *Thought projection, a psychic shield, and now the ability to throw energy. You're right, Annika. It's time to figure out who you are.*

Flames In Her Heart

Captain Donauska

He stood listening for a moment outside the door before knocking. Tracy opened her office door, and Annika peered around her from her spot on the couch.

"Hello, Gran. Annika." After they nodded back, he continued in rapid Ausurnian. "I hate to inconvenience you, but today's one of those rare times both Dad and I have off work. I observed her displaying psychic abilities at the lake, and we'd like to discuss it in private. The lake incident has also reached the papers, which is another problem. The article casts me as the bad guy for diffusing the situation and says our family is aiding a witch. Could you pick up Tiana and come to the house? You can leave the shop in her care, right?" Captain glanced back at Annika, concentration furrowing her brow. *Is she trying to translate? Good luck with that.*

Tracy shifted further out the doorway and whispered, "Why didn't you call me first?"

"It's better if we all discuss it together at the house. Try to keep Annika away from the news, too."

"Fine. I'll pick up Tiana and come over," Tracy sighed, turning around.

Annika leaned in; her eyes searched his grandmother's face. "I need to run to my son's house for an emergency meeting. I know this is the first time leaving you in charge, but you're ready." Annika stood and rolled her shoulders, nodding. "Stay busy. If the customers don't want help, either take down their phone number for me or leave them alone. It's their loss if they don't want you to help them." After a quick glance around, Tracy grabbed her purse and handed over the shop keys. "Ignore anyone who asks why you're here. Also, the lake incident was in the news, so tell anyone to talk to me if they have questions. I'll be back soon." Then she followed him out the door and to their respective cars.

* * *

Captain waited by his car as his grandmother parked.

"What does it mean?" he heard Tiana ask as she walked around the car.

"It means Annika is special. She's a gift. But it's turning out to be a chore to convince your uncle and cousin," his grandmother said, shooting a sideways glance toward him.

"I'll help, Grandma." Tiana took hold of her hand and gave it a reassuring squeeze.

Commander Donauska opened the front door. "Come in. We'll talk in the family room." He gestured to them. "I'll try to keep it short."

Upon reaching the family room, Captain sat in one of the two high-backed brown leather armchairs; his feet planted on the ground as each hand's fingers drumming on the armrests.

His grandmother sighed as she sat on the adjacent couch with Tiana. "So, what is so urgent you call two people away from their jobs?"

Captain tilted his head up. "It's time you two told us the truth of what, and who, Annika is."

He spied Tiana wringing her hands in her lap as his grandmother spoke. "Like I said, she's a Rovalkian who desires to learn and make a difference in this world. *You* don't want to accept it."

"Oh, I know what *you* think she is. But are you going to tell me she's already flown through all your psychic training with no prior knowledge? Every single level?" Captain folded his hands in his lap.

Commander Donauska mimicked his son from the armchair to her left. "I'm curious about this too, mother."

She looked from her son to grandson. "What do you mean, *all* psychic training? All I've taught her is how to read the energies of both the herbs and the customers in my shop. I also told her to work on her psychic shield to protect herself."

Captain Donauska tilted his head forward. "So, you're telling me you haven't taught her psychic shielding, thought-projection, *or* energy throwing?"

"What are you talking about? I knew she could build a weak psychic shield and could do a bit of thought-projection when I hired her, but she found out about those, and aura reading from a book on Rovalkia's old faith before coming here. That's why she came here—to learn from our people. Do you know what they're doing to people like her? It's a literal witch hunt. Burnings, public executions, evictions … the list goes on and on. Regardless, she's a quick study through just observing and listening, so her personal growth doesn't surprise me at all." She raised her chin.

Captain shook his head. He'd have to tread carefully. This was the previous Queen of Ausurnia, after all. "Grandma, the line of witches died out long ago. Dad and I speculate it's just an excuse to arrest people that aren't loyal followers of the new leader."

"Doesn't Annika's presence contradict that?"

The commander rubbed the side of his hooded face; his calloused fingertips scraping against black stubble. "Or they could be doing the opposite and secretly breeding people with witch lineage for their own gains against us. They may have figured out our game."

Tiana squirmed.

"Ah-ha!" Captain pointed to his cousin. "What do you know?" She jumped, her face blanching.

"Oh, really. Stop scaring your cousin. She's not training Annika," Tracy admonished, laying a reassuring hand on Tiana's back. "Tiana hasn't mastered energy throwing and you know it."

"She's right, son. Take it down a notch. This is a discussion, not an interrogation," echoed his father.

Captain took a deep breath and relaxed back into his chair. He waggled a finger at Tiana. "She knows something. Body language never lies."

His father implored, "Tiana, please tell us anything that may help. You're not in trouble and neither is she. We know you are friends with her and may have more insight."

"It sure sounds like it," Tiana mumbled, scowling at her cousin. "I'm worried I may have planted the notion of energy throwing into her head. But I blame Ciara first. She's the one who threw an energy blast at Annika. If it weren't for Annika's shield …" Her voice trailed off. "And Annika said those soldiers were holding her down underwater. I would've tried to blast them, too, if I were there. Like grandma stated, she's an adaptive learner. Like a sponge. But she is acting guarded …"

"No, it's nothing you did," Tracy assured her.

"So, she's a runaway? Did you tell her to come here, Tiana?" Captain turned his whole body to face her.

Tiana shrank under his gaze. Tracy folded her hands in her lap and said, "I suppose it's time I came clean. I hired Annika on the spot when Tiana introduced me to her. She was here just to visit, but when I saw this young woman whose old soul emanated through her emerald eyes, I had to learn more. Nothing about her dress or demeanor said runaway, but her pulsating psychic energy *was* alarming. I couldn't believe how psychically developed she was, considering she was an outsider. She escaped without being detected. Perhaps that's why she didn't tell anyone she left. She may be an anomaly, and she understood the danger she was in. Maybe she was playing by the rules until she got out, and Tiana innocently helped her with that."

Both men leaned forward, radiating their eagerness to hear more, as Tracy continued. "It impressed me throughout the first morning how Annika had kept a psychic shield around herself. It's such a rare thing for any non-Ausurnian to generate one. She also projected her desire for the job to me after I made her an offer. I didn't know if she knew what she was doing. It was more important to see the extent of Annika's psychic powers and get her to stay."

Captain raised his index finger toward her. "Why didn't you tell—"

"How do you plan to keep her here now that her government knows where she is? Our rules about outsiders haven't changed." Commander Donauska spoke over his son.

"I filed the paperwork to become her sponsor for a work visa, and Karaxin approved it the next day. Lucky timing, I think. I never grilled Annika about the reason she accepted the job so fast. I was too excited that someone appeared after my vision, and her psychic energy level was so much more than any outsider I've met. I still think she may help us— with training, of course."

95

Her grandson raised his hand. "Gran, wait. That's so dangerous. What if she is a random girl just wanting to run away? Or one the Rovalkian government sent in as a spy under the guise of a friend or runaway? This could all be an elaborate lie or trap. What if she's one of the 'rounded up' individuals, and they offered her freedom for help?"

"No! She'd never," Tiana cried. "You never give people the benefit of the doubt. Why do you have to be such a pessimist all the time?"

Tracy grabbed one of her granddaughter's hands. "Tiana, it's going to be all right. Your grandfather's death is why we all have some level of reservation, and your cousin was the closest to him." She paused and looked pointedly at the men. "Think about it, you two. Rovalkia sending someone with advanced psychic ability to use for espionage? With her looks? I don't think so. Spies need to blend in, and anyway, there's pain in Annika's heart. She hides it down deep, but I can sense it in her aura. It's what fuels her."

Captain drummed his fingers against the armrests. "So, we're back where we started. Fine. We'll play along. Where do you suggest we go from here, Gran?"

"There's more to her story than we know. She feels so much. She could help us gain a deeper insight into Rovalkian suffering. It's not like she's a child, although with her closeted upbringing, she often acts like one. We'll continue to play the political game instead of resorting to the outright violence outsiders have always assumed of us. There is time. Get close." She raised her hand in anticipation of her grandson's protestations. He slouched back into the chair. "This has nothing to do with my belief she would make a good Ausurnian. That'll have to work itself out. We have bigger problems right now. Especially if her name is in international papers. Give her a chance. Try being a friend to an assumed enemy. The insights you gain may surprise you. I've learned that much in my long life."

Her son nodded. "Fine advice, mother. This will be the path we'll take while we investigate her and her government further."

"Fine. I'll get close, but only to gain information." Captain rubbed his hands on his pants, suddenly feeling nervously excited, like when he traveled abroad on a mission.

Tiana turned to the commander. "Annika can stay in Ausurnia past all this, right?"

Commander Donauska stood up. "We'll need to work within our laws, Tiana. You know I never make promises I cannot keep."

"So, that means you're not making any promises to keep her safe or offer her a safe place to call home," Tiana goaded.

"Our country comes first, young lady," Commander Donauska reminded her.

Tracy grabbed hold of Tiana's hand. "We'll just have to help her prove her worth, dear. I can see this meeting has run its course. Let's get you get you back to the diner, Tiana." She stood and addressed the men. "I hope you two understand the gravity of whatever path you choose."

* * *

Heat rose from Pontagu's Main Street, weighing the captain down on the outside while his thoughts on the gossip he'd just overheard at the clubhouse played in his mind:

"Annika, a dangerous witch—"

"That's what Calageeh Times said in the—"

"Who told—"

"It said a close, concerned insider—"

"Who?"

"Dunno."

"Because of the lake incident?"

"Maybe?"

Annika's no witch. There have been no cross relations with outsiders in a hundred years ... But she's hiding something. Up ahead, silvery-blonde hair glinted in the sunlight, cascading down her back in waves as her face hid behind an open newspaper.

He closed in with silent steps, holding his breath. Energies in the air shifted, feeling heavier now. He unfocused his eyes to see her aura swirl in an amorphous shape. Captain refocused and looked at the front-page picture while Annika's white-knuckled grip crumpled the edges down. Bright orange flames swallowed up a two storied building, and in front of the burning building, Rovalkians crowded around a hangman's post. A masked figure hung from the noose, ripped book pages pinned to the body while more pages swirled in the air, burning like floating candles. He squinted to see the large red letters spelling HERETIC on the pages pinned to the victim's chest. He grimaced as he read the headline.

ROVALKIA MAKES EXAMPLE OF TRAITOR TO ONE TRUE FAITH.

Captain inched closer. "It's getting pretty bad there, huh?" She didn't respond, so he cleared his throat.

Annika jerked her head up. What little color lived in her cheeks drained away, and an extra watery look reflected in her eyes. She stepped back. The booth owner looked up from his paper, stood up from his stool, and pointed at the newspaper in Annika's hands.

"Miss, I'm going to have to insist you buy that paper in the state it's in."

Annika's eyes darted down in a look of panic as she desperately tried to smooth the edges.

"I'll get it." Captain jammed a hand into his pocket, fished out coins, and handed them over to the kiosk owner. He turned back to Annika, who stared at him, shame washing over her face. She proffered the crumpled paper toward him, but he waved his hand. "No, it's yours."

She lowered her hand, not breaking eye contact. Her eyes reflected a crying soul. He'd seen eyes like those before from refugees and victims of war from the world over. *What are you hiding, green eyes?*

In the next instant, Annika snapped her posture straight. Her shoulders went back, making her collar bones more pronounced, and a hard look returned to her wet eyes. She nodded once and stepped around him, walking away with quick steps.

"Hey, wait up." He sprang forward to walk alongside her. "Where are you headed? I'll walk you there."

Her terse reply came without a sideways glance. "Back to work."

"Why are you so upset when you're safe here?"

Annika stopped short, still facing forward. Her hand not holding the newspaper clenched into a fist. "Even if they don't care about me, that doesn't mean I don't care about them." She turned around, gesturing wildly. "I still have my siblings there, and there's no life waiting for them. There's nothing left for anyone. I'm no better than those monsters if I just stand by and watch."

"Someone obviously cares. Do you know who put an article in the paper about your disappearance?"

She stepped up to him, jabbing her fingertips into his chest.

"Don't touch me," he growled.

She didn't pull away, and a whiff of vanilla entered his nose. *There's that scent again. I thought it was Gran's shop candle, but no, it's her scent.* Her eyes stared, unblinking, while her lip curled up. "Wouldn't you like to know, your highness?"

"You have no idea how much more I know than you. It's my job to know. I'll find out, so why don't you just save us both time and tell me?"

Annika shook her head, wisps of silver hair swaying about her face. Her fingers touching him curled into themselves, and she lowered her fist. "Look, all you need to know is that I'm estranged from my parents, and my abilities will get me killed if I'm found out. But now I have been because someone went to the newspapers about me." Her voice tightened. "I *will* find someone to teach me and somewhere to become a fighter. I *will* find people who care like I do. My cause *will* prevail when I return to Rovalkia. And if I must fight, so be it. And no one, you included, is going to get in my way."

Captain noticed people looking at them. He leaned in, sweat moistening the hair beneath his hood. "Might we continue this conversation inside, away from nosy ears?" he hissed through gritted teeth. "Gran's shop is two doors down and she's already standing outside looking at us."

Annika whipped her head around to see his grandmother standing outside the shop with her hands on her hips. Annika hastened toward her, stumbling over a loose cobblestone, then righted herself.

"Give me a break, will you?" he muttered at her while keeping pace, hand at the ready to catch her if necessary. Outsiders always seemed such a clumsy bunch. "You're the one who popped up here. I have an entire country to protect."

Annika's emotions were on full display, her shields down. *She wants me to feel her pain.* He could hear her anger, *see* her anger, but so could everyone else on the street.

Once they got close enough, Tracy beckoned to them. "Come inside, you two. Come cool down." She turned to her grandson. "Lock the door behind you and flip around the 'open' sign. I think it's time we three had a chat."

They made their way into Tracy's office. Captain sat down in the desk chair while Annika sat on the couch cushion furthest away from him, staring out the small office window. Her hand still clutched the newspaper, its horrific front-page picture facing Tracy.

"Let's begin our talk with the article in hand. I'm guessing it's contributed to your heavy mood, Annika. It's time Captain here understood what makes you, well, you."

Annika looked down at the paper in her hand. Captain leaned forward. In a soft tone, he asked, "Was it a building in Karaxin?"

Her eyes darted up and around the room. They stopped to stare at the far wall. Tears pooled in her eyes. The girl's aura swirled faster. Tinges of red flashed here and there as his grandmother sank down onto the other side of the couch.

"It's all my fault." Annika said tightly. She blinked hard and looked back down at the front page. Her slender fingers glided over the picture. "Andrei was the closest thing I had to a friend. His bookstore was my oasis." A tear splashed onto the page, followed by another.

Captain gripped his knees. Tracy signaled for him not to speak. *"Let her tell her story,"* she thought-projected to him. *"She needs to be heard."*

Annika wiped her eyes. "It was the last used bookstore in Karaxin. Andrei enacted all the new laws and rules as decreed. I'd been going there for years. I'd run there when I had free time, and we'd talk about books. Or I'd read in a quiet corner until I had to go home. It was my playground, my escape. I loved looking at the large atlases of the word, pretending I was sailing the oceans. It's where I found a book on the old faith." She looked up at Tracy with red eyes. "If I'd known the consequences of bringing it home, I would've never touched it."

"What happened when you did?" Tracy whispered.

A single tear ran down Annika's left cheek. Captain remained quiet and licked his lips. Annika's eyes lowered back down to the newspaper. "You should've seen his face when I brought it to the counter. *'Where did you get that?'* he screamed at me. Andrei had never raised his voice to me before. I told him it was on the back shelf. He had shaken his head. *'No, I know every book in this shop. I've never owned that. Take it away. Right now. Get out.'* I tried to give him money, but he said, *'No, it's yours. Go home. And never come back.'* I'm not stupid, but I realize I acted naïve. But they drafted the book like a history text, not religious. I thought the government was still allowing history books on the subject to teach us about the past. Or what they call, The Great Mistake."

"How'd you get caught?" Captain asked. For all her secret keeping, he assumed she'd be just as good at hiding actual items.

Annika glanced in his direction. "I showed it to my parents."

"Why?" Tracy and her grandson gasped out.

"You have to understand." Annika slouched back onto the couch, tossing the newspaper to one side. She stared up at the ceiling. "I grew up under strict rules and curfews. My family was my entire world. And my father had a room full of books too, so I was never bored. He always encouraged reading, and they never batted an eye when I went to the bookstore. I was his smart girl. He never once told me what *not* to read. Teaching us kids what *not* to do was the job of our church leader. But every time we went to church, it was the same thing: Kraxxan is God, fear his wrath, and the old faith is bad because it gives power to the undeserving, blah, blah, blah. But there was never an explanation of why. I tuned it all out from boredom when I was younger, and out of annoyance when I was older."

She shifted to sit up. Her eyes were less watery as a blueish-gray hue swirled about in her aura, and she stared straight ahead. "When I saw a passage in the book explaining my ability to feel energy in my hands and to feel other energies, I got excited. My parents were getting frustrated with me any time I tried to talk about what I felt. They kept saying there's no place for feelings in our world. I wanted to prove to them I wasn't a monster by showing them the book."

Annika suddenly gripped the edge of the couch cushion. Red flashed through her aura, blooming here and there in spurts. "The last thing I thought would happen was my father ripping the book from my hands and hurling it into the fire. He was so mad. It was so sudden. He told me to be out of the house within a week. My poor siblings knew nothing; I had sworn not to tell them anything, or else I could never see them again. So, I told James and Sarah I was going on a grand adventure." She spread her palms open, facing them upwards. "Do you see now? His death is on me. My parents knew I went to that bookstore. They could've turned him in. I didn't think to warn him. I never went back. My priority was to find a job somewhere far away and wallow in self-pity. It's why I need to fight now. It's why I need to reshape my government. I need to go back and join the underground fighters. Soon."

"That's a lot for you to take on," Tracy sympathized.

"I know. But for all my asking, they have offered me nothing but empty promises." She shot a glance at Captain.

He leaned forward and said, "I understand you're upset. I do. But like I told you before, we don't go charging into another country without probable cause."

"*THIS* isn't probable cause?" Annika shoved the paper in his face. She stood up; her body shaking. "Or is it because this wouldn't be lucrative enough for you, your *Highness*?"

Captain sprang up. His chair flew back with a *bang* against the desk, and he towered over her, baring his fangs. Annika sneered back into his face. Not a speck of fear hid under her fierce gaze.

Tracy raised her hand. "Annika …"

"Why should I trust you anyway?" Annika continued to shout. "Why should I conceive you'd help me at all when you've been in a relationship with Ciara?" The captain's jaw dropped. "Yeah, I know about you two. How long did you reckon that was going to stay a secret?"

"Annika! Knock it off," Tracy shouted. "Stop acting like a child and sit down."

Annika stared at her wide-eyed for a moment, then sat. Captain balled up his fists, trying to suppress the fury he felt. But not towards Annika; Ciara and her friends had clearly gotten their claws into her. Their meddling would ruin the entire operation. He leaned closer to Annika and said with a calmness that was soaked in venom, "Gods above, girl, you sure like to take things out of context. First, I dated Ciara waaay back in school—for all of three days. And it wasn't because I liked her, it was because I thought it was the right thing to do as a future heir." He took a deep breath.

Annika sucked on her lower lip. "I didn't know that."

He sighed and glanced out the window. "What are you doing listening to them, anyway? Everything they say is for their own selfish reasons. And second, we know Rovalkia is in trouble. Trust me, we're your neighbors. We see everything. But something bigger must happen before we spring into action. It's a game of politics. The World Intelligence Committee is tracking them, too. Everyone knows. Be patient."

Annika's curled lip lowered into a frown. "If you say so, but my family's in there. You wouldn't be patient if it were your siblings, parents, and friends stuck in there." Tightness had come back into her voice.

"Annika, listen to me, if no one else," Tracy directed. "We *are* forming a plan."

Annika blinked and turned her attention to Tracy. Captain pulled the desk chair back and sat down.

Tracy smoothed her skirt over her knees. "My grandson *is* going to provide you with training."

"You are?" Annika's head whipped to gawk at him. Suspicion emanated from her before he sensed her psychic shield spring up.

He relaxed his hands upon the chair's armrests. "That's right. We can't deny your psychic abilities anymore, regardless of where they came from or who you are. My father decreed it is me who trains you so you don't get anyone, including yourself, hurt. There's no way we're going to let you go back—right now, that is."

Annika turned to Tracy; her lips parted. Tracy nodded. Annika turned back to him and scooted forward. "Okay," she whispered, nibbling her lip, then glanced up at him. "Psychic and physical training? It sounds like I'll need to fight more than before." Her hands clenched, relaxed, clenched again.

"As time permits, but let me be clear," he cautioned as he raised his finger to her. "I will not give you any military training, only basic self-defense. This is to give you a fighting chance for whatever you choose to do in the future."

Annika rolled her shoulders back. "I want to take down the Rovalkian government. Now. I need to go back. Maybe I can convince my dad to help, if I can break through his brainwashed mind …"

"But what about bloodshed, Annika?" his grandmother asked. "You don't know the horrors of battle."

Annika's eyebrows shot up, her eyes darting from her to him.

"Tuck yourself in, girl." Captain relaxed back into his chair. "You're going to be training in Ausurnia for a while. We will not be used as a quick means to your ends. You want to do this right? You must put in the time."

Annika's mouth popped open. "But—"

"I agree," Tracy said. "Your long-term presence here will, if hasn't already, get the Rovalkian government's attention. And they have a copy of your work visa to reference, too. We need you to keep a low profile while you learn and harness your powers. You sign your own death certificate if you go back any sooner."

Annika stood up and rubbed her hands together. "Fine. Can we start tonight, Captain?"

He stood up as well. "Tonight? No. I'll contact you when I have a free evening. We'll work around *my* schedule, not yours."

"What am I supposed to do in the meantime?"

"There's so much you can do. Learn more Ausurnian and have fun exploring the town. You are young and free. Live a little." Tracy offered a smile. "But right now, we need to make money, so please reopen the shop while I have a few private words with my grandson."

"Yes, ma'am." Annika turned to the door.

"Wait." Captain called out. Annika froze mid-step. "How could your dad help?"

Annika's eyes darted to Tracy and held her gaze while she bit her lip. Tracy tilted her head. "You can trust us, Annika. I know it's hard to do, but we're here to help."

"Well, you know how I said my dad is an office clerk?" she asked. "This is going to sound bad, but he's actually an office clerk … in the capitol building."

Captain gasped. *The gods are on our side! Finally!*

Tracy gaped, whispered, "Gracious me, child."

Captain brought his hands up and let them slap against his thighs. Then he leaped up from the chair. "Okay. Okay." He paced the two strides of space in the office, then pointed to Annika. "This—this could help us. Don't speak of this with anyone else. Do you understand me? Unless you want to end up like your friend, keep your mouth shut. Fear kills, Annika, and there's no exception for pretty girls. What kind of clerk is he?"

Annika's lips parted and closed. "Uh. Umm …"

"Quick, girl. I don't have all day." He snapped his fingers.

"I … I don't know." She looked at Tracy. "Honest. I never asked. It was never anything that interested me, so I never wondered." Annika hung her head. "I'm sorry. I didn't mean to keep it a secret. It scared me

106

to reveal too much since you warned me to be careful about what I say to anyone, Mrs. Donauska."

Tracy sighed. "It's okay, though it would've made our lives a little easier. This has been a tremendous culture shock for you, I'm sure, and we're all on edge these days. I should've told you that you can trust my family. I want us to trust each other." She looked over at her grandson. "*All* of us. We'll make faster progress."

Captain rubbed his chin as bits of a plan and wild theories flew around in his mind.

"Well, while my grandson digests this bit of news, please reopen the store, Annika."

She nodded sullenly and shuffled out, closing the door behind her.

"Why do you and your father linger in the past? It's holding you back from forgiveness and makes it impossible to build new relationships. Must I always be the glue holding everything together? What is there to even mull over?"

He leaned back in his chair, placing one hand on his chin, tapping in time with the other hand on his knee. "Grandfather's assassination was a warning. Rovalkia has its sights on weakening us. We thought Annika was using an alias. We can't find any other Mullways in public records. But something she said gives me an idea. Between us, dad and I have a growing suspicion that their elected leader is a puppet. The guy popped into existence right before the election, and we can't find a record of him either." He worked his jaw, jutting it out and in. "Out of frustration or actual fear, Annika's parents cast her out." He stood and leaned against the side of the small window, peering out. Too many theories were muddling his train of thought. "Then there's how the bookstore owner acted when he saw the book in Annika's hand ..."

"I need you to complete a single thought before moving onto the next, dear. I don't see the connection."

He faced her. "You know the way Rovalkia is rounding up the people they claim to be witches in the name of religion? I wonder if the Rovalkian government had the book planted at the bookshop as a reason to arrest the owner. Maybe he wasn't voting the way they liked or wasn't acting like them. Or maybe it was bait for self-proclaimed witches. But when Annika brought it home instead, it thwarted that plan." His voice rose to an excited whisper. "Her father could've been in on it. That's why he overreacted when he saw the book in his daughter's possession. If he's a clerk in the capitol building, that would explain why there's no record of her family name. They may run the Rovalkian government differently from what everyone believes, keeping the identities of their employees a secret. We've suspected it's never been a democracy like they play it out to be. The poor shop owner didn't stand a chance."

Tracy raised her hands to her face. "Should we tell Annika? Or request more information from her? It would infer her dad would've known about the plot since clerks and secretaries are skilled listeners by trade. Does this mean she *could* be part Ausurnian? I thought those family lines died out."

"We have records of those family lineages. They died out—I double checked. And any abilities they had paled compared to hers. I don't know what she is. She's … she's unique." He stood up straighter, stretching. "Maybe the outsiders are starting to have genetic variations like we do. We just need to figure out the whole truth first. It may take a while. We have men trying to sneak into the capitol building. Besides, there's no need to drop more stress on her than she already has."

"That's kind of you," his grandmother whispered.

"You know I dislike being a mean guy, right Gran?" He tilted his head. "I must be this way for our survival. It stings when family members act like *I'm* the monster."

Tracy exhaled slowly. "I'm sorry. You're right. We all have so much going on. There's a country to run, and the world is closing in around us. Here I am *retired*, and you're still climbing destiny's mountain. I forget how much responsibility is on your shoulders. I still see you as my little grandson, but it's important we're all on the same page when it involves Annika."

"I don't even notice the weight anymore," he lied. If his father and every Donauska first born before him could rule, so would he someday. A breathy laugh escaped his lips as he crossed his arms. "You're having a tough time retiring, huh?"

She smiled at him and stood. "When you've dedicated your whole life to service, it is tough. Helping others is in our blood. And our innate strength is why we are the rulers of this country."

Captain made to leave, his hand reaching for the doorknob. "Annika may well be a missing piece to the puzzle. I'll talk more with dad about my theory. There may be credence to your visions, after all. Maybe that's what it means—that grandpa will rest in peace finally, that we all will when Rovalkia gets restructured. I'll see myself out."

The Ausurnian Male

S he peered over the top of a shelf. "Captain, wait. Do you have a moment?"

He turned mid-step. "I have *a* moment."

"Why'd you warn me not to get bitten? Why all the open-ended threats if you want me to stay?"

"It was a genuine warning," he said, crossing his arms. "We inflict nasty bites because of our sharp teeth. Most Ausurnians nip when they fight. We use what the gods gave us. And *you* are gaining a track-record. Your shields won't protect you from a physical assault. It wouldn't be so important, but we have different bacteria than you outsiders. We don't want to treat you for a blood infection. There's no cure." The side of his mouth stretched up, adding to the sinister undertone of his words.

"Sounds more like something out of a fantasy novel. Are you messing with me?" Her narrowed eyes, frown transitioning into a smirk. "Lower your shields and let me read your truth."

"Not even over my dead body, girl." He bared his teeth. "I'm too old to be playing mind games. You can accept my advice or not, but don't waste my time." He turned and strode away.

"But when are you going to train me?"

"It's already begun if you've cared to listen," he shot back before the front door slammed behind him.

* * *

Annika stood eating an apple. *How can I train myself while Captain drags his feet? Think, Annika, think.* She nibbled around the core and thought back to her first days in Pontagu. At her bookshelf, she picked up a checked-out library book at random and started scanning the pages without thought or reason. Dry page flipping sounds filled the dim apartment. *Bingo.* Her memory of going to the clubhouse with Tiana popped up. *The clubhouse gym. I can work out right before it closes. There's bound to be fewer people.*

She placed the book back in its place and changed into the closest thing to workout clothes she owned: a pair of black sweatpants and a black cotton blouse. "Don't put off until tomorrow what you can do today," Annika said to the room. "I will avenge you, Rovalkia."

As she tied her shoes, her thoughts drifted back to Captain Donauska. *What cologne was he wearing? Did he rub against a tree? Mixed with the smell of his leather vest ...* "Ugh. Stop," she shouted to herself and left for the clubhouse. *You're not here to swoon. We need to free Rovalkia.* Her pace quickened. She looked anywhere but at the Ausurnians she passed. *Stupid Captain. Why does he have to be*

111

handsome? Well, the bottom half of his face, at least. I'll just have to run him out of my head.

At the door, Annika paused and peeked inside. *Good, no sight of Ciara.*

"Annika! Miss Mullway?"

She spun around, still holding onto the door handle in case she had to run inside. A familiar-looking, plain-clothed man stood next to an open car door. He waved, closed the door, and hastened over. As he closed in, he extended his hand and grinned a brilliant smile. "Theodor Donauska." Volumes of black wavy hair fell every-which-way atop his head, with strands falling forward into his eyes. His other hand traveled up, fingers combing back the unruly mess, while golden brown eyes connected with hers. Annika felt herself blush, placing her hand delicately on his to shake.

"I've heard so much about you! If there's anything you need, let me know," he said with a wink.

Annika blinked, her mind traveling back to Captain, wondering if he had the same eyes, the same hair. She fumbled to compose herself, embarrassed to meet another royal looking as she did.

"Aw, don't worry, Annika. I just came from the gym myself. It's a perfect time to go. The place is empty. I've seen you around town, so I know you don't normally dress like that. Hey, maybe we can grab a bite sometime, my treat? I feel like I know you already the way Tiana raves about you. And my mom sure likes you … What do you say?"

"I—uh, yes. It'll be nice to make another friend." She gave a wavering smile. Once again, Captain's hooded face invaded her mind like a jack-in-the-box.

His tiger eyes searched her face. "Great. We could all use one more friend, right? Especially during these times." He glanced around. "Well, I'll see you later. I'll come into Grandma's shop sometime and we can pick a day and time." Then he shuffled back to his car, looking over his shoulder twice as she stayed rooted in place.

After giving herself a good shake, Annika tiptoed into the clubhouse lobby and looked around at the various branching hallways.

"What do you want, Rovalkian?" came a sneering voice from the receptionist's desk.

Annika pivoted and strode toward the woman, whose black hair was loose and her red lips pouted. She was about Annika's age and poised in the middle of filing her nails. "Hi," Annika chirped, leaning over the counter. The lady leaned back in her chair. Annika spread a fake smile across her face. "I'm headed to the gym. Which corridor is it down?"

"Uh, no," the receptionist said matter-of-factly.

"No, what?"

"No, you may not use the gym. Or anything else in here." She motioned with her nail file like a conductor's wand and then pointed it at Annika. "You don't have a membership."

Annika dropped her smile. "Okay. May I have a membership?"

"Yeah, no. You need to be a citizen to be a member." A triumphant smile stretched across the woman's face.

How I would love to slap that smile off your face! Annika took a deep breath. "I have a work visa, and there's no rule about having to be a citizen to be in here. Tiana Donauska would have told me. So why don't you drop your racist act and give me a membership?"

The receptionist's smile became more toothsome. She leaned forward, more confident in her power over this conversation. "Pretty soon you won't be here, Rovalkian. Ciara's making sure of that."

Annika took a step back, pointed at the lady. "I knew I recognized you. You're one of Ciara's minions."

The woman held her nail file aloft. "What's a minion? Your Truscan is weird." She tilted her head and frowned, then resumed filing her nails.

Annika slammed her hand down on the counter. The woman flinched; her nail file dropped from sight. "What's Ciara up to?" Annika shouted.

The receptionist's face became impassive.

"Hey!" a male voice shouted from behind. "Keep it down. I'm trying to teach a class."

Annika spun around. "Damn it, Capt—" *Whoa. That's not Captain.* The man standing in a far hallway packed the space, his broad shoulders filling the upper half and spread legs filling the lower. Then movement at her side took her attention away from the mountain of a man. She spun back around in time to see the receptionist point at Annika and mouth something. "Hey!"

"Knock it off," he shouted again. "Get on with your business quietly. I won't tell you two again."

"Yeah, do your job," Annika taunted.

"And I told you, no citizenship, no entry. I didn't make the rules." The receptionist eased back in her chair. "There are trails out back leading into the woods. Hopefully you won't get killed." She scrunched her nose at Annika, feigning sympathy.

Annika backed away with her fists balled up. The teacher scrutinized her, so she held her head high and smiled.

The receptionist yelled, "Good luck." Annika lost it. She spun, held up both middle fingers in the girl's direction, and ran out the back door.

She kept running from both the adrenaline of her actions and fear that the enormous man may run after her. With light still left, she picked a trail at random and ventured into the woods. *Let's see how this goes.* She slowed to a jog as heat pierced through the forest canopy. Sweat beaded on her forehead before running down to her chest. She pumped her legs; her nose cleared. Deep smells of rotting leaves and evergreen were inviting and familiar. She inhaled. *Captain must be in here all the time to smell like this.*

Little creatures scuttled through the ferns on either side. Birds flapped their wings, and an animal giggled. *Giggling?* Annika started scanning the woods. *I hope it was just the vocals of a squirrel, and I'm psyching myself out.* "Ouch." She winced as pain shot through her side. Twigs cracked off to the left of the brush. Annika gritted her teeth. *Run through the pain. No pain, no gain.* She heard louder sounds of underbrush moving to her right. *Whatever it is, it's keeping up with me. But it doesn't sound like a big predator.* Annika jogged on. "Ow," she groaned and stopped. A sharp cramp seared across her waist. Bending over, she held her side and tried inhaling into the aching muscle. All the sounds in the forest quieted. "Hello?" she called out, scanning the path up ahead.

"Hello."

"Ah!" she yelped and spun around, sucking air in through her teeth. Four children half her height stood together on the path. Three boys with their shirts and shoes off exchanged big grins. The one girl wore a pink shirt covered in dirt, and mud covered her bare feet. Sweat trickled down into Annika's eyes. She blinked hard and used the back of her hand to wipe it away. Soaked hair clung to her hand as more plastered her face and neck.

The little girl took a step forward. "Hello." Big, round black eyes stared up at her. Black hair stuck out in all directions from a once neat braid pinned about her head.

"Hi." Annika took a step back. *Ausurnian kids. I should've guessed.* She wiped her sweat covered hand on her shirt. "Uh, am I in your way?"

115

The girl tilted her head to one side, as if not understanding Annika's words, even though she was speaking Ausurnian—well, trying to. One boy stepped up next to the girl. Mud smeared in an arc across his chest. "You don't recognize us? Or me?" he asked in Truscan.

"No, sorry."

"It's me." The boy pointed to himself. "Tiana's brother. From the lake, and these are my friends." He rested an arm around the girl's shoulders.

Annika squinted. "Oh, it is you," she lied. "You guys were fun to play volleyball with before those soldiers ruined it."

"You're not like other girls your age," the little girl said, pointing up at her and speaking Truscan, too. She smiled as sharp looking canines poked over her lower lip.

"And you're speaking Ausurnian, though you're an outsider," another boy piped in.

"Ah, well, I didn't want to assume you knew Truscan. Plus, I need all the practice I can get."

Tiana's little brother took another step forward. "We have language lessons every week," he said with his chest puffed out. He turned to look at his friends before turning back to her. "You seem nervous. But don't worry, we like you. You proved yourself by jumping off the jetty. Can we speak Truscan to you while you speak Ausurnian to us for practice? Want to run with us?"

The young girl hopped forward, grabbed Annika's hand before she could reply, and pulled her into a jog.

"Come on," all four kids cheered. "Keep up."

"Where'd you come from?" Annika gasped, holding her side.

"We own these woods," one boy crowed.

The rest howled upward, causing the birds to take flight above them, their wings buffeting the foliage. Leaves fluttered to the forest floor, and the kids surrounded Annika, pushing her forward. She stumbled, throwing her hands out in front of her. One kid grabbed the back of her shirt and pulled her upright.

Annika slowed to a stop. "Go on," she gasped. "I have to turn back."

Tiana's brother skipped past her. "You should become an Ausurnian, then you could keep up. See you tomorrow night?"

"What? Tomorrow?" Annika bent over again, massaging her side. "Uh, if I can get away, yes. I'll run this way tomorrow."

With a wave of his little hand, the young Ausurnian boy ran after his friends. Annika turned back, looking over her shoulder to make sure they weren't sneaking up on her again. The setting sun threw flecks of orange light through the trees. She turned her walk into a slow jog. *How would being a citizen make me faster? Strange kid.*

The shape of the clubhouse came into view as the last remnants of light retreated west. Annika slowed to a walk as she spied groups of kids weaving in-between buildings. One girl in long pigtails waved at her. Annika waved back, then rolled her shoulders. *It's nice knowing the creatures of the night don't mind my presence. What a story to tell James and Sarah.*

* * *

Sorrow plagued Annika's mind the next morning. She hummed a burial song while getting ready for work. *I hope Andrei didn't suffer. His death is a perfect example of why I need to reshape Rovalkia. Ouch, my legs are sore. But the more I run, the stronger I'll become. And I'll become stronger still with Captain's help.*

She entered the shop and went about making tea. Tracy came out of her office moments later. "I'm surprised you arrived to work early, Annika, considering the circumstances of yesterday."

Annika peered over her shoulder. "After the conversation with you and Captain, I feel like my new goal is more attainable. There's so much to do. Andrei's death is heavy on my mind, but it also motivates me. I can't wait to train with your grandson. The sooner I can get back into Rovalkia, the more lives I can save. And can we double down on language lessons? I want to speak conversationally."

Her boss's eyes widened. "I think we can do that, but I've told him to go easy on you at first. Training is hard."

"Then it's a good thing I'm determined." Annika drank down her tea and grabbed up the duster. She rattled off verbs and nouns in Ausurnian, dusting and rearranging bottles as she went. Tracy interjected to correct her or give her an extra word to use with the verbs. The mail carrier looked astonished as Annika whisked the mail from his hand in a spinning move. "I'm practicing being light on my feet," she explained to him. He left, shaking his head. When no one looked to be around, she did pushups against the counter.

The bell above the front door sounded, announcing a new customer. Annika looked at the clock on the wall and scolded her usual two o'clock patrons, "You three are a minute late today."

"Hey guys, she *can* speak." The closest leaned over the counter toward her. "And here we thought you were shy."

Her cheeks heated; she ducked down to get the box for them.

"Gentlemen," Tracy said, padding up from behind.

The trio stood up straight and saluted her with a fist over their hearts. "Ma'am."

Tracy gave the cadets a hard look as Annika watched, rising from her crouched position behind the counter. When Tracy disappeared into her office, the cadets relaxed. Annika looked them over. *The only way to tell these guys apart is their chin shapes. Drat these Ausurnian military uniforms.*

"Alright, gentlemen, here's Pontagu Military Base's order. Randall, I believe it's your turn to tell me the latest joke or prank you three are up to? I could use some laughter."

Cadet Randall leaned in. "We poured glue into the bottom of the archery instructor's quiver. When he went to pull out an arrow the next day, the whole quiver went flying out of his hand!" He made an arcing motion with his hand.

"You *didn't*. I bet the instructor was livid." Annika took a step back, drawing a hand to her mouth to mask the escaped smile.

All three men smirked. Cadet Jenkins elbowed Cadet Palmer. "We did. And we would've gotten away with it had Palmer here not burst out laughing."

Cadet Palmer let out a belly whoop. "It was worth it. Even for all the floor and toilet cleaning we will now have to do for the next month. I'd do it again."

Annika stifled a giggle as Tracy's stern voice rose from behind the half-closed office door. "Gentlemen. I know you're on the clock."

"Yes, ma'am." The three bowed their heads in the matriarch's direction and shuffled away. Cadet Palmer raised a hand to hide his continued tittering.

Randall paused halfway to the front door and whispered to his mates. He turned around; Annika raised an eyebrow at him. He grinned at her and once the others had left, motioned her over to him. She looked to make sure her boss's attention was back on the computer screen before walking over.

"What?"

"My little brother and his friends ran with you last night, and he couldn't stop talking about how fun you are. He was also at the lake with my mom. I told him it couldn't be the same pretty, shy girl at the shop, but he was insistent. So, I was wondering," he glanced over Annika's shoulder, "if I may take you out for a meal tomorrow night? Here in town? Nothing too fancy. Us cadets are more like unpaid interns."

Annika felt her eyes widen. Her mouth parted. *My first date.* "Yeah, I suppose so. Yes, I'll go out with you."

"Great." Randall's smile was all teeth. "I'll pick you up at seven. Where do you live?"

"Pick me up in front of the shop."

"Great. See you then," he said as he walked out the door.

Tracy strode past Annika and up to the front display window just as the tinkling of the door's bell faded away. Her hands went to her hips as her head tracked the cadet's car driving away.

"Mrs. Donauska? Is everything all right?" Annika took two steps forward, trying to read her boss's well-shielded energies.

Tracy turned back around, scrutinizing Annika. "I had a feeling … I'm sure it's nothing. And don't bother trying to read me. You'll never get past these shields." She traipsed back toward her office. "Once you lose a loved one, your shields become impenetrable. You'll understand someday."

A Desire for Lies

Annika rolled back her shoulders and threw herself into her work as her thoughts buzzed. *What does one wear on a date? I'll have to think up conversation topics. Do I pay for half of the meal?*

When her shift ended, Annika ran upstairs. She took out leftover soup from the night before to reheat. *Tiana can help me. I'll call her after dinner.* Her phone rang as if on cue, but the call back number was unknown. She answered with a tentative, "Hello?"

"It's Captain Donauska. Are you home? I need to take you to the base to have a chat with my father. Can you be ready in the next ten minutes?"

"Wait, what? No. I'm heating dinner up and still in the clothes I wore today."

"I'm sure whatever you're wearing is fine," he shot back. "Let the dinner lay. I'll have dad get food sent to his office. This is important, Annika. I'm on my way."

"So glad I have a say," Annika huffed. She turned off the heat and washed her face before raking a brush through her wavy hair. Then she took a moment to stare at herself in the mirror and pondered if the meeting would be about her training. A car horn sounded outside. Annika spritzed body spray over her red blouse, applied lip gloss, and snatched up her keys before running out to hop into Captain's idling car.

Captain Donauska

He stood up, car keys already in hand.

"Don't forget to make it feel and look real, son. The fact that her father works in a government building could be a game changer for us. Start slow, as if you *are* falling in love with her. Give small hints in body language and voice—nothing over the top," his father said as he stood up from behind his massive desk. "I want you to be so convincing that your public show of affection falls just short of the real thing—a deep fake."

Captain wanted to roll his eyes, but with his hood in place, there was no point. "I understand. Slow and steady wins the race. She's vulnerable, so it shouldn't be too difficult."

"Yeah, well," his father cleared his throat and tugged the hem of his vest down, "there's a fine line between pretend and real with the fairer sex. I know you have little time for a personal life, but with our line of work—well, you know. Just do your best and see if you can't coax out any more personal information from her. We need a win. Get into character and stay there for as long as it takes to figure this mess out."

"Okay. So, when are we going to reveal that there're no rebels for her to run to? That it's us exacting revenge by starting those riots and protests?"

"Probably never. Rovalkia is a bigger problem for us than her. Besides, your grandmother needs her at the shop. It's a win-win for us."

Captain stretched his lips thin, gave a curt nod, and strode out.

Annika

"You don't need to be nervous," Captain said at the first red light.

Annika looked down at her lap. Her hands were hard at work, twisting the strap of her seatbelt. She released her grip and watched the strap spring back to its original straight form. "I should hope not. But you *are* taking me to a place I've never been, and I don't know who you are from moment to moment. A prince? Law enforcer? Or just someone helping his grandmother? That's what has me nervous." She stole a glance his way. His chin was stubble free this evening, and he detected a whiff of his woodsy cologne. *Now I'm extra glad I cleaned myself up.* Her hand shot to her necklace to make sure the charm was facing forward and that the clasp was behind her neck. *Grandma Mullway, give me strength.*

"I'm all those things all the time. But my whole family *is* on your side, and so am I. We have no choice, since our name is now being dragged through the mud along with yours. Abetting a bona fide witch, they say. So now you need to trust us Ausurnians to accomplish what we need to do." His head turned toward her.

"I am trying to trust, and I'm sorry your name is being sullied too. Bad press can't be good for your image."

"No, it's not good." He turned off the highway and onto a road along an imposing barbed wire fence. The lowering sun blazed through the windscreen, and Annika squinted through her upheld hands to look at a guard house ahead with a metal structure beyond. The car in front of them paused inside the overhang before driving on when a green light flashed. Captain spoke with the guard in Ausurnian while handing over his badge. A guardsman handed back his badge along with an additional badge on a lanyard, and Captain handed the visitor pass to Annika.

123

"Do not lose it," he said as they idled in the structure. "I'll have to hand it back when we leave."

She placed it around her neck. "What's this box?"

"It's a scanner to check for bombs, weapons, and anything or anyone not in the registry." The green light came on, and he drove on to park in front of the foremost building.

A flagpole towered above the building near the front doors, and two flags whipped southward. The clanking of the flag chain against the metal pole drew Annika's attention. The top flag was Ausurnia's, but she didn't recognize the second. It had a large shield with stars in the center, and two swords crisscrossed behind. "What's the second flag?"

"It's my family crest. As long as those two flags are flying at full mast, all is well in Ausurnia." He laid his fist over his chest.

They entered and walked through a door-framed metal detector. "I don't think Rovalkia has anything like that car scanner. They have metal detectors like this one, though."

The captain and soldiers behind the reception desk cackled, and Annika looked from one face to another. "Rovalkia wishes they had our level of security. For such a fear-imposing country, it is easier to break into than an unlocked door," Captain explained.

"Good to know," Annika said, smiling.

All three men looked at her and dropped their mirth, with one receptionist handing back the passes and the other pushing a button without another word. A door swung open.

"She has dreams of revenge on her country," Captain explained to them. They nodded; one guard exhaled.

"Guess I'd better watch what I say in here, huh?"

"The less you say, the better." He led her through more doors, down a hallway, and through another security checkpoint. Annika remained silent. He stopped at a desk in the hallway where a soldier was clicking away on a keyboard. The soldier nodded toward the adjacent carved oak door. Annika stared in awe at the man. *He's the first not to acknowledge the Prince of Ausurnia.* Captain pulled her by the arm through the door.

Inside was a massive oak desk with carved legs and two plain chairs facing it. Behind the desk sat Commander Donauska in a high-backed leather chair. *Like a throne,* Annika mused. His attention was on the folders open before him.

The captain stayed standing, so Annika did, too. She kept a little behind him, waiting for a sign of what to do or say. Commander Donauska made a notation on what he was reading, then looked up. "Have a seat, you two. I'm having food delivered in a minute. I've heard you've had an eventful week, Miss Mullway."

"A little stressful, sir. I don't know about eventful." Annika looked straight at the commander. Rule Fifty-Four: Never show fear or inferior feelings, no matter how powerful the person is.

The side of Commander Donauska's mouth stretched up into a half smile. "You've gained more confidence since we first met at my house. I've heard you can now speak some Ausurnian and are mastering your psychic abilities." He folded his hands on the desk.

Annika sat up taller, feeling small in the ordinary chair.

"Those boys at the lake didn't know who was in front of them, huh?" The commander chuckled and leaned back in his seat. Then his mouth straightened, and he pointed at Annika. "Under the circumstances, I'm letting it go, but there will be no more energy blasts against my citizens, you hear? My son's going to teach you the proper way to react in those situations if it happens again. Energy blasts can stop a man's heart if it hits the right way."

"Yes, sir," Annika said, raising her chin.

"Don't, Annika," Captain warned.

"What don't you want her to do?" Commander Donauska asked.

"She's got that stubborn glint in her eye. She wants to argue."

"Speak your mind, Miss Mullway," the commander directed.

Annika rolled her shoulders back. "Sir, I will abide. But if any of your citizens threaten or hit me with an energy blast again, I'll hurl all I have back."

"Hold on." Commander Donauska leaned forward. "Who did that to you?"

"Ciara. My first week here. It's how she found out I had a psychic shield. Your son intervened before I had time to fight back." She jabbed her thumb in Captain's direction.

Commander Donauska looked at his son. Captain shrugged. "I must have forgotten to mention it to you. I had to intervene. It was her and Tiana against Ciara, and you know how Tiana hates her. Ciara didn't stand a chance. The pile of paperwork I'd need to do if she filed a report against Annika would've been a nightmare, too."

His father nodded. "You're right. Not to mention the lawsuit from her father. No matter what her family does, it always ends in a headache. Speaking of which, Annika, my mother and son suppose there may be a connection between Ciara and the recent increase in your name in the international papers. Thoughts?"

Annika contorted her face into a snarl, and her nails dug into the armrests of her chair. The bloody woman was going to be the death of her. She leaned her head back to stare at the ceiling. "So Ciara *is* up to something. I heard my name was popping up but haven't had time to get a hold of any news agencies to clear my name. Mrs. Donauska said it could just be a bit of town gossip, but Ciara and her friends have been threatening me. She's going to get me kicked out of Ausurnia." She let out a pent-up breath and looked at the commander. His mouth set in a straight line. She glanced at the captain to find his expression the same. "Your uniform hoods don't allow me to read your faces. Someone is going to need to say something. I don't know who's submitting the articles. I keep to myself."

"Well, Miss Mullway, Rovalkia *has* gotten wind of these rumors." Commander Donauska stood up and trudged around his desk toward them. He leaned back, facing her. "Personnel from their Bureau of Consular Affairs have been in contact with me. They know you're here, and they claim to be concerned about your welfare."

Annika opened her mouth to rebuke, but he quickly held up a hand. "I know, Annika, but there's more. The most recent phone call has me wondering what their interest in you is specifically." He paused. "They've requested for me to deliver you back home."

She recoiled, her heart thumping against her ribcage. "No. I won't go. I can't go back. They'll kill me. They killed my friend. And with all of Ciara's lies—" *I have to get out of here!* Annika vaulted from her seat.

Captain's hand caught hers, holding her in place. "We won't make you do anything or go anywhere you don't want to, Annika. Please sit back down. My father and I have thought up a plan to get them off our backs."

The commander hadn't budged from his leaning posture. She looked down at Captain's gloved hand holding hers. His long fingers wrapped around the entirety of her own. A shiver danced across her shoulders as his grip tightened. She looked up at his hooded face. He nodded, and she sank back down, still looking at the hand Captain held. Firm but gentle.

"Eh-hem." Commander Donauska cleared his throat.

Annika yanked her grasped hand back into her lap, but the feeling of Captain's soft leather glove lingered.

"My son spoke the truth. It's our name on the line, too." Commander Donauska's voice had an edge to it this time. "We'll continue to harbor you if you do your part, but you need to trust us. Can you do that?"

With a gulp, Annika nodded. "I think so, sir."

"Good." The commander rose from his lounging position and drifted to the window on the far wall. Both Annika and Captain's heads followed his path.

Beyond the parched grass yard, Annika could see troops running in formation back and forth. *Is there enough Ausurnians to protect their country if Rovalkia invades?* She shook her head to get rid of the thought. *Captain said they have more security measures. Rovalkia would be stupid to get the idea in their head. But then again*—The commander spun around. She jerked her head up at him.

"We're going to play the game back with a media campaign showing you happy and healthy; to prove your desire to be here. To show the world the rumors about you and us are wrong. Something they won't believe as staged."

BZZZ. A static sound came from the desk phone. Commander Donauska leaned over and answered it on speaker.

"Your food is here, sir," announced a voice.

The commander retrieved a bag and handed Annika and his son one package each. He then sat at his desk with one for himself.

As the two men opened their packages without a word, Annika followed suit. Her jaw dropped as sliced meat and vegetables spilled out the ends of a warm, folded flatbread. Annika's mouth watered at the peppery tang emitting from the meat and dressing. She looked at the men. They were two bites in. Her stomach rumbled. She bit down on one end and pulled back. It looked like a mere nibble compared to its sheer size. Annika attacked the wrap repeatedly. The ingredients were good, and she was hungry. An amused hum came from in front of her. She froze mid chomp, then lowered her hands to see where the sound came from. Commander Donauska had set his food down and appeared to be watching her. She peeked to her right as she chewed. Captain's head turned toward her as well; one corner of his mouth turned up. She wiped her mouth with the back of her hand, swallowed, and stared back at the commander.

He leaned back in his chair. "I'm glad to see you're a healthy eater, Annika. Sorry we delayed your dinner. Finish and we'll do the photo shoot." He reached over and grabbed the last remains of his dinner.

The portion still in her lap looked like a mountain of a task, and Annika's stomach pained with sudden fullness. She wrapped up the remnants. "I can't finish it, sir. I'll take it home and eat it for lunch tomorrow."

"You won't want to eat it. It'll be soggy," Captain said, rising from his chair. He extended his hand toward her. "Give it here. I'll put it in dad's fridge and eat it later."

"You will? But I've had my mouth on it." Annika stared up at him, her eyebrows scrunched together.

"Waste not, want not, Annika. Give the man your sandwich. A little Rovalkian spit won't hurt him. Ours will you, though." Commander Donauska got up and marched out the door.

Annika handed her sandwich over, and she tracked Captain as he strode over and placed the leftovers in a mini fridge in the room's corner. *So, is it true? Are they part monster, like the stories say, or is it a ruse, so I don't get too close to an Ausurnian?*

The soldier behind the desk outside was still there. He hung up the phone and stood with a notepad in hand. The man then fell in step with the commander. If Commander Donauska said something, the soldier scribbled on the notepad. Annika picked up her pace to walk next to Captain.

"Is he your dad's personal Shadow?"

Captain looked down at her. His mouth twitched. "It's Dad's personal secretary. He would protect him as I would. So, yes, I guess he is."

"Where are we walking to? What are they going to photograph me doing? Picking flowers? Laying in the grass?"

"You'll see," he said. "I came up with two out of three plausible scenarios."

They marched down hallways and up a flight of stairs. Commander Donauska entered a room, and they followed. Someone had set up the room like a photographer's studio. Annika remembered a room like this long ago when her parents had taken them to get a family portrait done. James and Sarah were still babies, and they all wore fresh clothes with their hair pinned up in mom's fancy hair clips. The backdrop had been a cheery landscape with clear blue skies and green grass. This backdrop was stark white. *That'll convince them*, she thought, rolling her eyes.

An Ausurnian man in a crisp three-piece blue suit with a lanyard around his neck stepped forward. "Good evening, sire. If I could have Miss Mullway and His Highness, Captain Donauska, stand in front of the screen. I need to make sure the lighting is right before proceeding."

Captain placed a hand on the small of Annika's back, guiding her toward the white sheet draped on the wall. "Give me your lanyard. I'll keep it in my pocket until we finish."

She handed it over. *Why is he in the picture?* She stood facing the camera, set on a tripod, with Captain standing at her side. "This isn't promising, Captain," she muttered out of the corner of her mouth. "A white backdrop? Really?"

"It's a screen. The computer will insert a backdrop into the picture. You need to trust us. It won't look convincing if you don't. Each emotion you feel plays on your face in full view. We can read you even with your shields up."

Annika clamped her mouth shut. *Each emotion? Every time? Void swallow me now.*

"So, Annika." Commander Donauska turned to her from the huddle he was in with his secretary and another officer who had stepped into the room. "This is our head of Information Exchange. He thinks we have one scene that will tick all the boxes."

"Scene B?" Captain asked.

His father nodded. Captain muttered under his breath. Everyone turned to her.

I hate it when they do that. She stood taller. *Here goes nothing. Let's see how far trusting will get me.* "I'm ready."

"Good girl. The less fussing there is, the faster we can all go home. Son, take your position," the commander instructed as he strode over to the photographer.

Captain came to stand right behind Annika. She felt his aura press against hers, their psychic shields resisting each other, as she forced her shoulders to untense. "Uh, can someone at least tell me what it's going to look like?" *Like why Captain is standing so close? His scent is so distracting.*

Captain's lips tickled the top of her right ear. "The most convincing scenario is one where it shows you in an embrace with a man," he whispered.

Annika jumped away, rubbing the ear into which he had spoken. "Who is this supposed to convince?" She spun to face the commander.

"Your father," Commander Donauska barked. "With his influence, if he has any, he will see you happy and tell his superiors to call off the dogs. Or it may piss him off enough to call for negotiations. Either way, the situation needs to fall back into *my* control. Now get back there. It must be a high-ranking soldier who's embracing you to get the desired effect. He's going to hug you from behind, and you two are going to gaze into each-other's eyes. It needs to be convincing. Why are you being so difficult? It's slowing us down, which puts you in more danger."

"How did you expect me to react when I found out?" she shouted. "No one gives me enough time to process *anything*!"

"Because *everything* having to do with you is a matter of national security. One more outburst and I swear I'll toss you on a train back to Rovalkia myself," the king roared back.

Annika flinched. When she opened her eyes, he had turned on the photographer, hollering in Ausurnian. Captain's hands grasped each of Annika's upper arms. "Dad, stop. I've got this." He nudged her until she looked at him. "Annika, look, it's been a long day for all of us. I understand this is a sudden development, but it's how we operate. These quick decisions are how we survive. There's more to it than your safety. This photoshoot will help to flush out the bad guys." Captain lowered his voice. "We've been doing this a long time. We know what we're doing."

At his soft tone, Annika shivered. *Why does he have such an effect on me?*

"Would you prefer one of our other officers do the shoot?"

"No," she shouted. Her hands shot up to cover her mouth. Not only her face, but her mouth seemed determined to betray her, too.

Everyone in the room turned to her. Annika glanced up at Captain. She couldn't read the expression on his lips, a mix of smirk and frown. Heat rose in her face as she pulled her hands from her mouth. "I mean, no. I know you better. I—" Annika flexed her hands. "—I trust you."

His face relaxed, and he guided her back to where they had stood for the lighting test. His movements were slow and controlled, and when he nodded to her, she turned back to face the camera.

"We're all yours," Captain said to the photographer.

Commander Donauska stepped away from the suited man who was mopping his brow. He crossed his arms; a deep frown set on his face. *Okay, Annika. Trust, trust, trust,* she repeated to herself.

"Miss," the photographer motioned with his hands to her, "Please lean back and to your left. Gaze up at His Highness with a smile."

Annika pursed her lips and leaned back. Captain's hands wrapped around her hips. She sensed him take a step back. *He's going to let me drop!* She grabbed at his hands to catch herself as her right shoulder found his chest, stopping her descent.

"I won't let you fall," he whispered. The lilt of his accent was like a feather against her ear. She felt his hands tighten around her waist and inhaled sharply through her teeth.

The photographer adjusted the camera. "Better. Now if you would look at His Highness and smile, Miss Mullway."

She released her lower lip and looked up and over her right shoulder. Her stomach muscles tightened. Captain was already leaning forward, looking down at her. His scent of pine and leather intermingled with his minty breath, and butterflies took flight in her belly. She imagined touching his full lips, how soft and firm they would feel pressing against hers …

"Near perfect." The photographer's words split the silence. Annika blinked. "Captain, lean closer, please. Both of you smile big."

Captain inched closer to Annika's face, and inexplicable laughter rose in her throat. She tried to stifle it, causing a strangled noise to escape.

"Huh?" Captain pulled his head away a fraction of an inch.

Trying not to move, Annika replied under her breath, "If my father sees this, his reaction will be volcanic. He never approved of any man asking to date me back home. And knowing he doesn't have control over my life anymore, well, imaging him react to seeing me in the arms of the Crown Prince of Ausurnia has made me realize how free I am now. I can't really describe it."

Captain's face moved, and both sides of his mouth stretched equidistantly apart. His white fangs dazzled as they poked their tips over his lower lip. *He's smiling! And it looks genuine. Sigh. Of course, it's handsome ... and sharp.* Annika grinned back, her lips parting as the smile stretched further up. *I wish this were real. I wish I had impressive canines too.*

CLICK. CLICK. CLICK. The sound of the camera shooting photo after photo shattered the illusion that she was alone with Captain Donauska. Butterflies danced to the beat of her heart as she stared into his hood where his eyes were. *If only I could see your face. If only you felt the same.* Annika let her smile soften to match his, still hyper aware of every point where her body was in contact with his. Warmth emanated from him, traveling through her thin blouse.

"Perfect. We have what you're looking for, Your Majesty," the photographer announced.

Captain inched forward, using his chest to levy Annika back up to a standing position. He stayed behind her with his hands on her hips. She grasped at them to steady herself, feeling light-headed. She closed her eyes, trying to steady her breathing and slow her rapid heart rate. His body heat radiated against her back. When she reopened her eyes, Commander Donauska was reviewing the photos on the digital camera as the photographer clicked through them.

"Stop." The commander tapped the man's hand. He looked up at Annika and his son; an unamused, tight-lipped expression crossed his mouth.

Annika and Captain dropped their hands and Commander Donauska turned his attention back to the photo. He pointed to the screen. "This one. Use this one." Then he looked at Annika and Captain once more, gave a slight nod, and left the room. "We're done here," he yelled over his shoulder.

Captain touched the side of her arm. "Let's go."

As they made their way out, Annika paused next to the photographer fidgeting with his camera. "May I see the picture chosen?"

The photographer snapped his head up, surprise etched in his face. "Sorry, miss. I was told this is a top-tier security shoot. But you'll see it in the newspaper soon, no doubt."

"Annika!"

With a nod to the suited man, Annika ran to follow the captain.

Captain Donauska

He stormed down the corridors toward the front of the building. Looking behind him to make sure Annika was still in tow, he remembered how her body felt against his. It had sent shivers through him, shivers of excitement. *Don't cross the line. Don't fall for her.*

They went back through the security at the front door and made their way to the car. Thank the gods she wasn't playing twenty-one questions as his mind muddled between what happened and his next moves. He glanced over at her when they were back in the car. She was biting her lower lip, and he shook his head. It took all his focus to concentrate on the road, trying to push down the urge to lean over and taste that lower lip of hers

SMACK. He blinked and glanced over at Annika, who had struck her fist into her other hand, looking at him with a playful smile. His focus on the road disappeared.

"If it *is* Ciara who went to the papers, how are we going to deal with her?" Annika licked her lips.

Oh, don't do that. Captain gritted his teeth. *Damn girl is too distracting. "We?* No. I'll deal with her under our laws. *You* focus on your training, and don't get into any more trouble." *Or get me into trouble.*

Out of the corner of his eye, he spied her slouch back into her seat. With a sigh, she stared out the passenger window. When they passed an Ausurnian couple walking hand in hand down the street, she asked, "Is it really true that Ausurnian saliva is deadly?"

His gloves creaked against the wheel as his grip tightened, pondering a plausible answer as he parked around the back of his grandmother's shop. Annika was still looking at him when he finally turned to face her. Her eyes glowed in the moonlight. "The truth is—and keep this to yourself—it is when our saliva gets into your bloodstream."

"Like a werewolf?" she sputtered, leaning away from him.

He shook his head. "Yes … I guess. But we're not man-eating monsters. We're just, well, different." The full moon illuminated the back street as he gazed out the windshield.

"Uh, okay." Annika glanced at him warily when he again turned to her, but her shoulders had relaxed. "But can I go on dates?"

He gaped. "Why? What dates?" Annika's eyes widened as they continued to search his face. "I mean … yeah, I guess." He tightened his grip on the steering wheel. "Look, I should get back to my dad. We still have a lot to figure out. Just stay safe. I'll see you later, okay?"

A tormented look quickly passed through Annika's eyes. He had the urge to grab her hand, to console her, but the soldier inside warned, *stay away*. Annika exited the car and ran up her stairs without a backward glance. Captain idled the car, staring at her closed door. *What had she wanted me to say?*

Covert Workings

Her fingers blurred across the dial pad as she chewed on her tongue. "Tiana, I need your help. I have my first date tonight and don't know what to wear."

"I'll be right over."

KNOCK. KNOCK. Annika looked at the clock. Only five minutes had passed.

"Did you teleport here? How fast were you driving?"

"You call an Ausurnian for help and we appear. Who's your date?"

"Cadet Randall. He's nice when he comes into the shop, so I thought I'd test the water. He's taking me out for dinner in town, he says."

"Ooh, are you going to kiss him at the end of the night?"

"No way," Annika said, shocked. "Why would I? Should I?"

"I did on my first date with Second Lieutenant Baar and don't regret it. I'm crazy about him—knew it the first time we met. You don't know until the moment arrives." Tiana shrugged. "Now, about this outfit. Let's go through your closet and mine and get you looking like a goddess."

After a silent moment of rifling, Tiana whistled. "Oh no, Ro." She closed the dresser drawer. "Is this all you own? These other drawers are empty. This won't do at all." She shook her head.

Annika crossed her arms. "I have what I have. It's not like I could transport a cartload of clothes from home." *As if I had anymore to begin with.*

"I'm sorry." Tiana stood. "Why don't you come over to my house? I bet we wear the same size." She looked Annika once over.

Annika relaxed. "That would be amazing. I'll—" She stopped herself. *Whoops, I almost said I'll owe her.* Rule Seventy-One: owe no one anything. *That lesson makes sense now. What if I couldn't "pay" her back?*

"Get in, Ro. We're wasting precious time. I have a ton of clothes for you to try on," Tiana called from the driver's seat.

Annika chuckled, pulled from her jealous thoughts. "You never slow down, do you?"

"Nope!"

Within minutes, they were in Tiana's bedroom. She opened a door to reveal a walk-in closet crammed with clothes and accessories. Tiana wiggled her eyebrows at her friend as she brought out five short skirts. Annika gasped. It would've been scandalous to show her knees back home, but Tiana insisted she take one. "In case the mood strikes you."

Annika tried on everything Tiana tossed her way: sleeveless blouses, long dresses, short dresses, all in muted earth tones. She checked the time. "I'd better be getting back soon. I still need to shower and style my hair. Let me help you hang this pile of clothes up."

"Oh, just leave the clothes," Tiana said, snatching up the car keys. "And don't stress about giving back the ones you're borrowing. They look better on you, anyway."

Captain Donauska

"I fold. You're too good at this game." Theodor set down his cards and disappeared into the kitchen.

Captain chuckled. "You're the one who suggested playing. Hey, have you run into Annika yet? I want to know what your impression is."

"Oh, so it's Annika now? Not Miss Mullway, or the outsider?" Theodor teased. "Yes, I've had the pleasure. She was going to the gym the other night just as I was leaving."

"She fancies herself a revolutionary. Wants to change the world and is desperate for help. The girl doesn't know the first thing about politics, and yet, her father is the clerk of something in the capitol building in Karaxin." Captain reshuffled the cards while staring out the back patio window. "But the way she processes information, how she wrangles in her emotions, and hints at political training … Add in her psychic abilities—"

"And looks," Theodor added, coming back from the kitchen with his drink refilled, wiggling his eyebrows.

"That has nothing to do with it," Captain spat. He tossed the deck back down on the glass coffee table, and cards slid across and off the surface. "She's kidding herself with these grand delusions. She'll be dead before she gets anywhere near the capitol building. Dad and I are trying to figure out how their government operates. They keep demanding we return her, and dad wants me to get close to her, so she doesn't go anywhere." He shook his head, leaning back to stare at the ceiling; then sat up, looking Theodor in the eye. "Your sources have heard nothing new, have they? Even though we know her dad works as a clerk, there's no trace of him. It's like they erase government workers' identities."

"No, I haven't." His brother leaned forward in his seat, picking up the scattered cards. "But Grandma says she's special and is excited about you training her soon. Is that how you're going to make her think you like her?"

"Maybe. Maybe not." Captain rubbed his face with one hand. "I don't know. There are these layers to her, and it's driving me crazy. Her psychic strength is powerful for one her age, especially with no formal training. I don't know what to do next."

"Maybe you should enroll her in a class instead."

Captain snapped his head up. "She's not a *child*. She's your age, I think. She thinks we're a nation of warriors who go about attacking and invading, and every time I mention we play a good political game, she thinks I'm lying. I can't change her mind."

"I'll talk with her again. We set a dinner date."

Captain frowned. "Date?"

Theodor held up his hand. "Hear me out. I understand Dad wants you to be the one to take the lead on this, but I could teach her a thing or two about being an activist. I could help steer her away from her murderous thoughts. You must admit I'd be good at it with my background in activism and underground networking. At least give me a chance. She and I have a good rapport—at least I got the sense we did. It sounds like everyone has a personal stake in her now. I might as well join in on the efforts."

"Hmm." Captain rubbed his chin. "You are compassionate with outsiders, which is weird to me. You don't wear the uniform, so she may naturally feel more trusting toward you, especially if the stories of how Rovalkian soldiers treat their citizens are true." He pointed to his brother; Theodor sat at attention. "But watch it. Don't toy with her. She trusted me first, and I worked hard for that. Annika's intelligent. Don't lie to her, or she'll figure it out. Work around the truth."

"Whoa." Theodor threw his hands up. "I get it. Try not to be too charming." He winked and stood up. "Damn, you're protective of her. That's the last thing I expected." Captain gaped, but Theodor continued after a quick glance over. "It doesn't surprise me. She's easy to talk to, and she's attractive, isn't she? Is she single?"

"Don't go down that road," Captain growled. "I'm serious. We are so close to getting some answers after all these years." He rubbed his hands across his vest. "Let's get food. The diner is usually empty right now."

"You never were good at pretending, so if you feel it's easy to be around her; if you think about her a lot, you like her for real." Theodor ducked away, avoiding a cuff to the head. "Fine, deflect as usual. Anyway, you can catch me up on more of what I've missed. I'll meet you at the diner in a couple of minutes. I have to run a quick errand."

Annika

She decided on Tiana's knee length dark gray pencil skirt, her own short-sleeved red blouse with a small ruffle at the collar, and Tiana's skinny black heels she insisted made Annika's legs look a mile long. Tiana had also tossed a makeup palette in the bag to round out the look, and she'd pointed out which colors Annika should wear to highlight her emerald eyes.

Annika untied her hair rags to reveal loose waves and applied the smokey gray eye makeup. She looked down at her exposed legs. *My knees are too bony.* A wave of nausea made her sway, her hands white-knuckle gripping the edge of her bathroom counter. In her peripherals, the hour hand on the wall clock moved. *Too late now.* Annika pulled on

141

a borrowed black cardigan, checked her necklace clasp, and prayed she wouldn't break her neck walking in the high heels.

Cadet Randall leaned against a car parked in front of the shop. He hopped up and hurried over. "Whoa, you look—wow." A wide grin exposed his fangs.

Annika averted her gaze and pulled a strand of curls back behind one ear. "Thanks." Her other hand fidgeted with the bottom button of the open sweater.

He offered his left elbow up for her to hold. "I'm going to take you to the diner tonight, if that's alright."

She applied a light handhold to his arm. "Best food in town." She leaned her head toward him and sniffed. Soap and leather. Nice, but not as intoxicating as the captain's cologne.

As they ambled in the diner's direction, Randall cleared his throat. "So, that's a peculiar necklace you have. I'm guessing it was a gift from the Donauska's?"

Annika drew her free hand to the pendant. Her fingertip grazed the raised garnet set on one side of the bent arm of the horseshoe. "No, it was my maternal grandmother's."

"Did she get it in Ausurnia?"

"What?" She looked up at him, confused. "No. I don't think so. I don't know if she ever traveled outside Rovalkia." Her left foot wobbled on a crack in the sidewalk, and she gripped Randall's arm tighter.

He stopped walking as she steadied herself. "You girls wear dangerous fashions to impress us guys."

Annika frowned. "I'd much prefer to wear a uniform like yours. These female societal constructs are ridiculous. Why'd you think my necklace was Ausurnian?"

"The horseshoe is a symbol of luck and protection in our beliefs. But being a descendant of a Rovalkian witch sounds plausible, too."

"Excuse me? I'm not a descendant of a witch. My grandmother was a proud Rovalkian with deep faith. She was loving and protective. There was nothing arcane about her—that I know of." She pulled her hand away from Cadet Randall's arm.

His other hand grabbed hers, placing it back on his arm. "Hey. No need to feel offended. The rumors say you're psychic. We know outsiders cavorted with us in the past, and that is how they have a bit of our gift. Their descendants are called witches. Ausurnians are the only race who is psychic by nature, so it's a plausible link. I meant it as a compliment. Come on, we're so close to an enjoyable evening. I'll change the subject. What's your favorite place in Pontagu so far?"

Annika looked at him, wondering if she had overreacted. Tracy had said anyone could be psychic if they tried hard enough. But since no one, to her knowledge, had ever thought to test that theory, why argue? She relaxed, shot him an apologetic smile, and tossed her hair back over her shoulder. "You're right. Sorry for overreacting. I guess I'm still on edge since the lake incident." He patted her hand.

A server near the door ushered them to a booth, and Annika slid into the side with a view of the front door. The woman placed a second menu across from Annika when she didn't make room for Randall.

"I'll sit here, I guess," he mumbled.

Annika flashed a nervous look at the server, but what could the girl do to calm her nerves on a first date? The server winked, and whispered, "I'll check on you, don't worry."

"What'd she say?" Randall asked.

"I didn't hear," Annika lied. "I picked to sit on this side because it's safer to sit facing the entire room—I feel like I need to explain based on your expression."

The cadet tilted his head. "But I'm here. I'm the male. *I* should sit over there."

She shrugged. "Next time I'll let you. It's just a force of habit. And to answer your previous question, the wooded path leading to the lake is my favorite place so far, besides swimming in the lake. Or maybe it's the library. No, that would be my second favorite. Oh, and here, I guess."

Cadet Randall choked on his sip of water. "The forest? Really? I'd think that would be the last place you'd like. And the diner? Why?"

"I feel at home in the forest, and I like Tiana and her mom." She shed the sweater, folding it down to her side. The cadet's eyes bore into her, and Annika stared back at him, her cheeks warming. "Yes?"

He shook his head, a sly smile stretching across his face. "You keep throwing me off, little lady. How old did you say you were?"

"Twenty-two."

Randall replied with another question, but she didn't hear what it was. A familiar aura was pressing against her psyche, and she slid her eyes toward the diner's front door. The outline of a tall soldier approached them.

Annika raised her head for a better look. "Captain," she hummed, smiling. There was something about being in the same room as that surly man that made her feel safe. Cadet Randall asked another question. "Huh?" Annika asked without diverting her attention from the captain. Her date leaned out of the booth to look. Captain Donauska stopped short.

"Cadet Randall," the captain stated with a frown.

Randall nodded. "Captain Donauska."

"Annika." Captain tilted his head toward her. The feel of his gaze sent butterflies dancing through her stomach.

"Hi." She gave a small wave, then averted her gaze so he wouldn't be able to read her.

Captain remained standing; his head still trained on Annika.

She raised an eyebrow. "Is everything alright?"

"I need to speak with you, but you're—" he turned to the other man "—occupied."

"Yes, sir." Cadet Randall raised his chin and turned to Annika. "We're on a date."

Annika looked from one man to the other. "Yeah, we can talk later."

The Captain's frown deepened. "We'll speak later," he muttered and turned, walking deeper into the diner. He took a seat in a booth against the opposite wall; his face turned in their direction.

"Do you two have something going on?" Randall asked, clenching his fists on the table.

Annika turned back to the menu, still feeling Captain's gaze on her. "What? No, of course not. Don't be silly. He's an acquaintance. He keeps track of me because I'm an outsider."

Cadet Randall frowned, scratching his chin as if in deep thought. Annika pursed her lips. Randall shook himself, and a smirk spread across his face. He leaned forward. "A beautiful outsider, if I may say so."

"Awe, shucks." Annika rolled her eyes.

Another figure entered the diner, and she looked over, smiled, and waved.

"Who's it this time?" Randall asked with an edge to his voice.

Theodor winked over at Annika, and she felt her cheeks warm up as Randall growled from across the table. The Donauska boy smiled and waved. Theodor then sat down across from his brother. They were in deep discussion right away, turning to look at Annika every few seconds. Annika finally turned back to her date.

Randall sported a frown so deep, Annika wondered if it was going to extend past his bottom jaw. "I'm your date, if you've forgotten," he pouted.

"He's just a friend. Relax."

The young server returned to take their orders. Once the server left, Annika glanced back at Cadet Randall. "Are we okay?"

"Damn those Donauska men, they're everywhere." He tossed his crumpled napkin onto the table and sighed.

Annika blinked. "Don't be like that. If Tiana walked in, I would've waved at her too. Just a couple of acquaintances, I promise. I work with their grandmother, remember? You'd be just as protective if a foreigner was working for your grandmother. Now, enough about them. Tell me about yourself."

She felt his aura recede and lighten as Randall eagerly jumped in, regaling tales of bow hunting in the south and being with his troop. "Every male in my family has served in the military. I couldn't wait for it to be my time, so here I am. But enough about me. What does a girl so far from home like to do?"

"I enjoy reading. And learning new skills."

The server came around with the food. They thanked her and dug in. Cadet Randall's head tilted to one side. "Now what skills is an already independent young woman desiring to learn?"

"Combat and stealth," she replied between bites.

His fork clattered to the table, and his mouth flopped open, drawing attention from nearby patrons. "Why would you want to learn that?" he choked out.

Annika sat up straighter, waving her hand in front of her mouth. "You Ausurnian's and your spice!" Then she lowered her voice and said, "To help the cause back home."

"But you're a girl," he said, pointing at her with his knife.

"Yeah, so?" She laid her fork down and narrowed her eyes at him.

"Men fight the wars," Randall stated before shoving a chunk of meat into his mouth. "Besides, Rovalkia is going to the dogs. Why bother?"

Annika grimaced. "You're wrong. I've heard of women officers and Rovalkia isn't going anywhere. It's only doomed if all its citizens give up."

The cadet raised an eyebrow while chewing. Once he swallowed, he shrugged and asked if she wanted dessert.

"Nooo," she drew out, drinking down the rest of her water to quench the inferno traveling down her throat.

"Okay. Let me settle the tab and I'll walk you home." He got up and went to the cash register at the diner's main counter. Annika turned around and spied both Donauska men following his movements. Then they looked toward her as she stood from the booth. She waved goodbye, and Randall scowled, having turned back around at that exact moment.

Once outside the diner, Annika inhaled the fresh evening air. Randall laid an arm around her shoulders, and she stiffened. After his last comment, she didn't feel like allowing him to get close. He stopped but didn't take away his arm.

"You act like you've never been on a date before. This is what we do. It's an innocent gesture. I get you are friends with guys here, but I can assure you I know more about dating than those Donauska boys. The men in that family put their country ahead of everyone, including their partners." He smiled down at Annika. "I'm also helping to stabilize you. You certainly aren't used to walking in heels."

Annika let out a bark of laughter. She shook her head and allowed her shoulders to relax. "You're right on both accounts, I think. If these shoes were mine, I'd chuck them into the lake … I get that they're royalty, but their partners should be their equals, right?"

"I can only assume they think everyone is below them," he said sympathetically. They stopped at his car. "Can I drive you home?" He looked around. "Where is home?"

"Oh, I live up there." Annika pointed above the shop.

"I didn't realize there was an apartment up there. I'll walk you up." He strolled with her down the alley. Annika hesitated at the base of the stairs.

As if reading her mind, Randall said, "I want to make sure you get to your door without spraining an ankle. If I knew you lived around back, I'd have picked you up at your door."

Annika led the way up the stairs. A tingling sensation at the base of her skull sent an alarm through her psyche. *Relax, he's just being nice.*

On the landing, she shivered as the wind swirled around them on the unprotected landing. "Thanks for the pleasant evening. Do you ever go running in the woods? It'd be fun if you joined me next time with your little brother and his friends. Kids here are so sweet. They remind me of my little brother and sister."

Randall grinned, reaching up to tuck a loose strand of hair behind her ear. "I'd love to spend more time with you."

Annika's cold cheeks warmed at his soft touch, and she dug for her house keys in the cardigan's pocket. They jangled in the quiet evening as she pulled them free. The cadet stepped forward, closing the distance between them. She felt his left-hand wrap around her hand that held the keys while his right ran up the length of her arm. His warm breath washed over her, still spiced from dinner. She swallowed hard, trying to suppress the shiver that traveled down her back. Randall's hand caressed its way back down to her wrist and snaked around her waist, closing the minuscule gap between their bodies.

She gasped as his chest pressed against hers. "Why don't we get you inside?" He coaxed in a husky voice. "I'll wrap you in a blanket and keep you warm all night." His head leaned forward, his lips parting.

Annika clenched her keys tighter, snapped her head up, and leaned away, her back coming into contact with the cold wood of her front door. It wasn't just that she didn't want to kiss him; it was the mistake Randall just made. His energies were suddenly readable: solid and dark; reminiscent of Captain's attempt to overpower her during their first meeting. Warning bells pealed through her body. She turned her head in time for his lips to connect with her cheek. "Whoa, Randall. I appreciate the thought, but you're coming on too strong. I don't know you well enough. There's no reason to rush things."

"What are you talking about, Annika?" He frowned when she peeked back at him, his face only inches away. She felt his body lean forward. Her back was now firmly against the door. She had nowhere to go. "You don't want to prove Ciara right, do you?"

"Excuse me?" Annika's pulse quickened. Energy swirled down her arms and condensed in her hands. She turned her head to face him, and her voice came out like venom. "Neither you nor Ciara know who I am. You've ruined this date. Just go." The air thickened. Sounds around them faded.

Randall leaned forward so the tips of their noses touched, baring his fanged teeth. Annika kept glaring into his hood, though her pinned body quaked in fear. He hissed, "Ausurnian's never compromise. This is *our* land and *our* country. Go home if you don't like it. We don't have time for your silly witch games. Your government is doing us a service by rounding up all you psychics. We don't need outsiders muddying up our bloodlines."

Annika scrunched her eyes shut as Randall's breath continued to wash over her frigid face. *What would Captain do?* She popped her eyes open and directed a furrowed glare at him once more. Then she pocketed the keys and maneuvered her hands so that her palms faced his torso. He looked down, taking a half step back.

"What're you doing?" he asked, his grip around her waist loosening.

"I'm *not* a witch," she hissed through gritted teeth. Then she released the hold of energy in her palms and shoved against him. "I am Annika."

"What the—" He stumbled backwards. His hands shot out to the railings, halting his descent. He snarled at her, still steadying himself.

"You will not intimidate me!" she screamed through thought-projection at him. Her body shook, and her throat burned. The front door, landing rail, and towering dark form of Randall blocked her escape. His right hand shot to her doorknob, startling her. His six-foot figure blocked the stairs and a fifteen-foot drop waited behind the railing. Annika dared not blink as she stared into the dark cavernous hood of his, waiting. She felt him replace his psychic shield as he straightened up to full height. The porch light caught Cadet Randall's gleaming fangs.

"Go," she snarled at him in Ausurnian, bracing for an assault.

"We'll expose you for what you are, Rovalkian. The Donauska's can't protect you all the time." Randall took another step forward.

An armored car careened around the corner and skidded to a stop at the base of the stairs. Randall spun around and tore down the steps. He just missed being hit by the driver's side door as it swung open. Annika yanked her keys out of her pocket as a soldier leaped from the car and called after Randall. But the cadet didn't stop running. He turned the next corner and was out of sight.

The soldier from the car turned to Annika. She gasped, lowering her eyes to the lock as she tried to jam her key in.

"Annika! Wait!" the soldier called out. "It's me, Captain Donauska."

She whipped her head toward him, her hands gripping the door handle. "Captain?" Her voice shook as her mind tried to decide what to believe.

"Look at my vest. My captain's insignia is right here." He pointed to the largest patch, then held both hands up while taking slow steps toward the stairs. "I sensed distress as I was driving by. May I come up?"

Without letting go of the doorknob, she nodded, blinking back tears, her body shivering. She looked around at the darkening shadows as inky blackness replaced the dark blue sky. "I ... I ... " Her key still hadn't found the lock and was sliding this way and that, moving from metal to wood as her eyes remained locked on Captain. He took the steps one at a time, slow and precise, holding his hands up in front of him. Then he stopped two steps from the top.

"How can I help? What can I do? An innocent man wouldn't have run and you have a look of terror in your eyes."

Annika shook her head, confounded. "I—I don't know. I'm cold. Can you stay a minute?"

"Of course." He nodded and gestured to the doorknob.

"For Bandau's sake," she muttered and took a deep breath, slid the key into the lock, and stumbled inside.

When she looked back at Captain in the doorway, her knees wobbled. *He's even bigger than Randall. What am I thinking, letting him in?* Captain had barely taken one step inside the door when she grabbed the kitchen counter to steady herself. Her breath came out shaky. *Using my powers will be my undoing. I'm surprised he hasn't handcuffed me yet.* "My life is becoming a living nightmare," she muttered, pulling herself up and looked up at the ceiling.

"Annika?" Captain's voice sounded worried.

"Oh," she startled, having forgotten his presence and wall of energy. "I forgot you were there." She strode toward him. "You can g—"

He caught her as she stumbled forward. "Whoa there. You'd better take off those shoes."

She held onto one of his hands and pulled the high heels off, sighing in relief. "Thanks, that's better. I'll kill Tiana for suggesting I wear those."

"Can I ask what happened?" he asked as he tilted his head to one side.

Annika looked down at the heels in her hand. "He ... he was toying with me, acting like such a gentleman. But he was just another one of Ciara's followers." Tendrils of energy swirled around her fingers. She shook her head. "I was kidding myself, thinking someone would have a genuine interest in me. Here, of all places." She took the cardigan off and padded over to her dresser. "You can go, Captain. I'm just feeling sorry for myself."

"Did he hurt you?" The captain's voice sounded dark, and his accent was thicker than usual.

Was she imagining it, or was he acting protective of her? She turned back to him. "I—no, but he was *acting* like he wanted to. He scared me and made me angry." Annika cringed, remembering Randall's hands on her waist. Her hands twisted the sweater over and over. "I know your father told me not to, but I attacked him with an energy blast to get him to back off." She stepped forward when Captain opened his mouth. "Please don't tell your dad. I had to. It was too much, and I don't know how else to fight." He remained silent, and her heart sank. "I was too trusting. You're going to send me back to Rovalkia, aren't you?"

His mouth snapped closed, and in three quick strides, he stood in front of her. Both his hands came up to hold her shoulders, steadying her. "I will never send you back there. You belong here, you will be safe here. We just need to get you trained. Tonight. Right now. Just you and me."

Exposed

S he stared up into his face. Since when did he reconsider? Her head swooned. "But Randall—"

"Cadet Randall will get what's coming. Trust me," Captain snarled. "You need to be trained."

"But the clubhouse is closed, and I'm not in the mood to exercise. I just want to go to bed." She peered over to her bed. Comfortable and safe, that's all she wanted to be.

"No, trust me. Your body will thank me." Annika shot him a suspicious look, and he held out his hands. "Sorry, terrible choice of words. All that adrenaline in your system needs somewhere to go." Then the left corner of his mouth stretched up. "Do you forget who I am? I've got a skeleton key. We'll have the whole place to ourselves. Go change into your workout clothes." He released his hold on her shoulders and stepped back, pulling out his phone. "I'll get someone to collect Randall."

She turned to the dresser. Her hands shook as she pulled out the running clothes. *A pauper's outfit to wear while training with a prince.* With a heavy sigh, she trudged to the bathroom.

Captain Donauska

He glanced at her. *Her workout clothes are pajamas and a blouse?* She finished plaiting her hair and stood waiting. "Text me when you find out anything," he said into the phone and hung up.

"I felt that look. I don't need your judgement right now. Just your help," she muttered.

"Fair enough. Let's go."

They parked around the back of the clubhouse. He unlocked a door and walked into the dark room, flipping on the light switch. When he turned back, Annika was blinking in the new brightness. He looked around the room. "Do you know how to use any of these machines?"

When Annika didn't answer, he looked over. She tapped the wrestling mat laid out on the ground with her shoe while rubbing her arms. Annika looked up and shook her head.

"Alright," he sighed. "Go get a fresh towel from the closet, and we'll start out on the punching bag."

He gathered the hand tape and made sure there were no tears in the bag. She drifted over with the towel and swung at the punching bag. A small *THUD* resounded, and the bag moved a little. "You were wrong about me from the start, Captain."

"Ah, well, you're a fluke," he said, rubbing his cheek. "You're something I haven't figured out yet."

"Good." Annika raised her chin into the air and punched the bag again. "I never want to be figured out."

"Is that so?" He felt the corner of his mouth twitch. "Well, what I *can* tell you is you're going to have bloody knuckles if you keep punching the bag that way. Come over and let me tape your hands. Then I'll show you the proper form. You're going to bruise yourself without doing damage to anyone that way."

She edged closer to him and held out her hands, dropping the towel on the floor. He pulled his gloves off, and Annika's eyes opened wider, staring down at his hands.

"You're acting like you've never seen a man's hands before," he said, pulling the tape off the roll. He grabbed one of her hands and wrapped the tape around her fingers.

"I haven't seen *your* hands. You and all the military personnel always wear the full uniform. I only know what the exposed bottom half of your face looks like."

He wrapped her other hand, aware of her locked gaze on his family ring. Its wide, black band had an imprint of a shield atop two swords, his family crest, and glinted on his right ring finger.

"It's my family ring. I'm still single."

Annika blushed deeply, and he chuckled, switching his focus from the softness of her hands to her face. He could get lost in those eyes.

"I thought those gloves of yours would keep your hands soft," Annika observed. "But yours aren't, and really tan."

He pulled his hands away. "I don't wear these gloves all the time. They're more for public image than anything. You expect a soldier to have baby soft hands?" He shoved his hands back into the leather gloves.

"No. That's not what I meant. I didn't know what to expect … you're an enigma to me. I'm still learning my surroundings." She lowered her eyes. "The only male in your family whose face I've seen is Theodor. It's harder to trust when I can't look into your eyes."

"So? Isn't the saying it's what's on the inside that counts?" Annika gaped, blushing. He paused, remembering the mission, the gray area between fake and real flirting narrowing. "We look alike, obviously, since we're brothers. Except *my* eyes are darker. Now, come over here so I can show you how to punch someone the right way."

Annika stepped closer to the punching bag, holding her fisted hands at chest height. "How much darker?" she asked, her voice low and eyes imploring.

"Almost black," he whispered, trying to inject mysticism into his voice. She hummed in response; her eyes became lidded. He froze, his eyes locked on her lips. No amount of training could have prepared him for how that noise affected him. He cursed at himself and told her, "Focus." adjusting her arms while taking a stance close behind her. "Your hands go up higher. Use your elbows and arms to deflect attacks. Now jab." He took hold of one of her wrists and guided it to the bag. "Note the motion. Now do it slow with the other hand. Good." He registered her fragrance of warm vanilla as he leaned to the side to observe her movements and inhaled deeply once, twice.

"Captain? Why are you smelling me?"

He opened his eyes. She turned toward him with one eyebrow raised, waiting for his response. "You smell good. Like a bakery."

She twisted toward him more. "I smell like bread?"

"Like frosting. Like vanilla. Now turn back around," he coaxed, using his shoulder to nudge her. "I'll show you how to do an upper cut, an overhand, a hook, and a cross. Then you'll do combos." He slid his hands along the length of her arms to her wrists, locking her body into a forward position. Her shoulders tensed. "Keep your body relaxed and fluid, but keep your core strong." Her shoulders relaxed. "Good. Now pay attention," he said low in her ear. They went through more punching techniques, and Annika's energies vibrated.

"Why are you nervous?" he asked.

Annika looked over her right shoulder. "I'm not nervous," she said nonchalantly. Goosebumps danced along his forearms. *Curse your effect on me.*

Her breath smelled of sweet mint mingling with the vanilla of her body spray. "Your aura is telling me otherwise," he taunted. *Or is it because I'm so close to you?* Captain smiled as he allowed imagined her arms wrapping around his neck while his hands tangled into her silver hair, both their lips parting at the same time …

"I'm anxious, I suppose. To—to learn all I need to. The realization I have much to learn is becoming apparent, and the psychic power I possess may not have the impact I want it to have. There's also your level of expectation."

Captain turned his head away, releasing himself from the daydream. "That's because there's no such thing as perfection." He stepped back and to her side. She repositioned into the original pose with her fists in front of her face. *Perfect form. She is a fast learner.* "You've got an advanced level of psychic ability, but a reality check never hurt anyone. Now jab five times in a row. Then five upper cuts. Then back to jabs. I'll change it up and tell you when to stop. Fast this time. Go."

SMACK, SMACK, BOOF. Her fists pummeled the bag. Three minutes in and Annika was puffing. He watched little beads of sweat roll down the side of her face and disappear into her shirt.

She continued to do combos for two more minutes as he threw Ausurnian wisdom at her in time with her hits. "You are stronger than the nightmares that haunt your dreams." *SMACK.* "You have nothing to be afraid of." *SMACK.* "Your mind is your best weapon." *SMACK.* "Fear is the root of all evil." *SMACK.*

"Okay, that's good for now. Walk a lap around the mats to slow your heart rate. Then get on the treadmill for a run." He pointed to the L-shaped machine with a rubber pulley. She nodded and walked away.

He checked his phone for messages. One text said to call his father at the base. "Hop up and I'll start the machine. Stay on this rubber part. I'm going to set it in workout mode. Keep up your speed and it won't hurl you off. I need to make a phone call." He turned the treadmill

157

on. "Use your core for balance and don't hold on to the hand bars. If I catch you doing that, you're going to start all over." She nodded, her white shirt shifting as she sucked in her stomach, her breasts now more pronounced. He gritted his teeth, impatient for the machine to beep into the selected mode, and slipped to the other side of the room to call the base.

"Are you with Annika?" his father asked. When Captain confirmed, Commander Donauska's voice came out calmer. "Good. Cadet Randall is in custody, and he's singing like a canary. Ciara's parents started an anti-outsider group with a secret monetary backer, who produced propaganda from outside Ausurnia, but the boy didn't know who. I need you to request Annika's home address. The report came back from the most recent mission into Rovalkia. They keep their main capitol building spotless, and they locked everything up in cabinets without labels. They're good. Too good. They had too many janitors for our infiltrators to break into any drawers or computers, but our theory of them wiping government workers' identities may be accurate. The janitors may have been secret police for all we know. We need DNA."

"How should I ask her?"

"Make something up, my boy. Say, I'm placing a security detail on her family to make sure they stay safe after all the business with her name in the papers. But for your personal information, we need the address to gather DNA samples from their house. We need to figure out who's in the capitol building. We'll place a bug in their house, too. And we'll make sure her siblings don't need to be rescued out of the country. I feel sorry for the girl," Commander Donauska said, pausing. "I told you not to get too close. I warned you," he added.

Captain winced. He tried to play the accusation off. "Huh, maybe that's why their buildings are so easy to break into. To put a false sense of security into any intruder. I'll get it out of her and call you back." He pulled the phone away, then brought it back up to his ear. "Dad, are you still there?"

"Yes."

"How can you tell? I'm not in love or anything, but ..."

"It was the picture. I haven't seen a smile like that on your face since you were young, riding your first horse. And if I had to guess, she feels the same. That picture couldn't lie if it wanted to. Tread carefully, son, and get the information I need. I know she's new and interesting, but it can't distract you from the work at hand. Ausurnia comes first for us in this family. Always."

"Yes, sir." Captain swallowed and hung up. He took his time walking back over to the treadmill, his eyes traveling up her body. Annika's platinum braid bounced up and down with each stride, her arms pumping at her sides as her chest rose and fell. Her face had pinked from exertion, and sweat ran from her forehead, but the look of determination in her eyes told him she would run all night if told to. When did she pique his intrigue? Was it at the photoshoot? Or was it as early as when she turned around on the barstool that first night? *Bandau, help me.* "Huh, maybe you have more stamina than I thought." He had tried to inject approval into his voice, but she didn't seem to notice. "So, my father called. He requests to know where in the city your parents' house is."

"Why?" she puffed out; one eyebrow shooting up and the other scrunching down.

"With your name in the papers, we want to get a security detail on your house."

"You think they're in danger?" Annika gasped.

"No, this is a precautionary move."

"Uh, okay. Number five on D Street. Third on the left. The whole housing complex east of the Capitol is government housing." Her head turned to him. "You swear you'll protect them if necessary?"

Captain nodded, pressing the Cool Down button. "We'll even sneak your siblings out if necessary."

Annika smiled. "You will? Ah—" Her body jerked backwards, and she tumbled off the treadmill, landing on her side on a wrestling mat.

Captain slammed his hand down on the emergency STOP button, ran to her side, and kneeled, offering his hands to help her sit up. "Gods of the Void, you flew. I told you to stay on the running pulley."

She winced, rubbing her hip. "Thanks. Maybe wait till I'm off the running machine to pump me with questions?"

"Sorry. Do you need first aid?"

Annika grimaced as she repositioned herself. "Just to my ego. I'm so embarrassed." She buried her head in her hands.

He pulled her hands away. Her green eyes looked up at him, then down to his hands holding hers. He leaned closer and tightened his grip. "Don't be so hard on yourself. I'm a trained fighter and you've never used this equipment before. Let's stay sitting down and assess your psychic ability. There're no muscles required, other than your brain."

After looking around the room, she nodded. "Okay. Half these machines look like torture devices, anyway." She tugged her hands away from his. He loosened his hold only slightly, so her fingers still had to glide between his. Annika flashed her eyes at him, and he gave her a sly grin. She blushed, looking away.

Captain repositioned himself to sit cross-legged, facing her. She followed suit. "Alright, close your eyes and raise your psychic shield." He paused. She closed her eyes. "Now make the shield strong. I'm going to press against it with increasing force until I breach it. Tell me when you're ready." He unfocused his eyes to see her aura better. The swirling gray slowed to an even pace. A purple hue glowed on her forehead, and then radiated down her body. A gray mist rose from the floor, covering her and the purple light. *Whoa, the gray mist must reflect the fortress she's envisioning.* The gray in her aura continued to condense.

"Okay," she whispered. "I'm ready."

Captain closed his eyes. His extended psyche found her shield and pressed forward. It didn't waver. He applied increased pressure. Nothing happened. *That's my girl.* He extended his psyche again and envisioned himself knocking on her shield. When she didn't respond, he asked, "Do you sense or hear anything?"

"Yes," she replied in a breathy whisper. "You're pressing against my shield in the front. Then you knocked on it like a door."

"Very good. Now I'm going to try to thought-project through your shield. Don't let it down or diminish it." He peeked at her. She sat tall; her mouth set in a small frown. Through his psychic vision, she remained invisible. *"Hello, Annika,"* he called out to her. *"Can you hear me?"*

"Hello, Captain." A small voice replied from beyond his shield. He stilled, lowering his shield to better hear. The voice spoke again. *"I can hear you as if you're on the other side of a wall. Can you hear me? Am I speaking loud enough?"*

"Ah-ha!" Captain cried out. He opened his eyes and grabbed her hands. "Gods of the Void, girl. You can thought-project through shields!" Her eyes popped open. He felt the smile he wore down to his soul. Annika stared back at his smiling face; her mouth parted. Then she smiled, genuine and sparkling—like at the photoshoot. His heart thumped.

Cursing, he released her hands and rubbed his own together. "Sorry. That was the last thing I expected to happen." Pink tinged her cheeks. "Okay, let's refocus," he said, more to himself than to her. "The last lesson is a psychic ambush. I'm going to pierce through your shield instead of pressing through. We use this tactic when sneaking up on enemies to cause panic. Enemies are easier to capture alive if they're out of their senses with fright." He chuckled at the memory of seeing hardened drug lords scream and run from their protected spots. Annika stared at him. "I just remembered a mission. Okay, try the same with me, but no energy blasts. We all know you can do that."

"Yes, Captain." Her lips parted into a wide smile while she closed her eyes.

He shot his psyche out to the top of her head after raising his shield again. His extension found resistance. He threw psychic arrows at her. The same resistance met him, but no attack came from her. *"You're supposed to be trying to invade my shield,"* he hollered through thought-projection.

"Don't worry. I will." Annika's voice held a curious edge.

He sensed movement around the lower half of his shield. Uneasy, Captain added another layer to it. A hand grabbed his foot and yanked down. "Ah!" The captain opened his eyes. He unfolded his legs to see what had grabbed his foot. "What was that?"

Annika howled in laughter. He peered over at her. She had tossed back her head and held her knees while she pealed with delight. When she pulled her head back up, her eyes were sparkling even brighter.

A smile rose to meet the laughter in her eyes. "I beat you," she crowed. "I beat the Prince of Ausurnia at his own game." Annika clapped her hands together, but they didn't make a sound. She proffered her hands. "Can you take the tape off? It feels weird."

Captain scooted forward, pulling off his gloves and grasping one of her hands. "I will if you tell me how you got through my shield. My father is the only other one who achieved it, and that was by sheer force."

Her fingers wiggled in his hand. "I went under the floor."

"Under the floor?" Captain unwound the tape. "How? Why?"

"I shielded myself in a bubble, but yours is more of a box shape. It has an open edge along the bottom." Her still-taped left hand gestured a tunneling movement. "So, using your first ambush method I felt, I envisioned a tendril of my psyche shooting down into the ground and coming up beneath you."

Captain clucked his tongue. He rose, flicking the wad of tape into a nearby trashcan, and asked, "Can you not see auras like we can? You keep saying you feel or sense, not saw."

Annika gaped. "You can *see* them? That's so cool. What's mine look like?" She stood with halting movements, holding the side she fell on.

Captain tilted his head, un-focusing his eyes once more to have a better look at her aura. "It's still shrouded in gray. I'm guessing it's from the shield you built. But right before that, a brilliant violet light shone from your forehead. It means you have a powerful psyche." *Too powerful.* He refocused his eyes. *Too beautiful.*

"So, I have potential?" Excitement rose in her voice. "It'll come in handy to take out the Rovalkian leader, won't it? I'll sneak up and startle him. If an energy blast is required, I can do it now."

"It may. But this was the *first* day of training. Fighting will happen before you get close to the leader, if it's the path you choose. Don't get ahead of yourself, green eyes." Captain snatched up the towel on the floor and tossed it to her. "Wipe the sweat off your face and ditch it in the hamper by the door. It's getting late. I'll drop you back home."

Annika's smile stayed. "Okay, but you're going to have to come up with a better nickname for me than that."

* * *

A better nickname. A better nickname. Something nice and not too mushy like—BZZZ.

"Still at the base?" he asked into his phone, after glancing at the caller ID.

"Yeah, still poring over the intel coming in from Rovalkia. How's she doing?" his father responded, sounding exhausted.

Always on the job. Mom may be right about us. "She'll be okay. I took her training at the clubhouse gym. It went all right." *Do I tell him about her getting around my shield?*

Instead of the chuckle he assumed he'd hear through the receiver, his father let out a lengthy sigh. "Someday she's going to have to accept her limitations. She has tall dreams for such a small girl. How would you evaluate her?"

"Well, she has strength and stamina, but no formal military training. But is an adaptive learner and advanced in psychic ability. She processes information like a politician, which makes sense if her father acts at home like he does at work. I want more time with her."

"Does this request stem from your feelings for her?"

When he didn't respond, his father snorted. "Fine. We'll address that later. I need your honest opinion, though. Do you think she could be withholding facts to protect her family?"

"She's protective, but not underhandedly. She just has a lot of fantasies, like sneaking in and taking out the leader as if that's going to solve all their problems. It's not logical."

His father hummed, and a pen tapped on a desk in the background. "I agree with that. Let's see what their reaction is to the photo. The priority is finding out who the leader is, or who's pulling the strings. Did you get an address?"

Captain leaned back on his couch and rattled off the address. His father released a big breath. The sound of a pen scribbling came next. "Thank you, son. This'll help more than you know. The sooner we can put some names to faces, the sooner we can unravel the mystery of their government. It's baffling our secret agents. They also reported long caravans heading away from Karaxin, and an encampment being built on the outskirts. Something's going on, and we need to get ahead of. Get some sleep, you earned it." *CLICK.*

164

Rosebud

S he turned over, still hearing the phone ringing from her dream. As her eyes slowly opened, she realized it was her phone on the bedside table vibrating and tinkling with the melody of an incoming call. "Hello?" she croaked.

"Annika? Dear, are you okay? Are you up?" Tracy's voice sounded so loud that Annika pulled the receiver away. Her head pounded, and her eyes felt swollen and gritty.

"Um, yes. Ow." Her arm muscles complained as she threw the covers back. "Do you need me to work today, Mrs. Donauska?"

"No, dear. We're going to have a private meeting downstairs in the shop in a half hour. It involves you if you can make it."

Annika yawned. "Yeah, I can be there."

The back door slammed behind her by accident, and she flinched and fumbled with the kettle, her elbow knocking the coffee tin over. The bag of frozen peas had done little for her swollen eyelids. One of her hands reached towards the stacked mugs. They clanked as her fingertips collided with three at once, pushing them dangerously close to the ledge.

"Annika." Tracy rushed forward from her office. "Be careful." Captain popped up behind her.

Annika glanced into the mirror on the wall. Her loose hair bun was askew atop her head; strands of hair stuck out in complete disarray. She saw Tracy draw her hand to her lips in shock and understood why. Red-rimmed eyes stared back at her, and she stood at a bent angle. Annika ran a hand over her hair and tugged her shirt down, her eyes focusing behind Tracy on Captain's pursed frown. Was that concern she saw on his face? Either way, it mortified her she hadn't cleaned herself up before coming downstairs.

"What happened? You look like you haven't slept in days. Are you hurt? You're standing at a funny angle." Tracy reached her hands out, beckoning Annika to her. Annika turned away and leaned against the counter, bowing her head to avoid eye contact.

"Cadet Randall happened," Captain growled and took a step toward her. "I shouldn't have taken you to the gym. You appear worse off than when I dropped you off. She fell off the treadmill, Gran."

"No." Annika's cheeks warmed, and she turned away. "I'm just sore and tired. It was a rough night. I couldn't fall asleep." Her fingertips traced the edge of the counter. "My whole body is sore and, yes, my date went badly. I don't know what he would've done if Captain didn't show up." She peeked over her shoulder at him.

Tracy strode over and cupped her cheek. "Sweetie, you need to tell us if he hurt you. We can press charges."

"Or kill him," the captain muttered. "But he's in jail. You don't need to worry."

"That's good, I guess." Annika ran her fingers across the countertop. "It doesn't alter the fact the damage has been done, though."

"I'm serious about my promise, Annika," Captain growled.

"What promise?" Tracy turned her head from Annika to her grandson.

"To protcct—"

"I'm here!" Tiana came dashing through the front door with two large coffees in her hands. "I've got an extra-large latte for you, Ro."

Tracy and Captain stepped to the side as Tiana crashed into Annika. Captain snatched the coffees before they spilled. Ista came in behind Tiana and waved her hand, holding a newspaper. "Have you two seen the newspapers yet? Everyone is calling me. Is it true? Oh Annika, how're you doing, sweetie?"

Annika shrugged. Ista clucked her tongue as Tiana pulled Annika into another hug. Annika winced and pulled away. "I'm so sorry, Ro. What an awful first date ever," Tiana murmured. She stroked Annika's hair. "I'm so glad you found out his truth on the first night, though. Imagine if you had wasted more time on the guy."

Annika leaned forward, resting her head on Tiana's shoulder.

"Hold on." The captain stepped closer. "*That* was your first date, like ever in your life?"

Annika groaned.

"Way to focus on the wrong thing, cousin," Tiana sniped. He took a step back, frowning.

Annika spoke up; her head still on Tiana's shoulder. "I shoved Randall away when he became threatening. He fell down the steps and was coming back up to attack me … I think." She raised her head and looked at Captain. "That's when you showed up."

The visible part of Captain's face remained neutral, though his head tilted to one side. Ista wrung her hands.

"And why did you show up?" Tracy asked.

"I was driving by the shop when a wave of distress ran through me. Theo and I had seen her on the date earlier, so I feared the worst had happened. I told you cadets are volatile, Annika." Though it sounded like a reprimand, his voice remained low and gentle.

She scrunched her eyes in shame. The kettle whistled in the background, and she roused, turning off the power as she took a sip of the coffee Tiana brought instead. "Yeah, well, I forgot that little detail. He'd projected such a genuine interest in me. It could've gotten uglier, I suppose. At the moment, I had thought he was going to shove me over the railing." She took another sip and stared at the far wall.

Tiana put a hand on her shoulder. "How terrible, Ro. I wish we'd double dated. We'll do that next time, okay?"

Annika focused on her friend. "Who says there's going to be a next time?" From her peripherals, she saw Captain's mouth open and close as if he wanted to say something but decided against it.

Ista leaned back against the cash register. "Since when did the younger generation become so aggressive? I don't remember feeling unsafe around cadets as a young woman. I feel so ashamed, Annika. Is there anything I can do?"

"Does my government covet me because I'm a witch? Is it possible that one of my ancestors was Ausurnian? Randall said he was glad they're collecting witches in Rovalkia and that Ausurnia doesn't fancy our presence either."

Captain crossed his arms. "First, that man is an idiot. Don't listen to him. Second, it doesn't matter. They won't persecute based on who their ancestors were in *my* country."

Annika's eyes widened as she stared at the captain. There was something about a person standing up for equality that she found so attractive. The shadow of a smile grew across her lips. For all his faults, she could tell he was going to be a good leader. Perhaps the harder the shell, the softer the insides.

"Sound words, son. Now, will someone please explain this picture?" Ista pointed to the newspaper she'd handed to her mother-in-law.

Everyone looked over as Tracy held it up. The front page pictured Annika being embraced from behind by Captain; both sharing enormous smiles. Annika's silver hair cascaded over her shoulder as she leaned back to stare into Captain's face. His hands held Annika's hips, and the glint of his fangs shone through his smile. Sure enough, a computer had generated a backdrop of them by the lake shore on a sunny day.

Tracy squinted down at the picture. "What is this? Are you two—"

Captain pulled the paper from her hands and looked at it. Annika and Tiana slunk over and peered over his arm at the article.

"Wow, if I didn't know any better, I'd say it was an engagement photo," Tiana giggled. Annika smacked her arm, shaking her head.

"Engagement?" Ista and Tracy voiced aloud.

Captain looked at Annika. "Well, if our picture doesn't flush out who the bad guys are, I don't know what will." The side of his mouth stretched up as he offered the paper to her. "You photograph well. Want to keep this?"

Annika took the newspaper without a word. Warmth traveled from her cheeks to her neck as she tucked it carefully under her arm. Captain's half smile stretched again when she glanced up at him. *Do I have feelings for him? Does he have feelings for me? Or am I just reading into his friendly gesture too much?*

"Oh, okay," Ista drew out, turning to her mother-in-law. "I remember. It's a ruse they're working on. I forgot his dad mentioned dragging out a reaction from Rovalkia. And he also mentioned an inside organization to expose." Annika blinked out of her fantasy.

"That's cool, Ro." Tiana hugged her. "No one in the world will touch you now, and Rovalkia will be on its knees before long. But do you know what you and I need? A vacation. I've been craving a shopping trip to the city of Mortainy in Calageeh. Let's go together."

"No," Captain said.

Everyone looked at him.

"Why ever not? I think that's a grand idea. She needs distance from everything, and what safer direction than west?" Tracy asked.

"Because of security protocols. Because we still don't have a name behind who wants Annika returned. Because Annika's name is everywhere, and now there is a face to go with the name." He crossed his arms.

Tracy turned to Annika and Tiana. "If my son and grandson say there is a security threat, we need to take it seriously. I'm sure there's plenty to do here in Pontagu, or somewhere close by. I'll give you the time off."

"And I'm thinking I need to talk to dad more about this and ramp up the investigation," Captain added, looking toward the front door. Tiana's widened eyes reflected the anxiety Annika suddenly felt.

"It'll be okay, girls." Tracy rested a hand on each of their shoulders.

"What about a high tea at the Embassy Hotel in Fringur?" Ista piped up.

Everyone's head swiveled around. Annika couldn't connect what Ista said to anything they'd discussed. "Tea?"

"I'm sorry. It just popped into my head. The planner in me is always at work. Why don't the girls take friends to high tea at the Embassy Hotel? It's a secure building and they do a great tea service. I want to help, and this is what I'm best at." She offered a small smile to Annika.

"Let's do that, Ro. It is far enough to *feel* like a getaway, but we'll still be safe in Ausurnia *and* be back before dark." Tiana grasped Annika's arm. "Please say yes. Please?"

"Okay," Annika mumbled, turning to Captain. "And you'll keep training me while I figure out what to do in Rovalkia?"

He placed his fist over his chest and bowed.

"Does that mean yes?" she asked.

"That means you have a solemn vow from an Ausurnian soldier," Tracy explained. "It's unbreakable."

"Like the photo." Tiana winked, nudging Annika's arm.

Captain grimaced. "Stop, Tiana. Anyway, I'm glad we're all on the same page. Everything we have discussed stays within this group, apart from my dad, okay?"

Everyone nodded in agreement.

* * *

She ran the back of her hand across her moist forehead, squinting at the sun. "So, who all is going with us?" The sun was trying to melt her, she was sure of it.

Tiana counted them out on her fingers. "There's Gwen, the grocer's daughter, who's a huge book worm. Then Valerie, who moved here for work from the south coast. She's tough but sweet. And Daisy, a cousin from my dad's side. She enjoys baking like I do, too, and she also looks like me. I think we'll get along fine. They all passed my test."

"I trust you. It will be a pleasant day out to forget about all our troubles, right?" Annika opened the clubhouse door for them. "Oh no," she groaned.

"What?" Tiana whipped her head around. "What? There's no one here."

"Yes, there is. The receptionist. It's the same girl I flipped off when I came here on my own. Maybe I should wait outside."

Tiana pulled her forward. "No. You're with me. Why didn't you tell me, Ro? I would've set her straight." She furrowed her brows and her voice darkened. "Like I will right now."

The receptionist opened her mouth as the girls approached, raising her boney index finger.

"Oh, no you don't," snapped Tiana. "You're going to shut up and stay that way. Hand over the van acquisition form."

Annika leaned in to peek at Tiana's face. Her friends' sharp incisors were on full display. She then turned to the receptionist. Instead of scoffing like she had at Annika, the woman's eyes dilated. Her hands pushed her chair away from the desk. Tiana looked fierce, while the receptionist looked wary.

The receptionist began opening file cabinet drawers, mumbling. Tiana straightened and flashed Annika a triumphant smile before leading Annika over to a coffee table to fill out the form. "We don't fancy Miss Nosey snooping for Ciara," she scoffed, motioning her head back toward the receptionist.

Tiana marched around the desk with the completed paperwork. The receptionist sputtered, "You're not allowed back here!"

Tiana sneered at her. "Oh shut up, you annoying aphid." She slipped the page into the slot marked OUTGOING. "We know you'd try to tamper with it. Do. Not. Touch. It. Or I'll come after you."

Annika hid a smile behind her hand as the receptionist's mouth formed an O. Tiana came back around the desk, wove her arm through Annika's, and led her back out into the summer haze.

The leaves who hadn't survived the last heat wave skittered across the pavement in front of them. "Impressive, Tiana. Now tell me what you know."

Tiana let out a peal of laughter. "How did you know I have good news?"

Annika pointed to her head. "Intuition. I can feel your excitement bubbling away."

"It's too good, Ro. I got the text while we were walking this way. But I wanted to wait for the right moment to share the news." She stopped walking and grabbed Annika by the shoulders. Her brown eyes sparkled while the breeze danced with her long, black hair like an invisible marionette. "They got her, Ro. Captain arrested Ciara and charged her with conspiracy to harm you through malicious rumors. Isn't it fantastic?" She released Annika, clapping and hooting. "She's off to the reform school that's tucked away in the Haxtov Desert. My mom once said they make older delinquents work in the kitchens or something. Ciara, a house cleaner. It's too good."

"Whoa, seriously? I hoped Captain was on my side once I spilled my heart to him, but never got my hopes up."

Tiana stopped. "Your heart? When did that happen? And why aren't you celebrating? This is good news." A crease formed between her eyebrows.

"I *am* happy. Just—I don't know. It's nice to hear she'll face justice, if not a bit of humiliation. But the damage has been done." An armored car rolled by. *Where would I be without this royal family?*

"Ro? Are you okay? Come back to me." Tiana waved her hand in Annika's face. "What's wrong?"

Annika shook herself. "You know what? I won't let her path of destruction dampen my mood when we have such a fun outing next week. So long as I stay in Ausurnia, I'm safe, right?"

Captain Donauska

"Annika? You there? It's Captain Donauska." He rapped on the door again. The lock clicked, and she opened the door. A scented cloud of cinnamon spice enveloped his senses.

"What *is* that?" he asked. One of her eyebrows arched up. "The smell, I mean. I was in the neighborhood and thought I'd catch you up on news."

Annika stepped aside. "Sure. I made a batch of cinnamon tea cakes. The kettles on, too, if you'd like some tea?"

"I'd love a cup of tea if you're offering."

"Great!" Her face lit up. She gestured to the little half-moon table with three chairs. "Have a seat. I'll join you once I get the tea steeping. What'd you want to talk about?" She plopped down a plate of steaming sliced cake in front of him and spun back around at the kettle's whistle.

"You're picking up Tiana-isms. You dance-walk like her," he chuckled.

Annika winked over her shoulder. "Tiana has a beneficial effect on me. And knowing Ciara has gotten charged helps."

"Ah. Let me guess. My cousin let you in on my news, huh?" He shook his head and sat down. *Blasted girl.*

The teapot lid plunked down. Annika placed her hands on her hips. "Tiana isn't a gossip. Someone had texted her when she applied for the van to Fringur. Tiana vetted all the girls going." With the teapot in hand, she sat on the far side of the table.

Captain glanced at the empty seat between them, then looked over to the sink window. Annika's dahlia plant had flowered again, and the red tipped buds aimed skyward. He glanced back; her lips matched the red shade of the dahlia. He gave her a sly smile. "Oh, I don't know how much I'd trust her vetting. She became friends with *you*."

Annika's mouth dropped open; her eyebrows scrunched together. He chuckled, and Annika leaned over and punched him in the arm. After feigning shock, he shot another smile her way. "Good form, Rosebud."

She sat back in her chair and tilted her head. "Rosebud?"

"I was told to think up a better nickname, remember? I thought up Rosebud. Look." He raised his hand, mimicking the shape of a flower bud. "A flower bud is where all of a flower's potential energy waits before the big reveal. That's the stage you are in life." He then let his fingers splay outwards to mime a bloom. "And the classic rose symbolizes your favorite color, red."

Her eyes sparkled. "I like it." A smile stretched up, making her cheekbones rosy and plump. Her eyes focused back down as she poured the fragrant herbal tea into two mugs, her black lashes hiding her green irises. She took a slice of cake for herself, and he followed suit. The spicy scent of cinnamon wafted up, and the glistening pats of butter on each slice made his mouth water. The first bite reminded him of his Aunt Jenny's recipe, and the tea was a recipe from his grandmother's book: lemon balm, peppermint, and basil.

"This is great. Aunt Jenny and my grandmother's recipes are getting a run for their money, I see. And I'm glad you like your new nickname. It can double as your code name, too." Her eyes refocused on him. "I also wanted to speak with you about your trip. I want to go over safety protocols for travel, okay?" He ate the last of his cake and turned toward her.

After draining the last of her tea, she poured more into their mugs. "I'm all ears, Captain."

"Do you have a spare piece of paper and pencil I could use? You should know the route to where you're traveling beforehand." He paused. Annika nodded and trudged over to her dresser. While she rummaged through a drawer, he continued. "There's one highway north, so that's easy to remember. But what would you do if you broke down? Would you walk up to Fringur or walk back home?"

Annika placed a ripped piece of paper and pen in front of him. "Maybe I would call for help? Or go through the forest. I could find a trail, maybe?"

"No." He drew a rough map. "The forest becomes denser on either side of the road the further north you go. Only travel into the woods under the direst circumstances. I'm serious. Even an Ausurnian would get lost in those woods. Go westward into the forest to the first stream. Never go east, unless you intend to flee back into Rovalkia. The border is close to the highway. If, and I mean *if*, you must get back here, follow the stream south. It'll take you to my grandmother's backyard. She has cell service or might be home. And if she isn't, there's a key hidden under the back steps. But if you are closer to Fringur, knock on the closest house or business door," he said, flipping the page over to draw another map. "This is a rough system of street names. They go in alphabetical order from east to west. Adjacent streets are numerical like any big city."

A chair's legs scraped against the wooden floor, and Captain looked up from the paper to see her plop down in the chair next to him. She leaned in, looking at his scribble. "There's no cell service here?" She pointed to the squiggle line representing the highway.

He answered with his eyes trained on her face, forcing himself not to breathe in too deeply. The cinnamon cake smell would have overpowered her vanilla scented skin, anyway. "No. No one lives there. But I should clarify. There is cell service if you have a satellite phone— us soldiers of rank have them. The main takeaway from this lesson is to be aware of your surroundings. It takes about an hour to reach Fringur. Know when you leave Pontagu and keep track of the time. It's that easy. And a Pontagu soldier will drive you up, so consider this trip a practice run." He slid the paper over, and she picked it up, looking at each side again. *I wonder if her hair is as soft as it looks.* Single strands slid forward into her face. The wavy texture and varying tones of silver caught the light from the ceiling lamp. He imagined pulling a glove off and running his fingers through it from root to end.

Annika rose from her chair, startling him from his daydream. "I'll put this on my refrigerator and have it memorized by the time I leave." He hastily drank down the rest of his tea and stood as she turned back around.

"More tea?"

"No, thanks." He moved toward the door. "I have paperwork to catch up on. We may have caught Ciara, but there's still someone leaking our military secrets to the world." He caught her genuinely worried expression, kicking himself for ever thinking she could be behind it. "Don't leap to conclusions just yet. Those secrets have no connection to you. Our work is never done. But this was nice. Thank you for taking my lessons seriously."

Her bottom lip sucked in for a moment, making him inwardly groan. As she released its hold, a more serious look entered her eyes. "I heard what's happening to Ciara. Can I ask what will happen to Cadet Randall?"

"After his trial next week, we're planning to ship him up to Fringur Base before posting him to one of our bases on the other, less desirable, side of the world. That's what we do with troublesome soldiers, rare as they are."

Her lips thinned, then relaxed. She stepped forward, stopping right in front of him. Shadows sculpted her nose and cheeks, and his pulse quickened from their proximity. "Never hesitate to call if you need me." He crooked his first finger, touching the knuckle to her slender chin.

Annika nodded slowly; his finger stayed in contact with her skin as it moved. He opened the door with his other hand. *"Until next time, Rosebud,"* he thought-projected to her.

"Until next time, Captain."

Ambush

*H*ere's to more good days, she thought while lacing her black suede shoes. Then, as Ista had shown her, she tucked in the borrowed silk, short-sleeved blouse. "Your red blouse, though nice, will be too loud for the dress code at the hotel. This smokey blue one will be gorgeous on you." Annika turned in the mirror, checking that the back of the blouse lay flat. A horn sounded, and Annika strode out the door to Tiana's car.

They arrived at the clubhouse and parked toward the back where a four-door armored military van stood waiting. The other three girls had already arrived. Tiana began introductions, starting with Gwen, who held a novel in her hands. Seeing the novel had a picture of a knight and princess on the cover, Annika thought, *I'll have to loan her my book. Maybe we can start a book club.*

Valerie towered over everyone present. Tiana pointed to her and said, "The South turns out the tallest Ausurnians. We blame all the fresh sea air." The four Ausurnian girls giggled, but Annika stood, staring.

Valerie paused mid hair toss. "It's okay, Annika. She wasn't being mean. It's the truth. Relax, we're all friends here."

Annika forced the tension in her shoulders to release, and in her best Ausurnian, she addressed the girls. "That is great to hear. Us nice girls need to band together."

Tiana's look-alike squealed. She grabbed Annika's hand. "This is going to be so much fun."

Annika returned the hand squeeze. "I look forward to getting to know you all."

"Please stop talking in Ausurnian, Annika. You're speaking too formally, and it's freaking me out," Tiana laughed, and Daisy smacked her arm.

A tingle started at the base of Annika's scalp, and her eyes felt drawn to the van. An Ausurnian soldier came around the front and stood near the passenger door with a clipboard in hand. His focus landed on Annika and his psyche pressed against her shield, the same pressing sensation she'd gotten from Captain during their first meeting. She grabbed Tiana's arm and whispered into her ear. "Who's the driver?"

Tiana shook her head. "I don't recognize him. Why?"

"But he's vetted through Pontagu Base, right? There's something off about him. Do you sense it? My intuition is prickling."

"Let me see." Tiana went silent for a moment. "No, I sense nothing out of the ordinary or threatening. Oh shoot, he's coming over here. He must've felt me trying to read him."

The soldier sauntered over, a confident smile spreading across his face. Annika felt queasy. "Good morning, fine ladies. It looks like everyone's here. Shall we begin the journey, Tiana? Annika?"

There's something about this man. Damn my intuition for not telling me what it is. "How do you know my name?" Annika asked.

The driver waved a hand behind him. "Someone at the base told me to look for a pureblood-looking Rovalkian. And your name isn't Ausurnian." He showed her the clipboard.

I need to stall to figure this guy out. Captain's face popped into her mind. *Yes, he will know.* "Uh, fine. I just need to make a phone call first."

The driver nodded but didn't move. Annika reached for her phone in her pants pocket. Her heart sank. It was still laying on the kitchen counter at home. Taking a deep breath, she turned to Tiana. "May I borrow your phone? I forgot mine."

Tiana gave her a questioning look. "Why?"

Through her teeth, Annika demanded, "Give me your phone."

The soldier was still standing close by, so Annika addressed him. "Board everyone. I need to call my friend in Fringur to bring me my migraine medicine at the hotel. I have a headache coming on."

After taking a couple of steps back, the driver pulled his own phone out with a smirk. The other three girls exchange glances. Tiana waved her hand at them, and they headed to the van. Tiana pulled out her phone. "What medicine do you need? Who do you know in Fringur?"

Annika hissed through her teeth, snatching the phone away. Tiana took a step back, her eyes widening. Annika turned away from everyone. She scrolled through the list of contacts for Captain's phone number. Once found, she punched the dial button. It rang and rang. Annika tried to extend her psyche for him to pick up, but stopped after a moment. *He can't hear me through his shields at this distance.*

His phone stopped ringing and went to voicemail. She tried to make her voice sound chipper so she wouldn't sound suspicious to the driver. "Hey, it's Rosebud. I'm wondering if you or someone could meet me at the hotel with my *emergency* medicine I keep at your house. I *sense* a headache coming on. A *bad* one. It's starting at the base of my scalp and *tingling* upward. We're about to leave in the van with number 551V on the side. Please? You'd be a *lifesaver*. Hope to see you there. Bye." She sent a prayer heavenward to the Void for protection. *Even if it turns out to be a reaction from being nervous, it's better safe than sorry. These girls, who all possess a strong intuition like me, don't seem to sense any danger.*

She sighed, returned the phone to Tiana, and ambled to the van. The driver secured all the doors and drove toward the main highway. Annika sat in the back row with Tiana. Tiana checked her phone's call log and showed the screen to Annika, pointing to her cousin's number with an arched eyebrow. Annika snatched the phone and deleted the call history before handing it back, shaking her head. Rubbing her temples didn't help to ease the intense tingling. The eyes of the driver were on her; his face pointed upward to the rearview mirror. Annika focused her attention out the side window and made a mental note of any landmarks.

"It's getting closer," Annika groaned a while later. Her temples throbbed worse than ever.

Tiana turned around, pausing from her argument on the season's clothing color trend with Valerie. Gwen's voice rose higher in her discussion with Daisy. Tiana shouted to be heard. "What's getting closer?"

"I don't know. But my feeling about the driver is intensifying. All my senses are tingling," Annika whispered out of the corner of her mouth. She motioned with her head to the driver.

Tiana glancing at him but he'd turned his head back forward. Tiana mouthed, "What about him?"

POP! The van swerved and veered on the highway. The driver hobbled it to a stop on a grassy stretch. Tiana had grabbed Annika's hand and held on tight. Annika felt her insides go cold. Tiana's eyes widened.

"Oh, shoot, where'd my book go?" Gwen shouted. She unbuckled her seat and started rooting around the floor. "Pick up your legs, you long-legged freak. I can't see around them."

Valerie hugged her knees to her chest. "You're the freak, Gwen. It's just a book."

"Ooh, I think we got a flat tire." Daisy had her face pressed against the window in front of Annika. "The front tire looks flat, guys."

"A quick tire change will get us on the road in no time, girls. Get back in your seat, Gwen. Driver. Driver?" Tiana pulled her hand from Annika's grip and leaned forward. "Do you need our help to change the tire? The hotel doesn't accept late guests. Driver?" Tiana looked back at Annika. "Am I not talking loud enough?"

Annika slumped lower in the seat, holding her stomach. Daisy pointed outside with her face still plastered to the window, shouting above the rest. "Look. Men are coming to help."

Tiana and Annika leaned over to peer outside.

"Where'd they come from?" Gwen shouted, unbuckling her seatbelt to lean over Valerie for a look.

Valerie pointed out the window. "What's in his hand?"

"Those aren't Ausurnians." Daisy moved back from the window.

Tiana leaned forward again. "Driver!"

"Everyone, shut up and sit down!" the driver shouted, swiveling around. Everyone abided, but their heads returned to ogle at the two men dressed in military fatigues walking their way.

"Ew, are those Rovalkians? I'd walk home before accepting help from them. No offense, Annika," Valerie voiced with disgust.

"I said, shut up," the driver growled.

CLICK. All the locks on the doors popped up. The driver got out and strolled around the car, eyeing the damage with hands in pockets, not paying any attention to the approaching Rovalkians. He suddenly reached over and yanked open the passenger door on the forest side. The heat outside flowed in, sucking out the cool, air-conditioned atmosphere. Valerie flinched away. Daisy craned her head forward, looking out the open door.

Tiana hissed into Annika's ear, "What's he doing? This isn't the right protocol. The driver should've hopped out and kept everything locked. He's being too casual about it, especially with two Rovalkians walking out of our woods." Annika nodded, holding her breath. Her eyes stayed fixed on the new arrivals. They'd stopped short of the van and hailed the Ausurnian driver.

"You didn't need to shoot out the damn tire. I was going to fake engine trouble. Thanks for the extra work. I should make you two change it."

"That's not part of the plan, Ausurnian." The handgun wielder hollered back. "Hand over the girl and we'll be on our way. We don't want to be in your stinking country any longer than necessary."

The girls turned and looked at Annika. Gwen asked, "What should we do?"

Tiana proclaimed, "Annika is one of us. No one's taking her."

Annika's eyes darted from one girl to the next; each nodded to her.

"We outnumber them. And if we can get hold of the gun—" Valerie started.

"It's too dangerous. I can use a punching technique to knock them out." Annika looked outside. All three soldiers were still bickering.

Daisy reached back, smacking Annika's shoulder. "Heck no, girl. We've had the most training and never get to use it. You stay behind us. Girls, let us agree on a move."

"How about the Exploding Arrow maneuver?" Valerie spurred.

"Yeah!" The rest of the girls agreed unanimously.

Annika gaped. "Exploding what?"

"Hey, what're they whispering about?" one of the Rovalkian men shouted. "Shut them up and get the girl out here. We're leaving."

The driver pivoted around. "Get out here, Annika."

The girls nodded to one another. Valerie got out of the van first. Gwen winked at Annika before following. Daisy got out next, whispering curse words under her breath. Without letting go of her hand, Tiana led Annika out. Valerie stood in front of Annika. Gwen and Daisy stood to Annika's left while Tiana stood to her right. A warm breeze rustled their hair, yet everything and everyone else were still. There were no birds in the sky; no insects buzzing. Annika looked down. The uneven ground had tufted grasses and rocks. *If I can find a rock big enough,* she thought, glancing around. The armed soldier raised his gun toward Annika. She tensed.

"Lower that gun or I'll slash your throat," the driver menaced with fangs bared. Sunlight flashed off the dagger that suddenly appeared in his hand. "The Ausurnian girls are under my protection."

The Rovalkian lowered his gun as the driver sheathed his knife, and Annika bent her knees to hunker down.

Tiana called out in Truscan. "Calm down, sirs. We all had to get out because she was in the back. She would've had to climb over all of us."

The driver motioned with his hands. "Let her through now, ladies. These men are here to escort Annika back to her country. I'll treat you all to a nice dinner in Fringur. Speaking of which… " He motioned to the Rovalkians. "My reward as promised?"

The Rovalkian man closest grumbled. "You'll get your money when the girl is in our car."

Annika felt the energies of her friends darken before their shields sprang up. Her own energy swirled faster, condensing around her hands. Anger took over, and the Ausurnian girls inched forward two steps while Annika stayed rooted in the same spot.

"Hey, what's the meaning of this?" the unarmed soldier yelled, taking a step back.

"Annika, come forward. Everyone else, get back into the van," the driver shouted. "There's no need for such defensive postures. I said no—"

"NOW," Tiana screamed.

The girls dashed forward. Annika raised her palms, releasing her energy at the man holding the gun. His head snapped back as the blast hit him square in the face and he stumbled backwards, dropping the pistol. Valerie leaped at the driver. He ducked, but her long arm caught his cape. She wrapped her arms around him from behind, covering his face with her hands. The driver tripped, and they tumbled to the ground in a cloud of dust.

Gwen and Daisy jumped, drop kicking each of the Rovalkian soldiers. The man who lost his gun swung his fist out just as he regained his balance, catching Gwen in the face, her foot missing its mark. Annika jumped forward as the soldier reached toward Gwen's motionless, crumpled form.

"No!" Tiana screamed, yanking Annika away. "Run! We've got this. Run!"

Annika stumbled backwards, tripping over clumps of grass. She forced her body to turn, fumbling into a run down the highway. A loud mix of shouts rose behind her. Annika tilted her head down and ran faster. She veered right, sensing someone behind her.

"Aargh!" came a male's bay of frustration not far behind. "Get her!" came a second bark further back.

She plunged into the shadows. Dense old growth, thick ferns, and fallen branches barred her way. She forced herself through, stumbling over roots and forest floor debris. The snapping of twigs echoed behind her. *I have to make it to the stream.*

But the stream didn't show, and her pursuers grew closer. Her mind raced through options as she navigated the underbrush. The captain's lessons came to mind. *"Become stronger than the nightmares that haunt your dreams."* Don't be afraid, Annika. Think.

The men gained more ground, crashing through the underbrush. *How am I going to get out of this?* A memory popped up. *"What do predators do to catch their prey?"*

Her legs pumped up and down, and sweat moistened her face and back. Moist earth and wood smells filled her nose. The underbrush whipped at her limbs and face, snagging her shirt, pants, and hair. But in her mind, a nine-year-old recited her lessons. *"Predators disable their prey. They go for the groin, the legs, and neck."*

"And what does a predator do if the prey is too big or fierce, my smart girl?" Her father had leaned toward her while she stood at attention in the library.

"Predators incapacitate those. An animal can't fight back if it can't breathe or move."

One man shouted from behind as the other cheered him on.

A large, toppled tree trunk came into view. She veered toward it, skidding around a stump to avoid the outstretched hand of the nearest soldier. Annika then launched herself feet first. *Here goes nothing.* Her feet landed midway up the side of the fallen trunk. She sprang backward, aiming her foot at the man's groin, but he jumped back, and her shoe landed below his right knee. A sharp crack sounded. She jabbed him in the face, and he fell back with a roar.

She stumbled to the side, trying to regain her balance. The second soldier grabbed her by the front of her blouse. She yelped, flailing her arms to get out of his grasp. He shoved her away, and she crashed into the fallen tree on her side. Pain shot through her chest as she slid to the ground, wheezing. Holding out her good arm, she tried to prop herself up as the Rovalkian soldier approached her. *Not like this!* She panicked.

"For Ausurnia!" A war cry sounded behind the soldier.

He spun around. Someone, blurred by their speed, crashed into him. The Rovalkian soldier used their momentum to push the person away, and Annika could just make out the clothes, the black hair, the height of the attacker as they whirled back around. Tiana.

Growling like a crazed animal, Tiana came at him again. She leaped between his outstretched arms, grabbing hold of his shoulders. He tried to headbutt her, but she quickly moved her head. The soldier's face froze. His mouth opened, but no sound came out. His arms pummeled at her sides with no effect.

Annika leveraged the tree trunk to pull herself up, clawing at the side for a handhold as rotting bark crumbled under her fingernails, raining down around her. Something moved to the right of her while Tiana and the second soldier grappled in a weird silent dance as Tiana continued to do whatever inhibited the soldier from making noise. They fell to the ground, grunting and flailing. Annika took a step toward the other noise, her pulse pounding in her throat, not understanding the rationale behind her curiosity. Then came more spitting noises.

"Dammit. You broke my leg, you little brat," winced the first soldier as his face came into view. He dragged himself along the forest floor, spitting out the blood running from his nose.

Annika recoiled.

"Run," Tiana gasped behind her.

Annika turned. Tiana had stood up. The soldier she'd wrestled with lay eerily still. A thick, dark substance obscured his neck. *Blood.* Annika looked up. Red glistened on Tiana's mouth, dripping onto her shirt.

"What are you doing? RUN!" Tiana screamed at her, flailing her arms as if scaring off an animal.

Stumbling backwards, Annika fell against the tree trunk again. "RUN!" Tiana shrieked again. Annika scrambled up and crashed through the underbrush.

Picking Sides

Captain Donauska

Another meeting, another waste of time. He stomped down the hall in a fury. His number two, Second Lieutenant Baar, kept up. Captain pulled out his phone and saw a voicemail from Tiana. *What does that needy cousin of mine want now?* He checked his watch. They should be in Fringur by now. He put his phone on speaker while they continued walking. Unexpectedly, it was Annika's voice that came through. She even used her new nickname. Both men stopped in their tracks and re-listened to the message.

"Who's Rosebud? What's she asking for?" Baar asked.

"Oh gods. Annika's psyche is trying to warn her, and she doesn't understand. Rosebud is the codename I gave her. They must've gone anyway." Captain sprinted toward the front of the building, with Baar following close behind. "Call the clubhouse to see when the van left and who the driver is."

When they reached the front desk, Captain hollered, "Code 501" to the man stationed there. The soldier leaped into action. Alarms connected to red flashing lights pealed throughout the building. Captain grabbed two more men and his brother, who came sprinting from nearby. They hopped into a second armored car to follow. Once on the road, Captain made a call to his cousin in Fringur, Second Lieutenant Donauska.

"Code 501. Get two cars full of men and drive towards Pontagu, along the main highway. Keep your eye out for a van headed north with the number 551V on the side. If you see it, stop it, and detain the driver. Then get the girls on board to safety. I don't know what to expect. Call me if you catch up to them." He hung up without letting his cousin speak a word. Baar shouted into his phone in the passenger seat, relaying the message to others. The town of Pontagu flew by. A single siren blared out near Town Hall, the signal for all Ausurnians to get inside and stay there. Once outside of town, Captain shifted into second gear, and the landscape blurred.

Halfway to Fringur, a large black Ausurnian van came racing into view. It sat off to the side. Captain signaled to the car behind him and slowed down. He maneuvered the car around the front of the van and slammed his foot on the brake, causing a cloud of smoke, dust, and pebbles to shoot into the air. The second armored car did the same. All five soldiers sprang out of the cars, crouching around the back corner to survey the scene.

Two girls grappled with an Ausurnian soldier while a third girl lay on the ground, unmoving. A loud snap sounded, and the tallest girl, who Captain now recognized as Valerie, screamed. He ran forward, signaling where the others needed to go, and grabbed the soldier by the collar while his three soldiers pulled the girls back. Theodor ran to the fallen girl. Captain shook the driver; the man's legs flailed as he tried to regain his footing.

"Where is she?" he snarled in the man's face.

The soldier didn't speak. Captain Donauska punched through the man's psychic shield with ease. He thundered into the driver's mind, *"Where's Annika?"* The soldier flinched and passed out.

Captain threw the driver to the ground in disgust. His loud thought projection must have been too much for the man's mind to handle. *Pathetic excuse of a soldier.* "Arrest him," he shouted, and one of his men dashed forward, handcuffs at the ready.

Theodor called out to him, holding the fallen girl in his arms and pointing toward the forest. "There's another car half-concealed in the woods over here."

Captain jogged over to him. Gwen was the fallen girl with a perfect likeness to Tiana. She groggily looked around, bloodied and bruised on one side of her face. Theodor handed her off to another soldier, and he and Captain approached the mystery car with slow steps. "Keep your eyes peeled for any movement, Theo."

The car sat on an overgrown dirt road leading into the woods. "That isn't an Ausurnian car," Captain whispered. They looked inside and found nothing except for food wrappers. He rested his hand on the hood. "It's cool to the touch. This car has been here a while." Turning back to the clubhouse van, he saw it tilting to one side. "A shot out front tire. A planned ambush." Captain cursed under his breath. *Where are you, Rosebud?*

Theodor strode back toward the van. He stooped down and held up something in his handkerchief. Black metal glinted in the sun. "A pistol," he shouted. Captain jogged toward him while Theodor checked the magazine. "One shot fired," he announced, pocketing the remaining bullets. He pointed to the ground "There's the shell. I'll ask the girls if anyone was hit."

Two armored cars careened down the highway, coming from the north. Their tires screeched to a halt near the van. Second Lieutenant Donauska and three others jumped out of the first car.

"Will someone please go after them?!" Daisy screamed. Captain looked over at her and saw tears streaming down her face as she tried to elbow a soldier's first aid administration away. "Go away. Treat Valerie. She's in more pain than me." An angry purple bruise spread across a swollen eye, and she held a bloody cloth to her nose. "Tiana ran after them into the woods." She pointed across the street.

One of his men hastened over. "Captain, Valerie says there's two men after Annika. Two Rovalkian soldiers, and they knew the driver."

Rage boiled in him. *Their blood will be mine*, he vowed as his gloved hands clenched into fists. He barked at his cousin. "You and Theo, with me." Then he pointed to the other soldiers. "You three, secure the scene. And you, escort the women back to Pontagu Base for debriefing and medical attention. Baar, stay and make sure Pontagu Base knows what happened." He broke into a run as the last word left his lips.

The three men had no problem sprinting into the dense forest without a trail. They'd run wild in these woods as boys every day. They knew where to place their feet and how high and far to vault over brush. Nothing impeded their advance.

A voice howled from deeper in the woods, and Captain signaled for the others to slow. The three men crouched down and crept forward, keeping behind the trees, their footsteps muffled by the thick carpet of moss.

"Shut up, you Rovalkian trash. There's no escape for you," a female voice shouted. "Try that again, and I'll rip your throat out."

The wailing became more audible. A man's voice rose, cut off by a string of curses from the female. Captain snuck around another tree and he threw his fist up to halt their advance as he took in the grim scene unfolding.

A green-fatigued soldier was attempting to drag another along the forest floor. Tiana stood before them with her arms crossed, unconcerned. Dried blood stained her face and shirt while dirt and leaves stuck to her body. The conscious man half-crawled, half-dragged himself along the ground, pulling his unconscious comrade a couple of inches. One of the crawling man's legs was bent at an unnatural angle, while the other's neck was slick with blood.

The crawling soldier noticed the trio just as Second Lieutenant Donauska marched forward, grabbing him by the collar. The man attempted to spit in the lieutenant's face, and Captain's cousin promptly knocked him unconscious with one jab to the temple.

Theodor checked the lifeless man's vital signs, grimacing as he prodded the bleeding, lacerated neck and grasping onto a limp wrist.

"If he's alive, he won't be for long," he said, deftly wiping his bloody fingers on a nearby bush.

Captain stepped deeper into the forest with Tiana in tow. "Annika!" they called, but no reply came.

"The other guy has a broken leg and nose. Did you do all this, little cousin?" Second Lieutenant Donauska asked with a smirk.

"No," she spat and picked the leaves from her hair, swiping at the dirt on her shirt. "Annika got the first guy. The second had her in his grip when I arrived. They were strong, and I did what I had to do." She spat again. "I don't know which way she ran. I screamed at her to go." Her head tilted up to listen at a sudden rustling to their right, then she grabbed at her stomach. "I think I'm going to be sick." She ran off, and the sound of heaving soon followed.

Captain shook his head in frustration. He extended his psyche deeper into the woods, trumpeting Annika's name using thought-projection. *"Annika?"* No response. *"Rosebud? You out there? It's Captain Donauska. Where are you?"*

"Captain?"

193

He strained to listen. The voice had been so faint. *"Rosebud, where are you? Shout louder."*

"I'm at a tree. There's no creek. I don't know."

"Okay, Rosebud. The stream may have dried up. If you ran over it, I'll be able to find you. Stay put. I'm coming."

"Ugh. I think I swallowed blood. Did you find her? Where is she?" Tiana suddenly appeared at his elbow, a sheen of sweat across her brow. She tugged on his arm. "I can't hear her."

"Stop," he said, pulling away. "You two, get help to drag this scum back to the base. Theo, you're with me. And clean your face up, Tiana," he barked over his shoulder.

* * *

When they came upon a sandy, dry stream bed amongst dense ferns, both men crouched, scanning for footprints. "There." Theodor pointed. Embedded in the mud were shoe prints that laid a clear path of Annika's trajectory. They nodded to one another and dashed forward.

"Annika!" they called out, over and over. "Annika!"

No reply came. Captain signaled for his brother to stop. He thought-projected again. *"Rosebud, are you there? Can you call out or make noise?"*

"I'll try," came a weak projection back, weaker than before.

The two men strained their ears for movement. *SMACK, SMACK.* Captain ran. *"We hear you, Rosebud! Keep going!"*

SMACK. SMACK.

"Who's Rosebud?" Theodor wondered aloud.

SMACK. The sound echoed nearby.

"Rosebud, there you are." Captain stopped short, relief flooding through him. Theodor skidded to a halt at his side. There Annika stood, leaning against a gigantic pine tree with a large stick in hand. She let the

194

stick drop to the ground when she saw them, and a small smile crossed her face before her head fell back against the tree trunk. Like Tiana, leaves and twigs stuck in her hair and on her clothes. Her blouse was in tatters, the ripped edges dark and stuck to her skin. An open gash on her hand oozed.

Captain scampered forward, cursing. "Sit down while I have a look at you." He held out his hands, and she grasped them, sliding down the tree trunk, wincing. Then her head shot up, and he turned his head. Theodor froze mid-step. Captain rubbed the top of one hand with his thumb, slow circular movements meant to relax her as he grabbed his handkerchief to wrap her other hand. He spoke in a soothing tone. "It's okay, Rosebud. It is just Theo." She nodded once; her eyes never leaving him.

"Hey, Annika." Theodor gave a small wave. "I'm here to help, too."

Leaves woven into sweat soaked strands of hair stuck to her face. Captain gently tugged the leaves out. "Theo, give me your handkerchief. Can I wipe your face, Rosebud?"

Her hands shot up to her hair, clawing her fingers through with fervor, catching knots. Captain grabbed them. "It's okay, I'll get it." With gentle dabbing motions, he wiped her face and tenderly pulled the rest of the leaves from her hair. She stayed subdued the entire time.

"There, that's better. Your shirt is a lost cause, though. Can you stand?" Captain rose and held out his hands to help Annika up.

"This is your mom's shirt," she groaned, inspecting the tears. "That bastard threw me against a tree trunk. My arm and ribs hurt." She winced.

"Let me check for breaks. And mom won't care about the shirt. All we care about is your safety." He ran his hands along her arm and felt her ribs, pursing his lips when his fingertips traveled around her breasts. "Nothing is broken, but you'll have bruises. I'll carry you back," he said, one arm already around her waist.

"No, please, I can walk," she cried, wincing, as she shuffled to one side out of his reach, a dry hoarseness roughening the sound of her voice. He froze, staring at her. She looked back at him sheepishly and lowered her gaze. "No offense. It's my pride … You understand."

"You're one tough bird, Annika. Or is it Rosebud, now?" Theodor smiled, crossing his arms.

She looked at him and blinked. Captain rounded on his brother. "Leave her alone. Walk in front."

"Okay, okay. Sheesh," Theodor grumbled as he made a path for them.

"Thank you, Theodor, for helping," Annika croaked out. "Ah, my throat is so dry."

"You don't need to say anything, Rosebud. I've got you. Hold my arm. Let me know if you get too tired. I have water in my car."

"You're welcome, Annika," Theodor called back.

"ANNIKA!" Tiana came crashing through the underbrush. She spread her arms wide.

"Stop," Captain shouted as he pulled Annika behind him. "She's in shock and hurt."

"Captain," Annika huffed. "Let me go. She saved me, and you're hurting my hand.

Captain released his grip and turned to her. "I'm sorry."

"It's okay." Annika stepped around him and walked up to Tiana. "Are you okay?"

"I'm okay." Tiana smiled, her face and clothes wiped off, minus the bloodstains on her shirt. She grasped Annika's shoulders. "The bad guys are gone. I told you we wouldn't let anything happen to you." Then she pulled Annika into a gentle hug.

Captain's heart pained and swelled. "She's right. Come on," he said, ushering them forward. "Let's get back to base."

As he reached out to Annika, Tiana wrapped a protective arm around her, gave him a pointed look, and led Annika forward. "Come on, Ro. I've got you."

Annika

Every breath felt like sandpaper against her throat. She tried chewing on her tongue, but no salvia presented itself. Every sound made her flinch.

She froze when they reached the highway. The armored van still stood along the road. Her pulse quickened. *Where is everyone?* she wondered as the sound of metal clanking echoed.

"Wow, they sure cleaned up the space fast," Theodor exclaimed, jogging forward in front of the group. "Nothing like a bit of excitement to rally the troops!"

With a reassuring squeeze from Tiana, the girls walked across the highway. Annika steeled herself as they rounded the van, noting all the burned tire marks on the asphalt. Theodor began talking in Ausurnian to someone just out of sight.

"Baar," Tiana gasped. She squeezed Annika's bad arm; Annika gasped.

"Hey there, lovely," the Ausurnian soldier said, turning. He set down a toolbox and beckoned Tiana.

Tiana released her grip from Annika and looked at Captain Donauska.

"Go on. I'll take care of her," Captain assured her.

Tiana looked at Annika. "Go on, Tiana. I'll be okay with Captain," she rasped out, and Tiana ran into the soldier's outstretched arms.

A light pressure on her shoulder pulled her attention from the two embracing. "Let's get you water, Rosebud," Captain whispered in her ear. She shook herself, and pain radiated through every nerve.

With one hand on the small of her back, Captain led the way to another armored car parked nearby. Annika stopped; at her feet, a circle of red stained dirt and grass. She sucked in a breath, looking around at the ground.

"What're we looking for, Annika?" Theodor asked, coming up from behind.

"The gun. One of them had a gun. Oh, Void. Did someone get shot?"

"Oh, like this one?" Theodor pulled a handgun from his belt loop.

Annika recoiled and Captain stepped in front of her. "Put that away, you idiot. You didn't need to show her." He turned to Annika as she backed up another step. His hands went to the sides of her face, his thumbs caressing her cheeks, melting her brain. "It's okay," he soothed. "He took out all the bullets. We suspect the man shot into the air. It's okay. Trust me."

She took a deep, painful breath, and the captain stepped away. Theodor frowned as he tucked the handgun back in his belt. Annika swept her eyes over the surrounding area. Another vehicle stuck out from the woods. She pointed to it, jumping behind the captain. "That car. That's a Rovalkian car."

He laid a hand on her cheek once more. "Rosebud, focus on me. It's okay. Theo and I inspected it when we arrived. There's no one else here. Do you trust me? I need to hear you say it." He leaned in closer, their noses a breath apart. "No one got shot. Just a few wounds—like you."

"They're going to be alright?" she asked, staring back into his hood, the pressure of tears rising.

"Yes. The girls are going to be okay." He then straightened and turned to his brother. "Theo, drive that car back to base. The keys are still in the ignition. Park it in a garage in the back. Then find dad and tell him we're on our way."

Theodor nodded, patted Annika on the shoulder with two awkward taps, and walked toward the car. Captain took a firm hold of her good hand and led her to an Ausurnian armored car. The familiar smell of pine and leather wafted forth when he opened the car door. *Captain's car.* She sighed mentally and inhaled deeply after she settled down in the front passenger seat with her feet dangling out of the door.

"I'll be right back," Captain said and walked to the back of his car. Annika watched as Theodor drove the Rovalkian car out onto the highway and turned south towards Pontagu.

"Here." Annika drew her attention back from the shrinking car. A black shirt and canteen were in Captain's outstretched hands. "Drink everything in here. It's an electrolyte drink. Here are some painkillers, too. I also found a spare shirt."

The tang hit her dry throat as she knocked it back, and she threw her head to the side, sputtering and coughing.

"Easy, Rosebud. There's no hurry," Captain said as he laid the shirt on the dashboard to her left.

Annika paused between sips to observe Tiana. She and the other soldier sat on the side of the highway in front of the van. Tiana sat on his lap, and he wrapped his arms around her. Their foreheads looked to be touching. Annika glanced back at the van and saw they had replaced the flat tire. *What if they had gotten me in their car? What were they going to do to me?* "Why do they want me?" she asked Captain.

He stood up from leaning against the car door. "We'll try to make the driver say—provided he recovers from my knockout. I'll make a call while you change into the shirt. Do you need help?"

"N—No." Annika lowered her eyes as a warm feeling flooded her body. "I'm only bruised." She wagged her finger at him, trying to give a cheeky smile. "No one but my future husband will see me without a shirt on. Turn around, but stay close." She tossed the now empty canteen into the back seat and held up the long sleeve shirt. "Whoa, this is huge."

"It's mine," he said, returning her smile with a hesitant one of his own, and took his phone from his pocket. "Yell when you want me to come back."

She leaned out the side of the car to sneak a peek in Tiana's direction. Seeing them still preoccupied with each other, Annika glanced toward the captain. He faced away, talking on his phone. She hastily unbuttoned the black shirt. It felt different from any material she'd felt before. *Now it makes sense why the material looks different.* The silky texture had a feather's weight and slipped through her fingers like water. She ran her hand behind it, checking to see if it'd be too sheer to wear, then held it up to the sky. Not a ray of sun passed through. Glancing around once more, Annika eased off the blouse she wore, not looking at all the scratches and growing bruises she felt across her torso and arms, and grimacing when bits of dry, bloodied shirt pulled at her skin. She pulled on the shirt one arm at a time, shivering as the silky material laid cool against her hot skin.

"You can come back, Captain."

He spun around and trotted back. "Awe, you're swimming in it, Rosebud. I knew you were petite, but damn," he chuckled. His smile grew as the heat in her cheeks rose, and he stepped closer, lowering his head and voice. "The color suits you, though. Striking." Her cheeks flared, and her mind melted. Absolutely gone. *Will I ever become immune to his quiet charm?* He grabbed one sleeve while the smile continued to play on his lips and rolled it up. She stuffed the hem into her pants with her other hand, acutely aware of Captain's intense gaze.

Tiana and her soldier walked up as Captain finished rolling up the other sleeve. "It's weird to see you in all black, Ro, but it suits you. I like it." She held onto Second Lieutenant Baar's hand draping over her shoulder.

"So, it looks like you two made up," Captain said. "About time."

Tiana stuck her tongue out. Annika giggled and Tiana winked at her. Second Lieutenant Baar cleared his throat and pulled his arm from Tiana's shoulder, causing Tiana to frown. "You're such a moment ruiner, cousin. You feel better, Ro?"

"Be real, Tiana. Maybe you've forgotten in your wash of hormones that someone almost kidnapped Annika on our soil." Captain folded his arms. "Maybe focus on the seriousness of the situation instead?"

"Be nice," Annika and Tiana shouted at once.

"You'll never win, Captain," Second Lieutenant Baar stated.

Annika and Tiana burst out laughing.

"Oh, I almost forgot. Ro, *this* is Second Lieutenant Baar. My boyfriend and my cousin's second-in-command. As well as his best friend." Tiana placed a hand on the soldier's chest, glowing with pride. He saluted Annika with his fist to chest and bowed. "You can trust him with your life, too," Tiana added.

"Thank you, Lieutenant Baar. Nice to meet you," Annika spoke in Ausurnian.

"The pleasure's all mine, Miss Mullway," Second Lieutenant Baar replied.

"Alright. Let's get you girls back to base." Captain walked to the back of his car and secured the door. He surveyed the area. "Baar, you and Tiana drive the van back to base. I'll follow, driving Annika in my car. Dad's sending out more troops to secure this road in case Rovalkia sends in more soldiers."

As they drove back, way more slowly than Annika thought he would, Captain broke the silence. "We're taking this attempt on you seriously, Rosebud. I hope you understand that."

She let out a slow breath. "I'm sure you are. But let's be honest, I'm no safer here than back home." She turned her head toward him. "It may be time for me to move on. To the coast or overseas. No rebels are going to want me around, as high profile as I am now. And I don't see how I can be of help anymore. Perhaps there's nothing I can do for Rovalkia. Maybe I'll have to forget about my family and my dreams." Her voice cracked. "I'll probably never see them again." Tears sprang to her eyes, and she tried to blink them back.

Captain's leather gloves creaked against his steering wheel; his lips stretched into a thin line. The corner of the barbed wire fence came into view as he turned onto the base's private road. Then his hand jerked the wheel to the side, and he pulled the car over in a cloud of dust, hitting the brakes hard.

"Captain!" she shrieked, panicking. "What's going on?" Annika grabbed her seatbelt and looked around outside, straining to see through the settling cloud of dust around them.

"No one—" Captain's voice growled out as she spun around; his fangs visible behind his upper lip. Her pulse quickened. "—and I mean *no one* can protect you better than I. Do you understand?"

She licked her lips as her eyes widened. "I—I don't understand."

"Damn." He grasped the steering wheel hard. "Okay, this can't wait any longer. I need to say it." He abruptly got out of the car and came around to Annika's side, opening her door. "I have something to say to help make you understand …"

More Than Wants

Captain Donauska

He held his hand out for her as she exited the car, and led her, wide eyed, into the semi-privacy of trees a few feet away. As he turned to face her, he was suddenly tongue tied, his brain a pile of mush. All he could do was stare into the most beautiful eyes he'd ever seen; the most beautiful face he'd ever seen. "Annika, I—" He stopped himself. A look of curiosity replaced the shock in her eyes. He took both her hands in his. "Rosebud," he started. "Where's your favorite place to go? And why?" He watched as she tilted her head to one side, gazing back at him, a frown forming. "Please, just humor me."

Annika licked her lips again. "I used to think it was the path to the lake. Or the lake itself. Or the south coast of Rovalkia where we used to vacation. But now, I'm going to say the Pontagu train station. I remember how serene and beautiful it was when I stepped off the train. My first taste of freedom." She closed her eyes. "A strong breeze was blowing the tall green grass about. The sky was clear and blue, and birds chased each other in the sky."

He smiled when she opened her eyes. "That first day. I remember."

She gazed around him again, at the car behind. "Uh, why are we here? I feel calmer now. Isn't your dad going to be mad when we don't show?"

He tightened his grip, closing the distance between them with half a step. "They can wait. I need this moment … with you."

Annika gulped, her eyes widening. Much to his relief, she didn't look scared. "Okay," she whispered.

"What was your first impression of me?"

Her eyebrows raised, the ghost of a smile playing at the corners of her mouth. "You came across as a grade-A jerk and intimidated me."

"Do I intimidate you now?" he asked anxiously.

Her head shook slowly while her eyes stayed locked on his face. "No. You have a powerful psyche. But," she paused, biting her lip, "it's comforting."

Captain broke into a chuckle, the nervousness and flutters of his heart twisting his stomach. "Gods Rosebud, here I am trying to do my job and you keep pulling me off course, like an untamed horse." He looked down to see her cheeks were bright red, her bottom lip sucked in, and her eyes lowered. As if feeling his gaze, she raised her green eyes and shrugged.

"That's me, all drive and no direction." Her eyes darted away, shaking her head. "What a mess I was—still am." She sucked in a breath. He sensed sadness emanating from her.

"What's on your mind, Rosebud?" He tipped her chin up, and her eyes darted around his face, searching but unafraid.

"I've realized I haven't wanted to admit something to myself …," she began, pausing as he traced her jaw with his thumb, her chin resting in his hand. "I don't want to go home. And you're one reason," she whispered.

Captain's mouth went dry. He swallowed; his left hand still held her right one as her other hand came up to meet his. Annika's hand twisted in his, her slender fingers intertwining with his. He held his breath, watching her nervous smile twitch. "Rosebud," he whispered, not believing his luck. Closing his eyes, Captain leaned his head forward until his hooded forehead touched against her bare one. "I don't want you to leave me either," he said in a hoarse whisper, inhaling the faint scent of vanilla still lingering on her skin. "I can't deny your hold on me either." Then he tilted his head up and pressed a firm kiss on her forehead.

Annika

A ringing sound split the silence, causing both Captain and Annika to jump apart. Captain cursed and answered his phone. "Be right there," he said and hung up. "You're right. Dad's wondering where we are. We'd better go."

They hastened back to his car and hopped in. Annika sat on her hands, trying to control the swooning in her head. Then reality crashed down on her. Not two, not four, but six armed guards stood at the base entrance gates. When they saw who it was, they waved him through, shouting into their walkie talkies, announcing their arrival. Captain parked at the front doors and five armed soldiers ran out. They surrounded his car, facing outward; their rifles pointed out in every direction. Annika waited for Captain to come around the car, too scared one of those guns would point at her if she moved. Then, in a blur of doors, halls, and running figures, Captain led her deep into the base and to the hospital wing.

Under blinding neon lights, the medic gestured for Annika to change into a hospital gown before closing the door of the exam room behind him. Captain had excused himself moments before, saying he'd be right outside until the doctor let him back in. Annika squirmed on the exam table while they disinfected her wounds, her skin itching as a medic teased hardened dried blood from her scrapes.

A few minutes later, Tiana joined her in the room with a toiletry bag. Tiana hesitated before lightly hugging her. They whispered reassurances to one another about their wounds, commented on the increased security, and giggled nervously about their predicament. Tiana brushed Annika's hair, and they washed their faces before redressing, staying in a comfortable silence. Annika donned the captain's shirt again, and Tiana changed into a black uniform shirt as well. Annika patted her necklace laying against her collarbone, thankful it had survived the ordeal. Then the captain escorted them back down the labyrinth of hallways.

"Where are the others?" Annika needed to break through the awkwardness she felt. Captain had visibly twitched when Tiana linked an arm with her at the same time his hand went to grab hers. Tiana had given him a suspicious look before he'd cleared his throat and walked ahead of them.

"Um," Tiana swallowed hard.

"Baar escorted them to the town's hospital," Captain said over his shoulder, his countenance unfazed. "They'll be fine."

Annika looked to Tiana, who suddenly looked paler. Before she could ask what they were hiding from her, Captain stopped in front of a double wide door guarded on either side by an Ausurnian soldier. "This is the War Room. It doesn't mean we're at war. It's just a large, secure meeting room. What happened to you today was a serious breach of our borders. That road shouldn't have been there."

The girls shared a wide-eyed look as Captain continued. "Whatever is said in this room, stays in this room. The consequences of leaking information are severe. Do you understand?"

Annika felt her stomach drop as she and Tiana nodded. Captain then nodded to the guardsmen, who stepped forward and opened a door for them.

A long oval table and chairs dominated the space, and television screens lined the walls. A dozen ranking officers were taking notes from an agitated Commander Donauska. Spread before him on the table were large aerial maps, and he pointed at precise locations while speaking in rapid Ausurnian. As the door shut behind them, everyone stopped and looked over at the trio. Officers snapped their notebooks shut, and those who had been sitting stood, saluting Captain before Commander Donauska instructed them to take a five-minute break.

The commander motioned the three forward as the officers filed out of the room. Annika noticed how sweaty her palms had become and rubbed them on her pant legs. His deep, booming voice filled the room. "Well, Miss Mullway. I'm glad to see you in one piece. All you girls were brave. And Tiana, you did the right thing in telling Annika to run. You took control of a dangerous situation like a true Donauska, and I'm more than proud of you."

Tiana straightened her back, her cheeks reddening, and saluted her uncle. "Thank you, Your Majesty."

Commander Donauska turned to Annika. She gulped. Not only was he a commanding officer, but the king of a nation.

"Young lady, I'm also proud of you. The girls corroborated that the energy blast you aimed at the armed soldier may have saved at least one of their lives. When the enemy caught up with you, you faced them head on. Special patches on their uniforms show they're a part of a new crop of soldier Rovalkia's leaders are turning out. There's no way you could've taken out both highly trained men without help, so don't think less of yourself for listening to Tiana when she told you to flee. I'd say you were an Ausurnian if I didn't know better."

A tear escaped out of Annika's left eye. She batted at it, nodding to him in thanks.

Captain placed a hand on Annika's shoulder, his touch enough to reassure her he'd been right—she was safe. Annika raised her eyes to him, swallowed against her tight throat, and then let out a soft laugh.

"What's funny?" asked Tiana.

"Sorry, my brain wandered. I just remembered how I used to be drilled, year after year, on the importance of how to act in the presence of powerful leaders and enemies." She paused. "But they failed to mention how knowing one's own power makes you feel strong, no matter whose presence you are in."

"Wow Ro, that's deep." Tiana raised her eyebrows. She looked at her uncle and cousin as if to encourage their agreement and frowned. "What's with you two?"

Annika looked from Captain to his father, who both shared a gaping look. "Are they thought-projecting to one another?"

Her words broke their stare, and Captain muttered to himself. "Why teach that?"

"Did your dad introduce you to powerful people, Annika?" the commander asked.

"Uh, why?" Annika clenched her hands, her palms sweating once again. There *had* been the odd dinner parties and afternoon teas. Just then, the other officers began reentering the room, and, catching a whiff of their commander's agitation, slunk over to the table.

Captain looked at his father. "Another time," he said, motioning with his head to Annika. "Take them home," he added, waving his hand toward the young women. "You ladies don't need to stress about the Rovalkians or the driver. They are and will remain in custody. But stay in town for a while."

Captain ushered Annika and Tiana from the room, the heavy double doors closing with a loud thud behind them. While they trudged back to the entrance, he made a phone call. Tiana motioned for them to trail closer, and they quietly snuck up behind him. "Gran? Yes, they're fine. I'm bringing them to mom's house. I need to drop them off and dash back. There's been a recent development. They came in on a service road north of your house. Come stay with mom for a couple of nights— Yes, he *is* sending troops to secure all roads from the Rovalkian border— No, not yet." He hung up and looked over his shoulder. "Tiana, I'm going to drop you off at home and take Annika to get clothes from her apartment. I'll come pick you up again after. You both are going to stay with my mom and Gran for a few nights until we know there are no other threats."

"What about *my* family?" Annika choked. She stopped short, holding her hands on either side of her face. The image of men grabbing James and Sarah flashed through her mind, and her chest tightened.

Captain stopped walking, causing his cousin to collide with his back. Ignoring Tiana, he grabbed ahold of Annika's shoulders. "They're fine. We have security details on them at all times. I promise. Whoever is after you is not after them."

She stared into his hood, hating how she couldn't see his eyes. "But they're my baby siblings. If anything were to happen—"

"Nothing's going to happen to them, Rosebud. They're safe. They've been safe. Your father must have a protection detail on them, too. We've seen them playing with friends in the street outside your house while Rovalkian guards patrol the street every half hour." He paused before adding, "The people affected are a caravan of citizens leaving the capital city. And from what we can tell, they don't appear well-off enough for it to have been their choice."

"So, the leaders are purging the city?"

"That's what it looks like. There are many unanswered questions right now. Do you still trust me?" His grip tightened on her shoulders, causing her to wince in pain. He released his hands. "Sorry."

His psyche receded from around her. "Go on, Rosebud. Read my truth. I need you to keep trusting me."

She closed her eyes.

"What's going on?" Tiana asked.

He shushed her as Annika extended her psyche toward him. She felt his emotions swirling fast and strong around him. Anger and determination were the loudest, but beneath was agitation and fear. "I trust you." She sighed at the same time he did, hearing the relief in her own voice, and pushed the longing for her family down deeper.

"You let her *read* you?" Tiana burst out. "Since when do you let *anyone* read you?"

Captain growled, "Let's go."

He dropped Tiana off and helped Annika pack her bookbag with a couple of days' worth of clothes. They then went through her fridge to determine if anything would need to be tossed, watered her dahlia plant, and locked up. She hopped back into her seat, and he cupped her cheek with one hand while his other held the car door open. "I'll check on your apartment and you every night before going home to make sure all is well. When things calm down, I'll take you out for a nice dinner—our first date. A *real* first date." Annika smiled brightly, her aches and pains subsiding. He kissed her on the forehead, and she melted into her seat.

Jenny, Tiana, and her little brothers came out to the car together. Annika barely touched the ground before Jenny caught her in a tight hug. "I'm so glad you girls are safe. Never do that to me again. You kids are my entire world." Jenny turned to her nephew while holding tight to Annika. "You keep her safe, you hear?"

"Yes, Aunt Jenny. I swear."

"I'll be your personal bodyguard when I'm older, Annika." Tiana's little brother, who had run into the woods with her, brought his fist to his chest and bowed. "Me too," cried the younger boy, copying his brother. Everyone but Annika laughed. She approached them and crouched down to their level, laying a hand on each of their shoulders.

"It would be an honor to be guarded by such brave young men. But right now, I want you to become strong for your family, okay?" She tussled the hair on both of their heads until they giggled, pointing at each other's mushed hairdos. They then ruffled each other's hair until Jenny ordered them back into the house. "Stay safe girls. Call me every day, Tiana."

Ista and Tracy were already waiting outside of Ista's house when the trio arrived. "Brace yourself, Rosebud," Captain warned. "Be prepared to be mothered within an inch of your life."

"That's okay. I could use a little parental smothering. It's been a long time."

"Can't say we didn't warn you," Tiana crowed.

Before getting out of the car, Annika turned to face them. "You guys are my best friends." She glanced at Captain and whispered, "and more." Then she raised her voice again. "Thank you for helping get me through today and, well, life right now. I'm not sure what I'd do without you."

Tiana smacked her on the arm. "No, *you're* the best, Ro. Look, you've got my cousin at a loss for words which *never* happens. Come on, I'm sure Auntie and Grandma have a list of activities to help take our minds off everything. I already smell Grandma's famous stew."

Annika gave Captain one more grateful smile when his hand shot out and squeezed hers. Then she hopped out of his car into Tracy's outstretched arms.

Captain Donauska

It was nice to see the town back to normal after three long days of patrols and border checks. He had checked Annika's apartment and sent her reassuring texts each day, no matter how tired he was, and each time she had texted back painfully short, single lines of dialogue. He sighed as he skimmed through their messages, searching for any hint of attraction they admitted to days before. *Why is she acting so guarded with me?*

Everyone, including Annika, had gone back to their own homes and jobs. As expected, the Ausurnian secret salve had Annika's bruises and scuffs healed in two days. When he was a little boy on his grandmother's knee, she explained how one Elder had permission to make salve. The recipe didn't change hands until that Elder died. *Is all this power worth it, though? All these secrets?* He gritted his teeth, annoyed with himself for letting his emotions get the better of him last night. He had shattered a glass, slamming it onto the counter after yet another single line of text from Annika.

He sighed, forcing his shoulders to relax. *Mom will at least appreciate these flowers as my thanks for looking after her.* He'd only just placed the bouquet in his car when a child shouted nearby.

"Look, the papers say the fair is coming to town after all!"

He looked up. The youngster and his friend had already dashed down the road, the newspaper waving in their hands. He looked around. A small rack of the local free newspapers sat to the left of the florist's front entrance.

DESPITE RECENT EVENTS THE INTERNATIONAL AUSURNIAN FAIR IS GOING FORWARD.

As he continued to read, it said the fair would be open to only Calageeh and Ausurnian residents this year. Pontagu would ensure every security measure and precaution was in effect. The article beneath stated how the transcontinental railroad stopped running through Ausurnia. He slammed the newspaper down next to the flowers and sped to his parents' house, grinding his teeth in anger the whole way there.

"Thank you for the flowers, dear, but why are you so agitated?" Ista asked while placing the bouquet in a fresh vase.

"Did you know dad's allowed the Ausurnian Fair to go ahead? How's that going to work?" He began pacing. "It's asking for trouble," he grated.

"Why don't you ask him yourself? He's in his study right now." She pursed her lips and nodded in the general direction. "I'm sure he has a good reason."

He stomped from the room and to the closed door of this father's study, rapping his knuckles twice against the door frame. "Dad, can we talk?" he shouted.

A gruff reply came from within, and he entered the room. His father had files open on the left side of his desk, and the laptop screen illuminated his hooded face. It took a moment for Captain's eyes to adjust to the darkened room.

"What do you want, son? I'm busy."

"You're always busy," he replied, moving closer to his father's desk. He peered down at the open files, curiosity overriding his anger. He saw more reports from secret agents in Rovalkia. A list of fingerprints and names were on the opposite page. "I take it we're getting closer to figuring out who's who in Karaxin. But since we don't have a name for the actual leader, why'd you okay the Ausurnian Fair to move forward?"

His father leaned back in his chair and closed the laptop. "Because the surviving Rovalkian soldier was a dead end. He was following blind orders from a handler. Because we need *more*. More intel, more names, more … facts." He looked up at his son.

"How's the fair going to provide more of those things? You must know Tiana's going to take Annika. What am I supposed to tell her?" Captain crossed his arms.

"I'm counting on them going."

"*Counting* on it?" he gaped. "Do you truly expect me to stand by and let you use Annika as bait?"

"I *expect* you to do your job. Your duty is to serve me and our country. When you're the leader, you can make your own decisions for the welfare of our people, but don't think for a second that I enjoy doing this. I've thought about it from every angle, and if they figure out we're trying to oust the leader, they'll stop at *nothing* to get her back into Rovalkia…or worse." He paused. "But she will be safe. Your grandmother's going to have her help at the booth, and I've little doubt that Tiana will be by her side at every moment. Son, our people depend on the fair for income. Understand, there's more at stake than Annika's safety. You'll work at the fair, regardless. I'll even let you pick the location."

He thought for a moment. "Post me at the front gates. We'll scan all who enter. And I'd like to take any soldier who isn't working and offer them overtime to shadow her from a distance. I'll pay the overtime if necessary." He gripped the edge of a nearby filing cabinet for support, forcing his next words out, low, and terse. "I don't care what faith you have in our military. These recent incidents have proven there are holes we need to plug."

"I'm well aware of that, son. Trust me, I've heard all about it from none other than Ciara's parents. They call me every week, demanding Ciara's release from the reform school. They've even tried threatening me with an uprising… Now they taunt me with the leaked military secrets." Captain opened his mouth, but his father held up his hand dismissively. "Yes, we all know they're the ones behind the leaks, but I don't have hard enough proof yet to build a lawsuit. Besides that, the detail on them has reported they've stopped their secret meetings and coded phone calls for the time being."

"I'll give them something to squeal about," he mumbled.

"No, you won't," his father warned. "First, we need to figure out who they leaked the info to and who the leader of Rovalkia is. After that, we'll deal with everything else. You need to remember to prioritize these things and leave your heart out of it."

Captain licked his lips. "No."

"Excuse me?"

"I won't leave my heart out of it. I've made my decision and have told Annika how I feel about her. She feels the same—I think. There's no more 'pretending' to love her for the press. It's real. And I'm not sorry. So, stop seeing Annika as an object."

His father ran a hand over his face and opened his laptop. "Your love life is your own business, but your future is already set." He pointed to his son's chest. "If I feel like Annika interferes with the safety of our country, I *will* intervene."

Tilt-My-World

Come to the diner. Annika read the text from Tiana. She dressed and scampered down Main Street. She found an empty booth with a newspaper left by the last patron and spread it out on the table to avoid someone asking her to move.

"Good, you're here. It'll be a minute before my break. I'll have Milly bring you coffee." Tiana wiped her floured hands across an already flour dusted black apron. Wisps of her long, black hair had escaped from her topknot and were unwinding, but her brown eyes sparkled.

"Oh, Tiana. Did any flour get in the bread? You'd make a ghost jealous."

A couple passing close by burst out laughing, and patrons turned around to see the source of the commotion. Obliviously, Tiana waved her hands over the table, making ghostly "Ooo" sounds while showering everything in fine cake flour.

"Get back into the kitchen before I chuck you in the oven," Jenny roared from behind the counter. "Gods, give me strength—And clean yourself up."

Tiana winked at Annika and danced her way back to the kitchen. All the diner patrons burst out laughing. Annika folded up the various pages of flour-covered newspaper in haste. A young girl came by with a pot of coffee and a cloth to clean up the powdered destruction left in Tiana's wake. "Give me the cloth, Milly. I'll wipe down the booth. Sorry."

"It's okay, Annika." Her tight dark curls bounced. "We're used to it." She smiled and took Annika's order of toast and coffee.

"Guess what time it is?" Tiana inquired as she plopped herself down.

"Geez Tiana, you're lucky I set my cup down, you startled me! It would've been a hot mess in our laps." Annika then bit down on her toast to stall for time. She shook her head while inspecting her friend's face for clues.

"The Ausurnian Fair!" Tiana threw her hands in the air. "You'll get to experience it with me. They've already started setting up at the grounds near our border with Calageeh. It's why there's more people in town this week. It's the most enjoyable time we Ausurnians have all year." Tiana bounced on the seat. "We're going to have a full week of games, concerts, food, and fun. My mom and grandma promised me I can take time off to show you. Oh Ro, we'll go on the Ferris wheel at night, too. The view is to die for."

"Alright, slow down. If you say it'll be fun, I'm sure you're right." Annika turned to see Jenny exiting the kitchen. "Look, I should go before your mom kicks me out for distracting you. We'll talk soon."

Captain Donauska

The two brothers neared the diner just as Annika exited.

"Whoa there, Rosebud. Watch where you're going." Captain gripped her shoulder before she bumped into him. She froze an inch from his chest, muscles tensing under his grip, before raising her dazzling emerald eyes to meet his amused smile. Her muscles relaxed, and she smiled warmly. Then her attention darted to the right. His younger brother stood there, grinning. Her fingertips raised to tuck a loose strand of hair back behind her ear, and she returned the smile minutely. Captain elbowed his brother, frowning at him.

"Hi, Captain. Hi, Theodor." She paused, looking back up to Captain's face. "Sorry, I wasn't paying attention."

"See? I told you she's doing fine." Theodor beamed, slapping his brother on the back. "He got worried when he didn't see you through our grandma's shop window when we walked by and were just about to call you. She's tougher than most, our girl is."

Captain cursed. "She's *my* girlfriend."

"Excuse me. *Your* girl." Theodor rolled his eyes.

"Do you ever know when to shut up?" Captain growled as Annika closed her eyes while a deep pink tinged her cheeks.

"How about we head—"

Captain shook his head in warning, and Theodor cleared his throat. "Okay. *I'll* go in and let you two catch up." He winked at Annika before darting inside.

Alone at last, Captain looked back down to find her staring up at him, her lips bent into a frown. He glanced at the nearby alley. "Let's go over here," he told her, and pulled her by the hand into the shadows.

"Wait, why?"

"Your shields aren't up. I told you to practice being present at every moment," he paused, reaching toward her silver tresses, "And what's in your hair? Flour?" He started swiping gently at her head.

Her eyes widened, and she giggled. It was like the most beautiful bell ringing sound. It made goosebumps sprout along his arms. Annika batted his hand away, but kept an amused grin on her face as she tousled her hair herself. "Cake flour got everywhere when Tiana sat next to me." Then her voice softened. "It's nice to see you."

He exhaled, planting a long kiss on her forehead. She sighed contently. "I've been keeping up with my workouts. It's just been a long week." She rubbed her right shoulder. "Uh, so, are you going to the fair next week? Do you have any days off?"

He tilted his head to the side and frowned, surprised. His father's words came rushing back. *I'm counting on her going.* "I've got guard duty, but I'll be around. Why?" He grabbed hold of her hand.

"Tiana and I are going. I've never been to a fair. I was hoping, maybe, we could have our first date there instead ..." She sucked in her lower lip, slowly nibbling on it, and a rosy tint bloomed on her cheeks again.

"Captain," a soldier called from the alley's entrance, "we've got a booth and are ordering."

He waved the interrupting man away. "I'll try to keep an eye out for you next week when I'm on duty. I have Friday night off, though. How about spending the last evening at the fair together? We can call it a date if you'd like—our first of many." He grazed the side of her cheek with one finger.

Annika nodded, glowing. "A date it is." She beamed, her straight, no-fanged teeth on full display. He smiled back and felt his heart soar.

Annika

Local newspapers reported each day how far along the fair's construction had progressed. Annika and Tracy spent the week prepackaging herbs and bottling concoctions for the shop's booth. On the eve of the opening, Tracy drove with Annika to the grounds.

"You'll get to see the fairgrounds before opening day," the Donauska matriarch said as they drove westward. There were campers parked along the highway when they left Pontagu city limits. "The crowd tonight will be the Ausurnians running the booths and attractions. Even after all these years, it's still exciting."

The Ferris wheel came into view with its multicolored lights competing against the descending summer sun. White markers guided the line of cars down past visitor parking to a reserved area in the back. Annika rolled down her window, taking it all in. The sound of hammering and static in speakers echoed loudly above the car's tires as they crunched on the dirt road. Lined up outside and within the entrance gates were rows of booths, like sentries protecting the games and rides beyond. The sweet smell of hay and the pungent aroma of livestock stung Annika's nose without warning. She pulled her head back inside, coughing, as she rolled up the window. Tracy tittered. "It wouldn't be a Fair without livestock."

"Why would anyone want animals at a fair?" Annika wondered aloud, sticking her tongue out.

"They award prizes at size and weight competitions, hold live auctions, and have a petting zoo for the kids. You've never been to a fair, have you?"

Annika shook her head. Two mountains of stacked hay bales were now on either side of the road. A sign reading "Vendor Parking" signaled the private lot entrance. All around them, people loaded their wagons with merchandise, game equipment, and tools. They wove around the cars toward an open back gate. Annika looked up at the chain-link fence surrounding the park to see barbed wire strung along the top in threatening spirals. Tracy parked and stacked boxes in Annika's arms.

"Why make two trips when one will do?" Tracy joined in with others who sang in Ausurnian, while Annika followed behind in silence. Together, they strode past the farm animal section and a myriad of game booths. A Tilt-A-Whirl spun with no one on it to their right, its lights flashing fast.

Three rows over and five tents down, Tracy came to an abrupt halt. An elegant painted sign: **Mrs. Donauska's Herbs and Remedies**, hung above a makeshift entrance. The fresh wooden kiosk stood out from the monotonous cloth tents. Planks nailed to the side functioned as shelves and builders had fashioned a makeshift checkout desk near the back, complete with a locking money box and stools.

They got to work setting everything on the shelves to attract potential customers. Tiana and Jenny walked up with their hands full of small cardboard boxes and drinks.

"Hi, Ro. Hi, grandma," Tiana greeted, pulling Annika into a bone crunching hug. "We brought you pie and tea."

Jenny set the drinks on the counter before hugging Annika and her mother. Annika grabbed up a cup, eager for the heat and caffeine to help with her headache. She listened while the three Donauska women chatted about how successful the fair would be.

"And the Rovalkians won't be attending, so I feel safer already," Jenny was saying.

"Not all Rovalkians are bad," Annika interjected.

The women startled. "Good gods, Annika. I forgot you're a Rovalkian. You're right. Please accept my apology." She rose from her stool and gestured to her daughter. "We should go Tiana. We need to close our booth up for the night."

Tracy set her hands on her hips. "We should close up, too." They took the empty boxes, rolled down a canvas tarp from behind the sign, and padlocked it in place at the bottom.

The noise died down as twilight turned to darkness. Annika looked around, swearing she felt eyes on her, but nobody appeared where she looked. Bright stars twinkled in between the strings of lights, illuminating the inky sky. On Tracy's beckoning, Annika followed behind, heading back to the car.

They drove along the dirt path behind a line of cars. With the window rolled back down, the from baby animals carried on the breeze. The thousands of string lights danced across the fair's landscape.

"Get a good night's sleep, Annika. Fair goers from near and far will crowd the place," Tracy explained while Annika continued to stare out the passenger side window. "And I heard Tiana's planning on keeping you busy with fun until the last evening. A word of advice: leave the busier rides for the last day. We close the grounds to all outsiders early on the last evening, except you, of course, and we have the run of the place. Oh, and there's a concert and fireworks on the last night, too."

Annika sighed. "Will it be safe enough for me to go since Calageeh is where the malicious news reports about me originated?"

"Yes, my dear," Tracy explained gently. "Ciara's parents submitted those articles, my son says, so don't worry. Just stay with Tiana or come sit with me, and try not to use your powers, except shields, for the week to keep attention away from yourself. I think you'll have a wonderful time."

* * *

The door shuddered. *BANG! BANG! BANG!* Tiana hollered from the other side, "Annika, it's time. Let's go!" Then Annika heard her rush back down the steps.

She looked out the passenger side window, playing with the horseshoe charm on her necklace, letting it slide between her fingers over and over. The car ride dragged along with heavy traffic, all heading in the same direction.

"Us Ausurnians use our own parking lot while the Calageeh visitors fight over parking near the front entrance." Tiana turned her head toward Annika. "And don't worry about the quantity of military personnel present. Non-Ausurnian soldiers get a discount at the front doors as part of the 'cultural exchange' theme. And, of course, our military will be there for our protection."

The ticket clerk stamped the girls' hands as Annika voiced her observation. "There must be thousands of people in the park already."

The clerk smiled at them and said, "You better believe it. But you'll get used to it."

Annika shuddered at the memory of the crowds back home in the big city. A familiar wave of energy pressed against and over her psychic shield. She looked around, then up. "Is that your cousin up there?" She pointed to the roof of the entrance gate where Ausurnian soldiers were patrolling and looking down at all the people entering the fairgrounds.

"Yeah, but don't pester them. When they're on duty, they pretend not to know anyone. Same if you see them on the grounds. Don't talk to them unless they talk to you." Tiana urged her to keep walking as throngs of people pushed forward, threatening to separate them.

"I can't believe how few details I noticed last night! All this color makes me feel alive," Annika said in awe. Good smells, laughter, and the biggest bands in recent years playing through the speakers filled the air. "James and Sarah would love it here."

Tiana swept her arm around. "Now, do you understand why we dress plain every day? When you save the bright colors for special occasions, it helps you appreciate them even more." Four color coded rows of booths stretched out before them, and Tiana pointed around. "Each color corresponds to a different trade. The black is weapons and metalworks, red is our herbs and spices—that's where you'll find my grandma's booth if you want to see her. Beyond that are green tents for food, purple is clothing and orange is crafts." She steered Annika toward the closest row, black.

The first vendors were selling silverware and copper plated serving bowls, each with intricate designs hammered in. Pinging of hammers against metal kept a tempo akin to a beating heart. Annika tapped her fingers against her thigh in time. The further down the row, the denser the crowd became. The girls held tight to one another.

As they made it to the end, the vendors selling metal daggers with deadly glinting edges turned into one's selling fishing gear and bows and arrows. Annika let her fingers graze the soft feathered ends of the nearest quiver, a feeling of sudden excitement bubbling up within. The vendor caught her eye. "Beautiful," she stated. "Good energy." The vendor smiled, nodding.

The next row of tented booths was orange. A crowd was ogling over a pyramid of ornately carved boxes. Annika bounced on the balls of her feet, trying to get a better look at the nearest box with a rose carved into the lid, but Tiana tugged at her arm. "Oh Ro, look," she exclaimed, pulling Annika away to the opposite tent. Four glass cases were lined up end to end, displaying jewelry. They had organized each case with one half being silver and the other half gold, both with accents of particular stones. "This one is your case, Ro. Look at all those rubies. And this one would be mine. Can you imagine a wall of sapphire jewelry?" Annika's heart leaped at the beautiful jewels; then she looked at the price tags, her heart sinking. Each price tag was higher than the previous, higher than the amount she was going to allow herself to spend for the entire week. Two Ausurnian soldiers were suddenly at her shoulder, crowding her out.

"Let's keep moving, Tiana," she said, squeezing away from the pressing bodies. "I can't enjoy anything with this many people around." Missing the familiar press of the captain's shield against hers, she said, "I would've thought there'd be soldiers at the grounds last night when we set up. There's a lot of expensive stuff here, but I didn't notice a single guard."

Tiana felt a stack of thick black woolen scarves with her free hand. "Oh, they were there. Trust me. It's an Ausurnian military secret.

They retract their shields and psyches and hide in the shadows to observe. It makes them undetectable."

Annika whistled. "Wait. Is that what your cousin did when he intercepted Ciara's hand at the clubhouse? I hadn't felt his approach in the slightest."

"Exactly. That's how he knew we were the innocent party." Tiana nodded. "Hey, look at the clothing booths! Now you can see the differences between the clothing of midlanders, northerners, and southerners. Valerie wore more traditional Pontagu clothes on the bus, so you wouldn't have noticed before," Tiana said as she pointed out different people and clothes here and there. The patterns from the South reminded Annika of waves crashing, while patterns from the North were sharp and angular.

"Am I missing something? I don't hear any differences in accents."

"Our language is more intuitive and breathier than most, making all the pronunciations the same. C'mon, let's get some food."

Passing by the first three stalls, Annika observed the same red spice covering all the vendor food, just as Jenny did with her dishes at the diner. Bags and jars of the spicy blend towered around each cash register; one or more sold in each order. "Outsiders act like our signature blend is a drug—they're addicted," Tiana whispered in her ear. Annika leaned over a counter to watch as one woman generously shook the spice over her skewered corn on the cob.

"That amount would burn my tongue off," Annika mumbled. Her nose tickled as the red dust wafted over. "Ah-ah-achoo!" The vendor threw an annoyed glance her way as Tiana laughed and pulled Annika away.

"Alright Ro," Tiana drew out. "Let's go find a vendor who can appease your delicate palette."

As the hours went by, they rode the Tilt-A-Whirl, ate rich meat pies that left their fingers greasy, and wove through the throngs of people.

"Can we go home now, Tiana? I'm tired and there are even more people than before."

"Let's stay a little longer. I promised Baar we'd meet up with him when his shift ends." Tiana pulled Annika deeper into the fairgrounds. "Why didn't I think to ask where to meet? I bet we've passed him a million times already."

An intense flash of light bounced off something nearby and shot into Annika's eyes. She froze, closing and rubbing her eyes. When she looked back up with still dotted vision, Tiana wasn't by her side. "Tiana?" she called out, swiveling around, in search of her friend. She found no sign of her. Annika turned back the way she thought Tiana had gone, hoping to catch up, but a wall of Ausurnian teenagers was coming at her. One of them held a clown doll, and she stared transfixed as its googly eyes danced and a big, red-lipped grin reached its ears.

She tore her eyes away and looked around for an escape route, anywhere but here. People crowded around her left and right. She stood stock-still, praying one of these tall, young people would turn their heads to see her before it was too late. She stepped sideways, maneuvering between the clown wielding girl and cackling boy. She yelled, "Excuse me!" to little effect as their solid Ausurnian frames squeezed and knocked her off balance, the teens still completely oblivious to her existence. She stumbled, reaching out, and her head and left shoulder hit something hard, halting her fall.

"Hey, watch it, girl!" someone yelled close by. "You touch it, you buy it."

Stunned, she turned to see she'd knocked into the pole of a tent, its wares swinging from hooks above. "S—sorry," she said and turned back around, her heart thumping. *Where's Tiana?* Annika's chest tightened. More strangers pressed up to and past her, locking her in place. She dove between two couples locked arm in arm, trying to get back into the flow of traffic. She froze.

Twelve feet away stood her father. His blonde hair was longer than she remembered, and his piercing blue eyes stared right at her. H was shorter than an Ausurnian, but stronger than he looked. "Dad?" He had an indecipherable look on his face. Her breathing hitched and her head swam. "How?" she choked out. Every nerve ending tingled. The primal part of her brain screamed at her to run, but she couldn't move. It was like everything from her waist down had been stuck in quick drying cement. This was it. Goodbye Ausurnia. Goodbye freedom. *Captain* ...

A hand took hold of her arm. Annika yelped and lost her footing once more. The hand holding her tightened, keeping her upright.

"Ro! What's gotten into you? You look like you've seen a ghost," Tiana shouted as she pressed them both to one side of the flowing mass of bodies. "Hey, are you okay?"

"No," Annika whimpered. She pulled Tiana into a hug, her eyes searching the crowd behind her friend. "I lost sight of you, and then it was like nobody saw me and were walking into me as if I didn't exist. And then ..." she shuddered, pulling away from Tiana, but keeping her eyes on everyone walking by. "I *swear* I saw my dad. He was looking at me, staring at me. I froze. I wanted to run. I should've run, but I couldn't. And then you were here, and now I don't see him anymore." She stood on her tiptoes. "We need to get out of here. Like now."

"Annika." Annika's attention snapped back to the use of her real name. "There is no way your dad, or any Rovalkian, could've gotten in. No way. Ro, listen to me. Don't you think it is possible that maybe, just *maybe,* there's another man in the world that looks like your dad? Maybe he was looking at you funny *because* you were acting so disoriented? Listen to me. Calageeh people don't look too different from Rovalkians. We won't let anything happen to you. I promise."

Annika nodded, swallowing hard. The thumping of her heart was still loud, but it didn't sound, or feel, like it was going to break a rib as it had moments ago. "Yeah—yes, okay. You're right. I'm just—I think I panicked and—gods, I'm thirsty."

"Good idea. Let's go back to the food stalls. I could use a cold drink, too."

The first refreshment booth caught Annika's attention. She yanked a mumbling Tiana back. "Tiana, we'll keep looking for Lieutenant Baar in a minute. I need a rest. Let's get a drink here and sit a moment."

"But I want the both of us to hang out with him. I was hoping we'd find him and *then* get a drink."

"No, we're getting one now. And why? He's your boyfriend. It'd be awkward if I stood there with you."

"No, it's not like that. He's my friend *and* boyfriend. We can separate the two when necessary."

Annika took out her card to pay for the drinks. *I doubt it.* "Alright, I'll stay a while longer, but these crowds are putting me on edge. I can't take it much longer. I feel like I'm being stared at all the time."

"Relax, Ro. It's just the guys checking you out. We're in the prime of our lives. Why wouldn't they?"

"That may be the case for you. You don't have a target on your back." They sat awhile, nursing their drinks. "Tiana, I can't help but notice this is supposed to be a multi-cultural exchange, yet the groups remain segregated. Well, except for those Ausurnian soldiers talking with the Calageeh soldiers by the Ring Toss."

"Everyone's still leery. The Calageeh people have to be on their best behavior this week," Tiana explained while chewing on her straw. She turned in her seat to scan where Annika had motioned with her head. "It's him! You found Baar." She sprang up, smiling from ear to ear. The hand holding her drink waved in the air like a lunatic, while her other hand shot out and began pulling Annika forward.

"Ow, Tiana! You're going to pull my arm out of the socket." She looked from one soldier to another, trying to remember some feature of Second Lieutenant Baar's face. One of the Ausurnian soldiers noticed their approach and smiled. *Bingo. His smile is for Tiana.*

"Hello, Miss Tiana, Miss Annika," said Second Lieutenant Baar. "Gentlemen, these are my friends from Pontagu,"

The Calageeh soldiers locked eyes on Annika. Their unobstructed gaze bore into her. She frowned, staring back, feeling her palms moisten. Before anyone else noticed, they looked away.

"Second Lieutenant Baar, what a coincidence. We've been here all day and haven't seen anyone we know," Tiana flirted, stepping closer to him.

Poor girl is love starved. Annika tried to make polite conversation about the fair and weather with the others so the love birds could have some illusion of privacy. Everything screamed they were head over heels for each other just like when they reconnected on the side of the highway. Annika noted his constant smile, the little touches to her back and arm, and Tiana's constant fit of giggling.

Annika gave up on the awkward conversation and excused herself from the group. Through thought-projection, she told Tiana to come to her grandmother's booth when ready. The Calageeh soldiers also left. Annika felt their unwelcome presence following her until they finally broke away when she looked over her shoulder for a third time. She also kept her eye out for the blonde man.

"Mind if I spend the rest of the evening with you, Mrs. Donauska?" Annika asked, finally arriving at the booth.

"Of course. Where's Tiana?"

"With Second Lieutenant Baar."

Tracy pulled up another stool for Annika. "That explains it. Poor girl. They both sacrifice so much for this family and country." She then regaled Annika with tales of fairs past, when her husband was still alive and when the world seemed a brighter place.

Heart Beats

Every day was the same routine. Annika got used to the flow of crowds and became more familiar with the fairgrounds. She made a point not to look many people in the eye, though she felt their eyes on her. The two girls wore themselves out playing games, walking among booths, and finding Second Lieutenant Baar when his guard shift each evening.

Throughout the days, Annika's senses tingled, but like before, they never told her if it was friend or foe. After meeting up with Second Lieutenant Baar and playing a game or two with them, Annika would excuse herself to help at her employer's booth before the fireworks started. Every night concluded with a text or call from Captain Donauska. Did she have fun? Did she feel safe? He told her he missed her but that their date night was just around the corner.

The last day of the fair had arrived. Still groggy from staying up too late the night before, she donned the new outfit Tiana had lent her.

"This is one of the few days we get to dress up. Please do it for me. I sewed the skirt myself," Tiana begged. Its heavy weight hugged her hips and fell straight down. The forest-green material had a smoky blue design woven in. Its design reminded Annika of the fog that rolled into town every night. "Your eyes will pop when you wear this skirt," Tiana had exclaimed when Annika pulled it out of the bag. Annika applied smokey blue eye shadow, and a periwinkle blue top finished the look. She looked at herself in the mirror. With the low neckline, her necklace laid across her collar, out on full display. *If my silver curls were black, I'd look like an Ausurnian.*

Tiana squealed in delight when Annika got in her car. "You look like a goddess. You're going to have so many dance partners tonight."

"Dance partners?" Annika's jaw dropped. "I don't know how to dance."

"Don't fret about it. We all know how to dance. The guys can teach you."

Annika gulped, her stomach twisting. "Says the Ausurnian to the clumsiest Rovalkian who ever lived."

Their day at the fair passed by in a blur. They bumped into everyone clamoring to get one more ride in. Annika maintained a death grip on Tiana's hand. They went back to the booth with the ornate boxes again, but the vendor had sold out of the one Annika had her eye on all week.

Finally, a voice over the loudspeaker announced the early closing of the fairgrounds. A wave of Calageeh natives receded toward the entrance. Annika looked down to inspect her skirt for dirt and wrinkles, thinking of Captain walking up to her soon, asking her to dance.

"You look as beautiful as you did when I picked you up this morning, Ro." Tiana nudged Annika's arm. "Are you going to ask someone to dance?" She wiggled her eyebrows.

Annika rolled her eyes, laughing to cover up the nervous tremor shaking her core.

They made their way to the concert area where Second Lieutenant Baar joined them. Annika wrung her hands. "Lieutenant? Have you seen Captain around? He's supposed to meet up with me—er, us today."

He draped an arm around Tiana and gave her a kind smile. "They stationed me at the back today, so no. But he'll find you, don't worry."

They had decorated the picnicking field with solely Ausurnian flags. Throughout the week, flags from each of the allied countries had also graced the field. A gigantic circle chalked onto the ground for a dancing area had everyone crowding around the edge. Excited conversation circulated. "Here we go," Tiana jabbered into Annika's ear. "The speech will be in Ausurnian, so nudge me if you need help to translate."

A suited man with a sash stepped up to the podium. He rambled on about the success of the fair and the continued brotherhood and support of allied countries. Annika was wondering how he could have any more to say, when the speaker finally raised his voice and announced the first song and dance. Everyone cheered. Annika laughed and thought-projected to Tiana. *"I'm pretty sure they're cheering because he stopped talking."* Tiana burst out laughing, too.

Annika stood on her tiptoes to watch as couples entered the circle. "There's your grandma." She pointed at the Donauska matriarch on the arm of an unknown, gray-suited man. She wore a black skirt with white designs embroidered on it, and the stark white shirt she wore had long tassels hanging from the length of the sleeves.

Music beat forth ancient sounding rhythms. Beautiful vocals and soul-thundering drums had the dancers whipping each other around in perfect time. The women's colorful outfits painted a story as their partners, mostly dressed in black, functioned as the brushes. The songs that followed were more familiar, and those without partners created their own dance groups. Tiana pulled Annika and Second Lieutenant Baar into one group with familiar faces. Daisy and Valerie each took hold of Annika's hands and, around and around, they danced.

A mixer started up after three songs. Those taking part separated into a line and swirled around each other, changing partners at pinnacle times in the song. Sweat ran from Annika's forehead as she stepped off to the side, conscious of her lack of a dance partner, when a voice on the loudspeaker declared a last dance for the adults before songs for the younger kids began. Annika smiled at the dancing couples, covering up the worry that Captain might not show. A hand tapped her on the shoulder from behind.

"Have one more dance in you, Miss Mullway?"

She turned and froze. Captain Donauska stood there with his perfect jawline, day old stubble, and that barely there smile he wore around her. He bowed and offered her his hand. "I'm sorry I'm late. It isn't an excuse, but something came up."

"Where'd you come from?" she breathed. Once again, she hadn't felt his approach. "I mean, yes. If you help me."

The side of his mouth curled up. *"You look beautiful, Rosebud,"* he projected to her as he pulled her out into the middle of the circle, and though people stared, it felt like they were the only two people dancing. Annika gazed into his hooded face. His hands scooped her up by the waist as the song began picking up speed.

"Rosebud, you're anything but an outsider," Captain whispered in her ear.

She gasped, unaware she'd accidentally projected her thoughts, her foot missing a step. *"Well, less of an outsider, anyway,"* she projected as Captain guided her through the steps. When the music dictated a partner change, he drew her back to him in a twirl, her cheeks heating, beaming, and laughing in delight. Each time she looked up, he would meet her smile with a toothsome grin.

The chords played softer, everyone slowing to a stop with the song, and a thundering clap rose while others whooped and cheered. With a guiding hand on her lower back, he directed her out of the circle and over to their friends. Kids and teens rushed by them, eager to have their turn dancing. When Annika approached, with Captain's hand on her waist, Tiana's jaw dropped.

"You two *are* together? I thought that was just a rumor!" Tiana shouted. Second Lieutenant Baar leaned over and whispered in her ear. "Okay, but that pinch stung," she said, scowling at the lieutenant. She then threw a wide-eyed look at Annika. Annika proffered a small smile back and leaned into Captain to show her friend that, yes, they *were* together. Captain reacted to Annika's lean by wrapping a hand further around her waist, pulling her even closer.

"Let's all go get drinks," Daisy shouted above the music. Annika and the others agreed. They made their way toward the food section of the grounds. Captain and his friends offered to hurry on ahead to buy the drinks while their dance partners rested in a dim corner. They collapsed onto the benches, while Annika and another girl were left standing without a chair. Annika looked around.

"There," she told the others, and pointed. "I can see at least one chair between those two tents. I'll go grab it."

Annika strode forward and grabbed hold of the first chair. A dark form shifted in front of her. She squinted into the inky black shadows. It moved again. More forms joined it. She shuffled backward, keeping the chair between her and the advancing shapes. She glanced behind her. "Ah, girls." The others turned to look in her direction. Annika kept walking backwards as a group of Calageeh soldiers materialized. Annika reaffirmed her psychic shield and felt the rest of the girls follow suit. The men approached with exaggerated smiles, narrowed eyes, and a swagger as they surrounded the benches.

"Well, well, well, don't you all look lovely," one soldier jeered. "You all have a nice dance? We've never heard such demonic music. Drums up all sorts of … *feelings*."

Tiana came to stand by Annika. "Why in the Void are *you* here? They barred Calageeh residents from the grounds hours ago."

"Uh-uh." Another soldier wagged his finger at Tiana. "We have special permission from the commander himself. Drawn from a lottery. We get to experience the fair, just like the Ausurnians." He locked eyes with Annika. "Apparently your pet Rovalkian witch won the same lottery."

"The commander is my uncle, and he'd never allow it. You've overstayed your welcome. Get out," Tiana growled. Daisy and Valerie came to stand by Annika as well.

"I agree," Valerie stated, crossing her arms. She towered over half the men assembled.

Annika looked to the nearest Calageeh soldier, her senses prickling. "Wait. So, you're telling me Commander Donauska gave your group special permission to stay on the grounds tonight? Tiana's right, that doesn't sound like something he'd do."

The girls shook their heads in agreement. The first soldier who had spoken stepped forward. "No. Commander Donauska holds no authority over us. I'm talking about Commander Jackson, of the World Intelligence Committee. He's *particularly* interested to hear if you show your face here. And *we're* curious why an 'innocent' Rovalkian ran away from home and into Ausurnia. That article stating you're with Captain Donauska was a sad ploy. Everyone knows Ausurnians only procreate with other Ausurnians. We smell a rat."

"Alright, that's enough. Leave now or we'll make you," Valerie hollered, pointing at him.

Tiana crouched into a running pose but froze, her eyes widening. *"What's wrong Tiana?"* Annika thought-projected to her friend, her eyes scanning for another danger. Tiana grinned open mouthed as her sharp incisors poked down over her lower lip. She raised her chin and winked at Annika. A sudden wave of energy flowed against Annika. It felt like a group of Ausurnians had just materialized. Powerful auras settled around them like a protective force field. The Calageeh soldiers sensed it, too, and looked around.

Energy in the air weighed more heavily. Her friends' expressions changed one by one like Tiana's, triumphant smiles replacing their frowns. The Calageeh soldiers tilted their heads, looking at one another for answers as their concerned looks spread. The auras grew stronger and heavier. And the owner of one of those auras Annika knew by name.

Captain Donauska

He revealed his location with a simple turning of his boot toe on the gravel. The Calageeh soldiers spun around. Captain Donauska and his men slid a couple more steps forward, and more Ausurnian soldiers materialized from every direction. He rested one hand on the hilt of his sheathed knife on his belt. A four-drink carton balanced on his other. All around, the dim light bounced off the large, uniformed Ausurnians; their sharp canines pointed down out from their open mouths. Annika chortled suddenly, and Captain quickly thought-projected to her. *"What's so funny, Rosebud? Are you okay?"*

She smiled. *"You're still holding our drinks, as if stopping intruders is a normal occurrence."*

"You're right. A few rogue soldiers are but minor nuisances, and easy to dispatch of," he replied.

The Calageeh soldiers straightened their postures. One stepped forward. "Hey guys, we were just passing the time with these ladies. No need to get on the defensive. We were leaving, see? Here we go."

They filed between the Ausurnians and retreated into the shadows. Captain followed them with his eyes. "Wrong way, gentlemen. The front exit is the other way. I'll have my men show you the way out." He gestured to three of his men. To Second Lieutenant Baar, he thought-projected instructions: *"Gain more information from them. Use any force necessary. They're in our territory. W.I.C. can't protect them here."* His second in command nodded and led the two others to corral the Calageeh soldiers.

The girls' shields thinned, and a few collapsed back onto the bench. Tiana sat down next to Annika, pulling the hair out of her face. "Don't listen to them, Ro. I wanted to make him pay for what he said to you, but the guys showed up."

"No, Tiana," Captain interrupted. "If you had charged him, it would've caused another incident we can't afford to have. We just got over the last one involving Annika." Captain handed out the cups of lemonade.

"Cheeky pricks," Annika mumbled under her breath. Captain caught himself on the verge of laughing aloud, pride rising in his chest for his Rosebud. He shook his head to compose himself and laid a hand on her shoulder. "We knew they were going to try something, but weren't sure what. That's why it took me so long to meet up with you all. We've been observing groups of them all week. Anytime Annika walked by, they would follow her for a while."

"I knew it. I could sense eyes on me all week, but could never figure out who it was. Tell me there's a way to discern who looks at you from in a group?" Annika implored. One of her fingertips tugged her horseshoe charm back and forth on the necklace chain, while the other met his hand on her shoulder, their fingers intertwining seamlessly.

"It may take time, but yes, I can try to teach it to you."

"Come on, girls," Valerie suddenly announced. "Let's put this ugly mess behind us and go ride the Ferris Wheel one more time. Just us." Tiana's eyes were eager as Second Lieutenant Baar walked back up.

"No thank you, Valerie," Annika said, rising to stand, still holding Captain's hand. "I'm going to ride with Captain, and Tiana promised Baar she'd ride with him. There he is now. We'll catch up with you later."

Valerie raised her eyebrows at Tiana, shot a pointed look at Annika's hand holding Captain Donauska's, then shrugged and walked away, the other girls and soldiers trailing behind.

Annika

"Are you *really* alright?" he asked as they approached the mesmerizing, multicolored Ferris wheel. Annika swallowed, nodding.

"I think so ..." She passed the turnstile to get on the ride first. The buckets were double chairs facing each other. Tiana and Second Lieutenant Baar got in on one side and Captain Donauska slid in next to Annika. Baar immediately put an arm around Tiana, and she melted into his side. Captain slid a hand over to Annika's thigh, gently gripping it. Annika put her hand over his and held it there. Silence descended as their bucket door shut.

Tiana spoke up louder than Annika thought necessary. "Too bad Gwen couldn't make it here. Her parents were so upset about the kidnapping attempt they moved her to Fringur to live with relatives for a while. I forgot to tell you, Ro."

The men and Annika mumbled sympathetic words about missing Gwen. Captain brought Annika's hand to his face, kissing the back. "She'll be all right. She's strong like you." Then the ground fell away, and the stars came closer as the wheel rotated faster. Some riders shrieked while others howled in delight. Annika leaned her head back, watching the sky move like an accordion. She took a deep breath, noticing the scents of others as they tickled her nose from the wind generated on the ride. Somewhere in there, she sensed Captain's woodsy cologne. *Why didn't you tell me what danger there may have been for me here, Captain?*

POP! SSSHHH! POP! POP! Smokey trails streaked up like stalks of flowers before the sky lit up with the exploding fireworks. Everyone who'd been talking fell silent and leaned their heads back. Captain snuck a kiss to the top of her head while Tiana and Baar had their heads extra close together.

Each of the buckets came to a slow halt at the bottom for everyone to exit. They stood off to the side of a gathered crowd as the fireworks continued to light up the sky. A soldier stepped up to Captain Donauska and whispered in his ear. Then he and Baar excused themselves for a moment.

A bracing wind swept through the grounds. Annika rubbed her exposed arms and shivered. Others nearby exclaimed, "Brrr," and "Well, summer's almost over." Annika pulled her attention from the dazzling fireworks and glanced to her left. Second Lieutenant Baar walked up behind Tiana and embraced her. Tiana turned around and hugged him back, burrowing her face into his leather vest. Annika felt her stomach drop in longing, her mind wandering to her secret daydream. *Captain would walk up behind me just like that. His leather gloves would wrap around my middle, pulling me close. He'd say my name and kiss my neck until I turned around to ...*

Goosebumps grew along her arms. She attempted to rub them away with vigor. A prickling at the back of her mind alerted her that a powerful aura approached from behind. She stood still and readied herself, reestablishing her psychic shield. No attack came. Instead, a slow warmth caressed her back and grew around her like when she slipped into a bath. It wasn't his psyche, but a warmth she'd never experienced. Her chill went away, and she relaxed her arms, revolving on her toes to come nose to chest with Captain Donauska. She parted her mouth as his smell invaded her senses.

"I can't extend heat far. I have to stand close," he explained, his voice soft.

She stared up into his hooded face. *"I'm still upset with you for not telling me what was going on sooner, Captain."*

"I understand you're upset with me, but I *was* telling the truth when I said we didn't know you were the target. Dad informed us the W.I.C. commander had planned something and to keep vigilant. That lottery doesn't exist. I would've told you if I thought you were in danger. That's why I stationed myself at the front gates all week." He touched one of her arms and motioned for them to stand further from the others. Annika narrowed her eyes, but obliged. "We stood on the roof, scanning for anything suspicious. And the gates you walked through were modified scanners, like the one we drive through at the base. But keep that to yourself."

Annika nodded. "But how did those soldiers get past your psychic scan?"

Captain stepped closer as the wind picked up, his body acting as a natural barrier. "We *did* scan them. But they had nothing to hide, since they thought the lottery was legitimate. All that Baar got out of them was that W.I.C. Commander Jackson mentioned reporting back to him if they saw you."

"Oh." Annika frowned. "So, you really wanted to see me this evening?"

"Yes, Rosebud." He raised a gloved hand and caressed her cheek. Her cheeks grew hot, and she turned back around, smiling to herself. He stayed behind her without saying anymore. Then his hands gently encircled her waist, and he pulled her closer to him.

The fireworks display ended, and the rides shut down. The lights turned off in the booths and games, and everyone began meandering toward the exits. Annika peered over to find Tiana hugging Second Lieutenant Baar, who had burrowed his face into her hair. Her friend's back shuddered. Was she crying? *Poor Tiana. She deserves a happily ever after more than anyone I know.*

"They don't get to see each other as much as they used to. Tiana blames me. And she's right, since I'm his boss. But with everything going on, I don't have many days off either."

"I know. What should I do? She's my ride home …" She turned to him.

He rubbed his chin. "What if your boyfriend provides that ride home so Barr can drive her back? He came with me here, so we will leave no cars behind."

"Oh, yes. I'd like that." She smiled at him. "That works for me if you have a way to let Baar know. I don't want to disturb her."

He looked toward his second in command. Baar's head nodded once, and he hugged Tiana tighter. *Thought-projection is so useful.* Annika followed Captain, giving a silent goodbye wave to Valerie and Daisy, who still stood nearby. Captain walked in front and to the side of her, clasping her hand. He made a natural wall against the throngs of people. He'd turn toward her every few moments, and she felt his fingers twitch when he did so. *"What're you thinking? Thought-project it to me."* He turned his head toward her again.

"I can't see you through thought-projection."

Butterflies murmured in her stomach. She stayed silent as they got on the shuttle ride, while walking to his car, and even into the beginning of the drive.

"I had a fun time dancing. Where'd you learn the steps?" she blurted out as she pushed herself back into her seat, frowning. *Why'd I ask that? I know the answer.*

His head jerked toward her before turning his attention back to the road. "Uh, parents teach their kids to dance. My mom taught me, and someday my future wife and I will instruct our children." His hand hovered in front of the radio volume knob, then lowered back down.

She rubbed her fingers together, knowing full well nervous vibrations emanated from her aura. "So, you see yourself getting married someday?"

The corner of his mouth twitched. "Why do you ask?" Unable to form words, she wrung her hands. His gloved hand squeezed her thigh. "Sorry, I was just kidding. Of course, I do."

She felt herself blush furiously, which incurred a hearty laugh from him. They passed Pontagu Base, complete with its bright perimeter lights and ominous barbed wire fence. It wretched her thoughts back to the worry needling the back of her mind. "Captain? Why would someone from the World Intelligence Committee be interested if I were at the fair?"

His gloved hand gripped the steering wheel harder.

"Please, tell me the truth," she implored. "Is Ausurnia in danger? Am I the root cause?" She watched as the speedometer steadily rose. The lights of Pontagu grew in the distance.

"Annika ..."

Oh, gods. Here it comes. She gripped her hands together and stared out through the windshield.

"This is *extremely* sensitive information. If I tell you, you mustn't tell another soul." His voice came out hard.

A lump lodged in her throat. "What you say stays between us. It always has," she proclaimed.

"Once we quelled the spread of lies from the hate group started by Ciara's family, we needed to find out who they told the information to before it reached the newspapers. Our sources proved that their contact had leaked to the press, not Ciara's parents. There were also secrets leaked from our military documents. Of which none of Ciara's family is privy to. So, by logical thinking, their outside contact must be a military person with connections to us." Captain navigated through the crawl of cars heading home. He pulled down a wide alley and drove east behind the shops on Main Street toward Annika's apartment. "The only outsiders that know anything of our military prowess is the World Intelligence Committee. They aren't supposed to talk to the press about any country's military, and *certainly* must never take sides when two or more countries are feuding. The leaked information went to the press as Rovalkia started making inquiries to your safety and threatening us."

Annika slumped down in her seat. "So, I caused all this." It was a disparaging thought.

"No, you didn't. None of this is your fault. Never believe those lies. We'd never have harbored you if it were at all true." He stopped the car at the base of her stairs and turned to her. "You came into our lives as tensions were already boiling over. The leader of Rovalkia, whether it's the elected leader or someone in the background pulling strings, is losing control and pointing at us as an excuse. Thanks to Ciara's parents, your country has something to latch onto."

"Oh, gods. I think I'm going to be sick." Bile rose in her throat; she held her stomach. Captain jumped out, ran around the car, and opened her door. She fumbled to get out of her seatbelt, sucking in air to keep the sick at bay.

"Exhale, Rosebud. You're hyperventilating," he said, rubbing her shoulders. "It's a panic attack. You won't be sick. Look at me." He gave her a gentle shake. "Inhale. Keep inhaling until it hits the bottom of your lungs. Then exhale slowly through pursed lips." He demonstrated, and she followed his instructions. "Good. One more time."

As her rapid pulse slowed, the spinning sensation quieted as well. She let her eyelids close, remembering the faces of all those she loved. *You're not alone,* she told herself. *You have friends. You love them. They love you.* She exhaled again.

"There you go. Feel better?" He rubbed her arms up and down.

"I miss my family so much it hurts," she whimpered. "And anytime something happens, it makes me agonize over leaving them." Tears stung her eyes, and she blinked up at the night's sky.

"I can't imagine, Rosebud. But you have us. Forever. I'll protect you. Your friends will protect you. You have a solid foundation here already. You've been through an ordeal not unlike what us soldiers face in battle. No one ever comes out the same." His generated warmth enveloped her again; she allowed herself to relax in his grip.

She nodded, the side of her mouth stretching up in a half smile. "Thank you. I needed to hear that. I think I'm okay now." She titled her head to the side. "How is it you all are so much more—more evolved? Is that the word I'm looking for?" she asked herself more than him.

"That's a question for a much later time. There's so much you don't know and aren't ready for ..." He trailed off, turning his head away from her.

"I know, but who says I'm not ready? Here I am, stuck in this tricky situation, my country putting me on a wanted list because of their ignorance in the understanding of energetics. And now Calageeh and W.I.C. are siding with Rovalkia over Ausurnia. To top it all off, my work visa expires in a year. I have to be ready." She tugged at her long skirt as pressure built in her throat.

His lips twisted into a grimace. "The Ausurnian law says so, Rosebud. I'm sorry. They're ancient rules, but still applicable to this day." He took her hands in his. "And with the position I hold, I have to follow these rules more than anyone. Just know we want you here. We'll get through this and come out better and stronger for it."

Annika stared down at her hands. *I belong here.* She tried and failed to find her voice. Each time her mouth opened; emotions constricted her throat. She raised her eyes. "I crave a place to call home; where I'm not scared anymore. I'm tired of hiding and keeping to myself. I used to want to live alone and keep to my own devices, but that's not right. I have these abilities for a reason. I crave to do good and be good. I want to help people."

"Of course you do. You're practically a Donauska, like mom said." Unexpected chuckling rang out from him in the cool night air, and Annika stared at him. "My grandmother knew it when she hired you. She said you were special and told us to trust her when we voiced our doubts. Gran told me to let you come out of your shell in your own time." He smiled. "You know how empathetic she is."

Annika's mouth widened into an O. "When I met her, her energy had been so comforting and calm. She put me at ease like I'd never experienced. She helped me find my place. I'm so happy it turned out the rumors about Ausurnia were wrong. But I still have a lot of questions that need answers." She snuck a glance at the captain. His face and body were relaxed, not deceiving any emotion that may be bubbling inside.

"I don't mean to sound like a broken record, but patience is essential when living here. Everything happens in its own time. No matter how dark the night is, the sun will rise again."

She tried to muster a smile while scooting forward in the seat. His hands left hers, and he took a step back. She hopped down out of the car, and they walked over to the base of her stairs. "Thank you for the ride home. This week has been amazing, despite those few minutes with the Calageeh soldiers." She smiled before adding, "And thanks for not letting me make a fool of myself while dancing."

"Anytime, Rosebud. Oh, I almost forgot." He strode back to his car and got something out of the back. When he returned, he proffered a small, wrapped package to her. She took it as he cleared his throat and rubbed his hands on his leather vest. "I got you a little something … It's okay if you don't like it."

Annika tore the shiny red wrapping paper back. "You didn't have to. Oh!" she gasped. It was the carved box with a red rose on the lid. The exact one she had her eye on all week. "Thank you. I was hoping to get one, but they sold out. How did you—never mind. Doesn't matter. I love it. Thank you." She stretched up on her toes and gave him a peck on the cheek. When she stepped back, she swore he was blushing; a darker color covering his tanned face within the shadow of his hood.

"You're welcome. Tiana told me about your panic attack on the first day. I felt terrible that I wasn't there to help you, but she was right about you being safe. But don't let your guard down, okay? At least not yet. We're not out of the dark yet." His hand came up, thumb caressing her lower lip. She closed her eyes, leaning into his touch and nodding. When she peeked through her still lowered lashes, his face was approaching closer and closer. Annika's breath hitched, anticipating, as his lips lowered to hers. She closed her eyes as a sudden tickle at the corner of her mouth startled her, and she jerked her head back. Captain's head snapped back, too. "Too fast? I knew it … Damn," he muttered to himself, clearing his throat and taking another step back.

She shook her head. "Uh, no, I—"

"I'll say goodnight. I'm sorry again," Captain whispered, his voice hoarse. Then he stepped forward, placed a soft kiss on her head, pivoted, and marched back to his car.

Unsure what to do, Annika ran upstairs, her cheeks burning.

Whirled

Annika was assisting two customers while Tracy rang up another when Tiana burst through the front door, gasping for breath, one hand holding her side while the other waved a newspaper. Everyone stopped and stared. Tracy marched around the counter and grabbed the paper. She read aloud:

> "Two Ausurnian soldiers evaded arrest in Calageeh after seen attempting to seduce females at a nightclub. Calageeh officials, growing suspicion of Ausurnian soldiers in their border towns, began a call for action after bordering counties published more missing persons reports. Official reports submitted to the World Intelligence Committee by firsthand eyewitnesses tell of a 'pet' non-Ausurnian being paraded around their yearly International Fair. Officials are pointing fingers at the Immigration Initiative that went into effect five years ago.

"The mayor of Mortainy said, 'The Immigration Initiative was a military initiative first. Then that ambitious Ausurnian, Captain Donauska, had the idea to expand it to include anyone. Stop taking our women. This ends today.'

"Unless hard evidence is found linking the missing persons to Ausurnia, they will dismiss inquiries by the year's end. Because of rising tensions, Ausurnia now has military guards stationed along all borders, and the transcontinental train has stopped running until further notice. Commander Donauska was not available for comment."

Her boss then folded the paper up amid silence, running her fingers along each crease twice. Everyone's eyes turned to Annika. "Not again," she groaned. "And why are you all looking at me like that? I was the only outsider at the fair, and I'm here of my volition. I *want* to be here."

Tiana walked over and hugged her. "Why can't they leave us alone?"

"Politicians are always trying to find a scapegoat for the problems presented by their citizens. We're an easy target because of our independent existence," Tracy explained. She motioned for the customers to leave. They murmured sympathies to Annika and left.

The office phone rang, and Tracy nodded to Annika, prompting her to answer it. Tiana followed her into the office and sat on the little sofa.

"Mrs. Donauska's Herbs and Remedies. How may I help you?"

"Hi, Rosebud. Quick, do you still have all your legal documents?" a familiar voice asked.

"Captain?"

"Yes, it's me. I hate to be short with you, but it's an emergency. Do you have all your IDs, work visa, and birth certificate?"

"Y—Yes, I do. We just read the article. What's going on?" she demanded, trying to keep her voice steady.

"Once we started making inquiries to Commander Jackson and what business he has with the knowledge of your whereabouts, he started—well, we *assume* he started pulling his puppet strings with politicians. They started signing petitions the last couple of days for in-depth, in-person inquiries at our bases. It's within their rights, unfortunately. I implore you not to accept or make any international phone calls until further notice. We're close to the beast; things could get messy for a while."

"Easy enough to follow." She glanced over at Tiana. Her friend inspected the throw pillow a little too closely. Yes, she was listening in. "Interesting that this Commander Jackson is so concerned about me and the nature of your troops, when Rovalkia is having public hangings and leaving people displaced." Tiana's head shot up; she edged closer.

"Exactly. There's something happening there. I have to go, but I'll keep you posted. Stay safe. I miss you... You're my world." *CLICK.*

Annika pulled the phone away from her ear and stared at it for a moment. "You too, Captain," she whispered at it.

"What'd he say?"

"There may be an in-person assessment of Pontagu Base by a W.I.C. Committee. But they have no interest in the humanitarian crisis happening in Rovalkia. It's so, so wrong," Annika forced out through gritted teeth.

Tiana stood up, placing a hand on Annika's shoulder. "They'll get their comeuppance, Ro. Mark my words. Bad guys never win."

"Hmm, I've heard that before." Annika shook her head. "But it doesn't feel that way."

Her boss entered the office. "I heard what Tiana said." She walked over to Annika and cupped a warm hand on her cheek. "Have faith, my dear. You must keep faith that the world's good. Also, remember, people judge others based on their own insecurities. Bad to one person is likely good to another … as backward as it seems."

"I'm glad I was born to my mom. The thought of having to play politics my whole life makes me sick to my stomach."

The Donauska matriarch chuckled, taking her hand from Annika's cheek and placing it on Tiana's. "You have a heart like your cousin Theodor. We each have our place in this world. You feed the hungry while Theodor shelters the compromised and weary. Captain, along with his father, protects us all so we may continue on." Tracy shook herself and told Annika to take her lunch hour.

Annika followed Tiana out of the shop. "Now we just need to figure out *my* role in life." The low-laying gray clouds threatened to dump rain, and a sudden gust of wind made the trees shiver.

"You'll get there. You have a big heart and a fierce spirit. I think you'd work well in politics or humanitarian aid." Tiana linked arms with her. "But for now, let's get soup in you. Mom put a fresh pot on the burner."

While Tiana tied her apron behind the counter, Annika took a seat on a stool. "I always fancied myself a revolutionary soldier, fighting with my compatriots for the right reasons; for better days." Tiana opened her mouth as if to console Annika, but her mom pulled her backward into the kitchen.

"Hey there, Miss Annika," a male voice said to her right. She swiveled on the stool to find Theodor sitting next to her, wearing a big grin. He wore a black business suit with a dark blue tie instead of his usual pants and a button-down black shirt. His slicked back hair reminded her of her father's friends that used to come to dinner.

"Hi Theodor. You look nice." She met his grin with her own.

"Thank you kindly," he said, nodding his head to her. "I just came back from a meeting with a few finance guys who had personalities about as worn as their ledgers." Theodor's laughter reached his amber eyes. "The things I do for this country …"

Annika giggled as Jenny sashayed out from the back, sporting her usual pinned up braid and carrying two large bowls. She placed them in front of Annika and Theodor. "Eat up, my dears," she said, giving them a motherly pat on each of their shoulders.

"Hey, that booth just opened up," he said, gesturing toward it. "Would you do me the honor of sitting with me?"

"Sure," Annika nodded, hopping off the stool. "But I'm on my lunch break, so I need to eat fast." She turned to pick up her bowl as his hand went toward it as well. She snatched her bowl up with one hand and smacked at him with the other. The bowl's contents sloshed up to the rim. Theodor yanked his hand away, and his smile vanished.

"Sorry, I can explain," she said, hovering at the edge of the booth. Theodor sat down with his eyes locked on her. "I never let another person touch my food or the vessel it's in. It's something I learned as a kid." She lowered her eyes. "I'll understand if you don't want to eat with me anymore."

"Sit down. I'm not mad, just surprised," he replied as she slid into the booth. He twirled his spoon. "That's just not a normal lesson, is what I'm saying. Who taught you that?"

After a few moments of stirring her soup, Annika laid her spoon down on the napkin. "Umm, an acquaintance taught me—a long time ago. Rovalkia is a dangerous place for a young, single woman. He wanted to keep me safe. And I'm still here, aren't I?" Annika picked up her spoon again, took a bite, and smiled. The vegetables were just soft enough and had a hint of spice that threatened to make her cough. Warmth spread throughout her body. *Get used to the spice, body. This is what they eat, so it's what we eat.* She spied Theodor studying her again and ate another mouthful, pretending not to notice.

"Well, your past lessons sure lend themselves to your independent nature. I could use someone like you on my team if you're ready to take a more active role in changing the world." His brown eyes sparkled as he took a sip of water.

"Your brother explained we need to take out 'the beast' first, *before* I can think about changing Rovalkia. But I'm not sure if he means the person leaking military secrets or the leader of Rovalkia."

"Both are dangerous tasks and are, no doubt, linked."

"You think?" Annika was worried. "How's there a connection?"

"Politics and militaries are always connected, but I'm sure dad has it under control, though. What *I* can do is offer you a much safer vocation as an advocate in my underground network to help refugees and victims of war. My head office is based in Fringur with safe houses and allies the world over. You could get started at my office, learning the ropes. Then, if you desire to see the world and learn a new language, we could send you out into the field. Those who seek refuge don't stay long. We get them well enough for more traveling and they pick their next destination. It's tough but rewarding work. What do you say?"

What do I say? Leave everyone ... again? Leave Captain? Just like that? Her eyes narrowed, suspicious. "That's a nice offer, but I can't abandon your brother, or anyone else." She exhaled, causing the steam rising from her soup to billow toward Theodor. "I don't feel it's the right time, Theo. Maybe someday in the future, if the offer still stands, but right now, there are still too many loose ends." *And new beginnings with Captain.*

Theodor's lips moved between different facial expressions. Annika glanced at him between bites. After a while, he sighed. She set her spoon down to give him her full attention. "What's on your mind?"

He drummed his fingers on the table's edge. "I noticed how you said my brother first. He cares for you—wants you safe. He'd do anything for you."

"What your brother and I have—it's real. I love him." His eyebrows shot up, and she pressed on before he could say anything else. "I didn't choose this path originally. My parents and Rovalkia forced me to diverge, which led me here." She crossed her arms. "I'm not looking for violence, but it keeps finding me. I know he's trying to keep me safe, that you all are, but if defeating the beast means I must resort to fighting, I'll be ready." She raised her chin to him. Theodor threw his head back, roaring with laughter. Annika looked around to see everyone, including his aunt and Tiana, looking over at him.

"Shh," she hissed, waving at his face. His laughter subsided, and he rolled his head around on his shoulders.

"I needed that." Theodor smirked, rolling his neck again. "Laughter is great stress relief." He drummed his fingers on his chest.

"What the *Void* is so funny?" she reproached through gritted teeth. "You laugh like a madman."

"Oh relax. You still have a lot to learn, Silver Girl." A sly grin crept along his lips.

Annika raised a furrowed gaze to meet his dancing amber eyes. "Theodor, no more nicknames. I have more than enough. If your society weren't so secretive, I wouldn't 'have a lot to learn.' And you still need to answer my question. *What* is so funny?"

He cleared his throat, straightening his face and posture. "Fair enough. I've been affectionately told by my brother that you have a habit of raising your chin in the air when you mind is made up. Arguing is a moot point after that. There's a name for it in Ausurnian. *Cayusu.* It means solid mind. Or of solid mind."

It annoyed her that others could still read her like a book, but his mention of it being affectionately told by Captain softened her. She brushed her annoyance aside. "The prefix means rock, right?"

"You are correct." He pushed his empty bowl away. "Alright, *Miss* Annika, since there is no budging you, how about we work together—as friends? I've been brainstorming. What do you think about fliers?"

"What about them?"

"We've observed your city being littered with political and religious fliers now and again. Let's use that against them—for the people. We could write up our own fliers, use one of our stealth planes, and drop some propaganda of our own."

"Over Karaxin? Are you mad? They'll shoot the plane out of the sky!"

"Nah. We can fly under radar detection; we have been doing it for years. It's how we monitor you outsiders." He touched a finger to the side of his nose. "I can have my team brainstorm today."

She leaned forward, licking her lips. "You think that could really work? And not just in Karaxin, but in other cities as well?" He nodded with a serious expression. *Now we're getting somewhere!* "Let's tell my people the truth about how Kraxxan is not an all-powerful god. Tell them of his inert powers and how he is a symbol of reflection, not fear. Let's teach them the truth. Then they won't be afraid to join the rebels and make actual change." She leaned back, feeling that glimmer of hope reignite in her heart.

Theodor's expression became strangled, like he was fighting back saying something. Then it was gone, smoothed over with a smile. He glanced over her shoulder, and before she could ask what he was thinking, he said, "Didn't you say you were on your lunch break? You'd better get back to grandma's shop. You only have two minutes left."

She hustled out of the booth seat. "I forgot. Gods," she cursed under her breath as she fished in her pockets for her charge card.

"Go. I'll pay for your lunch. It's the least I can do."

Annika gave him a grateful smile, waved toward Tiana and her mother, and ran from the diner.

Captain Donauska

He froze at the diner's window. Annika rose from a booth at the same time an arm, a masculine-looking arm, rose and signaled to a waiter for the check. *Who's with her?* She rushed out the door, oblivious to his presence, and power-walked away. After deliberating whether to run after her or confront the male she sat seated with, he took a deep breath and stormed into the diner.

"Theodor?!" he hissed, stopping short of grabbing the man by the neck.

His brother started. "Geez, where'd you come from?"

Captain slid into the booth. "Why was Annika running away? What'd you say? Why are you dressed up?"

Theodor crossed his arms. "I met with accountants today. And she wasn't running from me. She had to get back to work—I had just finished trying to recruit her for my organization."

"And?" Captain's heart thumped harder. If Annika said yes, she would have to move to Fringur. Between their demanding schedules, he'd barely ever see her.

"Careful, your feelings for her are showing," his brother smirked.

"Answer me."

"Relax, she's as attached to you as you are to her. She even used the L-word." His smirk widened, then dropped. "I have to admit, I think I'm a little jealous …"

Captain released his held breath. "She said she loves me?" he whispered.

"Yeah. Don't you?"

"Of course I do," he snapped. "I just didn't know …" He shook his head. "What I don't get is how it's so easy for guys like you to just talk with girls. They're always comfortable around you. Why is it so hard for me to talk with my girlfriend? Why does it feel like it's taking forever to move our relationship forward?" Captain gritted his teeth, not liking to admit his vulnerable feelings.

Theodor leaned forward. His voice softened. "Our military uniforms and family position don't help. And you rarely, if ever, smile … and, from what little I've seen, your flirting skills need some work. Plus, you're always on edge."

"I *have* to be," Captain growled. "I have to protect her, our family, and the country. Rosebud understands."

"Okay. But you're still an intimidating guy. She can be in love with you and still feel the need to maintain a protective distance."

Captain slid out of the booth. "You're right. She's right. Damn. I *still* put work before everything, like dad. I need to fix this."

* * *

"Well?" Commander Donauska grilled from across the War Room table. Other captains and ranking officers from the breadth and length of Ausurnia sat around the table, their hooded faces turned toward the royals.

"She's prepared and still has no contact with anyone," Captain Donauska informed the room.

"And you're certain that we can trust her?" someone inquired from down the table.

Captain bared his fangs. "Who gives you the right to question who I trust?" he thundered back.

"We all have an equal voice here," his father admonished, rapping his knuckles on the table. "Gentlemen, we're here to agree on a course of action should relations with W.I.C. sour. So far, I've negotiated with Commander Jackson that he and his committee will only visit Pontagu Base for their so-called assessment. Every base leader in Ausurnia agrees we should be on high alert and have extra check points along roads and highways." Heads nod around the room.

"Commander Jackson is still insisting on an audience with Annika, isn't he?" Captain asked, the thought souring his stomach. "*She won't be in the room alone. Not while I still live and breathe,*" he thought-projected to his father.

His father waved one of his hands at him. "*Of course, she won't,*" he projected back. Commander Donauska then leaned forward in his seat. "Officers, we all need to agree on the fate of Miss Annika Mullway. Intelligence compiled says that Commander Jackson is in an allied situation with the Rovalkian leader. Even though we still haven't been able to confirm who that leader is, we know they have a personal stake in Miss Mullway. She'll be seen as a martyr to the poor in Rovalkia— giving them hope on some level and giving a reason for her government to catch and condemn her. There's no doubt in my mind that this W.I.C. committee will request her extradition to Rovalkia on their behalf and deliver us an ultimatum if we don't comply with their demands." He paused and looked around the room. "Raise your hand if you stand with us Donauska's in allowing Annika to remain in Ausurnia."

To Captain Donauska's astonishment, all hands went up—a unanimous vote. He knew why *he* wanted her to stay. But what's the main motivation of the others?

"Thank you for understanding the brevity of the situation." Commander Donauska shuffled the papers in front of him. "Myself, my son, and a few others will be present when the committee arrives. We'll update you at the end of the meeting. You are all dismissed."

The officers rose and left, except for Captain Donauska and his father. Once the door closed, Captain exhaled. His father's head raised toward him. "You need to have more faith in our people, son. They're not as selfish as you believe them to be. We are Ausurnians. Loyal down to the core. They took an oath to us, remember? They trust us. If our whole family stands behind an outsider, they understand there's a good reason." He paused. "I can only hope Commander Jackson will slip up just like those Calageeh soldiers and reveal more than he intends."

"He's a hard man," Captain agreed, drawing his lips in a thin line. "We'll need to get Annika to direct the conversation for a revealing answer." He rubbed the side of his face, dread filling his mind at the thought of Annika facing that soulless man.

Commander Donauska stood. "Yes. I've been mulling over those ideas myself. Though Rovalkia's leader wouldn't admit it, we know the kidnapping attempt showed how that picture of you two in the newspapers worked. Don't hold back on the PDA." He made for the door. "And don't forget to inform her. They'll be here in a few days."

TRENT

Tricking A Beast

All was quiet as Annika hurried past the library's front desk. Lettie, the lead librarian, suddenly popped up, holding a stack of books. Annika jumped. *Not as deserted as I hoped. Does that woman ever take a day off?* The woman's piercing scrutiny penetrated her back as Annika turned down the political section and scoured the shelves. She pulled out a large volume from the bottom shelf. *Political Committees and Their Roles.* Annika flipped to the index to find World Intelligence Committee, page 532. She hauled the book to a nearby table and set about finding the page.

BZZZ. Her phone vibrated. She looked around the corner, making sure Lettie remained at her desk and crept deeper into the political section to answer the call. "Yes?" she whispered.

"Rosebud? Are you okay? Why are you so quiet?" Captain implored.

"I'm in the library." Annika glanced behind her. *Were those footsteps?*

"Can you meet me out front? We need to talk. It's urgent."

"Uh—yeah. See you soon."

Lettie took her time inspecting the volume before she looked at Annika with an icy stare. "I don't know if I should allow you to check out this book. It's written in Ausurnian, and I'm sure it's too advanced for you."

"Captain Donauska requested I pick it up," Annika replied in Ausurnian.

The woman's eyes widened as she pushed the large tomb toward her. *BZZZ. BZZZ.* Annika hit the answer button. "Hello?"

Lettie gaped and pointed at the large poster that read no phone calls allowed in the library. "Yeah, Lettie's taking her time. I'm on my way out." Annika hung up, grabbed the book, and strode away, relishing her own boldness.

Captain's car sat idling alongside the curb. The car door opened as she approached. "There you are."

"That woman hates me. One book and she acts like I'm trying to check out the Ausurnian Constitution." She buckled herself in and held the book in her lap. "Oh, and I mentioned you told me to check this book out. I hope that's okay."

"Sure. What'd you get?" he asked as he turned down Main Street.

"*Political Committees and Their Roles.* I want to learn about W.I.C.," she said opening the cover. "There's something on it, but I haven't read it yet." The pages were crisp and bright white, as if the book had never seen the light of day.

"Great minds think alike. The committee meeting is actually what I wanted to talk to you about. They'll be here in a couple of days."

Annika closed the volume as he slowed to a stop behind the herbal shop. Twilight had already activated the little porch light by her door. "It's written in Ausurnian. Could I get your help with translations if I need them?"

"Of course." He reached behind her and grabbed a bag from the back seat. "I brought potato fries in case you're hungry."

Upstairs, Annika filled two cups with water and sat down. Captain sat down in the chair right beside her; his cologne wafted over. "You smell good, as usual."

He poured half the bag of fries on a plate in front of her. "Well, that's good. I aim to please my girl." Captain leaned over and kissed her cheek just as she bit a fry in half. Warm steam filled her mouth as the salty potato made her salivate.

The book sat on the kitchen counter, its brown leather spine facing her. She chewed slowly; her gaze landing back on Captain as her leg bounced under the table. "You said it was urgent that you speak with me?"

The captain swallowed. "It is. I needed to speak to you today. Do you remember how I said committee members are coming to the base?"

"Yes, to do an internal investigation." She dabbed at her lips with a napkin.

"And remember how Commander Jackson had those Calageeh soldiers keep an eye out for you?" He turned in the chair to face her.

She took a sip of water. "Where are you going with this?"

"He's retaliating, remember? One of his push backs is that he's requested a personal audience with you. In person."

Energy began swirling faster down her arms and around her hands. She raised one hand, looking at her fingers, then lowered it back down to rest on the tabletop. "Did you know that when I get angry, my energy pulsates faster down and around my hands? It's how I know when I can form an energy blast. But I still can't see anything. Can you?" She kept her voice soft, swallowing the urge to scream.

He tilted his head. "You're right. Your aura is swirling faster and thickening. Do you sense your shields forming?"

"Yes, it happens unconsciously."

His voice sounded in her mind. *"You won't be able to blast our problems away, Rosebud. If it were that easy, I'd have all our enemies mysteriously dying of heart failure."*

Annika picked at the remaining fries and shook one hand off to the side, trying to dispel the tingles. "I can't help it. I *feel* so much. If my family doesn't understand me, this Commander Jackson certainly won't. And he thinks he can, what, pass judgment on me? Why? Because I'm not running back into Rovalkia with their less-than-nice request? What *is* it about me? Tell me." She flicked at the now stone-cold potatoes, inadvertently sending one airborne. It bounced off the back of the kitchen counter, abutting the table.

"You're special," Captain said, one hand deftly depositing the flung potato on his napkin while the other gloved hand grasped hers. "And they didn't realize *how* special until you were gone. It's a power play. Power for what? I couldn't tell you. This is a new type of political game. That's why we're learning and strategizing in real time." His hand squeezed hers.

She looked back into his face, wishing she could see into his eyes and feel safe there. His lips were now back to their normal, full, relaxed form. "Okay, so what do they do at W.I.C.? Besides monitor the world?"

"They exist because we exist." The captain pulled his hand away from hers. "They exist because the world grew afraid that we would take over, since we've always been superior in technology, weapons, and obviously our psyches. Then there's our superior physical strength, sharp fangs, and cultural obscurity." One of his hands tapped out an indecipherable tune on the tabletop.

She placed her hand atop his, relishing the soft leather. "I'm not afraid, and they shouldn't be. The outside world, in all their ignorance, will continue to destroy themselves just like Rovalkia is because they're not seeing Ausurnia as a powerful ally. I've been here less than a year and am amazed by the resourcefulness and the community of the Ausurnian people." She paused and pulled her hand away. "I should tell you though, your brother propositioned me for a job in his refugee support network." His lips parted, but he remained silent. "I said no, of course. He means well, but I'm not about to abandon you. Your brother says I have a *cayusu.* But I trust your opinion more. Do you think my spirit is strong enough to be in the presence of Commander Jackson?"

Captain stretched both of his hands toward her face as a smile stretched across his own. His hands cradled the sides of her jaw, and he leaned forward. Annika closed her eyes, licked her lips. *This is it! Our first kiss!* His lips caressed the tip of her nose, then her cheek, and as they traveled from that spot toward her lips, her skin tingling in their wake, his phone rang.

"Dammit!" he growled, pulling away. "I am so sorry." He turned his head away as he reached for his phone on the table.

She sat back in her chair, mumbling that it was all right even though she wanted to stomp his phone into dust. He finished the call, hung up, shook his head, and cleared his throat. She took a deep breath as he said, "Security breach of our online systems. Dad's in Fringur, so I have to step in to give direction—"

"Say no more. You're a captain for this very reason." Annika stood, half tripping on her way up, and walked to the door, feeling embarrassed for letting her desire for him cloud the big picture. "It's probably for the best … I mean, if we're to defeat this beast, we *have* to be strong. If I ever desire to see my family again, *I* have to be strong. And the world shows me I am *still* not strong enough." Her voice caught, and she stared at the floor as if to memorize every grain of wood in the planks. Captain's boots and then legs came into view, stopping in front of her. "So, I should keep away from anything and anyone that could be a distraction—for now." Her voice was a mere whisper, and she pulled her hands behind her back while fighting back tears.

Captain swallowed; she peeked up at him through her lashes. His lips were in a tight line. "I've been selfish, Rosebud. You're right, we need to be in the same place before moving our relationship forward. This next week won't be easy. Dad wants us to lay it on thick with the PDA in the commander's presence." His head tilted toward her.

She gaped. "To show him what?"

"That you aren't going anywhere. That there's nothing W.I.C. or Rovalkia could say, or do, or offer, to get you to return to your home country. That you'd never say anything incriminating against Ausurnia because we're in love."

"That …" She thought about it. *What is more powerful than love?* "That could work." She stood straighter. "How could they argue with that? It would imply they'll start a war by breaking up people in love. They'd *never* do that. Would they?" she beseeched, wringing her hands.

The ghost of a smile played on his lips. "I sure hope not. We have something many can only dream of … We'll get through this together. And then I *promise* to make more time for us." His fingertips traced the edge of her jaw, from earlobe to chin, causing shivers to flow through her. "My smart girl," Captain whispered and kissed her just shy of her mouth. "I'll say goodnight, Rosebud. We'll iron out the details right before the meeting, so it'll be fresh in our minds."

Annika continued to stare at the wall where he stood only moments before. Once the door clicked shut, she turned the lock, her forehead resting against the cool surface while her fingertips traced the rough grain of the wood. His footsteps retreated down the steps. When she heard his car engine turning over, she squeezed her eyes shut. Hot tears slipped past her lashes and ran down her face. She wiped them away but more came. *Why'd he have to say that? Why'd he have to use those exact words? Why can't he just take me—*Her head snapped up at the sound of tires sliding on gravel outside. Annika went to the kitchen window, pulled back the curtain, and jumped backward.

Captain Donauska

Her words stung; they'd plunged into his heart, jabbing with each sentence. Why did she think that them being together would affect this fight with Rovalkia? What kind of upbringing did she have that made her want to stay emotionally isolated during hard times? What was she afraid of? What was *he* afraid of?

His foot slammed on the brake, and his hands turned the car around before he registered what was happening. Tires screeched and people honked as he flew through a red light. His car came to an abrupt stop at the base of her stairs and his hands were white knuckling the steering wheel. "Just do it," he urged himself before hopping out of the car and taking the steps two at a time.

BAM! BAM! BAM! He pounded on the door. "Annika! Rosebud! Let me in. We can't leave things like this. We deserve to be together—to do what we want. We're adults, for gods' sake. Please, let me in."

From within, he swore he heard a strangled cry, and the door opened a crack. "I'm not in a good place right now, Captain," she sniffled.

"I know. That's why I came back."

"I don't want you seeing me like this."

"I don't care. If you don't want me to kiss you, let me hold you instead. Let me be *here*—because I'm not leaving until we figure this out." He sensed her move away from the door. With his fingertips, he pushed at the door, and it swung open with ease. In the next instant, Annika was in his arms and wrapping her arms around his neck, tears streaming.

He gathered her up, closed the door with his booted foot, and carried her to the bed. She sat in his lap at the edge of the bed, hiccupping and gasping with his eyes closed, and her head pressed into his neck. He pulled her tighter to him, kissed the top of her head, her forehead, her cheeks, wherever he could reach. "I'm here, love. Deep breaths. I'm here. I love you. I'm not going anywhere," he whispered. Pain was dousing the fire within her, and he felt how fragile she was, this warrior of a woman who repeatedly stared fear in the face; facing moments that would shatter less prepared soldiers. Her strength was cracking, and he could only hope that his love would be the glue.

* * *

He wiped his hands on a dishtowel after breakfast. The morning fog had finally receded, and red leaves peeked out amongst the green trees. His thoughts drifted to Annika; the events of last night came rushing back. He grabbed up his phone to text her, aware her shift started soon.

Good morning, Rosebud.

No.

Good morning, how are you?

No, too formal.

Thinking of you.

No, too creepy.

He punched the backspace button and started again.

Bring you anything?

He stared at the text for a moment, sighed, and punched *Send.*

Damn, I'm bad at this. I'll call the shop.

"Hello?" His grandmother's voice sounded chipper.

"Good morning, Gran. How're you and the shop doing?"

Formalities first.

"Fine, dear. People are getting ready for the cold. We've been selling pounds of tea. Annika makes wonderful flavor combinations. She continues to bloom in her abilities."

Captain cleared his throat. "That's great to hear. Uh, how is she today?" His free hand tapped the kitchen countertop, awaiting her answer. His worry about her combined with the stress at work had his nerves twitching as if he'd drunk too much coffee.

Silence met him.

"Gran?"

"Well… She just walked in, so I can't say for sure. Hold on."

He heard her call Annika over and asked why her eyes were puffy and red. He heard his grandmother then ask what the matter was and why Annika had tears in her eyes.

"Captain just texted me. He cares. He cares even after what I said to him last night. I hadn't meant it, and he saw right through it. He'd called me his smart girl, which brought up some bad memories for me … because of who used to call me that, and, and I just lost it. But he came back. He held me and didn't leave. Do you mind if I text him back and then wash my face?"

"Of course not, dear. Take your time." The sound of a door closed, and the phone picked up again. Captain cleared his throat, trying to swallow down the sudden tightness. "Did you catch any of that?" his grandmother asked. She quickly followed with, "What happened?"

"Yeah, I heard. Well, it started yesterday afternoon. I broke the news that the visiting W.I.C. officers desired an audience with her." He sighed. "And then—it was my fault. I read the moment wrong and there was some awkwardness. She tried to dispel it in her own way, which made me think she was pushing me away, so I left. Then I realized I was being an idiot and came back. She's still tormented, just like you tried to explain to me in the beginning. I just don't know how to help her."

"Some things take time, dear. If her heart is hurting; if it's her past home life that's affecting her, that hurt may never go away. Remember, her small family was all she had. It's a cold, indifferent world where she comes from, and though she's embraced us to a degree, we're still a reminder of what she doesn't have."

"That sounds about right," he said with a sigh and sat down on his couch. "So, what do I do?"

"Do what she asks and respect her boundaries. If she's ready to accept love back, and give her love, you will be there. You have been there for her. No other man can boast that." Her voice was direct, but soft.

"I don't want to lose her, Gran."

"You won't, dear. I've seen the way she looks at you and heard the way she talks about you. Your relationship with her has matured. She's matured. I think now is the time for Annika to teach *us*."

He smiled to himself. "Ever the wisest, Gran. Thank you."

When he hung up, he dialed his father.

"Are we a go?"

"Yeah, dad. We're a go."

Hunting Season

Dawn crept in through the kitchen window. Annika turned over in bed. *BZZZ.* She opened one eye as a text popped up on her cellphone. She reached over and tilted the illuminated screen toward her face.

Time to get up, Rosebud. Text me when you're ready.

Annika groaned and threw the sheets back. Freezing air slapped her bare legs. "When did it get so cold?" she screeched out to the empty room.

Her fingertips fumbled as she tied up her shiny black Rovalkian leather boots and pulled the hems of her fitted black jeans over the high tops. She purposely left the top two buttons undone on her maroon blouse, exposing her necklace to the world. *Commander Jackson will see a Rovalkian before him, forged with a new strength from Ausurnia.* She flipped the kettle switch off and drank a glass of water instead.

In the bathroom, she brushed her hair and wound it up into a classic Rovalkian bun, tight and high. Turning this way and that in front of the mirror, she tucked loose strands in place. *You don't have to hide who you are anymore. You are Annika.* She walked back to the dining table and messaged Captain Donauska.

Ready for pickup.

The captain honked his horn outside just as she pulled on her beloved red woolen jacket. A glance around her little abode reminded her of what she had. *You're free.* They wouldn't take that away. *I'm no longer just "a smart girl." I'm a free, intelligent woman. You don't know what you're in for, Commander Jackson.*

* * *

"Try to let your actions speak more than your words," Captain said as he pulled into the base parking lot. "They'll read your body language the moment we walk in. Try to exude extra confidence and only a little anger—that keeps them guessing. If you have questions about what they say, thought-project to me. There's nothing they can do to hinder that, at least." One of his leather gloved hands creaked as it tightened around the steering wheel while the other gave her hand a reassuring squeeze. She wondered if he was as nervous as she was, but didn't want him to think she didn't trust him.

They parked, but he didn't unlock the door. She turned to him. He wore a frown, looking back at her. "What?" She looked around. "What did I miss?"

"Nothing. I'm thinking preemptively. I don't know who's watching and from where. You must act off me and I you. Ready?"

She looked out the window for a second. *Better get my shields up, too.* "I'm as ready as I'll ever be." She tried to smile big, but it felt weak. "I'm glad we're together. I hate pretending."

Captain pulled her hand to his lips, let a kiss sit on the back of her fingers until her smile transformed into a real one, and met that smile with his own. "Stay. I'll come around and open your door."

His firm grip reassured her. She raised her chin and kept her head forward as they went through security. The front desk personnel gave each a silent nod. Soldiers scuttled, by saluting Captain Donauska while indistinct murmurs emanated from beyond the few doors that remained open. It was an unsettling quiet, a stark contrast from last time. Annika gulped and tightened her grip on his hand. He returned the extra pressure. *"Do not be nervous, Rosebud. It'll turn in our favor in the end."*

The next hallway they stepped into looked familiar. Near the end, two Ausurnian guards, along with two guards of unknown origin, stood at attention on either side of the War Room doors. One of the unknown soldiers stepped forward. In Truscan, he asked to see their identification. Annika handed over her papers, and Captain proffered his military card. While the soldier inspected each document, Annika observed him and the others. Both mystery men wore the same military uniform design as a Rovalkian officer with angled wrist cuffs and missing collars. But their uniforms were a dark blue, instead of Rovalkia's dark green. Large gold embroidered W.I.C. letters stood out above the name badge, and they stood at attention, along with the Ausurnian officers.

That's when she noticed how formal the Ausurnian guards looked. They wore a sash this time and the black leather of their vest armor and gloves shone. *First impressions matter.*

The W.I.C. guard handed back their documents and briefly touched his ear, turning away to speak low to whoever was listening on the other end. Captain stayed facing forward, a serious frown on his face. The Ausurnian guards also remained motionless.

"Why are your guards not doing anything?" She thought-projected to Captain.

"We know who is here. They don't. And because they're in our territory, they're hyper-concerned about an ambush or about something going awry."

"Okay," the W.I.C. guard said aloud, and the two Ausurnian guards opened the double doors.

The room was brightly lit this time. Broad-shouldered figures occupied every seat around the oblong conference table. Captain led her inside and over to the Ausurnian side of the table. Only then did Annika sense the auras of the visitors.

Most were unaffecting, but as her eyes traveled down the table, the auras became heavier. Captain brought her to a halt behind his father, halfway down the table. Annika's gaze froze on the man sitting opposite Commander Donauska. Her scalp tingled. He stared back at her with beady, black eyes. His thick neck threatened to spill over his collar and red blotchy patches dotted his cheeks. Below the medals and stitched gold letters of W.I.C., Annika saw the name she loathed. Commander Jackson.

For a long moment, they stared at each other. The room remained silent around them until Commander Donauska swiveled in his chair. He nodded to them before turning back around. "Commander Jackson and esteemed guests of W.I.C., I'd like to introduce you to my son and heir, Captain Donauska. And his partner, Miss Annika Mullway." His deep voice boomed off the walls of the windowless room.

Heads nodded toward them. Annika's attention went to the end of the table where a blue W.I.C. uniformed officer stood and saluted them the Ausurnian way. He had a blue hood attachment like that of the black Ausurnian uniform. Captain Donauska acknowledged him with his right fist to his chest.

The last one to acknowledge them gazed at Annika, unperturbed. As she stared back, the black of Commander Jackson's eyes struck her. *There's nothing there. No life, no feeling. They say you can see a*

273

person's soul in their eyes, but this man's eyes are empty. She steeled herself.

"My God, you're the spitting image of him!" Commander Jackson shouted. Annika narrowed her eyes as everyone turned their heads to him. "Did Rovalkia grow you in a lab, girl? You look like the female version of Kraxxan." He cackled; the forced, sharp sound pinged in Annika's ears at wrong angles, and she grimaced despite herself.

"Her *name* is Miss Mullway. And you will address her as that, *Commander,*" Captain retorted. Annika looked up at her partner, admiring his sneer that allowed his fangs to be on full display, in all their sharp glory.

Commander Jackson chuckled, a sneer of his own aimed at Captain Donauska.

"Gentlemen," Commander Donauska boomed. "We must remember to speak respectfully to *all* in attendance. If you don't feel you can do that, please leave the room now." He scanned the room before pausing at Commander Jackson. No one spoke or moved. "Good. As I'm sure you have more important matters to address, I'll help make this brief and to the point. Miss Mullway is before you. You see my son. You are now witness to their attachment. Half of you are married with children. You understand that once a young couple is in love, there is no separating them until *they* decide to. These two are no different. Miss Mullway stays in Ausurnia because she is *welcome* in Ausurnia. We are not here to judge her life choices, as we believe that to be a job for the gods. So, I pose a question to you, Commander Jackson. What business of it is W.I.C. to intrude on this young woman's life?"

Commander Jackson steeled his cold eyes on the Ausurnian king. "*My* business is that of monitoring and understanding Ausurnia's secret ways. We know Ausurnia is connected somehow to those missing individuals in Rovalkia and Calageeh. The question is why? Are you using them as slaves? As sacrifices? I'll expose you, and I have a good feeling that Miss Mullway here will be your undoing—provided she is forthcoming with the truth."

Angry grumbling bounced around the table. Captain let go of Annika's hand and stepped up to the table's edge. He placed his fisted hands on the surface and leaned closer to Commander Jackson. "If those missing persons are running away versus being rounded up like what *we* believe is happening, it speaks *volumes* more about Rovalkia and Calageeh. There's *nothing* to expose here," he hissed. "And there's nothing to be said of Annika that will alter how I feel about her. Ausurnia will stand long after you and other countries crumble to dust."

Her stomach somersaulted. Annika stared at the two men locked in their verbal battle. *What's to expose?*

The corner of Commander Jackson's mouth twitched.

"Captain Donauska, please step back to where Miss Mullway is," Commander Donauska warned. "This is a discussion. No need to be so protective."

Captain Donauska stood back up. *"Rosebud, do you see what Commander Jackson is doing with his body language, his facial expressions? He's a ruthless, self-serving man. He savors how he thinks he knows something we don't. It's the real reason we allowed him here. To use his ego against him and get information. Remember, we're playing a political game. Ask him something and see for yourself."*

"Sirs," Annika said to the room. No one acknowledged her. She cleared her throat. "Sirs!"

Everyone turned their heads. Her heart dropped to her stomach as she glanced around the room. Captain Donauska straightened the rest of the way up and stepped back to her side. He placed a hand on the small of her back and she took a step forward, forcing herself to stare into Commander Jackson's soulless eyes. His grin widened to reveal yellow, albeit straight, teeth. Annika fought against the bile rising in her throat. "Commander Jackson, why am I *physically* here attending this inquiry?"

The commander leaned back in his seat, looking pleased with himself. He pointed at her. "Just like your father." Annika widened her eyes. Commander Jackson leaned to the side and pointed behind her. "I understand why you, a prince, would be interested in her. A great man raised her. Always straight to the point." He looked back at Annika. "I respect that."

"*You* have met my father, Orrin Mullway? Under what circumstances?"

Commander Jackson chuckled, still wearing a smile. "While conducting business, of course." Annika had the overwhelming urge to spit in his face as an unfamiliar voice spoke in her mind, deeper in tone than the captain's voice. *"Annika, this is Commander Donauska. Act like this latest information doesn't faze you. It'll drive him mad, which will drive him to reveal more. We won't let anything happen to you."*

Annika shrugged. "So what? My dad knows tons of people. He works in the government, so it goes along with the territory."

Commander Jackson's smile faltered as soldiers tittered, red blotches spreading across his entire head. He raised a finger at Annika. "Fine. I'll play along. So, you feel comfortable in your newfound position here, huh? Then prove to me that you're still a Rovalkian."

The room erupted into chaos. Accusations and questions shot across the table. Several officers stood, pointing at one another. *I don't understand. Prove I'm still a Rovalkian? I have my Rovalkian ID, and my work visa is still active.* She turned to Captain Donauska. *BAM!* Annika jumped at the sound and Captain caught her in his arms. "It's okay. Dad's just regaining order," he whispered in her ear.

She peeked back around; now aware how silent the room had become. On the tabletop, Commander Donauska's large, gloved hand stretched out. Slowly, he retracted his hand, letting it drag across the dark wood; the soft swiping of leather against the smooth lacquered surface sent tingles through Annika.

Commander Donauska folded his hands. "You're out of line, Commander Jackson. We need not question her nationality. You know the rules we live by, so you'd better have a *damn* good reason to waste our time on such a test."

Commander Jackson folded his hands on the table and leaned forward. "You do the test and present me a copy of the negative results, and I'll take my men and leave peacefully."

"Peacefully? Or what? And for whom are these results?" the Ausurnian King grilled, his voice razor sharp. "You're too intelligent to try anything stupid while in *my* country, sir."

Annika clamped her jaw together. *A test to check my ethnicity?* Images of people in lab coats holding large drills popped into her head. *"Uh, Captain. How does one test for ethnicity?"* Silence followed. Annika looked up at him, seeing his head give a minute shake.

"You misunderstand me, sir. I wouldn't dare break the rules that govern W.I.C. We'll leave regardless, I can assure you." Commander Jackson unfolded his hands and laid them flat on the table. "The test results are for W.I.C. records, of course."

Annika folded her arms, and her ears pricked at his words. "But you'll *bend* the rules. Like picking sides."

A deep, booming guffaw rose from the man in front of her. Commander Donauska's torso shook as his laugh grew louder. She glanced up to Captain Donauska to find the corner of his mouth twitch and stretch into a sly grin. He patted her on the back reassuringly, and Annika turned back to face Commander Jackson.

The red in his face had traveled down to his neck. He blinked three times in rapid succession, making his eyes appear wet.

King Donauska swiveled around in his chair to face Annika. She looked at him, balling her hands into fists, feeling a reprimand coming despite his laughter. "Child, you are a breath of fresh air, calling a man three times your size out like that. Very astute."

Okay, so not in trouble. "Sir, if I may ask. What is the test?" Annika opened and closed her hands, feeling tendrils of energy flow around each finger. *Is there a possibility the test will show an Ausurnian in my family history?*

A gloved hand took hold of hers and she followed the arm up to Captain Donauska's lips. "It's a simple blood test. They draw blood from your arm and run it through a machine that tells us your ancestral history. All in a matter of minutes."

"I don't fancy anyone having my blood," she said as she raised her chin.

"The medic destroys the sample once they complete the test, and will conduct the procedure in this room," Commander Donauska assured.

She looked into the commander's hooded face and sensed a confident calm about him. Then she looked up into Captain's face. He gave a small nod, followed by a squeeze of her hand. She finally turned to face Commander Jackson. The redness in his face and neck had receded to the constant blotchy spots on his cheeks. But a frown had carved itself on his face, and a sweaty sheen reflected the overhead light off his skin.

"If the King of Ausurnia requests I prove my heritage, I shall," she declared in Ausurnian. The Ausurnians in the room clapped while the redness in Commander Jackson's cheeks spread again.

Commander Donauska sent one of his men to fetch the medic and testing machine.

"Miss Mullway." Commander Jackson refolded his hands and leaned forward. "I do what I do to keep the peace. I understand you've been in Ausurnia for only a few seasons. That's hardly enough time to have such an informed opinion of a culture, especially one that is shrouded in so much mystery."

The energy around her fingers prickled and danced. "And you think *I* will be Ausurnia's undoing?" She rolled her shoulders back and lifted her chin once more. She felt ready for a good fight. "You're here talking about keeping the peace and doing business in Rovalkia while Rovalkians are the one's doing the disappearing, the killing, the displacing, and gods know what else. Did you know there was a kidnapping attempt on me recently?"

Commander Jackson shook his head. "Slandering your own country, how sad."

"No," Annika shot back. "How sad for *you*. We know—can prove, even—what you deny. It shows where your interests lay. You disgust me." The side of one of her nostrils ticked.

"*I* disgust *you*? Are you blind? You're in the middle of a country of monsters, Miss Mullway. Do you know of their poisonous blood? One bite kills in battle. What about their night stalking?" Commander Jackson tilted his head to one side, smirking.

A deep growl rolled from Captain Donauska, and Annika glanced over to see his barred his fangs. His father held up a hand, to which the captain's growl subsided. Commander Donauska then turned his head to the left. "Miss Mullway, you may continue to speak your mind and ask us any question in this man's presence. We've nothing to hide. This has become most entertaining ..."

Annika glared into the greasy looking face of Commander Jackson. "Oh, I have plenty to say. I speak their language, I read their books, I dine with them, *and* I'm in a relationship with the Prince of Ausurnia. You think I lack comprehension of the fact that, after a millennium of social isolation, there's a logical difference in their biological makeup?" Waves of energy flowed up and down her arms, and her mind cleared as her anger increased. "You claim to know my father, but it seems you don't know him as much as you should, if at all. For if you knew him, you'd know he has always placed education as the highest priority for his children. They taught me knowledge is our greatest weapon, and that a sharp mind is always sharper than a sword. So instead of playing with friends, I read. Instead of learning the craft of homemaking, I read. Instead of cooking over a stove, I read." She paused for effect. "Every single book in his library and more. I'm not so ignorant as to believe your slander, sir. Their teeth may be sharp, but they are not vipers, and your attempt to scare me has me thinking all the less of you."

The commander's mouth bobbed open and close, and Captain's hand tightened on hers. *"Calm your energies, love. We don't need an accident happening if you release it."*

The War Room's doors opened, and everyone's attention diverted to the soldier that walked in with a medic identification band on one sleeve, pushing a white machine on a cart. Commander Donauska directed them to set up near Annika. They set two extra chairs down. The medic sat in one while they turned on the machine; a whirling sound grew in volume.

Annika didn't move, instead she continued to stare at the medic. *Will they be able to find any blood?* she wondered as she felt the blood drain from her face. Just then, a thick plait of black hair slipped out of the medic's hood. Annika blinked, not believing what she saw. Captain pulled their held hands forward to direct her closer, and she obeyed. He didn't follow, so she had to let go of his hand.

She sat down while focusing in on the medic's lower facial features. A slender jawline hid within the folds of the hood. *The medic is a female? There are females in the Ausurnian army!* She smiled at the medic, and the woman inclined her head to Annika, returning the smile.

"My superior officer thought you'd be more comfortable with a female performing the test since you come from a more conservative society," the medic said.

Annika smirked and spoke in Ausurnian. "They're right. It is comforting. All this male energy can be a bit *much*." Chuckles resounded.

Beyond those chuckles was hushed, angry mumbling. Annika turned her head to see who it was, but she didn't see anyone except Captain standing nearby. The other Ausurnians were still seated in their chairs. Captain massaged her shoulder. "Ignore them, love. We'll get you out of here soon. There's nothing to stress about."

The medic took off her leather gloves and replaced them with medical ones. "And I'm good at this, so you won't feel a thing," she said, motioning for Annika to come closer. On a tray in front of the whistling machine, the medic had laid out a small glass tube, a plastic box, and a needle. "Please take off your jacket and roll up your left sleeve," the woman instructed. Her movements were slow and steady; trustworthy.

Annika unbuttoned her jacket with numb fingers, and Captain helped to lay it over the back of her chair. She tugged the long sleeve of her dark red blouse up and held it there. "May I ask your name?"

"Cadet Pasteur, at your service." She grinned at Annika, exposing brilliant white teeth. Her fangs were like Tiana's, shorter than her male cousins but no less sharp looking.

"You look fam—" Annika began.

"Hey, what's going on over there?" Commander Jackson bellowed. "I demand to see the test being performed."

A low growl sounded from soldiers on the Ausurnian side. "Calm down, gentlemen. He has a right. All of you, move a few inches to whichever side of the room you are closer to," the king ordered. Chairs and bodies scuffled down, and Annika rolled her eyes at Cadet Pasteur, who nodded in agreement. Annika glanced back to see the sweaty, beady eyed commander staring at them, his view now unobstructed.

Cadet Pasteur took a deep breath and muttered to Annika in Ausurnian. "Let's get this over with quick. That man is giving off terrible

281

energy." She scooted closer and swabbed Annika's arm with alcohol. Annika blinked at the cold sensation. "Thank you for having such easy veins to find."

She blinked again when Medic Pasteur inserted the needle. Pasteur pulled back the syringe handle, drawing millimeters of blood out of Annika's vein. When it reached a half an inch full, Pasteur pulled the needle out. She covered the wound with gauze and dispensed the blood into a small vial. The vial then went into a slotted drawer, which Medic Pasteur locked into the machine. She punched a button, and the box whined for a minute as different colored boxes flashed on the screen. Annika held her breath. Medic Pasteur hit the same button, and the whining stopped. She kept her attention on the screen as a quiet fell over the room.

"You, Miss Mullway, have ancestral DNA from Calageeh and Rovalkia ... but there is one percent that's undetectable. That just means it's so far back in your history that the DNA has little to no effect on who you are."

Annika pursed her lips. *Is that one percent Ausurnian? What are the consequences of having Ausurnian genetics? Why do these W.I.C. people think I have Ausurnian DNA in me?* Cadet Pasteur pushed more buttons and little slips printed out. Captain took the stack and handed them out. He handed the last one to Annika, and she stuffed it in her pocket without looking at it. She just wanted to go home. Away from all these strangers. Away from that black-hearted, black-eyed man. Annika watched as the medic placed the specimen and needle into a red bag with a biohazard symbol.

Officers around the table stood and collected their notebooks. Annika turned in her chair, Commander Jackson's stare meeting hers once more. His face became redder as he pointed at her. "I don't know what witchcraft is going on here, but I can tell you this young lady: they will *never* accept you. You will *never* be their equal. Mark my words, one day you will call us for help, and we will turn our backs on you as you have done with us on this day. Your father thinks we can save your soul, but it's very clear we have lost you to these monsters." With that, he heaved himself up out of his chair and stormed out of the room.

Captain Donauska laid a hand on Annika's arm. "Time to go, Rosebud. It's over."

"Good riddance," Medic Pasteur mumbled as she fussed with the machine. Annika only chewed on her lower lip.

"What's wrong, love?" Captain asked.

"What he said about my dad wanting to save my soul ..."

"He's pulling at straws. He made it up."

Or he knows my father, she thought.

The Beasts Sting

Captain Donauska

Logs crackled with an orange glow in the fireplace of the communal area, emitting a gentle warmth as Annika and Tiana sat deep in a discussion on the seats closest to it. Captain stared at Annika through his peripheral vision, contemplating how empty his world would be without her. Theodor set down the two refilled coffee cups from the snack cart and dropped onto the couch.

"Dang, Theo. If you sat down any harder, this couch would snap."

Giggles pealed from across the room. "Yeah, Theodor. We felt the vibration all the way over here," Tiana cried out.

Theodor chuckled along with them while Captain snatched his coffee and took a long sip, the scalding brew burning all the way down, reminding him of nights on missions when they tried to stay warm.

He glanced at his watch, knowing the recently returned troops from Rovalkia reported to his father hours ago. They just had to keep Annika preoccupied until his father gave the all clear, just in case the mission had gone south and a Rovalkian government employees were killed. It wouldn't help the situation if Annika thought her father was dead. The Donauska family had voted unanimously on the clubhouse as the location to while away the time. His grandmother had made an excuse to give Annika the day off when he and Tiana walked in.

His focus slipped to the fire, brooding about being left out of this major infiltration mission. A group of his soldiers, led by Second Lieutenant Baar, had broken into the Rovalkian capitol, and collected DNA samples from every room they could, as well as computer data and paper evidence. "You're too close, son," his father had explained. "We need whatever is found to get back to us in one piece, without distractions getting in the way. Commander Jackson's top priority is to take a bite out of us."

Captain had jeered at the mental image and rolled his eyes. "Like his normal teeth could do any damage."

"My cousin, Medic Pasteur, said you were nervous after the test results. How come?"

His ears pricked, and he glanced over at the girls, noticing his brother was doing the same. *That was days ago. Why is Tiana bringing it up now?*

"That was your cousin? That makes sense. She looks like you, from what I could see under her hood. Anyway, I let the things Commander Jackson said get to me. Rovalkia seems obsessed with me through my dad, but why? He's the one that kicked me out of his house. He must be pushing them to find me. He always has to be right and always proves it." Annika looked into the mug she held. "Maybe Commander Jackson somehow struck a deal with the Rovalkian leader. Maybe that's why those Rovalkian soldiers said the leader wants me."

285

"Don't listen to him, Rosebud," Captain shouted. Everyone turned their attention to him. "That man fights dirty with psychological warfare. Listen to us and remember how unaffected my dad was by his words. Have patience."

Annika responded with a small nod. The room darkened, and they looked up at the clubhouse's skylights as clouds passed overhead. He gazed back at Annika. She chewed her lip and laid a hand on her necklace.

His phone vibrated. He pulled it from his trouser pocket, sprang up, and snuck down a deserted corridor. "What's the news?"

"Not good," his father replied. "I triple checked the results because I couldn't believe them myself." He proceeded to fill his son in on various bits of information gathered.

"So, there is a connection—"

"Yes. And trust me when I say I *still* can't believe what I'm reading. Bring Annika here to the house." Then the commander whispered the results.

Captain whistled. "Good gods. Should I tell Theo and Tiana to go home?"

"They can come too. This won't be easy, and I'm not sure how Annika will react."

"And Gran? Should I pick her up on the way?"

"I know she cares, but she has her shop to run and is supposed to be retired. I'll catch her up later."

Captain hung up and turned around. Theodor had the girls' attention on his phone, probably having deduced his brother needed privacy for that call. He whispered a thanks to Theodor and then called out, "We're going." He tried to keep his voice steady as the girls gave him quizzical looks. "Our parents are having us all over for dinner and have news to share with Annika beforehand about the latest mission in Rovalkia." Annika and Tiana exchanged looks.

Coming over to him and grabbing his hand, Annika asked, "What's happened with the mission?"

Captain squeezed her hand but didn't—couldn't reply, and just shook his head once. *What's wrong is I can't protect you from the truth. And I hate myself for whatever comes next.*

Annika

The girls climbed into the back seat while Theodor rode up front with his brother. Theodor kept asking questions about the mission, and Captain answered in terse sentence fragments. Annika's pulse quickened, sensing his growing agitation. Main Street sped by. Outside, the colors of autumn were showing off with golden yellows, neon oranges, and fiery reds enlivening the trees bordering the street. The weaker leaves released their grip, brushing against shoppers and cars before joining their brethren on the cobblestones to become imprints underfoot.

She drummed her fingertips on her lap in anticipation as Captain pulled up to his parents' house. Tiana squeezed her hand. "I'm okay, Tiana," Annika said, trying to smile through the lie, hoping that it disguised the murmur of butterflies in her stomach. Tiana squeezed her hand again and looked out the front window, biting her lip.

Ista strode from the house, her arms outstretched, approaching Annika first. "Hello again, beautiful. It's been too long." She encompassed Annika in a hug and Annika hugged back, relishing the motherly embrace, but Ista didn't release her when she tried to pull back.

"Mom, you're smothering her." Captain admonished, pulling Annika away.

Ista released Annika into the Captain's arms and turned to fuss over Tiana for a moment before greeting her sons with a hand to each of their cheeks.

A heavier aura, coming from the house, pressed around Annika. She and the others turned to see Commander Donauska step onto the front stairs. He waved them in as a heavy mist began to fall.

Commander Donauska led them to the family room and motioned to the couch. "Have a seat, everyone. We need to talk first." He sat down in the biggest armchair. Captain sat on the couch, pulling Annika down beside him on his left. He intertwined their fingers while he curled his right hand around the armrest to anchor himself.

Annika wished she could enjoy the smells emanating from the kitchen, but any appetite she'd had fled. Ista sat down next to Annika and Tiana sat cross-legged in the other armchair.

Theodor settled down on the loveseat opposite. He sipped at a hot drink from a tray on the dining table and leaned back, allowing one long arm to stretch along the back. He made eye contact with Annika and winked, a toothy smile following. She blinked and raised an eyebrow in question.

"Knock it off, Theo," Captain barked.

Commander Donauska turned his head. "Sit up straight, Theodor. This is serious."

The young man obeyed, bringing his feet together as he crossed his arms and glowered down toward the floor. "I'm just trying to lighten the mood."

Annika glanced around the room nervously. *Is this the final judgment? Have they used every loophole allowing me to stay? But these are the rulers of Ausurnia. They must be able to bend the rules if they wanted.* Annika slid her left hand to the couch and under her leg. *Maybe the rebels agreed to take me in.*

At that moment, Commander Donauska pulled a folder from the side of his chair and laid it on his lap. Annika spied the big red lettered stamp, **CONFIDENTIAL,** near the top, and her shoulders quivered in angst. She swallowed, raising her eyes to study the King of Ausurnia's stern face. They sat looking at each other for an everlasting moment.

"Miss Mullway, we have concluded our hunt for the leader of Rovalkia," he said as his gloved fingers tapped the file on his lap. The light *TICK, TICK, TICK,* filling the silent room.

That wasn't what she'd expected him to say. She sat up straighter, trying to remain optimistic. "That's great. So, who is he? Is it the guy on the posters? We can go after him now, right?"

"It's more complicated than that, Rosebud," Captain murmured, his thumb rubbing the back of her hand along the scar left by the cut she got in the woods. "The leader has run the country into the ground. There's no point trying to take him out because there is nothing but a colossal mess to take over. The entire system needs to be rewritten. Rioters and peaceful protesters alike are being met with irrational violence." He paused. "Which tells us the leader is getting desperate for his hold on the country."

Annika stared into his hooded face. "That's easy to believe. Did the rebels' retreat or—"

"There were never any rebels," Commander Donauska grated. "We are past that now." Annika expected to hear the windows rattle from the boom in his voice. She whipped her head over to him, narrowing her eyes.

"What do you mean, never any rebels?" She let each word draw itself out.

"We were—" Captain began.

"Not yet," his father barked.

Annika turned her head from father to son, uncertain of whom to focus on. She looked at Tiana when neither man spoke. Her friend's lips and eyebrows furrowed as she stared at her uncle. There was no hint she knew what was going on, either. *No one's being helpful here.* As energy traveled faster down her arms, Annika looked at Ista.

289

"Try to remain calm, child," Ista soothed.

Annika whipped her head to the commander. "I'm *not* a child. Just tell me what the Void is going on so I can figure out what to do next." She heard her voice wobble. *My whole existence rests in the Donauska's control.*

"You're quite right, Miss Mullway. I'll get to the point." Commander Donauska's jaw worked, his neck muscles bulging. "You have a family member holding a high position in the government."

She scrunched her brows, her eyes closing as she reached up and massaged her throbbing temples. "That doesn't make sense. That'd suggest we had more money—because families share their wealth. More is what we never had. My parents live in the same housing block as all the other government workers, and we drove the same car my whole life. My clothes were the same as all the other kids. We learned from home because we didn't have enough money for private school. Public schools barely stay open with the little funding they receive. My parents saved every single penny so we could go to the coast for vacation. Why and how could they concoct such a big lie?"

Captain turned to her and grabbed ahold of her other hand. "Your parents didn't lie outright. Your country doesn't have money, full stop. They don't even have loans out with their allied countries. Since the revolution, your country's been trying to run with a hundred percent self-sufficiency, which doesn't work. Our men went into the basement and found ledgers showing how they've exported everything while leaving nothing for future generations."

She looked down at her hands, feeling the pulsating energy calm down. Ista repositioned herself on the cushion. Annika tilted her head toward the Queen of Ausurnian. *"I'm sorry for my outburst, Ista. My emotions got the better of me."*

"There's nothing to be sorry about, Annika," Ista replied aloud, rubbing Annika's shoulder. "We're here for support. But we'll leave you alone with my husband and son for privacy if you'd prefer."

"I'm staying," Tiana burst out.

Commander Donauska pointed a finger at her. "Tiana, you'll be the first I kick out of the room if I feel inclined."

Tiana shrunk back, mumbling, "Yes, sir."

Annika's gaze hardened on the king. "Okay, so we don't have money. I already *knew* that. What does this have to do with the leader of Rovalkia?"

Theodor leaned forward. "My underground contacts told us your family *is* the connection—"

"And we can trust these contacts? For all we know, they've been leading me to get kidnapped again." Theodor gave her a pained look, and she immediately regretted her words. "I'm sorry, Theodor. I'm just … scared."

"We know, Annika. I can assure you his part *was* pivotal. He knows who to trust and from whom to get reliable information," the commander explained. "It's his job."

Annika looked to the floor, then raised her eyes to meet Theodor's hard, amber stare. "Thank you," she whispered.

"Water under the bridge," he said, his eyes softening.

Captain's hand hold tightened. Annika looked up at his face and he turned toward her. "Your family—your father has been lying to you your whole life," he said. At the same moment, she felt a wall of energy block her from reading him as she reached out her psyche, and the stern frown on his lips brought her back to when she swiveled around on the barstool upon arriving in Pontagu. He hadn't given her permission to read him. She swallowed guiltily and willed herself to speak.

"Okay. So, what's *his* position in all this?"

"He's the leader of Rovalkia."

"What?!" Tiana screeched, vaulting off the chair.

"Bahahaha!" Annika laughed. *Of all the absurd allegations!* She closed her eyes and chuckled more. All her tension slipped away as she wiped her eyes. "Good one, Captain. I needed that." Then she looked up, noticing how no one had joined in the laughter.

Everyone was staring at her. Tiana still stood, gaping while Ista and Theodor had questioning looks in their eyes. The commander and Captain wore deep frowns.

"Why isn't anyone laughing? That was a joke, right?" Annika looked at Captain. "Right?"

He shook his head in one slow move. Annika turned to Commander Donauska and pleaded, "It's not possible. You must've gotten it wrong. There's no way. I would've known." She chewed on her lip when no one answered. "Ah," she said and clicked her fingers together. "They must've tricked you. How else could your men have gotten into the Capitol? Why aren't they retaliating right now? There's no way. Maybe my dad thinks I'll return home faster if I think he's in control?"

"Annika, DNA doesn't lie," Commander Donauska sighed, sounding too tired to argue. "His fingerprints and hair follicles were on surfaces in the basement and in the best guarded offices that only the highest-ranking officials have access codes to. And we know *he* wasn't the office clerk because we connected another man to that job." He tapped the file on his lap again. "And there *were* guards. Twice as many as last time. They were expecting our move, and they know we have too much on them to risk drawing attention to themselves. We finally have the upper hand. And you helped us with that as you promised from the beginning."

Annika stared at him as her stomach sank. She thought of the Rovalkian soldiers chasing her, of how big and strong they were. *Gods, what the halls of the Capitol must've looked like ... Bodies everywhere*

292

... Then she met Tiana's gaze and noticed her friend's sad eyes as she swallowed back the bile that rose in her throat. *I played a direct role in this bloodshed by playing along. Tracy tried to warn me about bloodshed, but I didn't listen.*

"Baar went, Annika. It's true. I wasn't allowed to tell you about the mission. But they found what they needed to find. They did their job. They wouldn't lie, Ro."

Annika stared down at the coffee table. "No, I don't believe it. I can't," she whispered. She turned to Theodor, pleading. "Couldn't there be a possibility one of your contacts is a double agent?" Theodor gave her a sad smile and shook his head.

"Rosebud," Captain implored. She turned to him. "There's more."

"Oh, gods. Are James and Sarah all right?" Her body went numb. *Please, no. Please.*

"They're alive and well, Annika. We told you we'd keep them safe. They and your mother are none the wiser. That, or your mother plays a good game, too. What he means is that we got hold of your family tree." Commander Donauska opened the file and pulled out a folded paper. "This is a copy of what my men took."

He passed it to his wife, who handed it to Annika. Then Ista moved closer to her husband and took his hand. Captain unfolded the paper when Annika didn't and held it out in front of her. She took it by the tips of her fingers as if it were poisonous. The color copy revealed a parchment with the 'Mullway' family name scrolled in opulent green looping letters along the top.

"I've never seen this before. Where'd you find it?" She let her fingers trace the lines downward. Her family tree's base began with her great grandfather; near the top were her, James, and Sarah's names; each recorded with their date of birth.

"In a guarded records room," the commander said.

293

Captain took the edge closest to him, look underneath, and folded it over. A stamp of the Rovalkian seal showed in gold wax and Annika leaned in closer, whispering, "I've only heard rumors about what the seal looks like." The image of a snake swallowing a sword, just like the one depicted on the flag, filled the center. Around the outer circle read: "Mullway to Govern Rovalkia, So Long as Kraxxan Is God."

Annika stood holding the paper. "They didn't proclaim Kraxxan as our only god until the revolution; during my great-grandfather's time when he'd started a family." The paper shook in her trembling hands as she paced across the room. "Why—"

"Does this mean Annika is next in line to be Rovalkia's leader? Is she like—like a princess?" Tiana hissed out.

Annika raised her head. She stared at the wall behind Commander Donauska as all the memories of her sheltered life and all her father's teachings replayed in her mind. One by one, every rule and lesson preached to her by her father fit together like a puzzle. The complete picture clicked into focus. *I was being groomed. Not only to work in government, but to be the head of said government. To be an authoritarian leader.* Her family tree slipped from her hands, sliding to the floor. She forced her words out through gritted teeth. "So, you're telling me that all the executions, arrests, poverty, fear mongering, and crumbling infrastructure are because of *my* family?" Her whole body trembled, and no one spoke. She opened her mouth to ask again, but the words stuck in her throat. *The words have to be spoken. The truth has to be told.*

She tried once more. "He killed my friend." Her voice trembled along with her body, and she cried out once more, "And I said I was going to *kill* the leader. I've said so many things ..."

"No one would ever hold you to those things," Ista said, her voice wobbling.

Annika sank down to the floor.

Captain Donauska

She dropped like a petal released from a rose. His Rosebud, wilting before she bloomed. No one else in the room spoke. *Do any words exist that could make her feel better?* Someone sniffled. He glanced over to see his mother wipe her eyes. His father handed her his handkerchief and said, "Everyone out of the room except these two." Theodor and Tiana scrambled out of the room after them.

Captain slid off the couch and crouched in front of her as she sat hunched forward, her legs bent to the side. She gazed at the parchment laying face up. "I can't kill my father," she whispered. "Nor do I desire harm to befall him. It's just not right. How could he do this to me?" She raised her tear-filled emerald eyes to him. "But my country needs help. I won't abandon them with what I know now."

He pulled his gloves off, and with one hand, placed his palm on the side of her face. She blinked. The tears ran down her cheeks, pooling at his hand and then spilling over his fingers. Her aura swirled, distorted and blue as an erratic vibration emanated from her. He cleared his throat and said the one thing that came to mind. "I understand."

Annika closed her eyes, leaning into his hand as more tears fell. He pushed the parchment further away and brought his left hand up to cradle the other side of her face. She opened her eyes, her absolute sadness hitting him in the chest.

"Let us help you, love. This is Theodor's area of strength. He helps people in struggling countries the world over. His networking skills mirror my military smarts. I can keep training you to become strong physically and psychically while he teaches you the power of words and how to weaponize them. The type of man your father is, he won't admit defeat easily. But with you on our side, we can pool our strengths and corner him until he bends to our will.

Her green eyes darted back and forth, raising a hand up and placing it tentatively on his wrist. He moved the pads of his thumbs over her cheeks, wiping away the sorrow glistening on her skin; weighing his heart. He pleaded to the gods to make her pain go away while saying, "You'll never be alone, love. One day, you'll see James and Sarah again. Remember, once they are old enough to make their own decisions, they can choose which truth to believe. Now is the time to focus on *you*."

"Time to focus on me," Annika repeated slowly. "Right. I want to go home."

Salt in the Wounds

The room erupted as everyone shouted their opinions.

"You should stay here."

"I'll go with you."

"She shouldn't be alone."

"Everyone quiet," Commander Donauska boomed in the crowded kitchen. Annika straightened her posture, ready to argue her case with the King of Ausurnia while Captain tightened his grip on her shoulders. Ista blew her nose; her husband laid a supporting hand on her shoulder and said in Annika's direction, "I understand where you're coming from with wanting to be alone, but I must insist on someone in this room staying with you to make sure you don't make any rash decisions."

"Come, love." Captain offered his hand for her to take.

Tiana stepped between them. "She's been my best friend for longer than she's been your girlfriend. *I'm* going with her."

"Over my dead body," Captain growled back.

"Excuse me!" Annika yelled. She reached around Tiana and grabbed hold of Captain's hand. "I'm the victim here, and I think I should pick the person," she spat, pulling him out the door.

Tiana caught up with them as Annika was yanking her jacket on in the entryway. "Ro, I'm sorry. I—Just know I'm always here for you. Text me later if you feel like it. Okay?"

"Okay," Annika mumbled, avoiding eye contact as she hurried out the door. At any moment, her fragile façade was going to shatter, and the floor would greet her once more.

Captain gripped down on the steering wheel with both hands, the leather of his gloves stretching tight over his knuckles. "Home or keep driving?" he asked.

Annika shrugged, tugging at her seatbelt as a sudden feeling of claustrophobia enveloped her. She rolled the window down and leaned her head out, inhaling the frosty evening air. As the clouds cleared and the bright stars twinkled in the darkening sky, Captain drove on in silence. Annika watched the fog roll toward them from the west, wishing it could wipe away her past. *I'd stand outside and let it roll over me, taking my pain with it.*

They parked, and he led her upstairs and to the blue overstuffed chair by the window. Captain then set about getting the stove lit; the cold having already seeped in. Annika hugged her knees, watching him as he turned on the kettle and opened the refrigerator. "Do you want something to eat, love? You have leftover soup in here."

"Whatever." Annika rested her chin on her knees, rubbing her palms on her legs. *Where do I go now? Will I ever feel at home somewhere? Tomorrow I'll be here, and the next day ... But do I want to stay?*

Captain walked over and squatted down so his face was level with hers. "You sound as hollow as a burned-out tree, love. Come, eat a little. At least one bite. Please?" He took her hands and gently tugged her out of the chair.

"When did you become so motherly?" she asked, easing herself into a dining chair. "Where's my hardened soldier?"

He pointed at her with a wooden spoon. "I'll be back to myself when you are back to yourself. We're all worried about you. This is a crazy situation. I'd be freaking out right now if I weren't a soldier."

"I feel numb."

"I know," he said as he placed a steaming bowl in front of her. "But you reacted like a soldier. Anyone else would've run." He paused, glancing down at his phone that had just lit up on the table. "Tiana's wondering if you want anyone to come by later. She says you're not answering her texts."

Annika sipped the hot broth, feeling the heat travel down her throat to her stomach. "My phone is still in my coat pocket. Can you text her back? Tell her I'm in a committed relationship with this bowl of soup." She shot him an apologetic look, adding, "And you, of course."

"Yeah, I'll tell her." He turned away, a smile curling up.

Annika polished off the meal, amazed at how hungry she'd felt after the first bite had hit her stomach. She turned to the owner of her heart, her rock, peering into the shadowed depths of his hood. "I—Thank you—for everything," she whispered.

He placed a hand atop hers. "You're my world now. There's nothing I wouldn't do—" His phone lit up once more, his father's name popping up in the notification.

"Oh, no," she groaned. "Do you need to go?"

"You can't get rid of me that easy, love," he smirked, typing out a reply rapidly before pocketing the phone. Then he grabbed her bowl, stood up, and went to the sink. Annika watched in admiration of his smooth steps; his perfectly fitted uniform hung over what could only be a godly figure beneath. Her eyes wandered from his back at the sink to the darkness beyond the little window where her red dahlia lived. The dim light outside from above her door bounced off the thick fog, settling.

Blinking hard, she refocused on her flowering plant, trying to think happier thoughts. A plant of true love, Tracy had said. A plant that has the same vibrational power as one has in love. *The energy reminds me of something ...* Annika glanced at her captain as he added more fuel to the stove. *Like you.*

She strode over to him as he straightened back up, wrapped her arms around his neck, and kissed him deeply on the lips, pressing her body against his to convey just how much she loved him. A soft moan escaped him, making her melt into the muscular arms encircling her. His hands reached lower, grasped her behind her thighs, and hoisted her up so her legs wrapped around his waist. Annika drowned in his scent, his taste, his touch.

* * *

She lay in bed staring at the ceiling as the morning light crept in, snuggling closer to him as the previous day's events interrupted her bliss. *Do I have more or less responsibility to Rovalkia now? How can I help them when I can no longer show my face in the country?* "Can we go for a drive? I'm feeling claustrophobic," she blurted out.

"Anything for you, love," Captain said as he leaned in. Annika relaxed again as his kiss melted her thoughts away.

Even though no clothes had come off during the hours of embracing and eventual sleep, she'd felt like she'd seen a deeper layer, and knew him in a way no other could imagine. And the tingles! Oh, how her nerve endings had fired everywhere his hands went. Everywhere his lips had touched was like fireworks under the surface of her hot skin.

Comforting heat continued to radiate from him and as she

inhaled, his lingering cologne calmed her mind. "What I must've done in a past life to deserve this one ..."

Captain pulled away from kissing her forehead. "Maybe the gods chose you for this path in life *because* of your strength in a past one. The gods saw you and said, 'Yes, this is the girl for the job. It'll be difficult, but we'll provide her with friends and a man that loves her along the way.'" He smiled as she arched an eyebrow, trying to remain serious. He touched his finger to the tip of her nose. "I'm thankful to have you in my life. You've turned my world upside down, love. And I wouldn't want it any other way."

A few minutes later, Annika kicked the sheets off and went to the kitchen, finally surfacing from another heavy make-out session. As the kettle filled with water, she watched him put fuel in the stove, reminiscing about his touch and taste.

"Keep watching me like that and I'm going to take you back to bed," Captain whispered.

Annika startled, her cheeks burning as she turned around to start breakfast while he chuckled.

As they munched on toast at the table, she glanced around the room. A corner of her suitcase peeked out from under the bed. *Where could I go if our next step fails? What's my dad's next move? Should I leave preemptively so he won't move against the Donauska's?* "Bah, stop," she chastised herself aloud.

"What's wrong?"

"My thoughts are getting the best of me," she said, standing. "I'm going to get dressed. I really need to get some fresh air to clear my head."

Captain Donauska

She hopped from foot to foot by the front door, holding the handle. He paused just outside the bathroom, and looked her over: red woolen jacket, black slacks, and black high tops. Her wavy silver locks were free-flowing and parted down the middle, and her eyes were big and bright. The dark gray eyeshadow she wore made them stand out all the more. *I don't stand a chance ...* "Well, you weren't joking about wanting to get out of the house." She shrugged and ran down the stairs.

He put the car in gear and turned up the heater. "Cold this morning, huh? I think Ausurnia's summers are the shortest in the world." He paused, tapping the steering wheel. "So, anywhere you want to go in particular?"

Annika's hands released the wound-up seatbelt. "Can we go to the train station?"

Why does she want to go there? he wondered, feeling his pulse quicken. "Uh, the trains aren't running through here anymore."

"I know—that's not why. Remember when you asked me where my favorite place was, back when we admitted our feelings for each other?"

"Then the train station is where we shall go," he said and turned east on Main Street.

When they pulled into the deserted train station, he grimaced. "Gods, we need to paint this platform." Annika said nothing. Instead, she jumped out of the car and walked up onto the platform. He followed more slowly, taking in the surroundings. The autumnal sky roiled with heavy, gray clouds, and the usual tall grass bent from recent rains; their color drained from the summer heat. "I bet you would've felt different if you arrived on a day like this."

Annika sat on the edge of the platform, swinging her boots back and forth over the train tracks below. She leaned back to look at him. "I don't think so. This place is magical." She paused, looking around. "I mean, yes, there've been times I felt unsure and afraid, but nothing like how scared I felt when my parents said I had a week to get out of the house. The only time I was more frightened was when those Rovalkian soldiers caught up to me in the woods. It's hard to override fear. I don't know how you soldiers do it."

He walked up to her; his footsteps creaking on each floorboard while the breeze tugged at his hooded cape. "This place *is* different—untamed." He leaned against a post next to her. "It's difficult not to feel fear when those you care about are involved. It's damn hard. Especially with you."

"All drive and no direction. Like I said before." Annika put her head in her hands. The wind picked up speed and flung her hair up and around her head. He pulled off his gloves and tried to contain her wild strands, but the wind kept pulling her hair from his unsuccessful attempts at gathering it all up. Annika giggled and held both hands over her mouth, her laughter becoming louder.

"Damn this wind. I'm trying to help," he grumbled as more strands of hair blew from his grasp.

"Stop," she giggled, slapping playfully at his hands. "You won't win. My hair is impossible. Here, let me." Her hands wrapped around his that held her hair, soft skin touching his in a sure grip, the touch enough to make his heart thump louder. "Stick to battling bad guys, Captain. My hair will never surrender. It if were a soldier, it would be invincible." She wound her hair behind her head with deft movements.

When her hands retracted, her hair stayed put, all contained within a knot at the nape. "Impressive," he said in admiration.

Annika

She stood up and brushed flecks of paint and dirt off her pants. "Thanks. Hey, something just sprang to mind. Do you think the leaders of the resistance will accept me now that we know what we know?" She still couldn't say the words aloud: that her father was the leader of Rovalkia.

"You have been accepted."

"I have? You've been in contact with them? Or was it Theodor? When can I meet them?"

"No, no." he waved a hand, sounding exasperated. "We have told you, or rather, my dad told you yesterday, there are no rebels. There never was. It's been us Ausurnians initiating the riots and marches. Your people can't seem to organize themselves."

She gaped. "Excuse me? How? Why? You don't—do *you* want to take over Rovalkia?" she yelled and took a step back, feeling her world turning on its head once again. "Oh gods, *you're* the beast."

"Rosebud, calm down," Captain said, reaching toward her. "I'm nothing like your father."

"No! You—you stay away. Oh gods, did you fabricate the evidence from the Capitol? Explain yourself. Now." Rage boiled inside her, and she clenched her fists, trying to suppress the urge to run.

"I promise you," he pledged. "I don't want to take over Rovalkia. But my family has been wanting to punish your government since they hired the assassins that killed my grandfather. W.I.C. and the rest of the world may have let your father off the hook, but Ausurnia will *never* forget nor forgive. So, what if we get your citizens riled up and give them the means to trouble the authorities? You were ready to do the same until a moment ago. We've just been doing all the work for you."

"Work? Like getting innocent people arrested and executed? Like making the streets unsafe for me and my family to walk?" Captain opened his mouth, but Annika continued. "No, I'm not including my father in that," she spat, pointing at him. "Thanks to these incidents, my people have lost their lives, homes, and livelihoods—this is on you." She began pacing the width of the platform, shaking her hands to dispel the energy amassing there. "You've been stringing me along, letting me hold on to this small ray of hope that I can be a part of something bigger *with* my people all this time, while I could've been doing something more productive." Annika turned on him. "You lied to me."

"We never said there were any rebels," he stated calmly.

"But you didn't deny it."

"It was per my father's orders. I asked when we should tell you months ago, but it wasn't pertinent for you to know until now. We knew what was going on, and you still needed to be assessed for being a potential threat and then trained when we learned of your innocence. Remember, love, you've only had one day in the gym, and look how that went."

"Don't 'love' me. I'm so mad I could blast you, you monster," she forced through gritted teeth. Then she turned on her heels and stomped away down the steps and past the car, continuing on the road leading back to town.

"Annika, wait," he called after her. "Where are you going?" She didn't answer, only marched faster.

A few moments later, Captain drove his car up, slowing down to crawl along next to her. His window rolled down. "Please get in. Let's talk about this."

"No. You betrayed me."

"How? This just became our reality—finding out the leader was your dad. And there's no way I would've let you take up arms in Rovalkia. You're the daughter of a politician, not a soldier. That's where your strength lies, in your drive and compassion for your people. You're better suited to work with someone like Theo—behind the scenes, not in the streets. You—damn, my dad's calling. Hold on," he said, his head disappearing back into the car.

"You have no idea what my strength can do," she grumbled, trying to walk even faster.

Captain's head leaned back out. "My dad and our allies are having a conference at the base, and he wants us there. Even my mom and grandmother are there. Can we set this argument aside and see what's going on? This could offer you some perspective. Please?"

She stopped short, causing Captain to brake hard, the car skidding to a halt a few feet in front of her. Annika walked up to his window and asked, "Why do they want me involved if I'm useless?"

"You're not useless," he said with a sigh. "This situation calls for the need to be flexible, to absorb intel as it comes, and then adapt. Your stubbornness is getting the better of you, love." he reached out, his fingertips grazing her cheek.

Annika took a deep breath and relented. "Fine." She walked around and pulled herself into the passenger seat. "I might as well use up my visa while I have one."

"Your visa has no bearing on your staying. You're my girlfriend first. I won't let anyone take or send you away. You'll get asylum regardless of how you feel about me after all this is over."

She slumped in her seat and placed her forehead against the window, aching at the thought that Captain might have used her, aching at the emptiness of not seeing her family, and mad for being the last to know everything once again.

Glitz and Guile

The military base was a hive of activity. She instinctively grabbed Captain's hand as they sped through the hallways. *"I'm sorry for keeping anything from you, love. I never meant to hurt you. "* The thought-projection from him echoed through her mind. She looked up and nodded solemnly, feeling the need for time to process how she felt, and now wasn't the time as soldiers flowed around them, coming in and out of every door. "Nothing will ever be the same, will it?"

"No, I don't think so," Captain replied grimly.

The two guards on either side of the large War Room doors rushed forward, opening the doors. She paused, mesmerized as she watched soldiers passing notes to the officials seated at the table from the phone lines attached to the walls in a silent waltz. All those seated had on headphones. She heard voices from the table speak one at a time, in their normal tone, and wondered how they kept their composure so well. Captain inched to the right; the soldiers flowed around them. She gulped as the faces of uniformed officials on the screens paused in their muted conversations and turned to scrutinize her. One by one, all the people in the room paused as well.

"Son, come this way," Ista's voice rose from nearby.

A path to the table cleared as more bodies moved, getting out of chairs. Ista stepped in front of them. She laid a hand on her son's face and hugged Annika with her other arm. "Whatever you need, Annika, we'll help you," Ista whispered into Annika's ear. "Have a seat."

Captain directed Annika to sit to his left, handing her a headset. "Put it on. This is how we seated around the table are communicate with those on screen and with each other. It's more organized and civilized."

She placed the headset on while Captain reached over and pressed a button on the side of her earpiece. The headset crackled to life. A light *DING* played in her ear.

"Are we all on?" Commander Donauska's voice spoke in her ear.

"We are," Captain answered. He looked around at Annika and motioned to his earpiece. *"You hear me?"* he mouthed. She nodded.

"Everyone, I'd like to introduce you to Miss Annika Mullway. To reiterate to our new attendee, one person speaks at a time. If you'd like to speak, push the button on the left side of the earphones. If you hear a bell sound, brighter than the one that played before I spoke, you are clear to speak. We'll all be speaking in Truscan for Miss Mullway's benefit," Commander Donauska explained. "We'll pause on trade embargos and begin a discussion on what we can do about Commander Jackson and his connection to Orrin Mullway."

DING. "Your Majesty. We received confirmation from our soldier at W.I.C. that Commander Jackson is attending the Allied Conference and dinner."

DING. "Good work. We should plan to get information from him there. Any thoughts team?"

DING. "Ista speaking. From what I've heard, Annika pulled a big reaction from the commander. We could bring her. Maybe seeing her would be enough to get him talking again."

DING. "Great idea, my dear. Rodgers, add Miss Mullway to the guest list."

DING. "Tracy speaking. I've met Commander Jackson. He may be egotistical, but he's also shrewd. He'd see the trap coming from a mile away, especially after what happened when he visited."

Silence followed. Annika touched the button on the left side of her earpiece. *DING.* "Annika here." She swallowed; her palms sweating. "I'll do whatever will help. If it's a room crammed with Ausurnians, I could dye my hair black to fit in a bit more. It'll jar the commander if I pop up like that." She released her finger from the button. *Or am I placing myself in the beast's own trap?*

DING. "Captain Donauska here. There's nothing we need to change. She's my girl, and it's time he and the world are witness to it."

Annika raised her chin, smiling, and pressed her speech button. *DING.* "What's my objective, Commander Donauska?"

Sniggering laughter resounded around the table; Annika narrowed her eyes. Those across the table that caught her eye covered their mouths in amusement.

DING. "That's enough," Commander Donauska boomed through Annika's earpiece. She winced. "Annika has been groomed to think like a leader without knowing it. Don't mock her. Annika, I apologize on behalf of my colleagues." She adjusted her headset as his voice faded. The commander's voice crackled back through. "The objective is to find out how close Commander Jackson is to your father. W.I.C. officers don't have allegiances to any country. They're supposed to represent the entire world to help maintain the peace, but Commander Jackson has developed a one-sided opinion about Rovalkia, and that spells trouble."

Silence followed. *"Any ideas, Rosebud?"* Captain's thought-projection rang in Annika's mind. She thought for a moment. *Rule Sixty-Two: Always speak to a person face to face to get a job done.* She pressed the talk button on her headset. *DING.* "Annika here. I'm tired of being the prey in this game of cat and mouse. Let's flip the game. Let me be the cat. If it's not too bold of a move, I'd like to request from Commander Jackson to see my father."

DING. "Preposterous."

DING. "What's this girl playing at?"

DING. "Silence!" Commander Donauska boomed. "Annika, that *is* bold. Can you explain your rationale?"

DING. "I can, sir." Annika sat up in her chair. She pulled her hand from Captain's and leaned over the table, her eyes scanning those seated around her. "My father taught me a lot. Every week was a new lesson to memorize, so when I joined him in his 'clerical position,' my transition would be smooth. Speaking in person to get a job done was one such lesson. He respects those who abide by his rules. He'd know it was me if Commander Jackson got the message back to him. We wouldn't have to go through with the meeting, of course. But if my father sends a message back to you, Commander Donauska, we'll have proof Commander Jackson spoke to him … Or at the very least, we'll know he sent the message along, hoping to incur more drama."

The soldiers stared at her, their mouths agape. Captain regarded her too, his straight-lipped mouth revealed nothing of his innermost thoughts. She sat back in her chair. *Well, at least I contributed. Even if it was a bad idea.*

DING. "That's a well thought through plan," Commander Donauska said. Annika took a deep breath and leaned her head back. "But I must warn you, for this to work, we need you to be alone with him. He must feel in control."

Annika chewed her lower lip as she sat back at the table, staring at the reflective surface. Those black eyes would haunt her for the rest of her life. *DING.* "I understand, sir. As you instruct, I will do it. I'll mention I miss my family. My father's bound to play off that." She continued to stare at the table. "I could try to muster a bit of agitation into my aura and lower my shields. Does he know how to sense auras as well?"

Heads swiveled toward Commander Donauska. *DING.* "You are correct. My father agreed, early in his ruling years, to teach a select group of young outsiders at W.I.C. about our abilities to gain their trust. The plan is well-rounded. I'll iron out the finer details with a select group the day before, and my family will prepare Annika for her role. Now, if you'll excuse us, my officers and I need to continue discussing other security matters."

Once out in the hall, Annika took a deep breath. She bent her head from shoulder to shoulder, two loud pops resounding from her neck. Captain pulled her further to the other side of the hall and hugged her, kissing the top of her head. Annika wrapped her arms around his torso, deciding to forgive him, for now.

"Rosebud, if you're okay, I'd like to join my father back in the room. The conference is in three days and there are a lot of security measures to go over. Can I leave you in my mother and grandmother's care and catch up with you later?"

She nodded while looking up into his hooded face. *This is real. The Ausurnian government and I are working together. I really am a part of this team. But will the lessons my father taught me and the Donauska's guidance be enough to get me through?*

311

Belle of the Ball

S omeone else was parked in the drive when they arrived at the house. Tiana hopped out of the car, waving.

"Alright, girls, there's lots to do," Tracy said. "Let's go inside and flip through the fashion catalogues in the family room. Annika needs a dress for the banquet. Yes, I said a dress, Ista. She needs to gain favor with the commander, remember?"

Annika bit back a laugh as Ista's jaw dropped. "How'd you know what I envisioned her wearing?"

"I saw the glint in your eye while Annika explained her plan," Tracy said, placing four mugs next to the kettle in the kitchen.

"But your vision's coming true."

"What vision?" Annika and Tiana asked in unison.

"As much as I'd like to believe it true, we have to remember it was just a dream." Tracy placed a hand on her daughter-in-law's forearm before glancing at Annika. "It was just a dream, Annika. Nothing more. We need the enemy to speak, and we both know that he'll scoff at her, if she's dressed as anything less than a lady."

Ista scrunched her face at the same time as Annika and tapped her fingers against the countertop's edge, humming in thought. "So, we dress her as a princess. A long gown, heels, and done-up hair. Everything, save for a tiara. She'll enter the hall draped on my son's arm, but *we'll* know it's all for show." She paused and smiled wickedly. "Yes, I can get behind that."

The tea kettle whistled. Tracy told the younger girls to look at the magazines in the next room while she and Ista brought the tea out.

Annika's jaw dropped as she started flipping through the first magazine. Scantily dressed, striking women sat in velvet chairs and clung to tuxedoed men. They left nothing to the imagination. Meanwhile, Tiana was oohing and tearing out page after page, placing them in a maybe pile. Annika glanced over and choked. The top picture showed a woman from another country wearing a mini dress made of see-through, black chain mail, leaving nothing to the imagination. With one flick of her wrist, Annika sent the stacked magazine pages skittering across the dining table.

"Why'd you do that? I had them all organized."

"Because this is absurd." Annika waved her hand over the table. "Chain mail? Are you serious? And this is definitely not the occasion for my torso to be exposed."

Tiana gestured toward the pages and said, "But you'd look trendy. Fashion is the name of the game at these events."

Tracy placed the tray down on top of pages picturing women in lacy, black dresses ending far above their knees. "Girls, end your squabbles. We don't need inspiration anymore. Ista and I talked. Annika will dress as a proper Donauska princess."

"That means a shopping trip to Fringur!" Tiana exclaimed, clapping her hands together.

Tracy looked at Ista. Ista lowered her eyes and shook her head. Tracy turned to her granddaughter. "Tiana, I need you here. You'll be filling in for me at the Elders meeting that's on the same night as the banquet."

Tiana's hands dropped to her sides and mouth formed an O. "But … Wait. I get to pretend to be you?"

"Not pretend, dear. *Be*. And I trust you'll do an excellent job."

"But I want to protect her," Tiana pouted. "And I want to dress up, too."

"Oh Tiana, these political banquets are a serious bore," Ista said. "And Annika doesn't need your protection. She'll be with your cousin all night." Tiana mumbled under her breath, her lip still pouted. "Your grandmother is entrusting you to a *very* secretive meeting. And there'll be plenty more banquets in the future for you to attend."

Annika stirred in her chair. "So, do I bump into him? Pull him aside? Stalk him until he walks outside?"

"We'll have to think of a clever meetup for old mister Jackson." Ista brought one hand up and tapped her lips.

"Who?" Tiana asked, turning to Annika.

"Commander Jackson," Annika replied, making a face. "I have to get him to admit he's working with my father."

Tiana's eyes widened, then she asked, "Do you want to wear a similar heel to the one on your date? I have them in a lot of colors."

"Why, for the Void's sake, would I agree to wear those death traps again?"

"What's your train of thought, Tiana?" Tracy questioned.

"Well, Annika's wobbly in them, that's why she hates them—"

"I'm uncoordinated in any shoes," Annika grumbled.

"But you could use them to your advantage, Ro." Tiana sat facing her. "Back in school, in self-defense class, our trainers taught us to take our weakness and turn it into a strength. We can use your discomfort against the commander. Pretend to wobble or stumble into him. Or pretend to sprain your ankle. He couldn't ignore you then. That would be ungentlemanly."

Ista went to her niece and wrapped her arms around her shoulders. "What a clever girl you are! As uncomfortable as they are, heels have their advantages, not to mention they make a splendid weapon in a pinch."

"See? I'm not just a pretty face," Tiana smirked.

"Pack Annika all the colors you can spare, Tiana," her aunt instructed. "Everything else is my treat." She turned to Annika. "We'll have a fun girl's day together. Don't look so shocked, Annika," Ista laughed, "The banquet lasts all night, and it takes hours to get ready. We'll need to get our hair and makeup done before getting dressed. We all have our roles to play in this family. Tracy and I have experience doing espionage work for our husbands, too. We make a good team— trust me."

"This is all so new to me," Annika admitted. "At home, my mother readied herself with the same dress anytime she went to a government event with my dad. That's another reason I still can't believe who my dad was—is."

"Well, now you have us to teach you about the real world," Tiana said with a smile.

Annika smiled at her friend. *If only the real world wasn't such a scary place ...*

* * *

I'm the bait. I must place myself in the beast's jaws and get him to talk. I must succeed for all who I hold dear. Annika stared at herself in the mirror affixed above her bathroom sink. Her grandmother's horseshoe pendant hung from its chain; the garnet sparkled as the morning sun shone through the little window to her right. *This is my life. I will pick my destiny.*

A car horn honked outside and downstairs she went, opening the back passenger door of Ista's car. A large bag on the seat next to her held all the colored heels donated from Tiana. Red, pink, and shiny black shoes stuck out of the top. She pressed her eyes shut and let her head fall back against the headrest as Ista pulled out onto the main road.

She squirmed as they passed the point where the van had pulled over, and Tracy reached back with her hand. Annika took a deep breath as she reached her hand forward to meet her employer's. The Donauska matriarch squeezed it firmly. "All those roads have been closed, sweetie. Every border entrance has a guard now. It shouldn't have happened in the first place and never will again."

Ista's face turned up in the rearview mirror, catching Annika's attention. "She's right, Annika. My husband held a vote on the matter. All of Ausurnia stands with you. You're home if you choose to stay here."

Annika broke eye contact and looked out the side window, blinking back tears. She wondered if she'd ever feel that same warmth; that same sense of safety as she had growing up. Could she really never have to move again? Could she and Captain make it work and be happy together? A lot of questions needed answering first though ...

* * *

Downtown Fringur approached, its skyscrapers rising into the low-lying fog bank. Ista drove further north into the heart of the city.

Eventually, she turned off the highway and joined a line of armored military vehicles just like theirs, all heading in the same direction. Every block had Ausurnian soldiers standing guard on the street corners with large guns held in their hands.

"I didn't know Ausurnians used guns. With all your gifts, I assumed you wouldn't need them. I've certainly never seen soldiers with them in Pontagu."

"That's because we have no use for them domestically," Tracy answered. "But it makes our allied guests feel safer, so we use them for show during these conferences."

"Are weapons allowed at W.I.C. headquarters?" *How did Tracy's husband get assassinated from within such a secure building?*

"The outside guards carry them. It's *supposed* to be a safe place, but since my husband's murder, we know that's untrue. We've been trying to weed out the evil seeds ever since. With your help, Commander Jackson may prove to be one of those evil seeds." Tracy turned in her seat toward Annika. "But don't press a confession out of him just yet. Remember to act natural. Your goal is to see if he gets you a meeting with your father."

"Here we are," Ista announced.

The cars in front of them were inching their way to the front of a tall hotel with gilded windowed floors that rose into the clouds overhead. Unfurled national flags draped above the front entrance. Each car paused in front of the entrance carpet, and hotel employees hurried forward to open the doors and help take luggage out.

"Are the delegates and representatives driven in from the borders?" Annika asked as she leaned forward to see out the front window.

"Driven or flown in," Ista replied, "We have secret landing locations for our planes. Their safety is in our hands once they enter our airspace. We take it seriously."

She parked at the front door and instructed Annika to take her seatbelt off, but to wait for the hotel staff to open her door before exiting. "Remember, you're a representative of Ausurnia and a Donauska royal guest. Go off of our example."

Ista and Tracy's doors opened, and they took the hand of the valet as they exited the car while Annika followed suit. Ausurnian officers marched by, and she turned to see if any looked familiar.

A hand touched her back, and she froze. "He'll be here in time, my dear. I know that it's unnerving being around all these unfamiliar faces, but you need to stick with us until the banquet, okay?" Annika turned, giving Tracy a small nod, and followed her to meet Ista at the hotel restaurant's entrance, just past the check-in desk and the bustle of valets going in and out of the gold elevators.

As they approached a round dining table in the middle of the dining room, Annika could see eyes darting their way and the heads of other patrons leaning close together, whispering and pointing. *I should have dressed nicer,* she thought, looking down past her red coat to her unpolished black boots.

Annika sat down and draped the cream-colored linen napkin over her lap after the others had done so. Only then did she allow herself to inspect the table. Glass goblets sparkled as the light reflected off the large crystal chandelier overhead. Annika feared to even sip her water, least a drop get spilled on the pristine white tablecloth. A server arrived to present a bottle of wine to Ista; she gave a nod after inspecting the label. Annika kept her primary focus on the center of the table, using her peripheral vision to see what the other two women did. Servers brought food to the table within moments, and she stared at the food in front of her. *Was there a menu? Who ordered this?* Rule Twenty-Three: Never accept food or drink not ordered by you. She looked up at Ista with the question on her face. Ista pointed to herself, and Annika gave a quick nod of understanding as she picked up her soup spoon. Tracy leaned over toward her.

"That was very smart of you to check who ordered it. Who taught you formal dining etiquette? You're doing so well."

"My mother," Annika answered out of the corner of her mouth.

Tracy nodded, and Ista smiled approvingly. The meal continued in silence. Servers placed a small dish of unfamiliar gray fish in front of each lady next. Tracy leaned over once more. "I can assure you it tastes better than it looks."

After taking a nibble, Annika smiled, the meat melting on her tongue. Infused lemon oil and other pickling spices reminded her of her mother's canned vegetables. A server cleared the plates once Ista had taken her last forkful. Then Ista, the Queen of Ausurnia, stood and led the trio out of the dining room under the nosy gaze of every guest and waitstaff.

"I *hate* how they seat us in the middle of the room every time, as if we're an attraction. Someday I'll say something. But let's get our gowns now, shall we?" Ista linked an arm with Annika and started down the boulevard.

"You ladies have a long life of attention grabbing ahead, I can assure you," the matriarch mused from behind.

Ista tittered. "Good thing for these psychic shields, huh, Annika?"

"Yes. I'd have melted into a puddle long ago if it weren't for my shields."

Ista patted Annika's arm. "I know the feeling."

Annika froze. Then she yanked her arm from Ista, causing the queen to stumble. "Annika, stop—" But she was already running, running toward the woman and two children that had just rounded a corner—her mother, James, and Sarah.

"Annika! Where are you going?" Tracy called out.

Annika rounded the corner and saw the trio was only a half block away. "Mom!" she called out. "James! Sarah! Wait!"

Just as she reached them, the woman spun around, wide eyed. The children also turned, and the little girl screamed. Annika skidded to a stop in front of them, her arm poised inches away from the little girl. It wasn't Sarah, or James, or her mother; everything on the face was wrong. They had brown eyes, smaller noses, and round faces. But the heights had been right, along with the blonde hair color, and the way they walked.

"Annika! What are you doing?" Ista called out sternly. Annika looked back to see they were speed walking toward her. She turned back to the petrified-looking family; the mother had now corralled the children behind her. Annika lowered her hand.

"I—I'm so sorry. I thought you were someone else," she said breathlessly. "You look like my family from behind."

The woman nodded and began taking steps backward, then turned around and bustled the ogling children away. Annika went into the shade of the building next to her and leaned her back against it, exhaling slowly to steady her heart rate.

"What were you thinking, young lady? That could've been the family of a delegate or refugees," Tracy admonished.

"I thought it was my family." Annika blinked back tears. "I thought Theodor may have secretly brought them out to his headquarters here. I just saw them and something in my brain snapped ... I'm sorry."

"Oh, sweetie," Ista soothed, brushing hair out of Annika's face. "I can't imagine how much you miss them. But you need to remember to trust us. We would *never* keep something like that from you. You'd be the first to know if they came here. I promise."

Annika nodded, concentrating on biting back the tears. Tracy linked an arm with her. "Come on, dear. Let's continue on. We still have a lot to do."

Ista wove around females going in and out of the shop up ahead, set in a black painted brick building. They entered and Annika stared breathlessly at the long slim gowns and multilayered ruffled creations that graced the mannequins set up on the sales floor. Row upon row of black dresses filled the right half of the shop, while the back left corner held racks displaying traditional Ausurnian skirts like the citizens had worn at the fair. Toward the other side of the store, more racks of dresses, organized by their dominant color, stood in view of the windows. Three store attendants approached them when Ista turned to Annika. "Pick out floor-length gowns of silk to try on. One of these gracious ladies will hold them as you peruse."

Tracy veered toward the black dresses, and one clerk followed her. Ista moseyed toward the colored dresses. But Annika stayed put and looked around. Overwhelmed, she turned to the third clerk that stood by her. "I don't know where to start."

"I'd suggest you begin with your favorite colors," she said kindly. "Pick one or two black numbers to try on as well. I can offer feedback on whether a dress would be appropriate for the banquet when you hold them up to look at. Her Highness called ahead to let us know what to help with today."

Annika walked toward the rack of solid red dresses near the front door. She found a section of her size and pulled four off the rack. The clerk gave a silent nod to each one. Annika then wove through the racks of black dresses and pulled one with lace sleeves, but the clerk gave a small shake of her head. Annika replaced it and kept flipping through the hangers. The woman leaned closer and whispered, "The less busy, the better, miss. Her Highness, Queen Ista, should have the most ornate dress."

Annika mouthed, "Thank you." Then she spied a dress with a sheer silver overlay on top of a black slip and showed it to the assistant.

"Now you're getting it," the lady smiled. "It really compliments your hair."

"Thank you. I think I'll try on these five first. I don't want to overwhelm myself."

As her attendee led her to the dressing rooms, Annika eyed both Ista and Tracy at the checkout counter. Her attendee coughed politely, and Annika turned back to her.

"You can use this dressing room. I'll be right outside if you need help zipping up. You'll find that our sizes are consistent," she said.

Annika's shoulders relaxed. "Thanks again," she whispered.

Loud whispers sounded from outside her door as Annika turned around in front of the dressing room mirror in the first red dress. She paused, straining her ears.

"Annika? Would you mind showing us each dress as you try them on?" Ista's voice called from the other side. "I brought a pair of high heels for you to try with the dresses. I forgot they were in my purse."

"Yes, ma'am." Annika placed her feet in the heels her attendant slipped under the door, and she hobbled out. The crimson hue, the darkest red of her choices, shimmered along the folds where the light hit. Its low neckline concealed her breasts while the shoulder straps were thin but sturdy. It hugged her curves in all the right places. *I feel like a movie star.* She paused in front of the Donauska women, who now sat in red velvet chairs. Ista waved her hand to signal for Annika to spin around.

"May we have a chair to see how the dress flows when she sits?" Ista requested. Annika hiked up the skirt at her waist and sat down, her ankles crossed. Ista and Tracy exchanged a brief look that Annika couldn't read, and then Ista said, "Okay. Let's do the same with the rest of your dresses."

Annika nodded and went back into the dressing room. *Gods, what if they dislike my picks? What if I don't fit the part?* She wondered, shaking her head as she pulled on the next red dress. This one had the same shimmer effect but was a lighter hue.

One by one, she modeled her picks, and each time, the Donauska women's expressions didn't hint at what they thought. Annika took deep breaths as she redressed in her own clothes. Her attendant took Annika's dresses and approached Ista and Tracy. The women muttered back and forth as Annika tried to distract herself by focusing on the various mannequins around her. When her attendee retreated with all the dresses she'd picked, she stopped shifting her weight from foot to foot.

"Were none of those dresses acceptable?" she asked.

Tracy marched over to her and grasped Annika's chin gently. "You were lovely in all of them. Ista and I have purchased two red ones and the gray one. The low-cut red dress will be perfect for tomorrow night as the neckline is more princess-like with the neck strap. It'll also bring attention to your grandmother's necklace, if you choose to wear it."

Annika touched her necklace. "I hadn't thought about it, but it makes sense to wear. It's become a symbol of who I am now." Then she snapped her head up. "How can I repay you? Three dresses? It seems like too many when I'll only be wearing one gown one night."

"Annika. My son is courting you," Ista said, smiling. "There'll be plenty more opportunities to dress up." She leaned closer. "And please don't question me or Tracy in public. It's not proper."

"Yes, ma'am." Annika's cheeks flared.

Ista took Annika's face in her hands, and Annika looked into her dark chocolate eyes. "Don't beat yourself up so much. This is a learning mission. Please take it as constructive criticism, and never forget I care for you as if you were my daughter."

No Prisoners

S he let herself sink in. The goose feather pillows yielded to her weight with a gentle crinkling sounding as she laid her head down, stretching out on the smooth sheets. *A whole king-size bed for me!* Annika kicked her legs into the air with glee.

She bolted up, looked toward the door adjoining the two rooms. It remained closed, and she relaxed back down. *I shouldn't act so childish, but a whole hotel room all to myself!* The rack with her new dresses stood in the corner and her old schoolbag slouched on a chair, out of place in its plush environment. *No more having to share a room with two siblings or sharing one bathroom with four others. No more half-portions because the grocers ran out of food.*

BZZZ. BZZZ. She leaned over and grabbed her phone from the nightstand. "Well, hello Captain."

"Hello to you, beautiful. You sound chipper. Did you have a good day?"

"It was a big day." She leaned back into the pillows. "But they let me have the adjoining hotel room all to myself. Can you believe it? An entire room to myself!"

"And more than one dress?" he chuckled.

"How'd you know?" she asked, sitting back up. "I got three!"

"Whoo-hoo," he puffed. "I can't wait to see you in them."

"Can't you stop by? Where are you?"

"Sorry, love. There's no fraternizing between non-married couples at political events."

She pouted, a sigh escaping her lips. "Darn. I want to remember the night dressed up with you before it all goes downhill after I stomp on Commander Jackson's foot."

The captain chuckled again. "There'll be a photographer at the banquet's entrance. I promise we'll get a picture together, love. And don't fret, I'll be nearby the whole time. Just try not to shatter his foot. Those heels are bloody dangerous. You need to engage with him, not disable him. That's my job."

"I can't make any promises," she replied, and he laughed.

"I'd expect nothing less. Now rest up. I'll meet you at the entrance of the banquet after the Allied Conference, okay? Don't forget to keep your shields up."

"I won't forget."

* * *

She traipsed into the salon after the Donauska women, and the receptionist ushered the trio into a back room where empty salon stations lined one wall. Ista and Tracy took a seat next to one another, and Ista motioned for Annika to sit on her other side while she rattled off what sounded like instructions in Ausurnian to the stylist that stood nearby. The stylists wrapped capes around their shoulders and got to work.

Annika flipped through a magazine while her hair got pulled and twisted. Every few moments, the woman rolling Annika's hair mumbled.

"Sorry, what?" she asked.

"Your hair is so beautiful and healthy. What do you do?" the stylist wondered.

"Um, I wash it when it gets oily, but not much else."

"Well, whatever you do, keep doing it." The stylist pulled another section of her silver hair back, wrapping it in curlers; Annika winced. When she opened her eyes and looked in the mirror, another three stylists had entered the room. One approached her, holding a metallic box. The man set down the box and looked at Annika. She stared back, trying not to fidget; her scalp ached from the large curlers pinning her hair up.

"Well, there's not much for me to do here," the new stylist declared.

Annika slid her eyes to peek in Ista's mirror and Ista looked back, smiling. "I know what you mean. Annika's a natural beauty."

"Your Highness is correct. Now look to me, Miss Annika." The stylist spun her seat to face him. "You can close your eyes while I work my magic."

She steeled herself for the touch of another stranger working on her face and hair, but as her scalp ache turned into a numb pulling sensation and the esthetician's warm hands wandered around her face with a delicate touch, she relaxed into the seat. With her eyes closed, Annika let her thoughts wander into nothingness. Curlers got teased out of her hair and they applied a clay mask to her face. Ista and Tracy's voices spoke back and forth in Ausurnian, and at one point, Ista acknowledged Annika. "How are you doing over there?" When Annika only managed a purr of content, Ista replied, "I know what you mean."

A warm, moistened cloth wiped Annika's face clean before a soft, bristled makeup brush stroked the contours of her face. The stylist went back to work on her hair, beginning with the top of her head. Setting spray rained down around her, alcohol and body powder choking the air. She kept her eyes closed and settled back into her seat.

The brush strokes on her face glided to her eyes. Over and over, the bristles tickled her eyelids. "All done, Miss Annika. If you'd like, you can sit up and look in the mirror. Please let me know what you think."

Adjusting to the extra weight of the makeup on her eyelids and the light of the room, she looked up in increments. *Wow. It's me, but like a more mature version of myself.* The dark eye makeup had brightened her eyes. Her eyelashes were longer and thicker, and there were now sculpted cheekbones and a stained pout. Mesmerized, she raised one hand to graze her face.

"Try not to touch your face," Ista warned from her right. "We didn't bring makeup like this for touchups."

Annika lowered her hand and looked in the mirror at her hair. There were loose curls cascading down from a half bun set atop her head. Little curls framed her face at the temples, and they bounced as she turned her head to the left and right. She smiled. "I love it."

"Then our work here is done. Thank you for being such a wonderful client." The stylists bowed and exited the room.

"Turn our way so that we may see you, too," Tracy called over. Annika swiveled around, and Tracy and Ista gasped and clapped; Annika felt her cheeks burn.

"You two look nice as well," she murmured. Ista and Tracy also sported curls that cascaded down their backs and their face and eyes had subtle makeup applied. They had nothing to prove. *Ausurnians are gorgeous by nature.*

Tracy checked her watch. "We should head back to get dressed. The conference will conclude in an hour, and the banquet begins shortly after."

327

Annika's stomach lurched. *Oh gods, It's almost time to face the commander.* She gulped, and Ista placed a reassuring arm around her shoulders, not letting go until they reached the hotel.

Once back in their rooms, Ista instructed Annika to sit down to a tea service with her and Tracy. "I'm not sure how this evening is going to play out, and no mission can go well when you face it with an empty stomach. I demand you to eat at least two of those finger sandwiches, Annika."

She ate obediently but tasted nothing, nor did the tea add any comfort like it usually did. "What a year," Annika groaned out as she leaned back in the chair. "I don't agree with what my father's doing, but is it wrong that I'm still holding out for the goodness in him—that he might change—because of how I remember him as I grew up?"

"Of course not, dear," Ista said. "It's something we all face as we grow up and become more independent from our parents. Sometimes we find out a person's outer image contradicts their inner one, and different situations call for different responses."

Annika eased out of her chair. "You're right. I should get ready." She trudged to her room, shaking her hands to get the nervous energy out. *There's no time to fret. It's like the morning I snuck out to get on the train. Nothing's going to stop me.*

She pulled on the red dress, tugging it over her hips and inserting her hair through the dress's neck strap first. Annika pulled the zipper up the lower half of her back and stopped. This dress didn't feel the same as when she tried it on. While looking in the mirror on the back of her room door, she felt the heavy satin material of the skirt and traced the tiny silver beads threaded into a looping design on the bodice. She didn't remember seeing the beaded design, but then again, she'd been nervous as she tried on each dress. At least the low-cut cowl neck felt the same. Annika swished her hips to see the full effect. Cool air hit her left leg. She kicked it forward, and her leg slid into full view. She gasped, seeing the dress's slit end at her thigh; the milky whiteness of her skin was shocking against the deep red of the dress.

"Annika? Do you need help tying the back?" Ista called out. Annika grabbed the dark red heels and went back into the adjoining room.

"Aren't you a sight," Ista cooed. "Do you like this dress? I had the girl swap the one you'd picked for it at the last moment. The silver beads compliment your hair so much. I couldn't resist. Oh, your bow is all lopsided. Turn around and I'll redo it." Annika turned to see herself and Ista in a full-length mirror. She took in Ista's dress. The queen wore a dark purple dress that shimmered like Annika's, complete with a subtle gold design on the bodice, and a cascade of diamonds twinkling around her neck. "You were born for this dress. Don't you agree, Tracy?"

The Donauska matriarch strode out of the bathroom. She wore a black dress with long sleeves. The neckline ended at her collar and an extra length of fabric draped across the front of the dress like a shawl. Annika detected a gold shimmer in the bodice as well. But it was nothing compared to the headband nestled in her hair. Four rows of black diamonds were layered along the entire length of the band. "Yes, I believe so," Tracy said, placing a pair of looped black diamond earrings in her lobes. "We must get your ears pierced, Annika. You've a wonderful face shape for them."

Ista snapped her fingers and grabbed a small black velvet bag off the dresser. "I want you to wear this tonight," she said, waiting while Annika finished getting into her heels. Ista drew a long, sparkling silver chain from the bag.

"A bracelet?" Annika asked.

"My crystal head chain," Ista explained, as she walked behind Annika, lifting her hands up over Annika's head. "Not quite a tiara, but worthy of a princess. And it won't clash with your necklace." She lined up the chain with Annika's forehead and pulled it back; the cool surface felt refreshing against Annika's warm skin. "This is your debut outing with my son, and I want you to make a grand impression. It'll also be a pleasant surprise for him to see the chain on *your* head, as it was his favorite for me to wear when he was young—before I became queen."

Annika shot her hand up as the chain slipped down her forehead when Ista let go. "Don't worry," Ista assured. "There's a third, tinier chain that lays over your hair to keep it in place." Annika danced her fingertips along the top of her head, registering the cool metal. In the mirror, she admired the teardrop crystal resting in the center of her forehead. "Come along, dear. And remember, rest your weight on the balls of your feet when you step. One cannot walk in high heels the same as in a boot. It's a workout, but the effect is glamourous. We are women and we take no prisoners."

One Head, Two Faces

B lack-cloaked Ausurnian soldiers lined every wall of the lobby. Every lamp was on, but dim. Annika felt the press of these soldiers' psyches as she got off the elevator as they scanned for uninvited guests. Foreign dignitaries wore uniforms ladened with medals of honor, while their partners wore silky looking gowns and suits in every color of the rainbow. Up ahead, the flash from the photographer's camera went off repeatedly by the banquet hall's entrance. Annika squeezed into the lobby behind Ista and Tracy. *"Captain? Are you around?"*

"I'm near the door, love. Mom will find us," Captain's voice said in her mind.

"Wow, Mom, you look grand," Theodor exclaimed.

"Yes, though I don't know why you chose not to wear your tiara. You are the queen, after all." Commander Donauska's booming deep voice broadcasted.

"I don't need to wear a crown for people to know who I am," Ista informed him, winking back at Annika.

"Grandmother, will you be my date tonight?" Theodor asked. Tracy blushed and lightly smacked his arm.

"Hello, gorgeous," a deep and warm, familiar voice crooned in Annika's ear. Captain's psyche wrapped itself around her like slipping into a warm bath. Giddiness traveled through her as she spun around. Captain stood before her with an enormous grin on his face. His sharp canines poked down as his head did an up and down motion. "You look—"

"Like a Blood Princess!" Theodor exclaimed, jumping into view.

"Theo, I will break your mouth," Captain barked.

"*Boys*," Ista scolded. "Behave yourselves. We're going to get pictures. See you in there." She reached out, giving Annika's arm a squeeze before she and Commander Donauska melted into the crowd.

"Don't forget to socialize," Tracy directed as she followed behind her son.

"My team is in position. You look beautiful, Annika. Knock 'em dead." Theodor winked at her, and he, too, melted into the crowd.

One of Captain's hands rested on her lower back while the other grasped her hand and brought it up to his lips. He leaned closer, and Annika inhaled his familiar scent. She sighed, and he smiled.

"I'd love to kiss you, but I don't fancy wearing lipstick myself tonight. No nervousness, okay? We're all here," he assured, and she relaxed more as he pulled her closer. "There are no words to describe how stunning you are."

Annika gritted her teeth as she tried to force the heat growing in her cheeks to calm down. "Gods, you make it hard for me not to kiss you."

He took her hand and draped it over his arm. "Let's get our picture taken first. Then maybe we'll find a private corner to be alone."

She slapped playfully at his arm as they shuffled with the crowd toward the photographer. She whispered, "You look stunning too, Prince of Ausurnia." His leather-vested armor shone, and she swore his hood looked silkier than usual. The corners of his mouth ticked up as his gloved hand patted hers where it held onto his arm.

"How did the conference go?"

"Oh, just a lot of catching up and venting about trade and economy…and Rovalkia, of course."

"I can only imagine…"

A photographer stepped in front of them. He bowed and pointed to one side of the opened doors. There were gold-gilded floral carvings on the door, and a giant floral bouquet on a pedestal stood further to the left. Captain pulled Annika to his side, so that she stood facing the photographer's camera with the fresh flowers directly right behind her.

Two bright flashes blinded her, and Annika dropped her smile as she blinked, spots dotting her vision. Captain Donauska then guided her into the banquet hall; the well-dressed people reflecting the glitz of the room. She looked around to see large, gilded picture frames lining the length of the walls, pictures depicting Ausurnian officials and landscapes. Chandeliers of gold and crystal hung from the ceiling, and a band played to her left. She couldn't see the end of the room. People meandered back and forth, shouting hellos and good evenings above the growing din. Annika still couldn't see over anyone's head, even with the extra height from her heels, so she focused instead on not stepping on her dress or any of the long skirts that brushed against her.

They drifted with the general flow of the crowd, heading deeper into the room. Annika kept glancing at the surrounding faces, not recognizing anyone. Most would smile at her or nod, but none attempted conversation. Younger women gave curious looks when they spied her arm on the Prince of Ausurnia's.

Captain greeted decorated officers to his left as their partners looked down their noses at Annika when introduced. She tried to smile, but it faltered as it reached her cheeks. Then she felt complete nervousness emanating from a woman shyly glancing at her. The woman looked a little older than Annika, sporting dyed purple hair and big gray eyes. Annika turned her full attention to the girl. "Hi, my name is Annika." She offered her free hand for the girl to shake.

The woman smiled and placed the tips of her white-gloved fingers in Annika's hand. "My name is Mabel. Your dress is stunning. Though, if I may be so bold as to ask, why didn't you wear a green dress to compliment your eyes? If I had eyes that green—not that the red doesn't fit you, it being a power color and all ..." she trailed off, glancing at Captain, cheeks reddening.

"I thought about it, but red is my favorite color." Annika leaned toward her, gabbing, "This is my first time at a banquet, and I sense it's yours, too? I'm a box of nerves right now." She winked and Mabel's eyes widened as she smiled, her pearly straight teeth glistening. The woman next to Mabel scoffed under her breath, and Annika shot her a dark glare. The stranger blinked, averting her gaze.

"I hope we run into each other again this evening," Mabel called to Annika as her partner led her into the moving crowd.

Captain guided Annika deeper into the room, and women placed a hand on Annika's shoulder as they drifted by, murmuring in her ear about how beautiful her dress was. They all did a double tap with their finger before withdrawing it. After the third incident, she thought-projected to Captain, *"Why are these women tapping my arm?"*

"They're signaling to you they're your allies. These women are savvy to your attendance tonight for your protection. My dad and brother worked out who'd be aware on the inside while my job was to get extra security hidden strategically outside."

The end of the room finally appeared as four panels of tall windows offered a glimpse of the dark blue twilight, glowing behind trees dripping with lights. Fewer people milled about on this side of the room as it was the furthest area from the music and food. Annika tapped Captain's arm, but he didn't respond, so she thought-projected: *"Captain, can we go outside for a moment?"* He gave a small shake of his head and strode forward, eventually stopping in front of a small drink bar.

"What's the matter?" she whispered out of the corner of her mouth as a bartender approached.

"A champagne for the lady," he ordered. Annika stared at him, confused. The bartender handed over the crystal flute, and Captain handed it to her. His lips drew into a thin line as he bent down to her ear. "Dad just projected to me that a skirmish has started by the entrance doors—uninvited guests picking fights. I need to go assist the guards. Stay on this side of the room, and don't go outside. I'll return in a minute."

"Okay. Sure." Then she thought-projected, *"Has Commander Jackson not shown?"*

"No word yet, love. Stay vigilante, though." Captain kissed her cheek and strode away into the crowd.

She stared after him, taking a sip of champagne. Bubbles danced on her tongue, the sweetness reviving her focus. She wove her way toward the far window, taking another sip every couple of steps.

"I see you haven't lost your appetite for the color red," a masculine voice said. She turned to see Commander Jackson leaning against the side of a window frame. He took a sip of his amber colored drink, and it made a tinkling sound as the ice slid forward in the glass. His head bent back as the last of the liquid drained into his mouth. "Ahh," the commander said, smacking his lips and setting down the glass on a small table under the window. "There's nothing like watching a sunset with a good stiff drink. I see you're working on your own liquid courage." He motioned to the drink in her hand.

Annika grasped the slim neck of the delicate goblet tighter as she observed him. He wore the same dark blue uniform with badges as at the base; his military cap sat high on his forehead. *He's not trying to hide his face even though Ausurnians despise him. Interesting.* The same beady, dark eyes stared down at her. *He must've been on the balcony the whole time if Captain didn't know he was here.* "I don't need to drink for courage, sir. Just as a formality." She raised her chin and sidled closer.

Commander Jackson placed his hands in his suit pockets, tilting his head to one side. "That's my smart girl."

"*Excuse me?*" Annika took another step closer, draining the last of her champagne. She slammed the empty flute down harder than necessary beside his glass. "If you've forgotten, my name is Miss Annika or Miss Mullway. And yes, red's my favorite color. It reminds me of who I am, just like those badges on your jacket. Which, unless I'm mistaken, is supposed to *mean* something."

The commander chuckled, and his eyes darted above her head. *Is he thought-projecting?* She looked behind her, but no one stood out. No one else nearby had on the blue W.I.C. uniform like his, either. She turned back to face him. "What's on your mind, Commander Jackson?"

He stared at her for a long moment, the uncomfortable silence making her shift her weight from heel to heel, fighting the urge to walk away. "You haven't lost your edge. It's as if you haven't been gone these past months," he said.

Annika smiled sweetly, shoving down her trepidation. "Well, the love I have for my family keeps me strong." She looked around and turned back. "Have you spoken to my father recently? I miss him—miss all of them," she implored in a hushed tone.

Commander Jackson broke into a bellowing laugh, and she caught sight of couples nearby pausing to glance over. "Oh, Annika. If you only knew. I'll give you a hint." He leaned his head forward. "I wondered if it was you who stole your grandmother's necklace out of the trash. Your mother went to retrieve it, wanting to sell it, but it was nowhere to be found. Don't worry, I won't tell."

Annika's mouth dropped open. She snapped it shut and clenched her hands. *What kind of trick*—stopping mid-thought, hearing a far-off voice. Annika relaxed her hands and took a few steps toward the window, pretending to see something interesting. Just as Commander Jackson was turning his head, she turned hers toward him, glimpsing a flesh-colored object in his ear. *Oh, gods of the Void, does he have my dad in his earpiece? This wasn't the plan!* Annika blinked at the commander, not daring to speak, not daring to move. *What do I do?* She looked around out of the corner of her eye. *Great, everyone is out of normal hearing range.*

"The necklace does suit you," Commander Jackson started back up, turning to face her full on. She looked up into his eyes and stepped closer, wanting her next words to be heard by whoever was listening in, whether it be her father or someone with a script. She startled as his left pupil went fuzzy like static on a bad television station. The commander suddenly blinked rapidly, and the left pupil dilated, the iris now more blue than black. She drew in a sharp breath through clenched teeth.

"I knew you'd run to these barbarians. You were always too curious about them. You asked too many questions. Then when that scandal piece on you got printed in the newspaper... Well, someone did all the work for me. I'll send a thank you basket once I find out who."

"No, it can't be—" Annika took a step back.

"And why not? You think I'd just stand by while my heir co-mingled with Ausurnians?" Blood drained from Annika's face as she listened to Commander Jackson repeat words only her father would say. This was no scripted act. Her father, Orrin Mullway, was watching, listening, and now speaking; from the comforts of a desk at work, or home—or closer. She gulped and glanced outside. The commander acted a hollow chuckle. "No child, obviously I couldn't show my face here. That's why I sent my right-hand man here in my stead."

Commander Jackson rolled his shoulders back, looking pleased with himself. "In hindsight, though, what a fantastic way to gain their trust and infiltrate their people. I'd worried I had lost my smart girl. But then we sat back and watched you work your magic on them—having them break into the Capitol, using their planes to shower religious pamphlets filled with gobble-di-gook about Kraxxan not being all powerful. What a stunt. But it got attention—your cry for *my* attention, your mother explained. I hated being so hard on you, but Rovalkia needs a strong successor. You've proved yourself, Annika. You've survived the real world and found your old man out. Now come home and tell me what you've learned. We'll exploit their weaknesses and start an empire for our hundred-year anniversary. Starting with *this* country." Annika's insides churned. She laid a hand on her stomach. *Don't throw up. Not now.* She stared into the commander's small beady eyes as she let her father's words sink in. *Has he gone mad? He thinks I did all this to prove my worth to him? And build an empire with what army?*

Her pulse quickened, and she flexed her hands. The energy prickled and swirled around her fingers. She raised her chin, and her anger expanded as a warmth trickled down her limbs. The commander smirked.

Annika frowned. She was tired of being used as a pawn in this sick game between nations, and her feet were aching in these heels. *This is not the father I loved growing up.* She took one small step forward, blinking back tears, and forced herself to stare into Commander Jackson's video eye lens. "Thank you, Commander, for bringing my father to me so that I can say this: You know, the old me would've leaped at the opportunity to come home. I want you to know that I left without telling you to teach you a lesson on respect. I am an adult and demand to be treated as one. I love you, but how can I believe you love me after all this? You taught me so much, and yet you never could tell me the truth about who our family was. Finding that out hurt more than you kicking me out. Were you ashamed of me?"

Commander Jackson's eyes glazed as he said, "You weren't ready. I needed to know our country had your absolute loyalty. But then you began exploring your psychic abilities without my consent. You were too strong, too natural at it, and your mother worried about our safety. I had to put a stop to it before my colleagues found out. Your independent streak set me back years. We Mullways only use our psychic abilities to remain in power and have never told another living soul. I was going to re-train you when the right time came. They shouldn't teach just anyone to be psychic, Annika. Imagine the chaos it would invoke here. These Ausurnians are going to lose everything because they flaunt who they are. Just look at how the world views them. And since someone blabbed to the press about your abilities, we can spin it as a ploy of the Ausurnians. Another point for Rovalkia. The world will believe us over them."

Annika swallowed hard and blinked twice, her chest tightening. "Am I solely a means to your end? Have you ever been interested in what *I* want? I want to help our people. They need us. Why do you have such an obsession with control?"

"You're too sheltered to know any better, and that's partially my fault. But look at the state of Rovalkia. There's no sense of direction, no drive by the people. They *want* to be led. If we didn't maintain control, it would be anarchy." Commander Jackson pointed at her as if to say, "I told you so."

She clenched her fists, her nails digging into her palms. The urge to punch him grew harder to resist as his eyes refocused on hers. "You've got that stubborn look in your eye, girl, so here's a dose of reality: If you were born into any other family, the police would've shipped you off to a labor camp or done away with you. *I've* kept you safe. That was and is my priority. I can train you to use your abilities, with no one being the wiser. And after we're done kicking out citizens who aren't pulling their weight in the Karaxin, we'll invite in those that *want* to work and this city will finally be a utopia for those loyal to us and our cause."

"That's tyranny," Annika told him through gritted teeth. "You can't *force* someone to be something they're not, and you can't *force* people from their homes because they refuse to bow down to you like servants. And having control for the sake of control is not a cause, it's a sickness. Psychic abilities exist because they connect us to one another, not separate. We would be a stronger people if we all learned them."

"I wish you understood the big picture, Annika," the commander shook his head, emoting as her father spoke in his ear, "Nobody cares. Fear rules the world. Our family ancestor avoided being documented by the Ausurnians because they wanted to be free of Ausurnian control. Their sacrifice allowed our family to become the strongest blood line in Rovalkia—of mind and body, which is why we deserve to be in charge— a page right out of the Donauska's book. Don't you see? Utopias don't exist. It's control or be controlled. Now is not the time for an ethics lesson, child. I still can't believe how much you fight against our way of life. Seeing how you've dressed up is maddening enough." Commander Jackson mimed a deep frown and crossed his arms. "You *will* come home. I *will* un-brainwash you, then retrain you. Commander Jackson, please escort her out as planned." The whites of the commander's beady eyes suddenly became visible. Annika smirked at his mistake. His right eye twitched as a voice screamed out from his earpiece and he puffed his chest out, closing his eyes.

Annika took advantage of the split-second his eyes were closed to draw one foot back behind the other, the fighting stance hidden from view under her skirt. Commander Jackson opened his eyes, and she followed his movements as he looked around at the door leading outside. "Let's take a walk, Miss Mullway."

"No."

"That wasn't a request, young lady," he spat. "March."

"First," she raised a finger to his face. "I'm staying here where I'm accepted for who I am and for what I want to do." She then raised a second finger. "And my second reason is the last lesson you taught me, and one you *both* should heed."

Commander Jackson cocked his head to one side. "And what's that?"

Annika bent her knees and balled her right fist. "Bad guys *never* win." She then thrust her fist up, putting all her weight behind the strike as it connected with the commander's right eye.

Commander Jackson stumbled backward against the panes of glass; they shook with the force of his impact. Glass shattered nearby at the same time someone screamed, and all the while Annika kept her focus on him. She took two steps backward, and a blur of black rushed in from both sides. Commander Jackson roared, lunging toward her. She flinched and shuffled back another step. Soldiers expertly ducked around his flailing fist as he held the other hand to his face, a single line of dark blood trickling between his thick fingers.

New Beginnings

Two hands grasped Annika's arms from behind. "Let go!" she screamed, kicking back with her heel.

"Stop! It's me," her captor shouted.

Annika swiveled around, brought her hands up to Captain Donauska's neck, and pulled herself to him. His muscular arms locked onto her. "It's okay now. Shh, it's going to be all right," he soothed into her hair.

"No. It'll never be all right. He won't stop," she managed before turning to point at the commander being led away. "He has an earpiece and an eye lens. He spoke my father's words. He was here—my dad was here. Commander Jackson was his vessel. He was here!"

Captain called out to a soldier jogging by, "Check the commander for wires and an earpiece. Have the medic try to salvage any eye lens he's fitted with." He looked down at her. "I'm assuming you punched him in the eye that was equipped with the device?" Annika nodded and looked at the waiting soldier. He nodded and disappeared.

"Why didn't you thought-project to me, love? I was too far away to see you." He rubbed the side of her arm.

"It happened so fast and didn't go as planned. I was supposed to trick him. I failed." She laid her forehead against his chest.

"No, love," he soothed, tightly wrapping his arms around her. "You haven't failed. He's a tricky man. No one could've known."

"Annika!" a female voice cried out from the crowd. "Get out of my way!" the person shrieked again. The crowd parted faster.

Ista and Tracy came rushing forward. Ista had her skirt hiked up past her ankles while Commander Donauska's bulky figure followed behind them. He suddenly veered left toward the retreating mass of soldiers still wrestling with a belligerent Commander Jackson.

"Are you okay, Annika? What happened? Our guards instructed us to stay on the other side of the room. First there was a terrible commotion by the front door, and then minutes later the back windows shook, and someone screamed. We thought we were under attack." Ista attempted to pull Annika from her son's arms, but his grip on her tightened.

"Mom, calm down. Show us to a private room before you fuss over her. She may need a medic."

"What happened?" Tracy implored.

Annika buried her head into the captain's chest as his gloved hand stroked her head. "The fights at the front door were a diversion while the commander isolated Annika. Let's get her away from all these people," he said and pulled back from Annika, dipping to one side and sweeping her up in his arms. She snaked her hands around his neck and laid her head on his shoulder, inhaling his scent to calm herself.

The crowd parted as the Donauska women led the way through the banquet hall. Guests shuffled further away at the sound of

Commander Donauska's bellow as he told everyone to move out of his way. Annika tightened her hold around the captain's neck when she spied the commander's snarl, his fangs on full display, approaching rapidly from behind.

"I'm so mad I could spit," Commander Donauska boomed. "Jackson's going to get away with this in court since calls over earpieces aren't traceable, and he knows it. It'll be Annika's word against his."

"Hush, dear," Ista soothed, waiting for him to catch up. "Not here. Annika's hurt and upset."

"And I'm sure she had a good reason to assault him," Tracy added.

"For Bandau's sake, mom. I'm not mad at *her*." The commander's hands went up in the air. He stepped around his mother and back into Annika's view, his hooded face now wearing a frown. Captain adjusted his posture to stand straighter and his grip on her tightened.

"Alright, let's get to a private room. Follow me." Commander Donauska turned and led the way.

* * *

Once a guard had secured the door, Commander Donauska poured himself a drink and turned to Annika. "Do you want anything before we get started?"

"No, thank you," she said, shaking her head. "I'd rather relay what happened before I forget any details." Captain tightened his grip on her as she settled into his lap.

"Alright. Mom, please sit down. If Annika can remain composed, so can you."

Tracy frowned, pulling the curtains tighter across the window, and sat down on the settee with Ista.

"Okay Annika, from the beginning please," Commander Donauska encouraged.

Annika started from when Captain left her at the bar. "His men had set up a fake distraction," Captain Donauska interjected.

"I guessed as much," she said and placed her good hand on his cheek. "I'm not upset about being left alone. I was prepared for that." Then she continued, retelling everything until the moment Captain had come up behind her.

"Anything else we should know, love?" he asked as his father went back for another drink.

She nodded. "He's trying to create a utopian city in Karaxin. Did I mention that? He proclaimed he and I should start an empire and conquer this country once I revealed all of Ausurnia's secrets." She looked over at the commander, who had paused mid-stir. "Sir, I would never."

"I believe you, Annika. That's not your personality." He set down the glass and placed his hands on his waist. "But it *explains* all the camps around the capital we've been monitoring. He must be recruiting for his military, which means a lot of long nights ahead of me. It's time to choose, Annika. Either renounce your citizenship to Rovalkia now and stay, or Theodor will need to secrete you away with a new identity somewhere in the world. It's not safe enough here because of the loopholes in our international law system." Then the commander took another step toward her. "I'm sorry it's turned out to be like this with your father, Annika. I wouldn't wish what you're going through on my worst enemy, which is your father, coincidently."

Annika blinked once, twice, then closed her eyes and leaned her head against Captain's shoulder; she didn't want to think about the decision she had to make. Everyone remained quiet in the room. Faint whispers of music seeped in through the door. She thought of life in a foreign place, a life without her name, a life without Captain, or Tracy, or Tiana, or Ista. She would have to hide her powers again. "No," she nearly shouted. Everyone's head jerked up. "No," she said again quieter as she gazed into Captain's hood. "I renounce my Rovalkian heritage and citizenship. I will learn and live by the Ausurnian code. I am home."

Suddenly, Captain's lips were on hers, kissing her deeply. She sputtered as she heard the others gasp. "Captain!" She pushed at his chest, and he pulled away slightly, a grin spreading.

Commander Donauska cleared his throat. "Alright then. That settles it. I'll get the paperwork drawn up in the next week or two. I think I can speak for all of us when I say, welcome home." Ista burst into tears, ran over to Annika, and enveloped her and her son in her arms.

* * *

"Commander Jackson may lose his eye. A bit of poetic justice, don't you think?"

"I don't care what happens to him, so long as he stays away from me." Annika pointed out the window. "You missed the turn."

"We're not going home just yet, love. We need to stop somewhere first."

"Where?" she asked, her hands twisting her seatbelt.

Captain's hand grabbed hers and brought it to his lips. "A place of calm before we have to face the world again." His lips pressed down on her fingers, and she relaxed back into her seat.

A few minutes went by in comfortable silence. Then Annika sat up taller, seeing his destination. "The station," she muttered. "Of course."

Captain had barely stopped at the stairs of the weathered platform before she threw open her door and ran out. She opened her arms to the sky and let herself sink to the wooden boards. Laying spread-eagled, she watched the passing clouds while waiting for Captain to catch up, his form casting a shadow over her.

"It wasn't supposed to happen like this. I was supposed to step back on the train and go home by summer's end. I thought I'd be going back to join the rebels." James and Sarah's young, smiling faces danced in her mind's eye. "But it's all gone. There's nothing to fight for."

Captain sat down and stroked her forehead and hair, and she closed her eyes at his touch. "This is our place," she announced. "Whenever one of us needs the other. This is where we'll come—no matter where we are or who we're with in the future. Okay?" A frigid wind whipped hair into her face. Captain smoothed her hair back, and she nuzzled into his palm.

"There's plenty to fight for. You and a better future for James and Sara to start with. Mom reminded me a while ago to slow down and listen to what the gods were trying to teach me. That's when I had the revelation that you were my other half, the better half I've been missing. I don't see us ever being apart."

"That makes me feel better … Gods, I miss my siblings … Would it be okay if I tried to thought-project to them? They may be gifted like me."

"Not until we know more about your parents, love. If they all have psychic abilities and hear your message, it may cause trouble. You need more practice, and my primary focus is your safety right now."

"Okay. What a pair we make, huh? I still don't understand why you like me. But I like you, so I'll allow it." Annika rubbed her face back and forth against the soft leather of his glove.

"I don't like you, Rosebud. I love you," he whispered. "Someday, I hope you love me back."

Annika raised her chin toward him, squinting from the sun in her eyes. "I *do* love you. You know that. But you also must remember that my heart feels tormented while my future remains uncertain. What if it's because of my presence here that causes a war? What if more people die? How could you still love me if that happens?"

"This political aggression has been going on since before you were born, remember? Nothing you have done would make me say any of this is your fault. Besides, I'd follow you to the ends of the earth," he shot back through gritted teeth.

Her throat tightened around the lump growing there. "But you're the Prince of Ausurnia and have a duty to your people. It's your bloodline that matters. You couldn't leave."

"I would. But that doesn't matter."

"Yes, it does," she argued back, twirling her necklace between her fingertips.

Captain pulled away from her and she glanced up. He crouched above her, bringing his upside-down hooded face inches from her own.

"I'm tolerated solely because I'm helping your father. But now we know the truth of everything. It's all over. Who knows what'll happen to me next?" *I'll never be accepted.*

Captain pulled away another inch. "You don't seriously believe that?"

"And I still can't even look into your eyes," she choked out. "I still don't know your first name. It's—it's not fair."

His hands cradled her face as his lips lowered, connecting with hers. They stayed there, pressing down, warm and soft. Tears leaked from her eyes. Captain pulled away and Annika blinked repeatedly as tears clouded her vision. She whimpered, desiring his lips and his touch. A soft cloth pressed against her eyes one at a time. When she opened them, Captain's face hovered further away. "Come here," he said, and she sat up in front of him. He held his black handkerchief in his left hand while his right hand rose and cupped her cheek, his thumb rubbing away the salty tear residue.

"I love you. That right there is stronger and far more important than any law, or rule, or—or cultural expectation. Never let yourself doubt how I feel about you. We're *meant* for each other." Captain leaned back, shifting on his heels.

Annika lowered her eyes, feeling a single hot tear roll down her cheek. *Why can't my head believe it when you're all my heart craves?* The sound of rustling material pricked her ears, so she raised her gaze and gasped, her eyes drinking in the exposed face before her. Her hands rose, shaking, grazing over his warm skin, starting at his chin and his lips. Then she felt his nose, the sturdy bridge, and her fingertips moved upward with her eyes, memorizing the feel and look of every inch of tanned skin. Her gave traveled up past his eyebrows and to the unruly black hair being tugged around by the wind. Finally, she willed herself to gaze back into the eyes she had longed to see for so long. The near black, warm depths with long, black lashes gazed back. The corners crinkled slightly, and he drew his mouth up in a smile.

"My name is Mikael Donauska, Prince of Ausurnia, and I am yours." His hands took hold of hers. "This is our time, and we'll figure everything out. Together."

"Together," she echoed.

End of Book 1

TRENT

Acknowledgments

There are so many people I'd like to thank. First, I'd like to thank my wonderful husband, Chris, for his unwavering support and love. You always pull me back up whenever doubt in my abilities needles its way into my mind.

Thank you to my editor, Ashley, for wading through the messy first draft and sticking with me through the proofread. I promise to implement all your editing tips in future novels.

Thank you to my cover designer, Rena, for making the endless changes I asked for and then making the finished product even better.

To my beta readers, Jamie, Jessica, and Sheila, you were crucial in making sure that Into Ausurnia became the page-turner I envisioned.

Thank you to my Instagram family and extended family and friends who keep believing in me and cheering me on. I promise book two, The Rise of Athelia, will be published a lot sooner than it took this one.

And lastly, thank you, the reader, for the opportunity to share the worlds my imagination has created. It's always been my dream to entertain and help others escape from reality when they need to.

TRENT

About The Author

Alisha grew up in San Diego, California, and attended university in Oregon. Shortly after moving to the Pacific Northwest, she met her husband where they still live with their two cats, Daisy and Twist. When not at her day job or writing, she likes to bake, paint, and take long bike rides.

You can follow her adventures and keep up with her latest writing projects on social media:

Instagram @alishas_lifeandpublications_

Twitter @AlishaT_writes

Milton Keynes UK
Ingram Content Group UK Ltd.
UKHW020639310723
426074UK00019B/1445